T0104566

Three Kingdoms

BRIAN PENTLAND

Order this book online at www.trafford.com
or email orders@trafford.com

Most Trafford titles are also available at major online book retailers.

© Copyright 2017 Brian Pentland.
All rights reserved. No part of this publication may be reproduced, stored in a retrieval
system, or transmitted, in any form or by any means, electronic, mechanical, photocopying,
recording, or otherwise, without the written prior permission of the author.

Print information available on the last page.

ISBN: 978-1-4907-8265-2 (sc)
ISBN: 978-1-4907-8267-6 (hc)
ISBN: 978-1-4907-8266-9 (e)

Library of Congress Control Number: 2017907870

Because of the dynamic nature of the Internet, any web addresses or links contained in
this book may have changed since publication and may no longer be valid. The views
expressed in this work are solely those of the author and do not necessarily reflect the
views of the publisher, and the publisher hereby disclaims any responsibility for them.

Any people depicted in stock imagery provided by Thinkstock are models,
and such images are being used for illustrative purposes only.
Certain stock imagery © Thinkstock.

Trafford rev. 05/22/2017

www.trafford.com
North America & international
toll-free: 1 888 232 4444 (USA & Canada)
fax: 812 355 4082

This book is dedicated to my dearest sister, Dawn

CHAPTER 1

Distinguishing Boundaries

Distinguishing Boundaries

The strong wind swept across the undulating hills, driving before it a misty rain. The grey sky heralded further rain for the afternoon. From above, this zone seemed like a giant green field, cut into neat squares and rectangles bordered by one hundred year old cypresses in sentinel lines in a determined dark green shade that served as wind-breaks and cover for the cattle.

This was a dairy-farming district, like most of Gippsland, but being only one and a half hours out of Melbourne made it commutable. Walvern had once been a thriving, late nineteenth century town that somehow remained old-fashioned, but in the 1980s the whole town was bypassed by a freeway that connected Melbourne right through the whole of the Latrobe Valley. So this town, which had pulled itself up to the head of an important commercial agricultural town little by little slipped back as a result of no through traffic entering its determined but sleepy existence. It was not a huge town, but with the suburban sprawl it went ever outward and whatever type of nondescript modern houses were required or demanded, they were available.

The older part of the town was Victorian, but as the land undulated the houses were depending on the layout of the land; either the front or the back of each residence was considerably elevated. As a result of the very high rainfall and the acid soil, rhododendrons and camellias flourished, as did all types of evergreen trees and those planted a century ago were now in a mature state that gave the whole town an

3

anchor into the ground. The trees that lined the street in the older part of Walvern were plane trees, with trunks of enormous girth. Unfortunately these street trees were cruelly pollarded, so they never had the opportunity to show their true splendour.

Outside Walvern the countryside rolled away and each little zone had had its own character. It was now almost invisible, but in the nineteenth and twentieth centuries these areas had developed their own personalities, and this was obviously determined by money. The properties around the town had never been very large, its being a dairy-farming area. Originally, large areas were no required. The land was hard won originally, but won it was. The clearing of trees, planting of fields and the development of a rich diary industry was established. But with time, with milk quotas, the farms that had done well before found themselves in financial difficulties due to the fact that the hectares were not sufficient, so cut-backs had to be made. Near Walvern, the people who owned the properties worked the land. There were very few who held the land and had share-farmers running their properties, simply because the hectares were not sufficient to allow this. But one or two properties did have this luxury, though it was relatively rare.

North of Walvern was a tiny hamlet called Aspel. At its height it had boasted a railway station, a general store, a local hall, Church of England and Methodist churches, a series of houses and a jewel of a state primary school of considerable architectural merit. That was it. In the mid-sixties, the railway was closed, a survey having decided it was uneconomical to keep it open. So the hamlet slowly slipped back into its own dream world. The general store closed, due to the supermarket in Walvern offering the same products at lower prices, as well as a greater choice. In time, both churches were physically removed to areas where the population was prepared to use them : the church-going population had fallen to basically nil, so it was not worthwhile to keep them open. There had never been a Catholic church in Aspel : all the Catholics were obliged to make the journey to Walvern to St Joseph's and still d0. The houses in and around Aspel were average Victorian and later houses that held families and the numerous outbuildings all served to support their domestic and economic survival. Not all were aesthetically pleasing. But Aspel, although forgotten, boasted, several miles apart, three houses that were different from the rest. Two of them were much larger and the third a fine house but smaller.

The first house we shall glance at was called Rosebae. If one left Walvern and continued for eight kilometres, it stood on a high embankment. The main road had been cut below and a high cypress hedge – or to be honest a row of unkempt cypress trees – masked the front and side of the house as well as serving as a wind-break from the strong winds that swept across the neighbouring valley and upwards toward Rosebae. Sheltering behind was a very large, weatherboard, late-Victorian house that was the home to Terry Williams and Simon Osler. The large house was not pretentious : it had a veranda across the front, with a central passage and was completely symmetrical. But one rarely used the front door, as, when they had re-developed the road system and cut the embankment into the side of the hill directly under the cypress hedge, it made access to the house from the front impossible. So one entered from the side road that was gravel and continued in a straight line down to the bridge and then up again to the crossroads. From there, if one went on, it left one finished up in the forgotten hamlet of Aspel : if one went straight ahead, one finished up at a little farm property : if one went right, the first house one saw was Killpara, a modest Victorian home, and then on to a 1960s modern home, and a little further on, behind a huge barrier of pine trees, the largest of these three homes, Houghton Hall.

Rosebae had been in Simon Osler's family since the lad was selected and at 37 he continued in the family tradition of dairy farming. He had met Terry Williams seven or possibly eight years before, and they had decided that they were well suited to one another, so Terry moved in and began an amazing transformation of the house and its surroundings. Terry was thin, blonde and with a sharp face. His arms, which in summer were always exposed, were so thin that they looked like two lengths of thick, pink rope, but he, for some odd reason, was very proud of them, always exclaiming that he was fortunate to have such elegant arms. He was tolerant until tackled and then if he felt insecure he attacked viciously; his rapier tongue was well-known among his small group of friends. Simon was exactly the opposite in character and appearance. He was much taller, dark and extremely well built, with thick dark brown, unruly hair and almost black eyes with bushy eyebrows and a full mouth and a strong nose. He had an obvious beardline and was very much the man of the country. He was extremely popular with everyone, kindness itself, and it was said that he did not have a cruel bone in his entire body.

The same could not be said for Terry. When he moved into Rosebae, the property was a little run down and, as he saw it, completely in disorder. This he set about rectifying at once. He began with the house. Simon's parents had been dead for some years and he had lived by himself for a period; housework was obviously not his forte. So Terry found the house to be in the most forlorn condition. As all entry to the house was through the back door, it most certainly did not give one a sense of grandeur and that is what Terry set about changing. He had a new veranda built, right across the back of the house, and transferred the front door with its leaded side light to the back and had a window fitted in place of the front door, allowing more light into the house. A great number of the rooms were damaged, with cracked plaster and water stains on the ceilings, from which were suspended the most rudimentary light fixtures, generally a plastic-coloured shade above a naked bulb. The roof was repaired, and Terry himself set about systematically, room by room, re-plastering and painting. He tore up all the old, damaged, cracked lino which had spread itself into every room and automatically changed colour and design at every doorway. The acrid smell of the burning of all this floor-covering was terrible. A dense pall of black-grey smoke signalled the finish of the stuff. Terry spent the next few weeks pulling nails out of the floorboards as the sanding machine would not tolerate this metal intrusion. And so, in a year, great changes occurred at Rosebae. Terry never stopped. He was always throwing himself into one project after another, and complaining bitterly until each was completed.

But he had a great love, apart from Simon, and that was bird life. With Simon, he built a most elaborate and decorative enclosure to house the hens and he was most attached to one that he called Tahlulla, that was black and white and, when he was working in the garden, was always with him. Tahlulla followed him everywhere. This grand enclosure of a hen house, with knobs and finials, trimmed with decorative cast iron he painted cream and highlighted everything with white. He then moved on to an aviary for parrots, and a large arrogant peacock called Pete. Pete was always to be seen strutting about the yard between the house and the sheds. He had probably absorbed some of Terry's attitudes and when together they seemed to be mimicking one another. The oddest thing to watch was the night exercise, when it was time for Pete to be locked safely away for the night. He would allow only Terry to pick him up, but the minute he worked out he was to be locked up he generally put up a fight and when finally pushed into his very decorative enclosure he always walked to a low perch and turned his back on everyone. No amount of coaxing would convince him to turn around or open his tail. He just looked at the wall and sulked.

Terry also began an overhaul little by little of the outer farm buildings, the replacement of rusty tin and then a paint job. He did everything himself. He was considered a human dynamo but he was actually more like a bee : if left alone, he made honey, but disturbed or criticised he stung.

The interior of Rosebae now was comfortable but it could never be described as high chic. It still had a mixture of furniture, and all the prints and one largish painting had the same subject, of course – birds. Every time Terry went to Walvern he immediately dashed to the charity shops to see if they had any statuettes of birds and so the house little by little began to fill up with china birds of all sizes and colours, not to mention a great variety of quality items, but this did not worry Terry at all, and Simon just smiled as every time Terry returned from Walvern with a find he then had to decide where to place it.

Simon was the one who rose at 5.30 to 6.00 every morning and set about his methodical rhythm of daily life. He assisted the share farmer and then milked 89 cows. Terry was not up at 5.30, but by 6.30 or 7.00 was in the milking shed also helping. The relationship was one of mutual trust and a genuine sense that they were doing the right thing, but lo and behold if someone decided to move in on the gentle and dark, good-looking Simon, Terry was extremely jealous of him and he was quick to defend his territory and his lover with a vicious verbal attack. This rarely occurred, due to their isolated living, so their friends were very few, as both of them, when this relationship began, were discarded by many of their acquaintances.

Terry was a good cook and really enjoyed it. He liked to make his own butter and could skim the milk for thick cream, so his cooking was rich. He caused a little drama once at Walvern when he found out via a friend of his, a true county matron, that the County Women's Association were having a one-day cheese-making course and was furious that because he was a man he was not able to attend, since he could not become a member of the Association. He wrote a scathing letter to the local newspaper, The Walvern Gazette, screeching sexism, which in a sleepy country own raised a lot of eyebrows. He was fortunate that his friend knew the lady personally who was giving instruction in cheese-making and invited both of them to her home where the lesson was repeated in private. But the letter to the Gazette was followed up by women claiming that although Terry was right, there were also many things in this town they were prohibited from taking advantage of, and so these letters continued to be published in a column called 'You Said It' for some months. There was also another column in this weekly newspaper that was called 'In and Out of Society', a poisonous column that was to affect most people living in and around Walvern directly or indirectly,.

If one left the asphalt road at Rosebae and took the gravel road to the side of the house, one went down a steep hill across a bridge and up again. Turning right, the land on this corner belonged to the O'Riley family and had for many generations. The property, Killpara, although it had more hectares than Rosebae, was a smaller residence but a little grander, because it was built on a slope that fell away at the back. It was built on a slightly more level piece of land but much further in from the road. It boasted a gabled front and a half veranda which terminated at the projecting gable front. It had four bedrooms, a large living room but a tiny kitchen with a large skillion section that stretched right across the back of the house, enclosing a bathroom, laundry and a large waste space with cupboards for all manner of things. On the long side, these cupboards were topped by louvre windows which overlooked the share-farmer's cottage, which was built only nine or ten metres from the main house,. Due to the sloping terrain, the back of the main house was a metre above the ground, whereas the front door was level with the ground. In front of the very austere cottage was a large square space; on the right was the hay shed, on the left there was a corrugated iron utility shed and the stable block. Directly in front but lower down was the milking shed. This was one of the few properties in this area that had a share-farmer : on most of the other properties the owner and perhaps his son and most definitely his wife were the sole workers.

Mr O'Riley was a surveyer, so that helped to supplement the salary, and his wife Joyce kept the house. They had two children. Thomas had left home sometime ago : he had finished university and worked for a very successful investment firm in Melbourne. He had only last week, with Joyce's sister Rose, celebrated his thirty sixth birthday in Rose's beautiful home in Toorak. Thomas had a sister called Patricia, who had decided not to go to university despite the avenue being open to her. She worked in Walvern at the local library and seemingly enjoyed it. She lived at Killpara and had no desire at all to take on the responsibilities of a flat in Walvern. This was a blessing to Joyce, as she and Patricia were quite close and good company for one another as Mr O'Riley, Samuel, was often away for work.

The interior of Killpara could only be described as very ordinary or suburban. The furniture was late Edwardian or 1930s, nothing special, but everything was functional. Joyce would not have it any other way. It was a cold house : it showed no warmth at all, and this may have been due to the walls being either a dull green or an even duller blue. All the original fireplaces were intact – there had been no re-modelling at all. The gems of Killpara were the exterior chimneys. These four had ornate cornicing around the top and decorative incised designs on the sides. They always seemed too grand for the structure. Again, as at Rosebae, the front door was rarely used. One generally entered up a steep ramp at the back, which had tyres cut up and nailed flat in horizontal strips so that in bad weather, which was often, one wouldn't slip.

As regularly as clockwork, every Sunday, a car would leave Killpara for the nine o'clock Mass at Walvern, as that was the closest Catholic church. Sometimes two cars left, depending on the arrangements later or the weather. The Timms family was going as well as the share-farmers were also Catholics, although Mr Timms generally had to be dragged out to go. Joyce always said in a soft joking way that there must have been a mix-up at the hospital. She was short and invisible;

in a certain sense if there was a group of people no one remembered if Joyce had been there. Quite often at a shop she would stand for five minutes before someone noticed her. Her sense of humour was childish and it was as if she had lived a very sheltered life. Her grey hair and sensible but slightly old-fashioned clothes and the fact that she wore no make-up gave her the appearance of a much older woman. The joke she repeated often about the hospital now made no sense, as it concerned her two children. Thomas was thirty six, tall, with black hair, electric blue eyes and a very handsome face. At school he had been everybody's heart-throb and not just with the girls, whereas Patricia was a true Irish girl in every sense, red blonde hair, green eyes and a gentle face covered in freckles. She was short and very thin and a more pleasant and kind person one would never meet. But they were complete opposites. Patricia was also ten years younger than the handsome Thomas. The fact that he had left home almost eighteen years ago and so few people actually knew him as an adult meant that the hospital joke made no sense.

The Timms family consisted of James and his wife Paula and a small daughter called Lynette. They had fallen on hard times six years before: the Parish Priest, when he heard that the previous share-farmers were leaving, begged Mr O'Riley to take them on, which he duly did. He was a charmer, James Timms, good-looking, tall and a good, honest worker, but with money he was hopeless. He made unsound investments, especially the 'get-rich-quick' schemes and always burned his fingers. Mr O'Riley, seeing this problem, and the salary several times having to be advanced so that the family could eat, insisted that a portion of his wage went into a separate account that his wife controlled, so at least there was food on the table for the three of them.

If one continued past Killpara, going away from Aspel, on the same side of the road as Killpara, one first of all passed a modern house and then, looming up as one continued, was a long line of century-enormous old pine trees. After this barrier, it was possible to see, set well back, a very large late-Victorian house with an orange terracotta tiled roof. This was the home of the Houghtons, and the property revelled in the name of Houghton Hall. If the name was pretentious, so were its occupants, or at least one in particular. The property had been in the hands of this family for three generations but never had it been so run down. At some stage, someone claiming good taste had painted the house blue, which took away a certain style from it. The house was by far the largest in the district but at some time, due to incompetent handling, the whole property had fallen into financial hot water, so a large section of the property was sold off and the smaller part that remained was let to the next door neighbour.

The cash flow of the Houghtons was exceptionally limited but if you had met Emily Houghton's son Barry, you would never have believed it unless you sat through some boring, pretentious story about his ancestors ten times over, which is what he would do unless stopped. He was the same age as Thomas, 36, five feet seven inches tall but exceptionally over-weight. He dressed in a manner he thought reinforced his own importance : a collar and tie when it was not required, a jacket but with a hole in the sleeve when he thought he would go one better than the locals. His pretentiousness or arrogance was such that he had very few friends, but that never seemed to distress him at all. Whenever there was a function at the Walvern Library or the Walvern Art Centre, Barry could be found boring someone to death while at the same time consuming as much free food and drink as possible. Although he knew the O'Rileys, he rarely spoke to them and if he had to it was short and to the point, this due to the fact that they were Catholics, which he saw as a social limitation. At this point the word 'bigot' can also be brought into the description of him. Although claiming to be C of E, as he put it, he never attended the Church of England, now called Anglican, except for funerals and weddings. Both these events meant free food and drink, not to mention a captive audience. Due to his excess weight, his face had ballooned and he had unfortunately large, pale, watery-blue pop eyes which seemed to project out of their sockets. He had a largish nose and very full lips, plump cheeks, bright pink with fine red veins, receding blonde hair and strangely short arms terminating in plump pink hands. 'Oh, I always have my shirts tailored,' he was often heard to say, the truth being the sleeves of ordinary shirts bought cheaply all had to have the sleeves shortened. It was quite an exaggeration to call this a hand-made shirt.

Emily Houghton was also quite sure of herself, tall, with blue-grey hair, good features but a slightly beaky nose. She dressed conservatively but always with a string of pearls. The locals joked that she most probably wore them to bed as she was never seen without them fastened around her slightly crepey neck.

They drove a 1970 Mercedes Benz, one of the very large ones, in a burgundy colour, which Barry religiously polished. Mind you, this was the only work he did : he was bone idle. He never lifted a finger to do anything or to help anyone. This old Mercedes, that always burned an extraordinary amount of oil, was always seen parked at Walvern in front of the most expensive shops, just so the locals could see how the other half lived. But the reality was exactly the opposite. Inside this large weather-board house was a series of sad, dull rooms. From the front door, a worn carpet runner directed one down the hallway to a huge reception room filled with dark, heavy late-Edwardian furniture and odd knicknacks that in the Houghtons' minds symbolised gentry. The rooms were always with the blinds down and there was always a smell of damp. The marks on the ceilings denoted a leaky roof but as cash was short nothing was ever done. No one ever called. This was due to the fact that no one was invited. The Houghtons were not unaware of the state of the house though. In the main living room, due to four cats, the genuine velvet settee and two armchairs that were purchased in the 1930s were in shreds. The arms were now like macramé, threads everywhere, not to mention the dust, as Emily and Barry lived in a tiny room off the kitchen, with the television set perched on a 1950 coffee table. A more squalid room would be hard to find. They ate in the kitchen and Barry did so ravenously. He had the most extraordinary appetite and it was washed down with great quantities of cheap red wine. 'I never touch beer – it's so common,' he was heard to say, so the reality of living in this, the largest home in the district, and its actual condition were two completely different things, as no one had seen inside it. It was assumed by all, and encouraged by Barry's vivid imagination, that he and Emily were living in luxury. Nothing could have been further from the truth.

The garden area surrounding the house was so overgrown that it was difficult to see what was growing, except a fine variety of weeds. 'Oh, the croquet lawn and the tennis court – we don't use them now,' he was often heard saying and that was absolutely true. It was impossible to use either, as the croquet lawn was now home to blackberries and wild briar roses, while the poles surrounding the tennis court had long collapsed bringing the wire with them and a tangled mass of wires, rotting wooden poles and cracked, broken asphalt. It now boasted two fig trees growing in the centre. Barry was oblivious to it all. He lived in the biggest house and didn't work. 'The life of a gentleman' was how he described his life style.

He had one friend called Stewart Searle, whose father owned the local newspaper, the Walvern Gazette, and was equally pretentious. Stewart worked on the newspaper. He had a plush office and wrote a column called 'In and Out of Society' and a more poisonous column would be difficult to find in any newspaper. Many of the locals purchased the paper just to read this column, to see who Stewart had decided was in or out. Barry and Stewart only ate in the Commercial Hotel dining room, never contemplating another, though in Walvern there were five altogether and each had their own clientele. As one can imagine, the Commercial was a little run-down but had very good food, due to the chef, Lenny Risley. This was Barry's existence – an empty one – but because he was so full of himself he never noticed. There were only two things that could strike fear into Barry's heart : one was the word 'homosexual' and the other was 'aunt', Emily's young sister, Aunt Thelma. Thelma and Emily were like chalk and cheese in their outlook. Physically they were very similar, except that Thelma dressed always in a mannish way, no jewellery, and a man's watch. 'You can never read those stupid girly things,' she said of women's watches. Thelma had married late and the marriage only lasted four years, when her husband died of a rare form of cancer. Thelma inherited everything, everything being a sawmill, a house in Walvern and a comfortable bank account. She could have sold the mill and never had to worry about money for the rest of her life but this was not Thelma. She immediately bought herself a couple of pairs of overalls and took over the running of the sawmill. She saw at once how to make more money by investing in the business and went from a staff of sixteen to one of twenty-three, all in one year. The trucks left the mill laden with timber for all over Victoria. Thelma was a hand taskmaster and not afraid to get out with the workers and help. She could also hold her own on Friday nights at the local hotel, drinking with some of them. She was a popular employer, with a string of expletives for everything that angered her.

So when it was announced that Thelma was making a call, Barry genuinely suffered a type of fear that was complicated by nausea. Thelma had no time for him. She considered him a lazy, slack arse and said so, much to his annoyance. Emily on these occasions found it wiser not to intervene.

'Why the hell don't you lose weight?' she said, looking at Barry. 'I'll give you a job at the mill.'

'No, thank you, Aunt Thelma.'

'You are such a lazy bastard,' she replied in an off-hand way, looking about at the ruinous condition of the house. 'I can't believe you haven't done anything to fix the roof. Why don't you get up there, Barry, and clean all the leaves out? That's probably the problem.'

He took another scone and cream and wolfed it down.

'Hopeless!' was Thelma's retort. She and Emily went on to discuss the social ups and down of Walvern society, while Barry sat like a spring ready to move quickly the moment that Thelma's departure was decided on.

If Houghton Hall was a forgotten place in summer, in winter it was, according to Thelma, warmer at the South Pole. It was freezing, with draughts whipping in from all angles and to see this small room that became the centre of their lives, with old newspapers stuffed in between windows that would not close properly and under doors, was a vision of super-poverty, such as in the industrial revolution in England.

There was no social exchange between the Houghtons and the O'Rileys, and absolutely no contact with the boys at Rosebae. This, for Barry was just out of the question. As a closet queen, he was terrified someone might be interested in his sexuality, the truth being that no one could have cared less. The fact that he cut such a comic figure meant no one ever put the words 'Barry Houghton' and sex together. He always considered he had been wronged and carried a chip on his shoulder as a result of his not having a large bank account. He never moved. He went from home to Walvern and returned, never going anywhere else for fear that no-one would know him. Here at Walvern at least the store owners and staff addressed him to his face as 'Mr Houghton' : behind his back was another matter. This Thursday, before meeting Stewart Searle for lunch, he had a dental appointment at Dr Mary O'Farrel's surgery, which he attended under sufferance, as the old dentist in Argyle Street had died, so it left Mary's as the only dental practice in Walvern.

Mary O'Farrel was a pleasant, easy-going woman of thirty five. She had been to school with Thomas O'Riley and both had gone on to university. They nowadays saw one another very rarely as Thomas was resident in Melbourne. When Mary graduated from the dental faculty, she returned to Walvern to work in her uncle's studio and when he died he left everything to her, being childless. She took over the practice, having worked in it for some years, and began to modernise the interior with more up-to-date equipment and computer programs. She had another dentist who worked two days a week and between them they managed the workload for now. But the practice received a social boost as a result of Mary's receptionist becoming pregnant and leaving. Mary had a close friend, Trevor Wise, and it was he who offered to step in and take the receptionist's position. This move changed her practice radically, at least in appearance. At school, Mary had been an over-weight student, full of fun: she kept four friends who remained as such for life, as the large Catholic school was co-educational in Mary's time, Trevor Wise, Simon Osler, the beautiful Thomas O'Riley and one woman only, Enid Wrighton, that being her married name. With the exception of Thomas, the others she saw often, though Simon less than the others, due to Terry's jealously. But at school they had formed a link and they were inseparable. Mary had, like a magnet, the ability to attract gay men; her male friends were really all gay, but especially Thomas, Trevor and Simon, all good-looking, all socially smart. Their youth was spent together with Enid, laughing and joking through their adolescence but the centre of their existence was Mary, who always knew how to add salve to a broken heart, especially as the boys fell in and out of love with the sporting teams every week. Enid was the learner on the side; she came from a home of five girls and a certain harsh economic reality so whenever there were excursions or extra money was required at school or out of it, the group or mainly Mary paid for her, something she never forgot. But with Simon well closeted by Terry and Thomas in Melbourne, it was Trevor who was Mary's constant companion, always laughing together about the man who got away.

Trevor Wise still lived at home, and why not? He lived in one of the most beautiful homes in Walvern, in Aspel Drive, an old residential area. The street was named after one of the city fathers who laid the town out and the hamlet near Killpara also carried his name. This street was lined with plane trees and the big Victorian houses were set well back in manicured gardens and most boasted a vast number of enormous rhododendrons in every colour imaginable. No. 17 Aspel Drive was home to Dr Paul Wise, his wife and their son Trevor, whom they found quite a social handful. Because money was not a problem, Trevor lived like a summer cricket, never assuming winter would ever come along. He never studied well at school, although he had the opportunity to go to university he did not take it, so post-school days saw him in the company of Simon and Enid, but work-wise there was very little. He liked being a big fish in a little pond. He felt comfortable. This could not be said of his father, who heard rumours that Trevor was certainly not just having a drink with Enid and Simon, but was casting his net widely and always drawing the same type of man – a married one. Trevor complained bitterly to Enid about it but his sexual activities were always with the same type, married men.

When Mary returned from university they were all elated and the enlarged group with Mary as the guide formed a new but pleasant balance. Trevor and Simon had had an affair but just that, nothing serious and this bound them even closer, much to Simon's present lover's annoyance. He loathed Trevor. So when Mary found herself without a receptionist Trevor stepped in and loved it, all dressed in white, looking very Dr Kildare. He had finally found his niche. Mary trained him to assist her and he was very quick at learning the skills. One of the first things he insisted on was a complete overhaul of the terrible waiting room. Mary complied but was not all that excited about the cost of it.

Trevor laughed. 'Think of it as public relations, darling,' he said. 'No one minds paying if they feel great but in that old railway waiting room I'm surprised they pay you at all.'

'Are you?' she asked, tightening her lips, so in a short time Mary and Trevor became a fixture: his witty comments and her expert work made for more comfortable clients. And again the group changed as Simon joined it, though less and less due to pressure at Rosebae. So it returned to three, Mary, Enid and Trevor and they always drank at the Oriental Hotel in Main Street, opposite the park.

Mary lived in her uncle's house in Aspel Drive that had been left to her but she had two brothers, one older and one younger who both lived at home. Keven, the elder, and Joseph, the younger.

Keven, according to Trevor, was completely feral. He moved from job to job and was now nearing forty. He had a matching group of loud friends who drank too much and then used other substances to keep the night going. Keven had been in trouble with the police several times and had been threatened that the next time he would be in real trouble. He was a small town hoodlum. He always got caught: he was not clever at all. He was mercilessly thin, with a very drawn face and constantly glazed eyes. Their colour was impossible to describe as they seemed to change all the time. He had a visibly long nose and always botches on the skin on his face. He wore the same uniform all the time, skin-tight jeans, decorated cowboy boots, a check shirt hanging out and a belt with a huge silver buckle. The effect was of an ageing rocker of the fifties. He had a very short temper and in a flash could start a fight with anyone, so he was considered by all as very shaky, especially when he used other substances to kick him along. He disliked Mary and saw her as a public banner of something he wasn't, mainly a success. He hated Mary's friends and made no secret of it, especially Trevor, who always put the knife into him verbally and twisted it. But he had this sixth sense that to physically strike Trevor would never be to his advantage, so Trevor was the only male that got away with sharp, sarcastic comments at his expense. He had no fixed girlfriend for the obvious reason, his dependence on drink and other things, and he was not attractive. Strangely, with Mary, his sister, a dentist, he had the most shocking teeth. The front two were black at the sides, when he smiled or laughed, gave him a very left-over look.

But if Keven had serious problems, so did Joseph, but in a completely different way. Whereas Keven was unattractive, Joseph was beautiful.

17

He was tall, well-built with a soft mop of light brown hair and the most splendid pair of pale hazel eyes, a good nose and mouth and a cleft jaw line – altogether a vision according to Trevor and anyone else who saw him. But he had a real problem. He was an introvert: he kept to himself and rarely, unless it was necessary, left his parents' home. He had just turned twenty three and still had not found any form of employment. He just couldn't get going. Everything seemed insurmountable for him. He hated sports and the only thing that gave him any pleasure was Mr Ollie's auction room, that he haunted when he saw fit to leave the security of the house. Mary had offered him accommodation with her, fearing that Keven was a bad influence, but he had refused, choosing to remain at home with Keven, drifting in and out. But he liked Mr Ollie, who saw Joseph not as a problem boy but someone who just wanted to work out for himself where he fitted in in this complex world. Mary always supplied Joseph with money when he asked for it and that was rarely, so she took to just thrusting twenty or fifty dollar notes into his hand and giving him a kiss. She was particularly attached to him and very protective, as Trevor found out to his dismay once when he tried to move in on him.

It had been a Sunday lunch and Joseph had been lured out of his burrow to join her and Trevor. But Trevor made the mistake of assuming that Mary would not be all that unhappy if he and Joseph formed a relationship. When Mary saw Trevor begin to show his 'dorsal fin', she immediately set the ground rules for life.

'Do what you like when you like, darling,' she smiled, as Joseph was not in earshot, 'but you lay one hand on Joseph and we are finished and so, sweetie, is your job.'

Trevor was genuinely surprised at Mary's sudden and forceful attack and the threatened consequences and backed off, but it was difficult to sit opposite this beautiful boy for lunch and have to realise that he could never be touched. Joseph seemed oblivious to Trevor's approach and this made Trevor all the more annoyed, thinking that the man that would end up with Joseph - and he was certain it would be a man - was going to be luckier than him.

Mary had tried every avenue open to her to try and interest Joseph in some activity but to no avail. He feigned interest for a moment and then abandoned the idea, much to Mary's exasperation. Still, he remained someone she loved dearly and she was very generous to him in time and money.

One Saturday morning, Joseph had made his weekly pilgrimage to Mr Ollie's Auction Rooms and as Mr Ollie was short staffed he asked Joseph whether he would mind helping him to move a wardrobe and table to another position. Joseph was quick to come to Mr Ollie's aid and the table was moved, then the wardrobe. There was a soft thud from behind the wardrobe when it was withdrawn from the wall and when they looked behind they noticed two picture frames had fallen to the ground. Joseph picked up the pair of very damaged Victorian frames and looked at them.

'What do you think of them?' asked Mr Ollie.

'Well, they're not exactly in good condition, are they?' he replied.

'No, they're not, but a smart lad like you could probably restore them. If you like them, take them – a gift.'

'Thank you very much.' Joseph gave a slightly embarrassed smile and left the auction rooms with them under each arm.

It was later when he saw Mary. He told her about them.

'Are you going to restore them?' she asked.

'I don't know how but I would like to try.'

Mary struck quickly. 'Just a moment,' and she disappeared down the corridor and into her living room. In five minutes she returned. 'Well, young man,' she smiled, 'Monday at 10.30 you are to go to Mrs Jan Wilson's house on Ash Street, number 32, for your first lesson in restoration of frames. She is a quiet but really nice lady of about fifty five. I think you'll like her – I know you will. She is dying to meet you.'

'Hmm,' was Joseph's only reply, smiling and showing a radiant set of perfect teeth, all due to Mary's work, with Trevor panting while handing her the instruments.

Monday arrived and 10.30 saw Joseph at No. 32, Ash Street.

'Come in, come in!' called Jan Wilson. 'I'm Jan,' and shook his hand.

'I am Joseph,' he said, shyly but instantly felt good with her and she with him.

'Come through to my workroom.'

He followed her down the passage of a suburban house to a room at the right that perhaps had been a bedroom, but was set up as a laboratory workroom. Unbeknown to Joseph, Mary had made a second call to Jan to explain about her beautiful brother and his inability to settle down to do anything, and she was willing to offset any costs just as long as Joseph found something he was interested in. Jan had listened patiently to Mary and then said that it would all depend on how they found and reacted to one another. She was surprised at this good-looking, tall youth and sensed instantly that he was exceptionally shy and so she worked very slowly at removing any social barrier that he could not handle, first names, little jokes. He noted she had cleared a space so she worked one side of the table and he the other. He felt completely comfortable for the first time in his life in a work situation and listened carefully to what she had to say. She was a general restorer, but damaged pictures or mirror frames made up a large part of her business so she was well skilled to begin Joseph's first lesson.

Even at school he had never been a high achiever. He had always understood the lessons but he made the minimum of effort. He passed his exams but only just: he was totally indifferent to being top of the class and did what was required but only that. He loathed sport of any kind: although he was a strong swimmer he flatly refused to swim in House swimming sports. He was considered by his peers and teachers as a round peg in a square hole. He just didn't fit. He had very few friends at school and was always seen alone, never in a group. Mary despaired.

It was when she returned from university and dental school that she took over looking after him. His parents had despaired of both sons. Keven, the elder, had been expelled from school at an early age and the staff were worried that they would have another Keven, but were pleasantly surprised at what they saw and his very gentle behaviour, but they lamented that his efforts were extremely limited. He went to the same school as Mary and Keven but he felt no real attachment to it at all. He had to attend that he did, but that was that. The very handsome Joseph was and remained a loner. Every year his report read much the same: 'Seeking to pass with the minimum of effort'.

'No, hold it like this. Great! That's got it!' exclaimed Jan and he began for the first time in his life to gain a sense of achievement. He spent the morning watching Jan make little rubber moulds of the pieces that were missing from his pair of frames and he soon picked up the knack of it.

'You will stay for a bite to eat with me,' she urged. 'I can't have my favourite apprentice disappearing on the first day.'

'I'd love to,' he smiled.

Jan was a divorcee and happy about it, after ten unhappy years with a man much her senior. She divorced him and settled down on her own to start her restoration business to supplement her limited settlement.

'I'm quite happy to help, if I can,' Joseph offered, confidently.

'Great! Looks like we are really going to make this business a 'goer'.' She laughed. 'What are you going to do with your frames when they are finished?'

'I don't know,' he replied, looking at her. 'I think I may just hang them on the wall, empty for now.'

'Were you good at art at school?' she asked.

'A bit – but I never got into it.'

'I was the same when I went to school. I wasn't so good at academic subjects but I really liked to paint. In fact, there is a painting class at the state school, an evening class. I was thinking of joining, but I'm afraid I am too old to go and people will just look at me as some old has-been.' She picked up her glass of wine and had a sip.

'I don't think anyone would say that about you,' he replied in an indignant manner.

'Thanks. You really are a nice lad,' she said, softly.

Joseph felt a need to support Jan, just as she was helping him. 'I'll tell you what,' he went on. 'If you make enquiries about the art class, I'll come too, so at least we can sit together.'

'That would be great. I just couldn't go alone, you know, with all the others just looking at me, but with you it'll be a different story. OK, I'll see when the new semester begins and see what we need to take. Oh, I think it should be fun.'

When he returned home, he called Mary to say that Jan was really nice and she was going to teach him everything about restoring frames and perhaps they would go to the painting classes on Wednesday nights. Mary was overjoyed. 'Joseph, that's fabulous. I am so pleased. Listen, I shall be at home in half an hour. Come over for dinner. I want to hear all about it.' Then she hung up. 'So, sorry, darling,' she said, turning to Trevor, 'I have an appointment with Joseph and by anyway aren't you going to the theatre company later tonight?

'Oh, yes,' he replied with a sigh, 'but I just thought a drink or two before . . .'

'Sorry! What are we rehearsing for this time?

'I haven't a clue. We have all been summoned for a meeting tonight. How dreary. Same tired old thespians.'

Mary laughed. 'Come on, darling, you know you always get the lead role.'

'That's only because no-one else can sing.' He laughed.

Trevor was a member of the Walvern Light Opera Company and every year or sometimes twice a year they produced a performance of varying quality, but it was a very important cultural part of Walvern's life: apart from the agricultural show and the Light Opera production, that was it for Walvern. Trevor had a particularly good tenor voice, so despite his earlier comment he was always in hot demand as the leading man.

* * * * *

'Come in,' cried Mary as she welcomed Joseph in, with an arm around his shoulder. 'Tell me all.'

He settled his handsome frame into a chair in the kitchen-dining room and recounted everything, and to Mary's surprise, with a great deal of enthusiasm. She was particularly pleased when he said he was returning the next day to do some more work on his frames. 'Darling, I wish you would come and live here. It would be so much better for you. The stimulus at home is zero, I believe, according to Mum. There was another fight between Dad and Keven.'

'They always yell and shout at one another. I hate it,' he answered sharply.

'Listen, Joseph, why don't we give it a try. Why don't you come and stay here for a fortnight and then if you want to go back home I promise I won't say another word for life.'

He smiled. 'I don't believe you, but I just might give it a try. Keven is really out of his mind. He has drugs in his room and I'm sure he is 'pushing' them as well. I just find it a bit creepy.'

'Creepy!' cried Mary. 'He needs a large block of cement tied around his neck and dropped off the end of a pier.'

Joseph laughed. 'He's not worth getting into trouble for. And, besides, if Dad stopped baiting him all the time, and telling him he's a loser, he just might make an effort.'

'He won't. I have one feral brother and one beautiful one and that's that. Now, darling, do open the bottle. I say, will you be learning to gild?'

'I hope so. Jan's really clever. She seems to be able to do anything.'

'She sounds a really nice person,' Mary commented and Joseph agreed.

She watched him fill two glasses. He really was handsome, she thought, and it's not just that he is my brother, what with his good-looking face and his excellent physique. She thought that someone was going to be very happy with her little brother, and, like Trevor, she had the feeling inside that it was more than likely to be someone male.

Joseph returned the next day to Jan's workroom and the pair of them passed a productive and happy morning together, with Joseph working on his frames and while waiting for them to dry began work, under Jan's instruction, on the repair of a large mirror frame that had apparently dropped off the wall and was in several pieces.

'We must work out a scheme for paying you,' said Jan.

'Oh no,' he replied, indignantly. 'You are teaching me and I should be paying you.'

'No, no,' she contradicted, 'fair is fair. We'll go halves on the mirror frame when it's finished and that's it.' She smiled. 'Oh, don't worry, I have at least twelve other old frames just waiting for us. You see what you have got yourself into.'

'I think it's great,' was his smiling comment, and so this continued for the first week, with a very excited Joseph and a very content Jan. It was the first time for ages she had had company like this. After her divorce, most of her female friends cut her dead as they saw her as competition for their husbands. An unhappy marriage is one thing but a divorced woman is entirely another, and the men she had known called her only for one thing, so she had been very much alone for several years now and Joseph was like a breath of fresh air for her. She found herself waiting for the doorbell to ring at nine in the morning so that they could sit opposite one another at the worktable and discuss all manner of things while working.

Joseph had been very surprised with himself. He suddenly realised that the change he sought or the goal he sought in his life was as simple as walking through a wall of paper. He had always imagined that it was solid brick, impossible to pass through, so change would be impossible. Now, with a second change, due to a terrible fight between Keven and his father, as the fight raged on he calmly went to his bedroom, telephoned Mary and said he was coming to live with her. He would get a taxi and be there in less than half an hour. He began to put his things into a large canvas bag and then he looked at them and tossed them out. 'Only what I shall use,' he thought and left through the back door with a half-filled canvas bag and what he had on. He knew in his heart he had not left anything behind. The cab he had ordered stopped in front of the house. He got in and didn't even look back. He gave Mary's address and knew comfortably he would never return to his parents' house – ever.

'Darling,' cried Mary, 'welcome home.'

'Thanks. I haven't brought much because I don't have many things.'

'Great, we will go shopping this week and pick up a few things for you. Oh, I am so happy you are here. If you want to use my car, the keys are here. I rarely use it and Trevor is just up the street: he picks me up for work every morning, so you can drive to Jan's instead of catching the bus. Oh, it's all just perfect. Come on, I'll show you your room.'

The house Mary had inherited from her uncle was a very large Victorian one in the best street in Walvern. It was immaculate and she showed Joseph to a large bedroom with a double bed and a private bathroom. 'Darling, if you don't like the colour or something, say so and I will have it changed.'

'Mary, it's perfect.' And so it was, as was the rest of this comfortable, elegant home that was to be Joseph's, though, as it turned out, not for life. He was still shy but his character changed dramatically. Mary challenged him on all social levels and he rose to the occasion. His movements were much less lethargic than before and he was much more prepared to change his past tendency to retreat. Now, with a new address and a good one, plus learning a skill he enjoyed, he changed completely. Even Trevor had to admit that his character was much altered and in a very short time. But his beauty remained unchanging.

If everything was improving for Joseph, it was definitely on the decline for Keven. The company he kept became more and more dangerous and the moving of drugs became more complicated, the great problem being that Keven was not a genius and only saw life on a day to day footing. He never thought ahead and his so-called friends used him shamelessly. He was too stupid to see it. The last run-in with the police genuinely frightened him, so now, as he knew what the consequences of another brush with the law would be, and as he was not keen on the idea of spending a stretch in prison, his native cunning told him to lie low for a while. This should have resolved his short-term problems, but his necessity for drugs for himself soon had him walking a very fine tightrope. When he was happy, which was often due to excess alcohol or some other substance, he would make a regular pilgrimage to No. 6A, a little shop on Main Street, and yet another tattoo would find itself transferred to his body. He was now like a walking billboard and none of the tattoos bore any correlation between one and another. Where he had a space, on went another one. Because he was such an recognisable person, he had no problem supplying drugs, as he stood out like a beacon, so for the 'respectable' people behind this lucrative business Keven was good as a trader, though his erratic behaviour sometimes made them very nervous. He only had two moods, up or down, and down produced a very ugly side to him, the thug. He was without mercy when he attacked someone for one thing or another and when he was down it only took the slightest thing and he would raise his fists in that direction.

His relationship with Joseph was odd. To Keven Joseph was invisible. If he was in a room he chose not to see him and the conversation was non-existent, much to Joseph's satisfaction, so when he moved out to live with Mary, for Keven it was a non-event. He never spoke to him before so he didn't miss him at all. His relationship with Mary was much more complex and for some reason he was afraid of her. She most certainly was not afraid of him and often challenged him verbally in front of anyone. He just stood there without any comment like a small child being reprimanded for having done something stupid. She had threatened him several times that if he ever touched Joseph she would deal with him personally and he would rue that day for the rest of his life. But the situation with his father was electric. They yelled and screamed at one another day in day out and occasionally fists would fly or a piece of crockery or a glass would go hurtling across the living room. His mother had just lost the plot. She continued ever onwards, seemingly in a state of hopelessness, like an old tired mouse going round and round on a wheel. She didn't even say anything when Joseph left to live with Mary. Perhaps, Mary thought, she was secretly glad that Joseph was in good hands and out of harm's way.

CHAPTER 2

Thomas

CHAPTER 2

Thomas

Mary and Thomas had left Walvern together, both destined to do well at the university in Melbourne, but with time and new friends they did not see much of one another. A train trip back to Walvern became rarer and rarer. To begin with Thomas missed his friends and Killpara but he had someone in Melbourne that soothed his way into a lifestyle he adored. This person was Aunt Rose, his mother's sister. Rose was ten years younger than her sister. Thomas and she had always had a close relationship and as she lived in Melbourne, but paid visits to Killpara it was she who took Thomas under her wing socially and financially. Rose had married a very wealthy investor and had a beautiful home in Toorak. It had been her husband's family home. She took over the re-decoration and found that she liked it. She developed a passion for antique furniture and having the finance behind her bought well, but was always out for the good offer. Her husband had died some years earlier, before Thomas came to Melbourne, leaving her very wealthy, but a shrewd businesswoman that directly cast Thomas's life. The two great passions in her life were antiques and gay men: she had very little to do with women. She never completely trusted them, and felt more than comfortable with her coterie of gentlemen friends. Her dinner parties were famous, the food splendid as were the wines, and conversation was hysterically funny all evening, in this glorious mansion. If she had an excellent eye for antiques and painting, she also had an excellent eye and was a splendid judge of character, especially when it came to gay men. She only chose the ones she wanted as permanent friends. The friend for two or three dinner parties bored her: she saw loyalty as something to be rewarded.

She had watched Thomas grow up and in her heart never had a single doubt of his sexuality. He was kind, had a brilliant sense of humour and was beautiful, so when he arrived in Melbourne everything was waiting for him, orchestrated by Rose. But even when he was young he shone. He was a beautiful child and as he grew to early manhood he became even more noticeable. At school with Trevor, Simon, Mary and Enid, the five were inseparable but the most beautiful was Thomas. Enid carried a torch for him all her life. He was the smartest in class, the best sportsman; at whatever he tried he was a success and it seemed with the smallest effort. With all this success one part of him remained private, his sexuality. He was secure in it and so had no need to prove anything to anyone, and although Trevor made many moves in Thomas's direction sexually, he always joked it off in a charitable way without ever actually saying yes or no. Trevor was always at the end of that sexual fishing line, just waiting for Thomas to reel him in, but it never happened. Even Simon, the school swimming champion, subtly attempted a liaison but again Thomas held out. Yet it did nothing to damage his popularity; he was adored by his peer group, both male and female, and quite a few girls openly bitched against Mary and Enid for keeping Thomas to themselves.

He loved Killpara: the fact that the land dropped away to the valley and in autumn and winter the whole valley was covered in fog. The sensation was, he felt, that you could just walk out on top of it like a large soft, white carpet. They had a horse, but his sister Patricia never rode. Thomas did and he would ride for miles or go to Simon's when his parents were alive and they would ride off together into this splendid English/Australian landscape of undulating hills and hundred year old cypress windbreaks.

The little town of Aspel was lined with an enormous avenue of plane trees that just followed the roadside and one of these now majestic trees had been planted as a memorial to one of the local boys who had fallen in the First World War. Originally, a little plaque at the base of the trunk named the soldier who never came home this tranquil part of the world.

Thomas had been closer to Simon than Trevor as Trevor could sometimes make his play a little obvious. Simon did not do that; he was always with Thomas at weekends. Thomas's life had been idyllic. He had never suffered a setback in his life, only encouragement and love, but the dominant figure in his early life was Rose. Each bounced off the other; even though she was much older it made no difference. If Auntie Rose was coming to Killpara then all his friends just had to wait and it never altered all his life, so when he was accepted into the university, Rose simply took over, as you do if you are Rose, and supplied him with a beautiful terraced house in East Melbourne that she owned, as it was so close to the university. The fact that the house was so superior Rose saw as incidental. She refurbished it with antique items but not before changing the interior completely. It had been let for a long time and was showing the wear and tear of time and tenants. But it was right for Thomas. Her coterie of male friends were well in with the decorating world, and she had great fun enlisting them to completely refurbish the terrace overlooking Darling Square. New bathrooms and kitchen were essential and so the work progressed.

After Thomas's final days at school, he went directly to Melbourne as Rose's guest and the pair of them chose all the furnishings. It was in this early period that Thomas also discovered he had a love of antiques and nothing pleased him more than a day at the auction rooms or searching about in antique shops. Rose was an expert and he learned quickly. She was more than pleased with his eye for furniture and his taste in paintings and so in his first month or so before he began university his social education took a leap forward thanks to Rose.

Whenever she had a dinner party, there were generally for eight or ten guests. She was the only woman, dressed elegantly and dripping in jewels. She loved to wear them at home amongst her friends but did so much less in public as she was very aware of the catty or bitch comments passed by envious women. She made no bones about explaining to Thomas his sexual destiny and he accepted as usual everything Rose told him. He had good taste in men and that pleased her a lot, but she adored him as her escort and as a result he saw the best of Melbourne from his first steps. One of the only things Rose forbade him to do was to call her Auntie. He laughed and said, 'Rose it is!'

'Thank you, darling. 'Aunty' makes me seem positively ready for the grave!'

Not only did Thomas receive the elegant terraced house as his, he also, due to Rose, received a bank account and a very healthy one, with a generous sum added every month. Rose loved taking him shopping for clothes and soon his wardrobe was bulging, yet despite this wonderful life-style, his personality never altered. If he met a millionaire, and in Rose's company there were many, or another student whom he paid a luncheon meal for, it was the same: he either liked someone or he didn't. In this sense he was a carbon copy of Rose. He enjoyed sex with men but he never formed a relationship. He might see them once or twice and that was that. He never felt the need to continue or develop anything and this was the pattern of his life. If the truth be told, although Rose lamented his not finding 'Mr. Right' she was not unhappy about the situation as it meant he had much more time for her. He worked hard at the university but found most of it came easily. He was always concerned that if Rose was paying for everything she deserved the best results he was capable of.

Rose's home in Albany Road, Toorak, was splendid, a huge neo-Georgian house in aged red brick, covered in manicured ivy, with stone quoins around the windows and doors. The house had been built in the 1920s and, at the time, had been considered an extravagance. It was set in large grounds, one of the few houses left to boast that, as many owners had sold off their land for apartments or even demolished the original house as well. But Rose's beautiful house and grounds remained intact. The building had been altered two or three times, but the character always remained elegant. From, the moment a car pulled up to the front door, and a maid opened it, a visitor stepped into a large entrance hall with a sweeping staircase directly ahead, and a black and white marble floor that was the perfect introduction to the rest of the house. To the right and left were the two large reception rooms, with identical Aubusson carpets, beautiful furniture, exuberant curtain arrangements, large marble fire places with overmantel mirrors and wonderful chandeliers. Truly this pair of rooms was from an elegant past. Behind the room on the right was another sitting room in emerald, absolutely overwhelming and on the other side was the larger of the two dining rooms in a soft raspberry colour. The walls and curtains were both in matching silk damask, the furniture in the dining room was the finest Victorian, with a table that would, when extended, seat twenty without a problem and a pair of large sideboards either side of the terracotta marble fireplace that groaned under the weight of fine silver. This was the home that Thomas came to before his terraced house was completed and even after it was refurbished he spent as much time at Rose's mansion as he did at the house in East Melbourne. Each time he returned to Killpara to see his parents and sister, he was very aware of the difference in the accommodation and although he loved Killpara each time he saw the house he was more than certain that eventually there would have to be an overhaul and a major one at that. But for the present his mother was content with it and as he was now not resident, he let it go. Any mention of getting rid of a piece of furniture and replacing it with a better piece generally brought the same response: 'I'm quite happy with the piece, darling,' and that was that.

Rose occasionally came up to Killpara to see her only sister and acted as if she had a matching home, never complaining or passing comments that might be taken the wrong way. Rose sat at the family table chatting as if she were in her own red dining room, surrounded by her usual handsome ten men.

'Well, Samuel,' she said, 'how's the surveying going?'

'The same, Rose,' Joyce's husband replied. 'Nothing much changed in my field of work.'

'Joyce tells me that you are considering a big job interstate with a mining company for six months.'

'Yes.' He looked sideways at Joyce. 'But I'm not sure about taking it. You see, it leaves Joyce and Patricia here alone.'

'What do you mean, 'here alone'? There is the share-farmer and his wife barely fifteen metres away.'

'It's not that. We are so desperate for money, but a bit extra always helps.'

'You know, if you are in trouble financially and you don't come directly to me, I shall never set foot in Killpara again.'

'Thanks, Rose. It's very kind of you but with my work and the share-farmer we do pretty well here – a bit better, I must say, than them up the road.

'What do you mean?' Thomas asked before Rose could ask the same question.

'Well, look at the Houghtons. They must really be in a tight corner. They have sold off the land and leased what's left. You can't be getting much of a return on that.'

'Hm, I suppose not,' Thomas agreed. 'Why did they sell off the land?'

'I suppose they were short of cash and it seemed the easy way out. And the saints know Barry Houghton isn't going to lift a finger. I have never known such a lazy person. His poor mother does everything for him.'

'Do you know him?' Rose asked Thomas.

'Only by sight. He's pretty pretentious. Someone told me that the big house is falling into ruin inside but I don't know. I've never seen inside it. Mum, tomorrow lunch could I invite Simon and Terry. I'm sure Rose would enjoy meeting them.'

'Of course. I saw Simon the other day at Walvern. He is such a nice boy, although now,' she smiled, 'he is a man. Yes, that would be nice.'

Patricia, when Rose was present, remained mute. She didn't like Rose and the feeling was mutual. Patricia thought her to be overbearing and bossy and the person who always knew best: whereas Rose thought Patricia dead boring and a bit of a mouse. The pair of them, for the sake of harmony, simply ignored one another.

It was obvious to all that Rose was never happier than when she was with Thomas. They went for walks at Killpara, joked, laughed and, as they thought alike, they complemented one another perfectly.

The Saturday lunch was organised, with Patricia not in such a good humour as she considered she was being used as a servant and that displeased her greatly. Rose had a soft spot for the share-farmer, hopeless with money but funny and honest. Whenever Rose came to visit Killpara she never forgot he bottle of whiskey for James. Saturday lunch was set for one o'clock, later than usual, but it gave everyone time to be there. Thomas and Rose had gone to Walvern in the morning in Rose's black Jaguar, which, when with Rose, he always drove. Rose's garage in Albany Road held space for the Jaguar and a black Mercedes sports. Both were at Thomas's disposal. He had telephoned Mary previously and they met at mid-day at the Oriental Hotel for a quick drink before dashing back to Killpara for lunch.

'Hi!' cried Mary, as she dashed in. 'Sorry I'm late.' She laughed. 'Tricky patient. Trevor's parking the car. You must be Rose. I'm Mary.'

'Pleased to meet you,' smiled Rose and meant it. It was strange that Rose she should warm to a woman but she did to Mary.

'Darlings, you would think we were in fucking Bourke Street, not a park. Can you believe it?' Rose gave a very generous smile. This was the type of man she knew and liked.

'Sit down, young man,' she said. 'Darling, I'll marry you tomorrow.'

He laughed. 'No one has called me a young man for years.'

'Oh, that's because you aren't one,' said Mary, dryly. 'It's OK, Rose, we work together.'

'It seems,' Rose replied, 'you are both very fortunate. You complement one another.'

'Thanks,' Mary laughed.

'Thomas, you look divine,' said Trevor. 'If I can't marry Rose it will definitely have to be you.' Everyone laughed.

'Well, what's all the noise about?' Everyone turned their heads to see Enid coming toward them with a tray of glasses and a bottle of champagne.

'This is Enid,' Thomas announced. 'I have told you about her. Our school group is only missing Simon.'

'How do you do?' smiled Enid.

'Fine, thank you,' was Rose's reply, but it was obvious to Thomas that Rose did not find Enid someone she would warm to. But she was very polite to her.

'How long have you had the hotel?' she asked. 'Oh, gosh, I married Paul not long after I left school, so it must be almost eighteen years now. Thomas, you look great.' Rose did not miss this last comment from Enid.

Mary and Trevor took over joking about the locals, much to Rose's entertainment.

'Oh, I must tell you,' cried Trevor, 'I am to be the leading man in the new production.'

'Congratulations,' said Thomas. 'He was always the actor at school,' and, looking at Rose, who was immaculately dressed, 'he has a great voice.'

Trevor looked at Rose and winked. 'Eat your heart out, Pavarotti,' which even had Rose laughing. He really is an entertainer, she was thinking. I hope the other two at lunch are as funny.

'We shall have to go,' Thomas butted in. 'I'm sorry, but I'll call, Mary, the next time we are coming up and how about we all go out to dinner. Of course, we can have dinner here.'

'Great,' came the reply and they left, to drive off in the direction of Killpara.

'I think Mary and Trevor are delightful,' said Rose, leaving Enid well out of the conversation.

Thomas smiled: 'She's had a tough life, Enid, but she is OK.'

'She is in love with you. Don't you know that?' Rose was looking straight ahead.

'Yes, I know. I always keep things on the level with Enid, but she is not a problem.'

'And Trevor?'

'Oh him! He's crazy.'

'He is very good looking,' Rose commented.

'Yes, I suppose so, but he isn't me. He is someone I went to school with and I like very much. But he is always the showman, with tons of style.'

'Yes, I agree with you. And I like Mary very much. She is a very real woman, very dependable and pleasant to be with.

'Mary's the centre of this little group, but now I don't see them much. When I do, I enjoy it. Mary always organizes everything. She's great. She is very generous. When we were at school, as Enid came from a very poor family, she always paid for her school outings and any extras and no-one ever knew. I think Mary is the only woman Enid genuinely adores. She hates other women but she would do anything at all for Mary.'

'Well, perhaps I have underestimated Enid,' Rose smiled again. 'We'll see.'

This was the first time Rose had met Thomas's friends from school and although he was now thirty six these people still held a bond together, which impressed Rose.

* * * * *

'You're late,' Joyce exclaimed.

'Sorry, Mum. A funny drunk at the Oriental.'

'Good heavens, I'm surprised you took Rose there.'

'It was fun,' Rose insisted. 'I met some nice people.'

'Oh well, come along and I will introduce you to some more.' They followed Joyce into the living room, where everyone except Patricia rose.

'Hi!' cried Thomas, and went over to put both arms around Simon. 'I haven't seen you for ages. You look great.' Simon blushed a little. 'Oh, Rose, this is Simon and Terry.'

'How do you do,' she purred.

The drinks were offered around and Rose sat back to watch. So, she thought, the good-looking Simon also has an eye for Thomas. Terry felt out of his depth, which was foolish, but he wasn't sure how to react. The moment that Thomas said that Rose and he had had drinks with Mary, Enid and Trevor, Rose noticed that Terry stiffened and instantly guessed that he and Trevor were not close companions.

The luncheon went well, with the exception of Patricia and Terry. Both were very quiet, and Rose had the feeling that they would both have preferred to be somewhere else. Rose found engaging Simon in conversation was a very pleasant experience but found Terry brittle, and as much as she tried to bring him into the small talk he remained by choice outside, so she left him there and joined in with Thomas and Simon, having a great time.

It was Joyce who said to Terry, 'Have you seen anything of Barry Houghton these days?'

'Hardly. He's not my type – so pretentious and so ugly.'

There was dead silence. It was a stupid comment and it made a certain acceptance of Terry impossible. This statement, whether true or not, was not good public relations at a dining room table where he hardly knew anybody. Thomas changed the conversation at once and said, 'How's Pete?' as Simon some time ago had told him about the peacock.

'Pete's fine,' was the clipped reply. After that no further conversation went in Terry's direction, and directly after lunch, he stated they had to go, and, much to the others' dismay, this also included Simon.

'That's a very insecure man,' commented Rose to Thomas later.

'I don't know him at all,' he replied. 'This is only the second time I have met him. He's not overfond of me.'

'I wonder why?' and they both began laughing.

* * * * *

At 4.30 Thomas pulled the car out on to the main road and he and Rose headed back to Melbourne.

'Do you think you could ever live at Killpara?' Rose asked.

'Not as it is now,' he said bluntly, 'but it would be nice to see my friends more often.'

'Without Terry, I presume?'

'Yes, he's a bit much. I'm afraid he hates Trevor.' When she asked why, he went on, 'Well, Mary told me that Simon and Trevor had a short affair and Terry is aware of it.'

'What a pity Simon and Trevor never made it work. I think they're well-suited to each other.'

He agreed and added, 'I don't know what really happened, but Terry is jealous of everyone, so I guess it doesn't matter who you are.'

'No, I don't suppose it does,' she said, looking at him.

* * * * *

41

Rose had a small dinner party planned for Sunday evening, so rather than go home he stayed at her home and two friends of theirs were invited to 'a casual dinner' which generally meant anything but that. Rose had had the little dining room decked with late spring flowers and the effect, as always, was splendid. It didn't matter at what time of the year one came to the house on Albany Road it was always full of freshly-cut flowers, giving a lived-in appearance to the elegant, formal rooms.

Andrew and Raoul were bidden for seven o'clock, and Thomas welcomed them in. They were old friends of Rose and him. Andrew had a beautiful antique shop and that had been the initial meeting point. They had remained friends, ever since that first encounter. Andrew's large shop was stacked with the most exotic things, but all of high quality – chandeliers from a Maharaja's palace in Northern India, painted furniture from Venice, Victorian furniture, Georgian furniture and so the list went on, all very tastefully arranged on the extensive floor space paved diagonally in black and white marble tiles. The walls were hung with tapestries and fine paintings. This shop really had something for everyone.

Andrew had met Raoul almost fifteen years before and it had been a relationship that worked. These two good-looking men had a beautiful house surrounded by a magnificent garden, as Raoul was a very talented garden designer. So the house was used as a showpiece for clients. Raoul had a very good business and in a short period of time had built up a good and steady list of clients of whom Rose was one. She helped him initially by recommending him to her friends and the fact that she had the confidence in him to give him 'carte blanche' with her large garden impressed her friends. Two or three garden parties helped enormously to promote him and he never forgot this generosity on Roses's part. As a result, anything that Rose needed for the garden Raoul had it organised immediately at extremely good rates.

'Good to see you,' said Rose, as she swept into the sitting room, heavy with the scent of two enormous vases of lilies.

'The lilies are just you,' Raoul said, smiling.

'Thank you, darling. Is Thomas looking after you, drinks-wise?' The answer was affirmative.

Raoul had a secret love for Thomas but was very careful to keep it exactly that. He thought him the most elegant and handsome man he had ever known : a smile from Thomas was sufficient to keep him walking on air for a week. But what he waited for was the summer parties Rose threw at the swimming pool. If Thomas was beautiful in clothes, in a mini swim brief Raoul thought he was the closest thing possible to a Greek god. Thomas was not unaware of Raoul's attention but out of respect for Andrew always kept the relationship platonic, much to Raoul's dismay.

Andrew was a much more extrovert character and always the entertainer. 'Rose,' he began, 'it's a pity you weren't here last night. Can you believe it, Sandra Kent had a dinner party.'

Here Rose interrupted with, 'Thank the saints I wasn't here. I can't stand her. She's so pretentious.'

'Well, that's the truth,' Andrew laughed, 'but you'll never guess what happened.'

Rose narrowed her eyes. 'Do tell.'

'Well, our Sandra was out to impress her husband's clients, so she thought she would have a table of ten for dinner.'

'What, in that dining room?' asked Raoul. 'It's minute.'

'Exactly. Many years ago Sandra bought from me a chandelier, but decided not to have it electrified as it still had the holders for candles. She had a ratchet system fitted so she could wind it up and let it down to clean and change the candles.'

'Really,' Rose murmured. 'I had no idea she had any creative taste.'

'She hasn't. The chandelier was far too large for the room and even when pulled up to its maximum height it looked a bit silly but she was convinced it was the best thing in town. Anyway, getting back to the story – and I know it well because Bruce was invited and went. Silly of Sandra, as Bruce has a megaphone voice and the telephone numbers of the best gossips in Melbourne. Well, it was raining, not heavily, but a nuisance, and as one of the women went to enter the front door, the mat was wet and the mat and the woman disappeared into Sandra's azaleas.'

Thomas began to laugh. 'I hope she was dressed for the occasion.'

'Oh, she was like all the rest – it was a black tie affair. Well, she was hauled out, looking very bedraggled according to Bruce and from this moment on everything went wrong. The woman was taken upstairs and sort of tidied up according to Bruce, but he said she looked as if she wasn't sure where she was. Do you remember the living room, Rose?'

'I've only been there once and that was sufficient. No, not really.'

'It's long and narrow and Sandra has managed to fill it to the brim with furniture and 'objets d'art' – in other words, tacky ornaments. This poor, damp woman walked past something and swung her arm around, sending a large porcelain figure hurtling to the floor and shattering in all directions. The woman was mortified and Sandra was cross, but pretended everything was fine. With ten people in that narrow, gutted room it was exceptionally difficult to move and one of the men plonked himself down on a gilded opera chair and fell straight through it to the floor. He was, as Bruce said, very overweight, not that Bruce could throw stones – he's enormous!'

'It sounds like a Marx Brothers movie,' said Thomas.

'Oh, it gets better.'

'Well, come along to the table and finish the story there,' urged Rose.

When seated, Andrew continued, 'Bruce said he never did it but I am sure he is the clumsiest and most stupid queen in town : apparently, when all were bidden to the dining room, as he got up he said someone bumped into him and he caught his arm on the edge of a tray and sent the contents clattering to the ground. Some broke, apparently. Sandra was now charged up and exceptionally nervous. The problem, it appeared, was to seat these ten people in this tiny room and there were some very solid guests. As she attempted to pass at the narrowest part to go to the other end of the table, she caught her lace jacket in some silver on the sideboard and as she turned quickly to save the silver she tore her jacket and slipped on the rug under the table. She fell down, bringing - as a result of grasping anything to support her - a silver soup tureen, a tea service and a chair, all on top of her. Bruce said it really was very funny but everyone was now terrified to touch anything lest they knock something over. The space was apparently so cramped that when you reached for your glass you had to be careful you didn't upset someone else's. Sandra had set three glasses in front of each person, all with very tall stems. The first one to be upset was a full glass of red wine, which then spoilt the table cloth. Sandra was beginning to get hysterical but was calmed down until a woman reached out for her glass just as a candle in the chandelier sent down a cascade of hot wax that split onto her naked arm. The scream should have been sufficient, but Bruce said she pulled back her arm, suddenly knocking over all three glasses and as she swung it back, caught a man in the chest with her elbow, causing him to lurch backwards. He grabbed the table for support but missed and took hold of the tablecloth.'

'I don't believe it,' cried Rose, laughing.

'He managed to upset most of the glass, as the chandelier continued to pour hot wax onto the table. Sandra, now over-excited, stood up rapidly, upsetting her chair and as she bent over to right it, stepped on the hem of her frock and a ghastly ripping sound was heard. Holding the front of the frock, she began to let the chandelier down to extinguish the rogue candle but in her agitated state let the ratchet handle go and the chandelier ended up nestled in the centre of the table with everyone wondering what to do. The candle was put out and the chandelier winched back up off the table and hung there, swinging about, so that small sprays of hot wax shot about.'

'It sounds a nightmare,' Thomas commented.

'Oh, it gets better! Sandra by this stage was so angry and upset she forgot the food in the oven and when she finally dashed from the table, now looking like a battlefield with no one able to laugh and all of them making very artificial conversation, she returned with the burnt offerings on a large silver tray with everyone saying 'bravo' – until she stepped on the front hem of her frock which was torn from the fall over the chair. Yes, you're right', he laughed. 'Down she went. The entire contents of the silver tray spilled across the floor and under the table. She was screaming, as the hot meat juice poured down the front of her frock. I would have killed to have been there.'

'What happened then?' asked Thomas.

'Bruce said at that point everyone left, leaving an hysterical Sandra and a demolished house.

'But why have so many people in such a small space?' asked Rose.

'Who knows?' Roaul said to her, joining in the conversation. 'You know how pretentious she is. Do you think she was trying to do an Albany Road?' Everyone laughed, including Rose.

But Rose had not always had this great deal of finance behind her. She and Joyce had grown up not far from Killpara in a modest home. Having a sister ten years her senior was like having a baby-sitter rather than a sister. When Rose was eleven, Joyce married Samuel and a year later Thomas was born, so Rose saw very little of her. When she finished school, she went to the university and studied economics, as Thomas had done so much later. She worked for an important investment firm, met and married the widowed owner, some years her senior, took over the running of the big house in Albany Road and indulged her passion for antiques. It was later in life, when Thomas was about fourteen, that in a certain sense she re-discovered Joyce. She found herself returning to her old stamping ground and enjoying it. If one met her on the streets of Walvern, you might have said her clothes looked a bit smarter but that was it, no jewellery. She didn't have to show off to say she had made it, it was not part of her character but when she began to see Joyce on a more regular basis she formed this relationship with Thomas. He wasn't the son she hadn't had, he was a million times more than that. He was a friend. Her sixth sense told her his sexuality was very much to her advantage and the first person he ever spoke about it was to her. They had more than just absolute confidence in one another, they had a real bond and this bond would remain all their lives. Rose had always attracted gay men like a magnet. They loved her and she adored most of them. She had the ability to judge in two seconds if she liked a person or not, and if the decision was in the negative that was that – she never saw them again, though if forced to do so socially it became quite clear that she was not interested. So when Thomas came to Melbourne to university this was a major turning point for her. Whereas before she had no central pivot in her life, her husband having died some years before, Thomas became the fulcrum of her existence. They had identical likes and dislikes, which made their lives together so much easier, although Rose had given Thomas the use of the terrace house in East Melbourne where he spent some time when he was at university. The minute he completed his degree, he was automatically elevated into an excellent position in Rose's late husband's investment firm little by little he spent more and more time at Albany Road until he virtually lived with Rose. He only used the beautiful terrace house in East Melbourne when he had picked someone up and it was somewhere to go. He never had slept with a man in Rose's home. She had spoken to him about it, as they spoke openly about everything and she had asked him why. He had laughed and told her the man that he brought to sleep with at Albany Road would be the man he would love for the rest of his life. Rose had smiled at that but realised what a supreme compliment it had been : only the very best would do to share her house. And so he had continued from the age of fifteen until now, at thirty five, still claiming he hadn't found anyone suitable to bring to stay at Albany Road.

Seventeen wonderful, carefree years had been offered to Thomas and he gratefully took them. He was now the managing director of Rose's investment firm and a very good one it was. Of Rose's private investments he had in a ten year period multiplied them by four. The staff adored this Adonis and it was not only the female members of staff who thought that, given the opportunity, they would certainly take advantage of it. He was popular with everyone. A full all-round sportsman, he adored sport and was good at it, especially tennis and swimming. Both these sports were well catered for at Albany Road and there was never a problem finding a tennis partner and absolutely no problem finding a swimming companion. As Raoul had said, in a swim brief he was a Greek god, which in roughly translated terms meant very, very sexy, and with an excellent body. But he was nearly always with Rose. So many young men sought an introduction to him via her, and she was quite aware of what they wanted and occasionally vetted them and offered the excuse that at the moment he was 'well, occupied'.

They were often at the races, both being members, and enjoyed it immensely. Rose had Thomas join the most important club in Melbourne, so, from being a beautiful country boy, in seventeen years he had become a very smart young man who fitted into all social circles, like Rose, and generally had a very good time. Owning this large investment firm, Rose could organise Thomas's time as she saw fit, so overseas travel was always something that happened regularly and as there was no shortage of finance they travelled well. Every trip always had an international freight company sending something back to Australia that they had decided they could not live without.

Rose noticed over the years that Thomas's choice of companion followed no particular look and as always lasted a very short time. The only exception to this was a young man he saw for a month or so. His name was Edward but everyone called him Eddie. He came from a family Rose knew, in fact she was instrumental in introducing the two of them. Eddie was also sports-minded as well as constantly at the gym. His family was well-off as a result of a prosperous construction company. He didn't appear to work but he enjoyed playing in every sense of the word and took to Thomas on their first meeting at a dinner party at Rose's. He was used to being the prima donna, the person everyone wanted, good looking, wealthy, and he had his nose quite put out of joint when Thomas paid no attention to him at all. This was the bait, obviously, but for Eddie it was also a slap in the face. This is always the price of arrogance and conceit, so this relationship took a while to get off the ground, as both Thomas and Eddie played the same game. They met at the races, at concerts, but that was that, no invitations were offered to one another; it just became chance when they were next to encounter one another.

'This is stupid,' said Eddie one evening to Thomas at Roses's for dinner with a large group of people. 'Why the hell don't we do something about it. I'll stay the night.'

'Not here, you won't,' said Thomas with a smile, 'but I might just be able to think of an address for tomorrow evening.'

Eddie returned the smile he had never had to ask for of anyone before, so he was aware that the person he wanted was special, yes very special, he thought. And so the appointment was made and was very much to the satisfaction of both of them. So the relationship began to develop.

'Well, Thomas,' said Rose. 'Am I to expect an extra face for breakfast soon?'

He laughed. 'Not yet, Rose, not yet.'

After the first month, which was based on fun and sex, Eddie began for the first time in his pampered life to become possessive and objected to having to share Thomas, especially with Rose.

'You'll have to accept me and Rose,' said Thomas sharply one evening when Eddie was not happy about not being able to see him the following evening. Eddie pretended that he understood, not wishing to cause a rift between himself and the man he now thought he loved passionately but he had made the fatal error of criticising Rose's position in Thomas's life and as a result Thomas began the inevitable winding down. Eddie was anything but pleased. He loved Thomas and to realise he was being slowly but surely dismissed angered him. This also had a great deal to do with his conceit, as he considered himself every bit as good-looking as Thomas, if not better, so it came as a real sense of rejection. The more Eddie performed, the more the door closed firmly, until Thomas told him outright, 'The relationship has been great.'

'What do you mean 'has been'?' snapped Eddie.

'Face facts. This can't last, so let's just be friends.' It was a stock comment of Thomas's when he wished to extricate himself from a relationship.

'Oh, great!' muttered Eddie, sarcastically. 'I'm dismissed and you go back to Auntie.'

Thomas caught the sharpness of the comment and as usual any comment that even slightly touched on Rose saw him on the attack. As they were in a restaurant at the time, he stood up, leant over and said. 'Goodbye and good luck,' and left the restaurant. Instead of going back to the terraced house in East Melbourne which had originally been the idea he and Eddie had had, he headed his Mercedes Sports in the direction of Albany Road, knowing there would be lots of conversation and laughter at breakfast time. And that was the pattern of Thomas's life and this was as he enjoyed it. Sex was one thing and a thing he rarely went without due to his good looks and position, but friendship was so much more, the stabilising influence in his life. It was this he pursued, especially with Rose.

'Darling,' she greeted him, seating herself down for breakfast. 'No more East Melbourne?'

'Not for a while. Aren't we supposed to be going to the Marshalls for dinner tomorrow night.'

'Darling, it's tonight. Black tie.'

'Great! I'll be home early.' He rose, kissed her, gathered his briefcase and keys from the hall console, then disappeared to the garage. In a moment the black Mercedes Sports was to be seen streaking up the drive.

'Oh, thought Rose, 'another man bites the dust!' She stood up, as the maid entered, then left to call the hairdresser for the evening's dinner party and the Marshalls.

While sitting in the hairdresser's in the early afternoon, she thumbed through a magazine not really looking at it. A strange thought came into her mind and made her smile. A month before, or was it two, she had been at Killpara and when Joyce and she were alone Joyce, for the first time in her life, began to broach the subject of Thomas's sexuality but in a very roundabout way.

'I suppose you must get so tired of all those women calling to see Thomas,' she said. Rose was, usual a step ahead. She knew very well that if Thomas wished to speak to Joyce about his sexuality that was fine but Joyce was not going to trick Rose into telling her what she obviously did not want to hear. Rose simply side-stepped the issue and Joyce seemed quite content. It was odd, she thought, that simply by not confirming anything, Joyce was capable of constructing in her mind a little world where everything that she thought was not challenged was correct.

* * * * *

'Darling, do give me a hand,' she cried. Thomas, hearing her, went into her very beautiful bedroom which had its own sitting room. She had taken from the safe a black box and when opened it displayed a magnificent diamond necklace.

'Can you fasten it for me,' she asked.

'You look great,' he complemented her. 'You should wear them more often.'

'Thanks. There aren't the places as there once were to wear a lot of jewellery.'

'We'll make the places,' he laughed, looking so smart in his dinner suit and black tie with his well-trained black hair and those blue eyes shining out. Rose was sure he was the most handsome man in the world. She was extremely proud of him, for in the seventeen years he had been with her his taste for fine things had developed to a high level – opera, concerts and, of course, travel and his attention to what she told him concerning paintings and antiques. And like Thomas with her, criticise him and you criticised Rose : she also went on the attack if anyone dared pass a comment she thought was unjust or unfair.

* * * * *

Rose and Thomas swept down the staircase. She always carried herself very elegantly and seemingly without effort. That evening, in a long black paper taffeta gown with a slight train and cut low at the back and front to show off the diamonds and matching earrings to advantage, at forty six years of age Rose looked very handsome and although she had had many suitors she had kept them all at bay. Her circle of friends was quite sufficient for her and Thomas: well Thomas was just the most perfect companion anyone could have – and Rose had him.

'We are a bit early,' he said. 'Let's have a drink first.' He disappeared and returned with a bottle of champagne and two glasses. They sat in the front sitting room, overlooking the late spring garden which, due to Raoul's expertise, looked splendid.

'He adores you, you know,' Rose smiled.

'Oh yes? Who?' Thomas asked in an offhand manner.

'Roaul, of course.'

'He's a great guy, but spoken for, and I like Andrew as well.'

'So do I, but it doesn't change the equation. He really adores you.'

'Listen, who's going to be at the Marshalls' tonight?' he asked, changing the conversation.

'I really don't know. I received our invitation and accepted and that's all I know.'

'Oh, won't it be fun if Sandra makes an appearance!'

'The answer to that, Thomas, is no.' She laughed at the thought. 'You never know – you may encounter Mr Right this evening.'

'You never know,' he responded.

When they arrived, he pulled the Jaguar right up to the front of the house and Rose got out. He then drove it out of the narrow drive and parked in the street. Rose waited for him, chatting to someone she knew. 'Oh, here he is. Thomas, you remember Craig Turner.'

'Of course,' came the reply. 'We met you at the races a few weeks ago.'

'Come along inside,' insisted Betty Marshall, and they were swept into a very large decorative living room with a marvellous view over the back garden with the best late spring show possible. "I'll tell you the truth, Rose,' she said, laughing, 'I was sure it would be pouring with rain tonight and the garden would be a disaster, but we are saved.'

Betty Marshall was a woman with so much energy she was always doing something, president of this association, secretary of another, a member of the Opera Society, and the National Gallery. She was on everything but there was one organisation that Rose was extremely proud of her being the President of, the fund-raising committee for AIDS research. Rose had always given very generously to any of Betty's projects : she had lost far too many fine friends to the virus, so she was as convinced as Betty was that a real cure had to be possible.

The evening moved along and when everyone was seated for dinner Betty made an announcement. 'I need to raise a relatively large amount of money for some new trials for the AIDS research. So now it's over to you.'

The eight seated guests were, to say the least, well-heeled, and so ideas ran between one and the other.

'Betty,' asked Thomas, 'what's your connection with the National Gallery like?'

'Good. What's your idea?'

'Well. What if we picked, or you picked, a hundred of the best or most prominent Victorian artists and got them to donate a painting each, with good publicity and $500 as the starting price? And you should be able to do a gala dinner before it. Add it all up and you should be coming close to your target.'

'Thomas, you are a genius!' cried Betty. 'Exactly, exactly! "One hundred of the best", that's the title. Oh, if the National Gallery won't come to the party, I know of several other venues. Oh, how splendid, Thomas! You're a genius.' She repeated.

The rest of the evening had to do with the ramifications of this exhibition and a sheet of paper was brought out, to be filled with the names of the most prominent painters. As the evening progressed, with laughter and constantly filled glasses, the company relaxed into feeling that they were on the way to raising the money required for the research.

As the evening wore on, the Marshall's son returned home, Rodney, all of seventeen years old and with eyes for only one person. Rodney had met Thomas many times at the races with his parents or at charity events or the theatre. He was a dancer and a very good one. His social behaviour may have been a little scatty at times but on stage he was discipline itself. At the school of dance they held high hopes that he would be accepted by the Australian Ballet Company, but he only had eyes for Thomas. He thought he was the most fabulous man in the world, and dying for him seemed a quite reasonable idea. Rodney and Betty had an understanding that was based exclusively on honesty. He had been an unexpected treasure in the sense that Betty was heading towards menopause when suddenly she found herself pregnant, both Betty and her husband genuinely considered the possibility of terminating the situation, but as Betty had just lost her most beloved brother to the AIDS virus, she was determined that this new person to enter the world would carry his name and so he did. He was good-looking, Rodney Marshall, with a mop of bushy blonde hair and Irish green eyes, just like his deceased uncle. Betty lived for him. Whereas most women of a certain age find motherhood extremely tiring, Betty thrived on it. Little Rodney was her brother Rodney reborn : but at seventeen years old his hormones were up and running and in the direction of Thomas.

As the dinner party had not finished when he arrived home, and not lacking in confidence, he drew up another chair and inserted himself between Thomas and another guest, just to be beside him. His head raced and to be able to speak to him about ballet, which Thomas understood, was such a plus. Rodney's confidence was such this evening that while Thomas was speaking to Rose opposite him across the table his eyes suddenly opened much wider than usual and he had a very surprised look on his face. This was due to his believing very much that he should strike while the iron was hot. He slid his hand down under the table cloth and upwards between Thomas's legs. Thomas pretended nothing was happening but quite firmly removed his hand, much to Rodney's dismay, assuming Thomas would be delighted at this offering. Here he made a mistake and Betty was to hear all about it.

Next morning, feeling very slow due to the wine she had consumed, she sat by herself in the breakfast room, along with a second cup of black coffee. 'I may never drink again,' she was thinking, only to hear footsteps across the corridor as Rodney entered the room. 'Morning, darling,' she said.

He sat down beside her, not saying a word, which was quite unlike him. 'Would you like some breakfast?' she asked.

He tilted his head. 'I love him more than anything in this world,' and looked directly at her as if she were suddenly going to give him the answer to his problem.

'Oh, Rodney,' she exclaimed, extending her arm around his shoulder. 'Are you sure?'

'I love Thomas with all my heart,' he responded and threw both arms around her neck and began to cry. The extreme helplessness that Betty felt was terrible. Here he was, a seventeen year old, in love with a man who was elegant, wealthy, everything that he should be, but was obviously not interested in Rodney. The boy was inconsolable. He wept bitterly, confessing how it was only Thomas he wanted, everything else was nothing, only Thomas. Betty attempted to right the situation by saying she would have a word with Rose but beyond that she could make no promises.

Rodney was elated. 'Oh, how fabulous! I know if we are alone everything will be fine. He will love me and it will be great.'

Betty had a slight hangover and with Rodney moving from the depths of his soul to suddenly walking on the roof tops she found it a very exhausting way to face a new day. 'Rose, if you promise to serve lunch without alcohol, I'll join you,' a very slow Betty murmured. 'I have a problem only you can resolve. You had better be ready for it.' She hung up.

Rose was most curious as to what Betty wanted, let alone her belief that she could solve it.

'Oh dear,' she said, as she listened to Betty opposite her. 'Is Rodney really sure that he is in love with Thomas?'

'I am afraid so.

'It doesn't appear to me that Thomas is at all interested in him sexually. I am sure he likes him as a young friend but beyond that I'm sure there is nothing.'

'Oh, what am I to do?' Betty lamented. 'He's breaking his heart for Thomas.'

'I'm afraid that even if Thomas were interested it wouldn't be fair on Rodney.' When Betty asked why, she went on, 'Well, in the seventeen years Thomas has lived here I have never known him to be with one person for more than a month and I'm sure that's not what Rodney is looking for, is it?'

'No, it's not. He is looking for happiness ever after.' Betty sighed. 'Do you have any ideas about what I can say to Rodney?'

'Well, you could perhaps say that as Thomas doesn't have any faith in long term relationships that he wouldn't become involved with Rodney as he thought a great deal of him and would not want to hurt him.'

'Rose, that sounds great - a gentle let-down. Oh, you would think that young gay boys would be so much easier, wouldn't you? And give me half a glass of champagne! I may well need it when I get home and have to explain this to the boy. You know, Rose, he has been the most wonderful thing that has ever happened to me and the fact that he's gay is a real bonus. It took his father a little while to accept it but now anyone who passes an anti-gay comment in our home Robert shows them the front door at once.'

'I think Rodney is very lucky to have two loving and supportive parents.'

'Thanks, Rose, but it doesn't really solve the problem of him being in love with Thomas. You don't think if Thomas spoke to him it would be easier, do you?'

'Put yourself in Rodney's position. What would you think?'

'I would be destroyed.'

'And so would Rodney,' Rose replied.

'Rose, I must rush. Thanks for the advice and thanks for lunch. That half glass has picked me up no end.'

* * * *

'What?' cried Thomas, when he returned from the office and was sitting having a drink with Rose. 'Rodney! Why, he's only fifteen or sixteen.'

'No, darling, he's actually seventeen and mad for you.'

'But I haven't ever encouraged him. I have known him, through you, from when he was a child.'

'Well, Thomas, children have this odd habit of growing up and falling in love, hence Rodney's problem. But, as Betty and I agreed, he has good taste in men.' Thomas smiled but did not respond. 'Don't forget it's Joyce's birthday next week. I said we would go up Friday night, if that's OK with you.'

'Yes, it's fine, but what the hell am I going to buy her for a present? She's so difficult.'

'Oh, don't worry. I asked her straight out what she wanted and she said she would like a new vase as the cat apparently knocked a vase off the sideboard and it smashed. I said we would buy a new one together.'

'Rose, you are fabulous. I would never have known what to buy and she would never have told me she wanted a vase.'

'I'll get the vase and perhaps we might collect two dozen roses to go in it, on the way up. I will order them tomorrow.'

'Dinner is served,' came the announcement of the maid and they moved through to the small dining room, arm in arm.

'I can't believe Rodney,' he said. 'He's just a child.'

'What were you thinking of when you were seventeen?' Rose asked, taking her chair.

'I don't honestly remember, but I think I thought that the captain of the hockey team was pretty good.' He laughed.

'You never felt anything for Simon, did you?'

'I thought he was great, but nothing seemed to come of it. I guess we were all young and inexperienced, although Trevor never missed a trick. He was always with one boy or another. Gosh, it all seems such a long time ago.'

* * * * *

At Rosebae, Terry had just come in from putting Pete in his enclosure for the night, threatening him if he wasn't more co-operative he might well end up on the dining table, well-roasted. When the phone rang, 'Hello, Rosebae,' was his usual response. 'Oh, I'm not sure but the moment Simon comes in he will call you back. Thanks very much. He hung up and suddenly realised he was becoming angry and it had nothing to do with Pete the Peacock putting on his usual evening performance.

Simon came in about three quarters of an hour later, having finished the milking. 'Thank goodness the days are getting longer,' he said.

'I've threatened Pete with the oven. He is such a bore,' complained Terry.

Simon laughed. 'You would die without him.'

'Hm, I'm not so sure. Oh, before I forget, Mrs O'Reily from Killpara telephoned. It seems it's her birthday this weekend and she has invited us as Thomas and Rose are coming up. Personally, I think it will be a bore.'

Simon knew that Terry disliked Rose and knew the feeling was mutual, but he was also aware that Terry was jealous of Thomas, so he realised from the outset that this birthday party was going to be very awkward.

Joyce had decided that for her fifty sixth birthday she would also invite Thomas's friends, as this would make for a more enjoyable evening, as she planned an informal buffet meal, so that she could invite a few more people than for a sit-down dinner. She had already spoken to Mary and Trevor and received an affirmative reply but Enid refused, due to her work at the hotel, though she wished her a happy birthday all the same. She had invited some of her friends and knew at the back of her mind Rose would be bored stiff but Thomas's friends would solve the problem, and Rose could chat with them. Patricia thought the whole thing was over-the-top and failed to see why Thomas's friends had to be invited just to please him and Rose. She knew that a great deal of the work in the kitchen was going to end up being hers.

'Come on, Terry, do you want to go or not? You don't have to.'

'Oh, I see. You would prefer to go without me,' he began.

'Stop!' interrupted Simon sharply. 'I have to telephone Mrs O'Riely and I must have an answer. It's as simple as that.'

'I suppose Rose is going to be there?'

'I would think so,' Simon replied.

'Oh, it sounds so dreary.'

'Do I take it that that comment means you aren't interested in going?'

'I haven't decided.' Terry sulked into the kitchen. He's getting just like Pete, thought Simon, and picked up the phone to telephone Killpara.

'Simon, how nice to hear from you,' was Joyce's response. 'I have invited Mary and Trevor so you youngsters can have a reunion. Enid said she was working and so can't make it. I take it you both can?'

'Well, I will be there but we are not so sure about Terry.'

'Oh, it's not a problem. It's a buffet, so numbers aren't so important but do tell him I would love to see him. Goodnight, Simon.' She hung up.

He put the receiver down only to see a silhouetted figure directly in front of him.

'Who's going?'

This will be good, thought Simon and explained what Joyce had said.

'Oh, it sounds just lovely,' Terry replied in a sarcastic tone. 'All school chums together.'

'You are more than welcome, Joyce said. She would love to see you.'

'She is nice, but the others – Rose and Trevor – no, I think I shall have a headache.'

'Well, please yourself,' Simon spoke rather sharply, getting tired of the drama. Every time they went out, Simon missed Mary, Trevor, Enid and especially Thomas, so an opportunity to see them was always welcomed. 'What should we buy Joyce for a birthday present? I haven't a clue.'

This comment instantly brought Terry back into the conversation. 'Hm, I think a nice tablecloth and serviettes would be suitable. After all, the house is pretty plain and to buy her something decorative she may take offence.'

'You're right. What a good suggestion.' And instantly the drama was over. 'I have been reading the Walvern Gazette. What a rag! That Stewart Searl is such a bitch. In his column he ripped someone – I don't know them – to shreds for having a christening party he considered kitsch. I'm surprised someone doesn't shoot him.'

'It's another good idea! Didn't you go to school with him?' Simon asked.

'Yes, but he was a couple of forms in front of me. I had the misfortune to have Barry Houghton in my form. What a drip! So pretentious even then. I can't understand him and Searl being friends, but then I suppose I can : they are both social misfits and both pretentious. The only difference is that Searl has a really vicious tongue and a newspaper column to vent it in.' It annoyed Terry that as Simon had gone to the Catholic College with the others, at times he felt out of it, especially when they were together, these five friends. They would joke and laugh endlessly and no matter how he tried there was always a sort of glass wall that socially separated him and it made him feel awkward, almost as if he was an afterthought. He genuinely felt it was a plot against him and the more brittle he became in their company, obviously the more distant they all became, so an evening at Killpara was not something he was looking forward to, but not to go, that was another equation altogether. Simon alone, with Trevor and Thomas, was not what he considered ideal.

Mary had tried to persuade Joseph to attend the birthday party but to no avail. He said he didn't know anyone and said he would prefer to remain at home, that now being Mary's. So like the others, Mary and Trevor wracked their brains for the ideal gift and genuinely looked forward to seeing Thomas and Rose as well as Simon, but both breathed a heavy sigh when they realised that Simon came with Terry.

Joyce threw herself into the party with unusual dynamism. She wanted to get everything just right. Even Patricia thought it was odd. Generally birthdays, especially Joyce's, were non-events but this year all the stops were being pulled out. Even Samuel was curious about this frenzy of behaviour. It was unlike Joyce to show any enthusiasm for anything. She was performing as if it was her last great show. So for Samuel and Patricia the last week before it proved to be a real headache, with Joyce checking and re-checking the same tiny details over and over again. She had even had new curtains made for the living room, not that anyone was going to notice them as they were almost identical with the previous ones that had hung there. She did her shopping like most people living in the country once a week but this week she had driven to Walvern every day for yet something else. New cushions for the divan : she spent a whole morning torturing herself about the colour of them and when purchased they too seemed very similar to the previous ones, except without the shredded fabric that was the result of the cat – and here Joyce would not allow the cat into the living room. Now Patricia and Samuel realised that this birthday was really serious and both confessed that they thought perhaps their gifts were a bit miserable but it would be difficult to right the situation in less than a week.

* * * * *

'Oh, Rose, it's beautiful,' exclaimed Thomas, having a close look at the beautiful Medici urn in gilt bronze. I don't think the cat is ever going to upset this vase!' It was indeed a beautiful urn-cum-vase. It looked like a champagne bucket with figures in relief around the central bowl, two small, false handles on the sides and an elegant stem that flanged out to form the base. All of this was mounted on a block of antique green marble. It had an inner liner in brass that could be removed for easy cleaning. 'It weighs a ton,' he went on, lifting it and returning it to the table.

'It's Victorian but the casting is very fine. It's French and I suppose originally there were a pair but as Joyce has asked for just one vase I guess we have managed correctly.'

'We certainly have,' Thomas said enthusiastically, looking at it again. 'Mum won't believe it.'

'I just hope she will like it,' Rose sighed.

'She will. Don't you worry.'

'I'll pack it now, but I wanted you to see it before we made the presentation for the birthday.' She lifted the urn and returned it to the box she had purchased it in, quickly wrapping paper around it. Thomas fitted and tied a big white bow. 'Here, darling, just sign here.' He did so with a birthday wish and it was done and in twenty five minutes he had stopped the car at the florist, the roses were paid for and deposited on the back seat and off they headed for Killpara.

'The traffic's not so bad tonight' he said. 'Generally Friday night is a horror.' They branched off and entered the freeway for an uninterrupted drive to Killpara.

'I wonder who Joyce has invited,' Rose wondered. 'I haven't a clue, but I will lay a bet this weekend is not going to be the smartest we have ever had. It's strange, when I spoke to her the other day on the phone she seemed a different person. She is generally slow and methodical but I'm sure I detected an urgency in her voice.'

'Really? That's most unlike her. She is generally the total country mouse.' They both laughed, but not uncharitably. They were both to be very surprised when they arrived at Killpara at the change in Joyce and neither had any idea why.

As they drove down the drive, they both looked at one another. The front veranda light was on. Everyone always entered by the back door but this light made it quite clear that the entrance was at the front, so the pair of them, with bags and present and a huge bunch of roses somewhat nervously used the big cast-iron knocker on the front door. To their utter surprise it was opened by a blonde Joyce. Neither of them said anything for a moment then Rose said, 'Joyce, you look wonderful.'.

'Mum, you look great,' Thomas added, wondering what the rest of the conversation was going to be like.

Joyce invited them in, they deposited their bags in their respective rooms and then went into the living room. It seemed tidier or neater than before. It was difficult to say how but changed it was. Greetings were exchanged with Patricia, who was as non-committal as always and Samuel, seeming to be in a daze, as Joyce whizzed around with a tray of hors-d'oevres, chatting as if she had been the 'hostess with the mostess' all her life. Her hair made her seem at least ten years younger, from the years of grey-brown hair (with more grey than brown) to a soft blonde colouring : it changed her completely, not to mention the smarter cut. Obviously, for Joyce, dull matron was out. She even had a little make-up on, something she never had done and her skirt and shirt with a jumper tied around her neck seemed as if, when one looked at her, she had had a total make-over. Rose and Thomas were genuinely complementary about this new look, which Joyce obviously appreciated.

'Oh, it's exactly what I want,' she exclaimed, giving Rose and then Thomas a hug. 'And it's is perfect for the centre of the buffet table and those pale lemon roses – quite my favourite colour. This will all be just so right for tomorrow night.' She disappeared with Patricia to organise the flowers and check the food.

'If I didn't know her better, I would say she was taking some sort of substance,' commented Samuel, pouring Rose and Thomas a drink.

'I think it's great,' replied Thomas.

'And so do I,' Samuel agreed. 'Don't get me wrong, but from this high, isn't there also a down?'

'Not necessarily,' Rose disagreed. 'Sometimes people reach a point in their day-to-day lives when they just, well how can I say it, yes, they turn a corner and all of a sudden the sun is in front and off they go.'

'Maybe,' Samuel spoke doubtfully, 'but I must confess I'm a bit concerned.'

The evening meal was anything but the normal. Joyce had decided to attempt a new look in every sense of the word. The meal was inventive and very good. Even Patricia had to admit that if Joyce was going to be a new woman and the cuisine picked up like this she was all for it. After a delicious meal the five of them retired to the refreshed sitting room.

'What happened to the portraits?' asked Thomas.

'Oh,' said Joyce, 'I took them down ages ago and put them in the laundry and apparently the humidity has made a mess of the frames. I have put them on top of your wardrobe. If you want them, take them. I have never liked them.' She spoke in an off-hand way about the portraits which were of Rose's and Joyce's great grandfather and great grandmother, average portrait work but in a later period the original plain, dark wooden frames had been discarded for a pair of very ornate gilt frames, which both Thomas and Rose thought superior to the paintings inside them. It was like the old saying that a new broom sweeps clean and so it was with Joyce. They all chatted on but were amazed at her. She now opened up on subjects that previously she would have remained silent about. This was the new Joyce.

Saturday morning, she told Rose and Thomas to lunch out as she was far too busy to organise a lunch and a dinner party, so they followed her instructions and needless to say, after completing another shopping spree for Joyce's big night, ended up at the Oriental Hotel for lunch.

'But we have been invited,' said Mary to Thomas, after giving him and Rose a hug.

'What, to Mum's birthday party?'

'Yes. It seems she is going all out.'

'So it seems,' he exclaimed, exceptionally pleased that at least he and Rose would have someone to speak to, as Joyce's other friends were a trifle staid.

'Trevor will light up the night,' laughed Mary. 'He's having drama with the Light Opera Company, but I will let him tell you the funny bits.'

Enid crossed the room, drew up a chair and smiled. 'Sorry, Thomas. I told your mother that I just couldn't make it this evening but I have a gift so don't forget to take it with you.'

'It seems Mum has invited everybody.'

'Well, almost everybody,' came a voice and Trevor swept across the room. 'Darling, a drink or I shall surely die.'

'I'm prepared to put that to the test,' Enid assured him, and he laughed as she signalled a young waitress to bring another glass. When she arrived, Enid looked at the bottle and asked for another.

'What should I wear tonight?' Trevor asked. 'Its not collar and tie, is it?'

'What did the invitation say?' asked Mary.

'I didn't get an invitation, just a telephone call.'

'Oh well, if that's the case, smart casual. What do you think, Rose?'

'I think that's good advice.'

'Enid,' said Thomas, 'what's for lunch?'

'Oh, I don't believe it. You are actually going to eat here at last.' They smiled and said they were.

'They have taken out good health insurance,' quipped Trevor with a treacherous smile.

'Bitch!' came the reply from Enid. She excused herself and went off to check the kitchen.

'I wasn't kidding,' Trevor went on. 'The food is so ordinary here. I have tried to convince Enid to drown her cook and get a decent one but you know what she is like – Mrs Conservative herself.'

The others laughed and what with the repartee and the continual laughing the food took a very second place, though stunning it certainly was not.

Rose and Thomas had a nap, if that was possible what with the noise and banging and shouts from the kitchen of Killpara. One could be forgiven for thinking there was to be a Papal visit at 7.30, not just Joyce's birthday party. The share farmers, both James and Paula, were drafted into the birthday team with specific jobs, with Joyce hopping about like a small wren from place to place, moving plates five centimetres this way or the other, in general making everyone feel uncomfortable. But the moment the guests began to arrive the evening relaxed and Joyce began to flutter from group to group, exchanging the most useless pieces of information which had everyone in hysterics.

'Hi, what a surprise!' exclaimed Thomas, as he embraced Simon and then a slightly stiff Terry. 'It's great everyone is here tonight.' Terry bit is tongue He hadn't wanted to come, but he had insisted only a week ago Simon accompany him to his niece's daughter's christening lunch and it was, even in Terry's words, 'Death'. So fair being fair here he was. Conversation became louder and people moved about but Terry felt very much the outsider, especially as he noted Trevor and Thomas laughing with Mary and Rose and quite often an arm was seen around Simon's shoulders.

'Would you like a drink?' came a voice behind him.

'Oh,' as he turned around, 'how are you, Patricia?'

'Don't ask. I hate these turns. What about you?'

'Well. It almost beats a funeral.' There was a silence and they both began to laugh. Terry knew Patricia from the Walvern Library. She had always found and obtained books for him on inter-library loans and had genuinely made an effort for him, for which he was most grateful.

'What are you drinking?' she asked and then noticed that he had a full glass of champagne in his hand. 'I can't bear the stuff. Do you like it?'

'No, not really,' he replied, in a slightly embarrassed way.

'Like a beer?'

'Now, you're talking.' He laughed as she returned with a glass of beer.

'Cheers!' she said. 'You men have a much better life than us women.'

'Oh really? Look across there at Rose.'

'Yes, Queen of Queens,' and they both began laughing. 'I'm stuck here in the kitchen. I can't cook, in fact I hate it and everyone is out having fun.'

'Well, not everyone.' He narrowed his eyes. 'But if you want a hand in the kitchen, I'm your man.'

'You're on,' she smiled. 'Come and have a look. See what you can make of it in here.' They walked through to the kitchen and Terry automatically took over. Suddenly he felt fine. He was wanted and he was a whizz in the kitchen so he and Patricia chatted on as he organised everything.

'I'm so envious of you,' she admitted. 'Some time ago I got you that book on raising parrots and when you had finished with it I read it. I was fascinated. I had no idea there were so many types and how sad that some of them are now extinct.'

'Yes, that's the sad bit here in Australia. We had so many types and some of the most fragile ones are just not with us.'

'I can think of someone who I wish was just not with us.'

'Now who could that be?' he smiled, leaning back against the bench having a drink.

'Barry Houghton.'

'Oh, forget him. He's a real loser. But why do you dislike him?'

'Well, it goes back to the parrot book.'

'Really? I can't imagine that poisonous dwarf being interested in parrots!'

'I don't think he is, but one afternoon I was just about to leave the library when the phone rang and it was Barry's mother, Emily, and she asked did we have a copy of a certain book. I checked and told her we did, so she asked if I could bring it home to her as she was just up the road and was not well. Barry was away with that Searl creature.'

'Say no more!' exclaimed Terry. 'A prize bitch.'

'Exactly. Do you read his column?' Terry said he did and so, it appeared, did Patricia.

'Anyway, I took the book up to Houghton Hall. I had only been there once in my life. It's very run down and after delivering the book I went back to my car and I noticed beside the hedge a huge aviary. It was in a terrible condition, with stinging nettles everywhere, a cast iron thing. But one side had fallen off, so I thought if it was restored and installed here perhaps I could breed parrots as well.'

'What a great idea,' Terry butted in, wondering why he had never spoken to Patricia in a social way before.

'Well, it turned out to be a real drama. I asked Dad if he would call for me and speak to Barry and that's where it all went wrong. Dad telephoned and asked if Barry was interested in selling what was left of the structure. Barry put on the full pretentious performance.' She started to mimic him. '"The heritage of Houghton Hall has no price and it certainly would never finish in the hands of people of Irish descent." Dad was furious and threatened that the next time he saw him he would give him a public thrashing. Needless to say, my idea of a Victorian aviary full of parrots flew out of the window. But if there has to be a funny bit, this is it - help yourself to another beer, by the way. About a month later, Dad saw Barry in Walvern and stormed over to have it out with him, Barry being the utter coward.'

'He was exactly the same at school,' Terry agreed, 'big mouth and nothing else. Now he can match his big mouth with his big stomach.'

'Well, when Barry saw Dad heading his way, he ducked into the nearest shop but Dad saw him and followed him in, to Mrs Robbins's shop for ladies' underwear. Did Dad bawl him out in front of everyone! He said that if he dared speak to him in that stupid, pretentious manner, and as everyone knew he was almost bankrupt, he would tie him up to the cenotaph naked and flog him. Apparently Barry went completely white according to Mrs Robbins and then Dad stormed out. Mrs Robbins said her shop assistant Jenny offered Barry a bra and panty set "for the more expanded and mature figure"! Mrs Robbins said the ladies in the shop went into peals of laughter as Barry left the shop with his tail well between his legs and a very embarrassed look on his white face.'

Terry screamed with laughter. He could just see Barry in a mature and expanded bra and panty set.

'What's happening here?' shouted Joyce.

'Don't worry, birthday girl! Food's on the way.' Terry and Patricia went on laughing and working together, joking about Barry in a bra and panties.

The other groups also had fun. Usually, Joyce's evenings were likened to a wake, but this evening no. Rose was in fits of laughter at some of the funny stories about them all at school together and Trevor couldn't be stopped as his stories came one after the other. The food was served and everyone complemented Joyce and Patricia on the splendid presentation. 'Oh no,' protested Patricia, quite loudly, 'it's Terry who has done everything,' and everyone applauded.

'No applause, just money!' he laughed and the party continued well into the night.

Thomas was speaking to Mary about having some frames restored. 'Look no further,' she said. 'Joseph is an expert and I am sure the price will be better than in Melbourne.'

'Great! I'll take the portraits back with me and when we go to Melbourne tomorrow I'll drop the frames with you.'

She asked what time he was planning to go back to town and was told between three thirty and four, so she told him to drop in for a drink and to meet Joseph. 'You remember him, don't you? She asked.

'No, I'm afraid I don't. Keven, yes.'

'Oh forget him. He is way beyond redemption,' said Mary.

'But he's so decorative,' and when Simon asked what that meant Thomas asked, 'Haven't you seen him without his shirt?'

'Hardly,' was Simon's answer to that. 'He's definitely not my type.'

'He's definitely not anyone's type,' responded Trevor. 'He is covered in tattoos and what a sight!'

Mary agreed, plaintively. 'He really is a sight and not an attractive one.'

'That, however, cannot be said of Joseph,' was Trevor's comment.

'Careful, sweetie'. Mary narrowed her eyes.

'Just an observation, darling. Quite the best boy in town.'

Terry came over and joined them. He related Patricia's story about Barry Houghton. There were peals of laughter as everyone knew exactly how pretentious and obnoxious Barry could be.

Joyce thanked all her guests for their gifts and the evening drew to a close at about one o'clock.

The following day, after lunch, Rose and Thomas collected the portraits and frames and headed off to Mary's. 'Welcome!' she cried, 'Come in. What a fun night!' This they were all agreed on.

'Where shall I leave the frames?' asked Thomas.

'Oh, you've just missed Joseph. He has gone to Jan's to help her out but he said he would be happy to do the frames for you.'

'What a lovely home you have,' remarked Rose.

'Thank you, but I can't take much of the credit. My uncle furnished it and I am so happy living here, and especially now as Joseph lives with me, so it's great company.'

After about twenty minutes they made their farewells then headed back to Melbourne, gossiping about the people at the birthday party.

The following week saw two events occur that involved Terry, the first being on Monday afternoon, when he and Simon returned from Malvern. They noticed on the doorstep a large bunch of flowers in cellophane with a card that read 'Dearest Terry, thank you so very much for the help in the kitchen at my birthday party. It was very much appreciated, love, Joyce.'

'How sweet,' said Simon.

'Yes,' agreed Terry, 'she is a sweet person. Whether it was the flowers that prompted him, or a plan was already in his mind but that evening, after dinner, he telephoned Barry Houghton. 'Rosebae House here' he announced in a very grand voice.

'Oh, hello, Terry,' came the reply.

'How are you?' asked Terry.

'Oh, I'm, all right. Mother is not so good. Another cold, I'm afraid. May I help you?' The voice was as pompous as usual.

'Well, yes, you may, but it must be very confidential.'

'Oh, but of course.

'I have a friend, and as you know, I breed parrots.'

'I'm aware of that.'

'Well, I need an old bird cage for a friend and as you have one you are not using – 'and then very quickly he continued the conversation before Barry could get a word in, ' – It would be a very discreet sale, of course.'

'Oh, of course.'

'What sort of condition is it in?' Terry enquired, knowing full well the state of it.

'Oh, a little bit of repair is required.'

'And what sort of price are you thinking of? Now, remember, no-one will know of this sale.'

'Oh, of course. Well, I don't really use it, and it is a bit of an eyesore. What about 500 dollars?'

'Don't you think 400 would be more the value of it?'

'Well, Terry, you do realise that the aviary is part of the history of Houghton Hall,' he began.

'Oh, so you don't want the money?' Terry interrupted hurriedly.

'Oh . . . Oh well, just for you and obviously this is to be a very discreet business venture . . .very well, 400 it is - but in cash.'

'I will send Simon and perhaps I shall come and collect it. Yes, cash it is. Goodnight, Barry.' He hung up, then immediately telephoned Killpara and first of all spoke to a buoyant Joyce, thanking her for the flowers but saying it wasn't necessary. She insisted it was, before Patricia took the phone.

'Terry, you are a darling. How brilliant! But for goodness sake get a receipt of some kind because if he finds out in the future that the aviary is at Killpara he may just cry theft.'

73

'You're right. He is sneaky. OK, I will get a receipt in duplicate. Simon and I, or a friend of Simon's, will collect it and then drop it off to you sometime next week.'

'Thanks so very much. I will drop the money off Tuesday when I return from work.'

'So why don't you stay for dinner Tuesday evening. We would love to have you.'

'That's very kind. Thank you, I shall look forward to it.'

Tuesday evening was indeed a pleasant time and Simon felt very comfortable knowing that Terry had found a friend on the edge of the five of them but it included him and this was the first time Terry felt part of this social group. Pete performed beautifully, with his tail spread in the air, until it was time to be locked away and then the antics started, which had Patricia and Simon in hysterics, while Tullulaha walked about under everyone's feet, clucking away. Patricia had never been inside Rosebae before and was surprised at the comfortable interior.

'It's all Terry's work,' Simon insisted. 'It was a real disaster before he started.'

Terry cooked a splendid meal and they sat about eating and drinking, discussing the removal plan for the aviary.

'I'll take a friend with me with an electric cutter for cast iron, because you can be sure that everything is rusted up.'

'Oh, while I remember,' said Patricia, opening her handbag and handing Terry an envelope with 400 dollars in it. 'I vaguely remember that the whole area around the aviary is covered in stinging nettles.'

'Oh, fantastic,' laughed Simon. 'I shall remember to dress for the event.'

It was relatively easy to take down the aviary due to its very poor condition. The big dome on the top came away thanks to the electric cutter, in four sections and they were able to lift it onto the truck.

'Do sign here, Barry,' said Terry. He pompously asked why, to be told it was simply a formality, at which he scratched his signature on the receipts, both of which Terry kept, and he then handed Barry the envelope with the money, which was obviously Barry's greatest concern.

'Discreet,' was Terry's parting word.

'Of course.' Barry smiled and waddled back inside, never thinking to offer them a cup of tea or a drink.

The truck delivered the aviary two farms down and James helped them offload the pieces. 'It's in a shocking state of repair,' he commented. 'You'll need an expert to make up the panels again so it can be assembled.'

Patricia, looking downcast, thanked him. 'I guess I never realised it was so bad.'

'Don't worry,' he reassured her. 'I know a guy who does this sort of work. You can have a bit done at a time. That way you can spread the bill.' She asked James to get him to come and have a look and give her a quote, since they might as well get started on it.

'Here's the receipt. I'll keep a copy. You never know our Barry.'

'A drink, boys!' came the voice of Joyce as she rounded the corner with a basket of beer and champagne. 'Oh my!' was her reaction as she saw the enormous heap of rusted cast iron. 'A bit of a jigsaw puzzle, isn't it?' Simon, do open the bottle.' They all looked at each other : was this really Joyce?

CHAPTER 3

The Oriental Hotel

CHAPTER 3

The Oriental Hotel

The only thing oriental about this establishment was its name, set in relief lettering in cement in the ornate Victorian entablature in the balustrading that encircled the roof. Paul Wrighton's grand-parents and in turn his parents had been the owners of this establishment and now it had fallen into his hands as owner and manager. The building had known better days; architecturally it had been a pompous Victorian building with a veranda that was double-storeyed and ran across the front with copious quantities of decorative cast iron.

All the five hotels in Walvern were in one street, Williams Street, the other four being on corners but the Oriental was between equally pretentious Victorian shops, so the look of the street was fairly consistent. The advantage of the Oriental Hotel was that it was directly across from a long narrow park, so aesthetically it was the most beautiful, the others being on noisy street corners. If the exterior, apart from a drab blue-grey paint job that covered everything, was completely intact and covered in advertising that could not be said for the interior. In the late Sixties the demand had been to modernise and most of the hotels in Walvern slavishly followed suit. Where there had been in most of them the main bar, ladies lounge, a mixed lounge and a dining room all of them, including the Oriental, kept the main bar and knocked the mixed and ladies lounges into one large space. Many also included the dining room as well so the internal spaces were one. And the joining of these rooms was done in the most unsympathetic way possible. In nearly all of them the ceilings were lowered and nasty asbestos or pressed cane ceilings were installed with harsh fluorescent tubes. The furniture was standard laminated tables and these were inevitably accompanied by multi-coloured vinyl chairs with tubular legs and back supports.

All the five hotels served counter lunches, and dinners in the evening : the quality of the food varied, the menus never. The Oriental was different from the other four in that the big dining room remained intact, although the ceiling had been lowered. The drabber the colour for the walls the better and if wallpapered the taste was exclusively suburban. The decoration as such was confined to souvenirs or narrow shelves holding sporting cups; photos of local cricket or football teams abounded. Occasionally there was a print of some part of Victoria but that was generally it.

For years these five hotels had managed to make an adequate living. Each attracted a certain clientele. Friday and Saturday nights were the busiest and this kept them all afloat. In country towns, hotels are the mainstay of a social equilibrium : the Commercial Hotel was probably the best one, not aesthetically, of course, but they considered themselves the right hotel. It traditionally had been the hotel where the wealthier Protestants drank and ate and it continued to attract this establishment class. Needless to say, Barry Houghton and Stewart Searl never drank anywhere else. The Oriental traditionally catered for a genteel Catholic clientele and continued to do so, but not exclusively. The other three hotels went down the scale slowly but surely until one reached the Star, which was a fine Victorian brick building and was known as 'the blood house'. There were always fights and the police were regularly called on Friday and Saturday nights to quell yet another brawl. This hotel was patronised by Mary's brother, Keven, and especially in this hotel certain substances changed hands regularly. Keven was a pusher but not a very clever or discreet one, so although his clients knew he was always about it became risky to be seen with him, especially exchanging finance for a small plastic container. As soon as the police appeared Keven would disappear, only to return when the coast was clear and then it was business as normal.

These five hotels had changed little over the years. The interior décor had become more kitch but the clientele remained attached for one reason or another to their particular establishment. The Oriental had traditionally made good money. It was well run and it was extremely rare that a fight was seen on the premises. If it did occur, the barman and bouncer put a quick stop to it at once. It had one peculiarity in that men generally drank at the main bar but the two rooms that opened now into one, with orange concertina plastic doors, was generally used by women of all ages and rarely with their male partners. It was known as a hotel where girls over eighteen or women could go to have a drink in secure surroundings.

But all of this was about to change, and the change was very much for the worse. The town Council and the Licensing Board approved a plan for a new hotel on the outskirts of Walvern, between the town and the freeway, so the building of this vast structure in the most ghastly taste began. The local hoteliers had petitioned the Council but to no avail : the plan was passed and that was that. The Oriental had been the first hotel to sound the alarm bells though the rest of the hoteliers were slow to join in.

Enid had married Paul Wrighton when she was eighteen years old. She knew exactly what it was to be poor and determined that her future would be anything but that. She came from a family of five girls, and being the second had it not been for a generous aunt who paid her basic school fees she might never have met the other four. She had a boyish look, always cut her reddish brown hair short and had a rather hard face : it was the eyes, the light green eyes that were slightly narrow, and that gave her a calculating look. If one knew her well, the calculating look and attitude were taken for granted. When mini-skirts were in, hers was always the shortest. She had good legs and showed them to advantage. She was a loyal friend, but if crossed it was a very different situation. She never forgot or forgave. She married Paul, who was fifteen years her senior, a tall, extremely good-looking man with black hair now going grey on the sides and the palest blue eyes. He had a very handsome face and a large chest with very strong arms that ended in full, largely developed hands that were always immaculately manicured. The bitching talk had always been why on earth he had married someone like Enid, who, after a short time, took over the running of the Oriental and was extremely efficient at it. From maids to waitresses to the cook, she demanded the best and paid well, but she was a hard taskmaster. She would not be corrected and found any advice galling to accept. For that reason, the hotel was well run and clean but static. Nothing changed because Enid did not think it necessary. Now she was having second thoughts. With this new hotel, which was called The Stardust, to open next year she knew very well she would lose all the younger clientele and perhaps a lot more as well. Something new, parking for three hundred cars, and business did not look too cheerful at all. She was very brittle on any subject of change but the future was something these five hotels were now very worried about and strangely, as the Stardust came to completion, the clientele of all the hotels looked forward to better things.

There were two events which led to a change for the Oriental. The first occurred not at that hotel, but at another, the Commercial, the staid, conservative hotel, and to those like Barry and Stewart the only hotel. It had been like any luncheon time, the same patrons with the owner, Robert Lachlan, as usual strutting about giving orders and attempting in his own pretentious ways to assure the clientele they were in the only hotel with class. This appealed to Barry and Stewart, who naturally assumed that every comment this overweight person passed about class included them. It had been a situation that was nothing, but with the personalities involved it escalated to a moment that seemed as if Vesuvius was to erupt again. It had a great deal to do with the arrogance which both the owner of the Commercial Hotel and both Barry and Stewart would not have considered anything to do with them, but Stewart passed a vicious comment about someone at the bar and Barry, as always, agreed. The problem this time was the man at the bar did not think that this pseudo-smart comment at his expense was very clever and said so. Stewart was stupid enough, with plump Barry across from him, to pass yet another comment about peasants. The man at the bar, and not without a certain stature, grabbed Stewart from his small table and threw him against the wall. Stewart was, to say the least, surprised, not to mention being afraid. The first punch sent him to the floor in a heap. Barry completely bleached white, assuming he was in for the same treatment.

'You dreary poofs!' yelled the insulted client, and, as he passed Barry, shoved him backward on his chair so that he fell to the floor with a loud thud.

'Where's the manager?' screamed Stewart with a throbbing sensation in his left eye.

Herein lay the fall of the Commercial Hotel. When Robert Lachlan rounded the corner of the now open section, the insulted client reported what had happened and as fate would have it not far behind Lachland was Lenny Risley, the best cook of all the hotels and someone who kept the Commercial on its toes food-wise. If you wanted to eat well, you ate at the Commercial. Lenny was a brilliant cook but he suffered under the extreme control of the owner, who refused point blank to have any fancy food on the menu. 'No one will eat it,' was his dull reply. So Lenny was limited in a certain sense. He was employed but that was it. Nothing exciting and no opportunity to expand.

Lenny was good-looking, tallish, with soft hazel eyes and a mop of blonde hair, a good face with the corners of his mouth always betraying a hint of a laugh – and a good body. In the morning, before work, he always spent an hour or two in the local gym but he was the most mysterious man in town. No one at all had any idea about his sexuality. He was everybody's friend but no one's lover. In a smallish country town a good-looking blonde generally has someone with him but Lenny never appeared to.

So as this debacle occurred in the side section and Stewart found himself flattened and Barry upturned, the insulted client told the owner in no uncertain terms that if he was expected to put up with fags like this he would be the first to go - and with a smile on his face - to the Stardust Hotel. Lachlan, the owner, stupidly didn't realise the consequence of his following comments: 'Oh, all these fags should be burned alive. They don't bring a cent to this hotel. And we are only relying on your type of clientele.' He smiled.

Lenny was furious, as were both Barry and Stewart, but Lenny had much the greater clout. He went immediately into the kitchen - and this was the full lunch period - changed and walked out. His last words to Robert Lachlan were, 'Get fucked!'

If Robert Lachlan thought he had heard the last of this, he was wrong, but a very similar situation occurred at the Oriental in that Enid criticised the cook, a certain overweight Ann Trevie, who in a moment of anger threw a whole container of *bolognese* sauce at Enid and found the target. Enid fired her on the spot and told her her wages would be terminated immediately. 'I couldn't care less. I am going to work at the Stardust and you and all the rest are going to be bankrupt.'

For Enid it was one hurdle after another. Her fortune was that Trevor and Mary were having lunch at the hotel at that moment. She tried to sponge as much as she could of the sauce off her clothes and popped her head around the corner of the kitchen door.

'Trevor!' she called. He stood up and went to see what the problem was. 'Darling, you serve it on spaghetti, you don't wear it!'

'I've fired her,' she spat out, 'but what am I going to do now?' She looked so forlorn.

'May I suggest you go upstairs and change. When you return we shall have the problem solved,' though he wondered how.

'Goodness,' exclaimed Mary when he told her. 'I have an idea,' she went on briskly. 'Don't you remember Joyce's birthday party? Terry took over in the kitchen and did a great job. Perhaps he could help Enid out.'

'Why not?' was Trevor's reply.

Enid returned and they suggested Terry to her. She listened for a moment and then fled into the kitchen to prepare and organise lunch.

In small country towns it does not take long before the gossip gets about. Trevor had heard about the debacle at the Commercial from a client in the dentist's studio late afternoon and immediately telephoned Enid.

'I don't have Lenny's telephone number,' she wailed.

'I do. He's a client of ours. Take it down and make the appointment to see him at six tonight. I want to be there. I don't want you fucking this opportunity up.'

Enid thanked him briskly and said she's see him at six. Trevor also asked her to tell Paul to be there as well. Then he hung up. He had a rescue plan for the Oriental in the back of his mind but he couldn't think of a way of forcing Enid into changing her very set ideas. He telephoned a Melbourne number and made some enquiries and the answer appeared to suit him.

'You look like you're going to war,' Mary commented as the last patient for the day left. Agreeing that he was, he quickly changed and drove to the Oriental and was just going in as Lenny crossed the street. He waited and they went in together. He looked at Lenny and thought 'not bad, not bad at all'. There were few customers and so Enid and Paul, Trevor and Lenny went into the closed dining room. Enid excused herself and returned with a bottle of champagne and four glasses. Trevor took over. He knew full well that if he did not take advantage of this moment he would never get another opportunity. 'Well, he said to Lenny, 'how much do they pay you at the Commercial?' When Enid heard what it was she was genuinely surprised as she paid her ex-cook more, but before she could say anything, Trevor continued. 'We will pay you A\$100 more a week and you have a free hand in the kitchen.'

'Completely free?' he queried, looking at Enid and Paul. Enid bit her top lip as she did when she was nervous and looked at Lenny.

'OK,' she said in a business-like way, 'you can have six months to do what you like. The only thing is I want a profit.'

'You'll get your profit on the condition you don't interfere.'

'Very well,' she said grudgingly, looking at Paul and then at Trevor who announced. 'We are going to overhaul the whole hotel.'

'It needs it,' returned Lenny, looking about. 'It's pretty bleak in here.'

Enid was about to say something defensive but it was Paul who said to Trevor, 'What do you have in mind.'

'I'll show you tonight. You are both coming with me to dinner. You, too, if you like, Lenny, and I will show you exactly what the Oriental is going to look like. If we don't start work immediately,' and here he looked at Paul and Enid, 'you will have to sell for what you can get and remember there will be another four hotels on the market, so don't expect much.'

If one thing in the world frightened Enid it was the prospect of being poor again. She had suffered badly as a child and the cold hand of poverty was something she was determined would never touch her again.

'Get changed,' Trevor went on. 'Paul, tell the barman he is in charge. Alert the staff. We leave in five minutes.'

Enid went upstairs and changed, the thought of bankruptcy flashing back and forth in her mind. She was now more worried than before. As Trevor's car swept out onto the freeway, with Lenny, Enid and Paul on board, he began little by little to unfold a design to save the Oriental. Every time Enid brought up an objection, the others, including Paul once or twice, shouted her down. She moved uncomfortably in her seat, staring out through the front windscreen.

'And if this idea fails? she asked, in a snappy tone.

'Then we are no worse off,' replied Paul slowly. 'I know I can get a mortgage easily, as we own the building outright, so that's not the problem, but it's all got to work well.'

'With Lenny in the kitchen, you can't fail,' insisted Trevor. Lenny smiled. 'Thanks, Trevor, for the vote of confidence, but I know I can do it. At the Commercial Lachlan would never allow any change at all so it was boring, as was the clientele. Lachlan could have made much more money but he just couldn't see ahead, the arsehole.' Although Lenny had accepted working at the Oriental, Enid was still confused as to why he had left the Commercial. She was sure it wasn't just a dull clientele.

After an hour and a half, Trevor pulled up in an inner city zone, to an hotel much smaller than the Oriental but feeling the same. It was twilight but they could see the cream-coloured exterior with white trim and up in the balustrading on the roof in gilded letters 'The Travellers' Arms 1856'.

'Well, come on. Your education now begins,' Trevor assured them. 'Don't miss anything.'

They entered a high-gloss black door and walked immediately into a largish room with a pair of tall, beautiful Victorian sand-blasted doors that opened into a second room beyond. 'May we help you?' queried a young man in a white shirt, black tie, black trousers and shoes, with a long black apron?'

'I have an appointment for three but we are four.'

'No problem at all. Would you like to take a seat? Come through here.' The waiter took them through to the second room, with large French doors overlooking a very well-landscaped courtyard. They sat down and the drinks order was taken. When the waiter returned, there was a small tray of bits to eat while drinking.

'Hi, Trevor!' came a cry and the owner, dressed the same as the waiter, came over and Trevor introduced the others to him.

'It looks great,' commented Paul, looking about.

'You should have seen it eighteen months ago. You wouldn't have said that.' The owner laughed and explained that in summer the courtyard was used for eating, and there was waiter service in the evening. But he said that last summer he had tried an experiment that had proved to be a great success. For Saturday and Sunday lunches, the clients purchased a ticket and that entitled them to a steak which they cooked themselves. There was a table of salads, and it was all smart self-service. 'The problem was that we had to keep refusing people, it was so popular. It appeals to the young, smart set, who don't want to go to a restaurant and want to eat out of doors.'

'What a good idea,' Enid heard herself saying.

The owner excused himself but not before smiling at Lenny. Enid looked about at the clientele – men. Hm, she thought, Trevor has brought us to a gay pub and her eyes strayed about the décor, pale walls, very subdued lighting, lovely heavy cream curtains which absorbed the sound and the fact that the two rooms were still intact. The wall broke the sound as well. At the Oriental the noise with a big crowd was terrible. The open fireplaces on the sides of these two rooms boasted Victorian marble mantels with huge mirrors over them and at the side of each mantel was a clear glass cylinder vase filled with fresh flowers.

'Well, what do you think?' asked Trevor. 'The waiter looks a bit better dressed than Maureen at the Oriental with the short top and a midriff of fat hanging out!' Enid narrowed her eyes but the point was taken.

As the evening set in the lighting came on in the courtyard, creating a very special, and because of the high walls, a very private space. Paul looked at Trevor and then Enid and Lenny. 'We have all this at the Oriental but I never thought to use it like this. I like it a lot.'

'You haven't seen the best yet,' smiled Trevor and no sooner had he said this than the waiter appeared and asked whether they would like to have dinner there or in the dining area - whichever you would like.' He smiled and Lenny returned the smile.

'I think we will try the dining area please.' They followed him to what must once have been the original dining rom. It was virtually an extension of the other rooms but much grander. It also had a view of the lit courtyard. Enid sighed. 'Well, to think someone bricked up the windows, leaving on a narrow slot at the top in the dining room at the Oriental.' Again, thick heavy curtains and a carpeted floor helped to cut the noise. In the first two rooms the floors were in travertine marble. The big marble fireplace was intact and again a huge oval Victorian over-mantel mirror stared out at the clients. They sat down.

'Look, Enid, the colour is white.'

'I can see,' she replied sarcastically as the reference was to the table linen : at the Oriental it was either red or gold.

'I hope you have noticed the furniture, darling. Not a piece of chrome or vinyl to be seen.' Enid narrowed her eyes and gave Trevor a very false smile.

Lenny studied the menu. 'It's not bad,' he said, 'and it's not over complicated – simple, but good, not an enormous choice but that's better because you can change it. Look how they insert a new menu into the cover each day.' Enid grunted, turning hers over, but again the mood was kept quiet, due to the soft light and an enormous chandelier that offered only a soft light from its dimmer system. 'A bit smarter than the fluorescent tubes, wouldn't you say, Paul?' asked Trevor.

Lenny was well aware that Trevor was making every point a winner and felt good that he was in at the initial planning of the reconstruction of the Oriental. The food was pronounced good and even Enid had to admit the wine list was quite extensive. Paul excused himself for a moment after they had finished and said he wanted to have a look at the main bar. He returned very enthusiastic as the Travellers' Arms had kept the ornate back bar fixture behind the bar with the shelves and mirrors to display bottles but was pleased to announce that the one at the Oriental was finer.

'Would you like the coffee and drinks here or would you like to move back to the other section?' asked the very pretty waiter that Trevor realised Lenny obviously thought attractive.

'Let's go back to the other room' said Enid, anxious to glean as much as she could. The table was readied in the other room with a view of the courtyard and Enid noticed that the waiter must have held a table for them, as all the rest were occupied. They sat down to the soft music that had accompanied them all evening. Although it had been a fact-finding exercise it was a really relaxing time - even Enid had to admit that - so after coffee and another drink they decided that an hour and a half's drive home meant they had better get going. Trevor asked for the bill but the waiter smiled and said, 'The gentleman has paid, thank you.' Everyone look at Paul. When he had got up and gone to view the bar area, he had discreetly paid the bill with a very handsome tip to the waiter.

On the way home Enid could not be silenced. Lenny drove due to Trevor claiming total exhaustion due to Enid, who defended herself with a string of expletives. 'But if we do this . . .' and it turned out the entire conversation was thrust and parry between, not Trevor and her but between her and Lenny, each bouncing off the other. Enid suddenly realised that although she and Paul had just this evening hired the best cook in Walvern she had also gained a friend and someone she was prepared to listen to without becoming angry. Lenny had been two years behind the group at school and so doing a quick calculation she put his age at 32 or 33. At school she only had vague memories of him, great at swimming but nothing else, a skinny kid with a long mane of blonde hair which always got him into trouble with the school administration. And here he was again, but this time he was in control in a certain sense. He was able to see much more clearly what Trevor had tried to show Enid and she was very aware of this and knew that he was most probably going to be the person who would save the Oriental. For that intelligent piece of reasoning, Lenny was one of the few that could take on Enid in a head-on argument and win, without Enid being stupid enough to threaten to fire him. She liked him also for another reason. Nothing has been said but she worked well with gay men. Of her four closest friends one was a woman and the other were all gay men., even Thomas. She sighed to herself : the beautiful Thomas. Whereas the others had no problem with their sexuality, Lenny was secretive, not that that mattered to Enid but she felt much more secure with him and as a result allowed him a much freer hand. Unbeknown to her and only when she was not present, the group, always in fun and behind her back, called her 'Noddy', as her name, Enid Wrighton, was so close to Enid Blyton and so obviously Paul was 'Big Ears; but not even her closest friend Mary would have dared call her Noddy to her face.

* * * * *

The following week saw frenetic activity at the Oriental. The mortgage was granted by the bank without any problem, transferring the sum to Paul as his solicitor guaranteed everything and so the Oriental was on the way to becoming a copy of the Travellers' Arms. Whenever they hit a stumbling block, Enid and Lenny or Paul and Lenny would dash to the Travellers' Arms for dinner just to check out what they had forgotten.

The debacle at the Commercial Hotel seemed years ago but in fact it was less than a week since it had happened, on a Thursday, the day the Walvern Gazette was published, so it was necessary for Stewart Searl to wait a whole week to vent his spleen on the management. And did he let fly! *'In and Out of Society'* was a column read by all, if only to criticise it, but there was a lot of people who had heard the story and with Stewart sporting a black eye everyone who saw him knew the next issue was going to be worth reading.

Someone who anticipated the poisonous column was Trevor, who invited Stewart (whom he disliked intensely) for a drink at the Oriental. Always ready for a free drink, he accepted. The staff were already primed, so when he arrived he was shown a good table, champagne was offered and he and Trevor were joined by Paul, but not Enid due to her particular loathing of him. Public relations began as they explained everything to a very curious Stewart, the courtyard development and Lenny's fine cuisine, 'much smarter than the Commercial Hotel ever thought of,' said Trevor, 'and it's going to be for people who understand class like yourself.'

Stewart took the bait easily. If there was one thing he was susceptible to it was flattery and after the three of them had finished the second bottle of champagne he wove his way between the tables and left.

'The things I do for you!' laughed Trevor.

'Thanks a lot,' Paul replied, smiling. 'You have been fantastic. Without you and this change that now Enid is crazy for we should have been in very hot water.'

'Well, let's see how we go and for God's sake take those awful orange concertina doors down tomorrow. They are so bad.'

'Do you know, in the stable behind we have the polished doors that were here originally and I know you won't believe it but behind this false wall here,' he pointed to a party wall, 'are the marble fireplaces.'

'You're kidding,' answered Trevor, turning around and glancing at the wall.

'Well, down they come and these hideous ceilings. We – I mean Enid, Lenny and me – have decided to do the dining room first, as it is rarely used and then we shall move to one room and then the other. We shall fit French doors to the courtyard, exactly like in the Travellers' Arms.'

'Fantastic,' said Trevor. 'I must be going. I have promised to have dinner with Mary and Joseph this evening.' As he left and walked to his car, a little thought crossed his mind. It crystalised and then dissolved. 'Enid, Lenny and me' – how quickly these three had formed the task force to save the Oriental. 'Enid, Lenny and me' – 'Lenny and me'.

The Thursday edition of the Walvern Gazette was a sell-out and for the first time ever a reprint was made. *'In and out of Society'* was a vitriolic column that was twice as long as usual. Robert Lachlan considered legal action but was told by his solicitor that this would be like petrol to a fire, but the article was poisonous. Everything that it was possible to criticise was criticised with a vengeance. Nothing was spared, from the ghastly décor to the unhygienic toilets and even the wonderful Lenny Risley leaving the rat hole; the worn carpets that were never cleaned and on and on he went. And the management's indifference to clients' safety, being attacked whilst eating lunch in a public place. Nothing was said about the fact that Stewart had baited with sarcastic comments the particular person who had struck him. This was not in the equation. Then he went on to praise the fact that the Oriental Hotel was gearing up for extensive renovations that could only be described as tasteful and smart, something Walvern lacked and was unlikely to find in the Stardust Hotel. If the Oriental needed the best publicity in the world, they got it. In one week Enid had five enquiries for large dinners and had to refuse them saying she would only be happy to receive their bookings when she was convinced the surroundings were good enough for them. Lenny's public relations routine had found a firm supporter in Enid. It was odd that someone like Enid, who found any type of constructive criticism as a personal attack, allowed Lenny to virtually take over. This handsome blonde organised not only the kitchen but also, when free, oversaw the renovations. He had a good eye and with Trevor in and out, Enid little by little accepted that all this change was due to her, something the others never corrected her on.

About ten days later the false ceiling had been totally removed in the dining room, the bricked-up windows were opened to the floor and newly made French windows were installed. Everything was going to plan and quite quickly, until a worker began to open up the false ceiling in the back room that was to overlook the courtyard. The hideous orange concertina doors had not as yet been removed and were closed. It was a busy lunchtime and patrons were squeezed into the one room with lots of apologies from Enid. 'We are doing the renovations for you,' she smiled, and helped out collecting plates. Then there was the most tremendous noise, a crash and the sound of splintering wood. All the lights went out. Enid spun around and dashed into the hall, then into the back room where a workman was extricating himself from the rubble, covered in dust and grime.

'What in hell has happened?' she shouted and then looked about as three quarters of the ceiling hung in bits and pieces, with the centre part touching the table and chairs.

'This whole section,' replied the worker, 'was in a very dangerous condition. You are damned lucky you didn't have patrons sitting here or they would have been very flat!'

Enid asked what had happened and was told, 'I opened up one of the panels near the walled-up fireplace and obviously the beam was rotten. With the pressure of opening, the ceiling just collapsed.'

'Oh fuck!' was Enid's response. 'See if you can open the windows to let the dust out.' Then she disappeared to telephone the electrician to say she had an emergency.

That evening Enid, Lenny and Paul decided it was impossible to try to continue in the state it was in. The main bar, at the other side of the building, remained open but they closed the large front room, not wanting a problem with the insurance company if the ceiling collapsed there also. So the kitchen closed and Lenny and Enid took over as helpers and organisers in an attempt to finish the work as quickly as possible. Lenny was the only one to keep Enid's spirits up. She was now becoming very worried as the renovation expenses continued and the revenue started to dry up. She was most afraid that this might well be what was to happen when the Stardust Hotel opened in only four months' time.

* * * *

'Mr Ollie!' she called, 'Mr Ollie!'

'Coming!' and he rounded a wardrobe. 'Oh, Mrs Wrighton, I see you got my message.'

'Yes, I did, thank you. Where are they?'

'Over here'. He took her to the left side of the action room and then to the junk section at the back. 'What do you think?' he asked.

Enid stared at four huge overmantel mirrors, not one of them in good condition, each of the frames missing a bit here and there and the most beautiful one obviously in the worst condition of all. She sighed : another problem, she thought and then remembered Joseph. She narrowed her eyes and took out a tape measure. With Mr Ollie's assistance she measured them.

'I only need three. Are they to be sold separately or as one lot?'

'One lot, due to their poor condition, but the mirrors are not broken.'

She slowly asked how much the reserve price was and was told there wasn't one, and so she said, 'Very well, I'll come on Thursday and bid. Thanks very much, Mr Ollie.'

'A pleasure to help you renovate the Oriental,' he smiled.

Enid left immediately, phoned Mary for Joseph's number and contacted him after accepting a dinner invitation for the evening.

When she got through to him, she started, 'Listen, Joseph, it's Enid. Mary gave me your number. Where are you now?'

'I'm at Thompson's hardware,' he replied.

'Great. Can you come to Mr Ollie's now?'

'Sure. I'll see you in ten minutes,' and in ten minutes precisely he arrived and the two of them went into the gloomy interior.

'What do you think?' she asked, anxiously. 'Can they be restored?'

'Yes, of course. Jan and I did one like that – someone had painted it yellow, so we cleaned it all off and re-gessoed it and then gilded it.'

'Does it take a long time?'

'Depends,' he said, non-committedly.

'All right. I'll buy them and can I send them to your workrooms?'

He gave her the address and asked her to give them a call first. She thanked him and said that she would be seeing him that night, and seeing his surprise explained that Mary had invited her to dinner. 'I have time off for good behaviour,' she said.

He smiled and saying, 'I'll see you later, then,' disappeared.

The Oriental was now taken back to its original state downstairs. The fireplaces were uncovered and the tall original ceilings, very damaged, were exposed. The walls were punctuated with holes that had supported the beams of the false ceilings. Bricklayers, plasters, electricians and carpenters were the only inhabitants of the reception areas, together with a very nervous Enid but with Paul and Lenny seeming quite content with the progress.

'You look exhausted,' Mary greeted Enid.

'I feel it,' came the reply as Enid placed a sack full of wine battles on the kitchen table.

'I've invited Trevor, so you two can talk shop or renovations. Joseph tells me you are going to buy some mirrors.'

'I hope so, but it depends on the price and not just the price at the auction rooms. It also depends on what Joseph charges.'

'Don't you worry. You'll get value for money with Jan and him. I'm just so happy he has found his niche. Jan says that he is very good indeed.'

'Hi, all,' said Trevor cheerily as he came in. 'I believe the Oriental is on fire.'

'What!!' screamed Enid, turning white.

'It's OK, darling, just a joke!'

'I will personally castrate you if you say anything like that again,' she retorted very sharply, as Trevor passed her and gave her a kiss.

'Just keeping you on your toes,' he murmured.

'Thanks,' she spat back.

Mary related the story of the mirrors and asked Enid what she was going to do with the fourth one.

'I haven't a clue. There is one that is a bit smaller. You don't want it for your living room, do you, Mary?'

'I hadn't thought about it.'

'But if I remember correctly, you said, some time ago, you were looking for one for here.'

'Well,' Mary laughed, 'I was, but I gave up. I'm just so lazy.'

'Well, we'll see what happens.' Enid smiled at her and both she and Trevor knew the fourth mirror was destined for Mary's living room as a gift.

'What about the upstairs?' asked Trevor, as he sat down.

'I think a coat of paint is about all,' answered Enid.

'Don't be stupid!' he argued.

'Who's stupid?' came Joseph's voice as he entered the large kitchen-dining room.

'Enid is,' Trevor teased. 'How are you, handsome?'

'Fine. Oh, Enid, Jan says we can go all out on the frames if it is an emergency.'

'Thanks, sweetie,' said a slightly more relaxed Enid, as she poured drinks. 'It comes naturally – must be the work environment.' She returned the bottle to an upright position.

Mary had some time ago listened to Enid one evening when there had been some discussion about Trevor's attention to Joseph.

'You can't keep Joseph under glass,' she said. 'Now he has greater confidence, let him use it. We both know Trevor is not going to take advantage of him. He wouldn't dare, with you and me in the background but it's important Joseph knows socially how to handle people like Trevor and if he can sort him out he won't have a problem with anybody.'

This proved to be true. In the past, if someone spoke to Joseph in a certain way, he excused himself and spent the rest of the evening watching television in his room. Now, that never happened, and he was learning to counter Trevor's remarks with his own, which kept Trevor at bay, but not supressed.

'You should see the courtyard behind the hotel,' sighed Enid. 'It's a great junk heap.'

'Well, take advantage of it and strip those ghastly bedrooms upstairs and start again. They are just hideous and some still have lino on the floor.'

'I know. I spoke to Paul only yesterday about it. He seems convinced that every room must have its own bathroom, and so the plumbers are looking at converting some of the smaller bedrooms into two and connecting them to the larger ones. I don't know where all this is going to end or how we shall pay for it all, although I must say we are right on budget.'

'What are you going to do with the courtyard?' asked Joseph.

'Well, I know what I want it to look like but how to get it there I haven't a clue.'

'What about Thomas's friend, that fabulous garden designer who did all of Rose's garden,' suggested Mary.

'Who is he?' asked Enid.

'I don't remember his name but why don't we call Thomas and find out?'

'Great idea, girls,' said Trevor, 'but not before the courtyard is cleared. It's asking a bit much to envisage paradise with all the rubble in it.' Enid agreed that he was right and said she would call Thomas the next day.

'Ask him if he has a chandelier – a big one,' Trevor suggested, smiling. Enid didn't reply.

The conversation moved on to the vicious column of Stewart Searl and the Stardust Hotel. The latter was well ahead of schedule and this large flat, rectangular structure with asphalted parking for three hundred cars was well under way : a glass disco floor, two front bars and a side bar, enormous kitchens and four large areas for eating and drinking, each one in a bright colour. It was good for the local youth, as it supplied occupation and part-time work, which meant that late school types had weekend jobs. They paid only award wages and no contracts, but still the young flocked for interviews for positions, as did the not-so-young. Two of the local hotels lost their chefs and the two bouncers from the Star were to take their new positions as soon as the Stardust was ready to open. Cleaners, maids and waitresses were ever ready to dash to the Stardust for an interview, hoping to be part of the new establishment. Enid had lost and found a cook; she had lost only one waitress, while the barman and other staff stayed loyal to her, something she did not forget in their Christmas bonus envelopes.

'You don't mean your overweight waitress is gone, do you?' laughed Trevor. 'Thank God! She was such a waste! I might just be able to fix you up with a young man.'

'If he's prepared to take direction, send him to me,' replied Enid in a business-like tone. 'We hope to have the kitchen up and running and the rooms ready in a fortnight.'

'Oh, he takes direction very well,' Trevor said, knowingly.

But it took more than three weeks before they were ready to re-open the rooms. They were still missing pieces, but little by little it all started to come together. Thomas had brought Raoul up to have a look at the courtyard; Enid and Lenny liked what he suggested very much, especially the fountain. As Raoul had said, you are only going to use the courtyard in summer and so for eight months of the year it's empty, while a fountain, splashing, always gives a feeling of something happening. He took measurements, suggested ideas for the paving, added large Italian terrcotta pots with lemon trees and smaller ones filled with one type of annual flower. He was a great success and they agreed on a price for the work on the condition that he oversee it and dine at the Travellers' Arms, which Thomas promised to take him to so he could see the sort of thing they wanted.

The owners of the Stardust Hotel were now desperate to open as they did not want to lose any trade. So they opened half of it, the two big section only, plus the disco part for the evening. It began as a great success. Everyone went, especially the young people. Everyone was curious to see it. The one great advantage was easy car parking. The older clientele that had remained faithful to the original five hotels left in droves. A huge self-service food section at reduced rates and special lunch deals emptied the local hotels : Enid, Lenny and Paul were now very worried. The fact that the Stardust had opened before they were finished was a blow, as the trade that might have come out of curiosity to see the newly renovated Oriental didn't bother. The exterior painting was now complete; all the old advertising signs had been ripped off and the building looked very smart indeed. By this time, the interior was more or less finished and two of the huge mirrors were in position, giving the place a much airier feeling. The courtyard was almost completed, but where were the throngs of people?

Everyone who did come loved it, but that was not sufficient. It was then that Trevor took over again and invited Stuart Searl to dinner. He had written a half-hearted column about the Stardust, as the owners had wined and dined him, but he found it extremely noisy and said so in his column, not to mention the colours being loud, though prices were all right. Enid realised that she would have to tone down her approach to Stewart if there was going to be some positive information in his column. But they need not have worried : Stewart genuinely liked it and Lenny's food was marvellous. And it took Enid ten seconds to realise that the new young waiter recommended by Trevor was going to be the draw card for a completely new clientele and she was right. Stewart thought Anthony, the new waiter, was a splendid addition to the décor and he paid him a lot of attention with smiles all evening. He was also fascinated with the idea of Saturday and Sunday lunches where one helped oneself. He thought the prices were fair and the wine selection excellent. The fact that he never paid for anything was another matter.

And so, on Thursday, an anxious group from the Oriental waited for the Walvern Gazette. The report was not just good, it was glowing. Every superlative was used : the food was excellent, and the Saturday and Sunday lunches concept. The only thing Stewart said as a sharp joke was that they would all have to wait for the chandelier in the gloriously restored dining room. He finished by saying that not to go to the Oriental, now completely refurbished in exquisite taste, was denying oneself one of the real pleasures of living in Walvern. It worked. The business came in a rush and a whole new type of clientele, young professionals filled the Oriental. After two or three visits the fascination of the Stardust wore off. Besides, the Stardust was aiming for a clientele between eighteen and thirty : the Oriental was looking at a clientele of twenty five to fifty and they just happened to have put together the correct formula. After the months of work and worry it all began to happen and for the first time in her life Enid was refusing bookings as the hotel was full. She was also very aware that it wasn't just the environment that attracted the clients, and as a result Anthony received a healthy rise in his pay packet. Enid was all for investing money where it paid off.

Enid had emailed the article Searle had written to Thomas and begged him and Rose to find her a spectacular chandelier. She gave them a budget and within two weeks the most beautiful chandelier, with what seemed like a thousand cut lozenges in crystal was hanging from the dining room ceiling with a dimmer fixed to it. The soft lighting worked perfectly. Stewart Searle always received a good discount when he ate there and he was always reporting whom he had seen and what they were wearing or the charity luncheon for the local hospital. On and on it went, always mentioning the hotel décor but never seeing it, only a waiter in a white shirt, black tie, black trousers and a long black apron.

Whenever Mary ate at the Oriental, which was more frequent now, Enid made sure that Anthony and another good looking boy, Walter, never placed a bill in front of her and she was always to be thanked for coming, as they did to the others. But Mary always received special attention. And her living room now had the smallest of the four mirrors: Joseph and Jan had restored it and it looked perfect there.

If business had had a turn-around for the Oriental, it was not so with the others. The Star Hotel, was the mecca for the young, with a dance floor, loud music and fights. On Saturday nights they were lucky to get twenty people now and even that number began to dwindle. The Star Hotel, with this young age group which had been their mainstay financially for a long time - and a very healthy mainstay it had been – could not complete with the Stardust, so the young danced all night on an illuminated glass dance floor with special lighting effects and lots of loud music, with Keven moving like a shadow, collecting finance in exchange for little plastic bags with all sorts of substances inside them. The fights continued, but the large asphalted car park was the venue for them. The bouncers only patrolled inside and up to the front doors.

The Commercial Hotel, even if there had not been the opening of the Stardust, would still have been in trouble, due to Stewart Searle's bitter column and even now, when he had the opportunity, he still fired venomous comments at the owner and the establishment itself. Lachlan was now feeling the squeeze financially. He had, as a result of arrogant management and not looking to the future, well overspent on unnecessary things. He was terribly over-staffed, generally with young girls that he thought were attractive and although they had been a draw card once the Stardust had more and they were prettier. His biggest problem was a vast overdraft he had at the local bank. When times were good, he spent and the bank lent, neither assuming that after a long plentiful summer and a good autumn there would come a very hard winter and this was now what he was feeling. He had trouble repaying the mortgage at the bank and began to fire staff. This did not make him popular and Stuart Searle was ever ready to give a certain ex-employee of the Commercial who had worked for twenty three years for Lachlan and was dismissed a free lunch at the Oriental in exchange for ammunition for his column. The lunch was an excellent investment and so each week there was always a poisonous sentence or two concerning the Commercial. Barry had also decided that the Oriental was now smart enough for him as well, and often joined Stewart for lunch, feeling he was doing the hotel a real favour. The truth was that after that eventful day when Stewart had been attacked at the Commercial and he was overturned on his chair, not to mention, horror of horrors, a direct attack by Lachlan on his sexuality, and the fact of being a coward, he never returned to the Commercial, not that Lachlan was concerned about him. But he most certainly was about Stewart, who never forgave him.

Of the five original hotels in Walvern the Commercial was the first to close, due to the bank foreclosing on it, so the hotel and contents went to auction. The original Victorian veranda system had been removed in the early seventies to make it what seemed at the time more in touch, so the hotel finished up as offices, as the façade was now so anonymous that offices were well suited to the building. Stewart Searle wrote an article on the history of the hotel and finished it off with a scathing attack on Lachlan as an incompetent hotelier who was the direct cause of an important piece of Walvern history being dismantled.

The Oriental was now making very good money; people now dined there as they would at a restaurant : Lenny's superb cooking and a splendid environment added to the success. There was an incident one evening, and of all people to witness it was Stewart Searle, dining with Barry. A group of young men in collar and tie had been drinking at the main bar and some of them decided to stay for dinner. One of them was quite loud, due to drinking too much alcohol. Enid moved quickly across to their table and tapped the drunken man on the shoulder. He swung around and to his horror glanced directly into Enid's narrowed eyes. She tightened her mouth and then quietly spoke. The table fell into silence.

'You can leave quietly now and return whenever you wish but if I throw you out you'll never put a foot in this hotel again.'

The young man had this odd feeling that at any minute two long fangs were about to come out of Enid's mouth and bury themselves in the side of his neck. He went to say something. 'I wouldn't,' said a stony-faced Enid. He stood up, went to the door accompanied by her. She smiled (or at least he thought that was what the look was) and said, 'I shall look forward to seeing you soon. Goodnight.' She closed the door behind him and moved back to the kitchen to see if Lenny wanted anything. A bouncer was not necessary at the Oriental : Enid was not afraid of anyone and out to protect and make her new clientele feel safe. To be told not to come back was to be destined to social oblivion, especially in a country town, where everything is always magnified.

Simon and Terry now, with Patricia, often ate at the Oriental. Terry and Enid decided that it was wiser to ignore one another but even Terry had to admit the food was great and it was a nice place to be. Mary and Joseph made a habit of dining every Wednesday evening, so if Simon was at a loose end, which wasn't very often, he dined with them. He noticed that each time he saw Joseph he seemed just that little bit more confident and as always more beautiful. Joseph was not unaware of Simon's dark good looks but nothing apart from funny repartee ever took place, especially as no one ever saw Joseph without Mary. Wednesday evening was for Trevor rehearsal night for the Walvern Light Opera Company and he always joined them for a drink : Enid or Lenny would have something for him to eat, even if the kitchen was closed. The moment the kitchen did close, Lenny always disappeared, unless there was a problem to resolve. 'The ever-mysterious Lenny,' thought Trevor. 'Who is he having an affair with?'

By this stage all the initial problems of re-starting the Oriental were solved and no waiters were employed permanently unless they were taken to the Travellers' Arms in Melbourne to look and learn. As a result of this investment Enid kept her staff smart and on their toes. If they were popular and brought in regular clients – and she did notice – she simply paid them more, so working for Enid became a sought-after job. She selected on two criteria, intelligence and, more importantly, that they were good-looking males. This formula netted her a very handy profit.

Whereas the Oriental after the restructuring was now working smoothly, this could not be said of the Stardust. After a sensational start, the crowds of young people became larger and larger and some of them were underage for consuming alcohol in a public place. This was only one of the problems, because they became drunk quickly and were out to impress one another. There was always a fight at some time during the evening but the two bouncers were always ready for it. It had the uncomfortable feeling that one had to be careful at the Stardust, and for that reason especially in the evenings families just didn't attend, so instead of building up a safe reputation the word was always out to be careful at the Stardust, especially late at night. Keven found business good and sometimes took unnecessary risks but managed to become invisible when the police arrived. So if the management thought they were going to capitalise on a smartish young crowd they must have been disappointed because it did not happen. The young did not drink expensive drinks and a great deal of them drank very little due to Keven's supply of an alternative 'happiness'. So the take each week was considerably less than they expected and controlling this vast number of young people became a real headache.

Thomas and Rose, when they came up one weekend met everyone for dinner at the Oriental and were amazed at the transformation. There was a night of laughter and drinking : as it was a warm evening Enid set them at a table outside, near the fountain, so the noise was not a problem to the other clients as Trevor, when everyone was together, generally performed and was noisy. Mary said to Rose that the frames that Thomas had given to Joseph were now finished and they could pick them up at her place before they returned to Melbourne. Joseph, needless to say, was not present. Rose related to the group that the paintings had at some stage been over-painted and when cleaned back properly had revealed that they were much better quality than they had expected.

'What are you going to do with them?' asked Mary.

'I don't really know,' Rose replied. 'Thomas will have to decide. Oh, so Roaul has designed this courtyard,' she added, changing the subject.

'Yes, he was just great.' Enid joined the conversation. 'So professional. Everything done without any drama. And by the way, Rose, your choice of the chandelier for the dining room was perfect.'

'Well, I can't claim all the credit. Thomas and I saw it at an auction sale and we thought it would suit you.'

'It's just perfect... Enid smiled and felt relaxed, a rare thing for her.

The waiter, Antony, arrived to check the drinks and Thomas was not unaware of his talent. He smiled at him. It was discreetly returned. Anthony was a very sophisticated young man and he knew exactly how to handle the clientele, but he also knew that to become involved publicly with any of them might just lose him the one thing he loved, his job. Enid had made it quite clear to the staff that a gentle flirt was good for business but at work it stopped there and that was that. So although he thought Thomas was a dream, he continued his work normally, so as not to incur a look from Enid.

The evening continued well after the last clients had left and the lights were turned off and doors closed. Enid went off for a moment and returned with a large tray of cheeses and splendid salt biscuits Lenny had prepared. He appeared with a matching tray with his vast assortment of sweets and cakes and for once Enid insisted he stay for a while and join them. Both Thomas and Trevor thought Lenny very, very attractive, a great body and the blonde hair and ever so charming, but as usual, after a drink with them all, Paul led him out and returned to join them.

'When we find out who the lover is, I can only tell you we shall all be surprised,' commented Trevor. 'Great body.'

'Great cook,' laughed Enid. It was a good night for her. Finally her and Paul's money worries seemed behind them and she was with the group of people she really loved. For Enid that was a very rare experience. She only relaxed in the company of these four people : they were the only ones to see her like this. Rose was fascinated with her, in the sense that work-wise she appeared to be without pity and seemed to live and work twenty four hours a day. This evening was the first time Rose had seen her genuinely laughing and totally at ease. There was no bill to collect : Enid thanked them all for coming and demanded that they make a date to come again together as soon as possible.

'She is a contradiction,' said Rose, as she drove Thomas back to Killpara.' She looks tough and I am sure she is – tough work-wise - but she has another side that she keeps well hidden.'

'I think you're right,' agreed Thomas. 'I guess she feels secure with us and so she changes like some insects when they pass from one coloured leaf to another. But Trevor has been fantastic. Without him the Oriental would have ended up probably the same as the Commercial – defunct.'

'He's so funny,' Rose added, 'but I also think Simon is particularly good looking. Thomas agreed at which Rose shot him a glance.

'No, no, Rose. I suppose I could have, but somehow we never did.' She said it was a pity.

The next day being Saturday was totally occupied with Killpara. Rose, for the first time or a long time, made a survey of the property, the house and its situation. To the right of the house and very close to the side of it was a gravel drive which the milk truck and share farmer use.

To the right of this again was a hideous modern garage that housed two cars. The garden was basically non-existent. Joyce was not a gardener and so it had degenerated to a narrow area of cut grass in front of the house and a few very tired shrubs which at this time of the year seemed to be crying out for water. The grass was totally brown. To the left was an old wire netting fence that divided the house from a bushy hedgerow and between this reasonably large space was the remains of an old orchard, now in very poor condition. At the bottom of it, parallel to the back of the house, was a fallen-down summer house with only two of the eight sides still vertical. The rest had just given up and slid into the now tall yellow grass that surrounded it and grown over the forgotten orchard. The total effect, Rose thought, was of indifference, not abandonment, just that no one really cared.

Mary had telephoned threatening death if Rose and Thomas did not join her for lunch on Sunday prior to returning to Melbourne. A threat like that was not to be ignored and as Thomas owed someone for the restoration of the frames they accepted much to Joyce's annoyance and Patricia's relief. The black Jaguar pulled up in front of Mary's home in Aspel Drive at exactly 12.15, the allotted time. It was a hot day, without any air, but before this precise timing Rose and Thomas, with his family, had been to Mass. Joyce, with her nose out of joint, had said goodbye to them at the church and they had gone their separate ways. 'She is so demanding these days,' commented Rose. 'I think she was easier before this change in her character.'

'I don't remember her like this,' replied Thomas, opening the car door for her.

'Come in!' shouted Mary. 'Trevor is already here, opening bottles. He is such a dear!' They made their way through to the large kitchen-dining room.

'Good morning – or is it good afternoon!' cried Trevor and swept around kissing them both. 'Imagine if I had done that to you at school,' he laughed.

'No one would have noticed,' Mary replied. 'If I remember, you seemed to be kissing most of the boys.' This produced a sarcastic laugh from him.

'Do sit down, Rose,' urged Mary, as Thomas placed four bottles of wine on the kitchen bench.

'Mary, it's such a pleasant house,' said Rose.

'Mine's better,' Trevor shot out. 'Two doors down. The only problem with mine is that it is infested with parents. A good fumigating is necessary.' Everyone laughed.

'I asked Simon and Terry but no go. It seems Friday night was all Terry is going to cope with.'

'He is such a bore,' Trevor said, 'but Simon is great.'

'Well, you would know,' Mary said with a wicked smile.

'Careful sweetie!' came the retort, passed just a little more sharply than usual.

'Well,' Mary asked, 'what do you both think about the transformation of the Oriental?'

'It's amazing,' replied Thomas. 'It looks fantastic.'

'Well, thank goodness we aren't there today.' When Rose asked why, she went on, 'Well, simply because it will be packed. Saturday and Sunday lunches are full house every weekend.'

'It's great for Paul and Enid.'

'But it's thanks to you, Trevor. We happen to know our Enid only too well. If you hadn't insisted they saw that hotel in Melbourne and changed her mind they might well be in a different situation.'

'I'll take a round of applause now, then,' was Trevor's response and they laughed.

'It's great,' said Mary, 'that Simon and Terry are out and about with Patricia. They had become a bit reclusive and as Terry and Patricia seemed to have hit it off we get to see Simon more often. By the way, how's Barry's birdcage going?'

He laughed. 'Oh, you mean part of the heritage of Houghton Hall,' and still laughing went on, 'I don't think it was such as bargain, as Patricia has this man out from Walvern every so often for three hours work welding or re-making all the broken parts. It's going to take some time before parrots are flying about in that aviary.'

'But it's much bigger than you describe it,' Rose insisted to him. 'It's actually a very large structure.'

'Yes, I think my sister got quite a surprise when it was delivered, but she is determined to have it standing and ready for its inhabitants before the winter.'

'Good for her,' Trevor muttered in a flat tone.

'Listen,' Thomas went on, directing his conversation to Trevor.

'Always!'

'Come on,' Thomas offered a smile that set Trevor alight. 'What's happening at the Light Opera Company.'

'Do you have three weeks to listen to it all? We can finish the boring bits in bed.'

'You're impossible,' laughed Mary.

'The show is a disaster, probably the most disorganised production I have ever been in and, believe me, I've had some very shaky performances here. But this is the worst. The producer and the director hate one another, two theatre gods of limited talent, so every night at rehearsals it just becomes more tense and dramatic. I only go for the drama myself.' He laughed. Then, 'Oh, the oven!' and rushed over to check that all was well.

Thomas had noticed that the table had been laid for five and had expected Enid or Simon but said nothing, assuming the extra person would be revealed at the right moment. Rose, too, had noted the seating and had hoped that the extra space would be filled by Simon. She liked him immensely. He was dark, good-looking, charming, intelligent and with a humility that was overwhelming. This, to her mind, was the perfect final partner for Thomas. They had been at school together, their parents had known one another, Rosebae and Killpara were close together. She knew that Simon was more than interested in Thomas – Friday night had confirmed that to her - the long looks, the hand on the shoulder. Oh, why was Thomas so difficult, she wondered.

'Have a look at the living room, Thomas,' said Mary. He stood up and walked to the room and was duly surprised, as not only was there Enid's gift of a large over-mantel mirror, but the nasty bricks that surrounded the old oil heater were gone, as was the heater itself, and a Victorian marble fireplace stood proudly in its place. The room had taken on a much more dignified feel. He looked about. It was a very pleasant, large room. He walked to the bay window and pulled the curtains apart, to see a beautifully manicured garden in front.

As he returned to the others, he was aware that there was another voice. He entered to see the back of a young man with bushy, brown hair and a broad set of shoulders.

'Joseph,' said Mary, 'let me introduce you to Thomas.'

As Joseph slowly turned around with the light streaming in from the window behind him, he had the advantage of sight. Neither of them said a word.

'Come on, boys,' said Trevor, realising there was an awkwardness there, 'kiss or at least shake hands.'

Thomas moved forward and offered his hand, as did Joseph, and at that moment Rose saw that all her hopes and dreams of Thomas and Simon being together had simply vaporised in front of her. None of the company had ever seen Thomas like this before. He was generally the bright, witty, good-looking man who kept everything going, but now a young man called Joseph had entered under his social armour and was making his presence felt without saying anything. The entire conversation during lunch was with the three of them : Joseph and Thomas were the silent listeners. If Rose had seen this impact, so had Mary and she was not at all sure that it was such a good idea. She knew very well Thomas's track record and to have her younger brother caught up in a no-win situation was the last thing in the world she wanted. But whatever it is that happens between two most unlikely people that produces a magic chemical reaction called, for the want of a better word, love, it was happening in front of them. No conversation or at least very little, just the assurance of a glance or a smile, that was all it took to trigger off this situation.

Trevor made it easier for them but Mary and Rose were much more circumspect. In Mary's mind, Joseph was just twenty three years old and Thomas a sophisticated and quite wealthy man was thirty six : there was a thirteen year difference, not that that was a problem but socially Thomas was light years ahead of Joseph and that was what worried Mary very much. She did not want this situation to put Joseph in a losing position when Thomas finished with him, as she knew this could only affect her long term relationship with Thomas himself, which at all costs she did not want to occur. But it was as if a net, so fine no one could see it, had been cast over the top of them and drawn them together and neither Thomas nor Joseph made any attempt to escape.

After lunch, as they had to return to Melbourne, Thomas pulled out his cheque book and asked Joseph how much the cost of the frames was, as he and Rose were very impressed with the workmanship. He gave a price that was exceptionally low. Thomas wrote the cheque and on another sheet of paper his telephone number. 'Call me,' was all he said as they loaded the well-packaged frames into the car. After their goodbyes, the car moved slowly down Aspel Drive and Joseph unfolded the cheque to find that Thomas had doubled the amount asked for. He folded it up and with the other piece of paper with the telephone number on it headed back inside to have another glass of wine - which was most unlike him. Trevor excused himself and said it was time to check the oldies. Mary sat down opposite Joseph and was about to start a conversation about the danger of Thomas when she noticed a glow that came from within him and spread across his face. She realised that any conversation or warning was wasted.

'He's beautiful, isn't he?' This was the very first time Joseph had ever made any comment about his sexuality.

'Yes, darling,' said Mary, helping herself to a glass of wine as well. 'He is very beautiful.'

Joseph just smiled. He seemed to have drifted into a mellow state and was absolutely content. Oh well, thought, Mary, if nothing else I suppose I can pick up the pieces.

Rose was driving on the way back and realised after a certain point that conversation was useless unless she wished to talk to herself. She had never seen Thomas like this before. He had always been the aggressor socially. If he wanted a man he went and got him, but today he was different. This beautiful twenty three year old had totally bewitched him and now, thought Rose sadly, he was going to feel what others felt when Thomas dismissed them. It was now going to be Thomas who was going to wait for this young man to call him. She sighed. I suppose it had to happen, she thought. Well, at least he is a nice young man. Let's see how long this lasts – we shall see.

CHAPTER 4

On With The Show

Thomas seemed distracted so after the first half of the week after he had seen Joseph Rose decided to give him a helping hand. Unbeknown to Thomas, Rose called Mary and the two of them, after a long chat, decided the same thing, to wait and see what happened. Rose had not realised that Joseph was so shy and so asked Mary whether she thought it would be improper if Thomas perhaps telephoned him. Mary had no objection so she gave Rose Joseph's telephone number.

Before dinner that evening, after he had had a swim, Thomas sat down beside Rose and had a drink with her. 'Darling,' said Rose, 'here.' She handed him a small sheet of paper and written in her neat hand was the name Joseph O'Farrel and the telephone number. Thomas took the sheet and looked at Rose. 'Not a word until you telephone him,' she went on, standing up. She began to walk back towards the open French doors.

When she returned, twenty minutes later, she noted a much more animated Thomas and realised that the telephone conversation had been positive. 'He's fantastic,' Thomas said. 'You will really love him.

'Does that mean I might just see him for breakfast shortly?'

Thomas smiled and his blue eyes shone. 'I hope so.'

It was then that Rose realised that this was a very important young man in Thomas's life and assumed that the visits to Killpara and Aspel drive would be much more frequent.

* * * * *

'She has a voice like chalk being scratched down a blackboard,' announced Trevor. The auditions for the Walvern Light Opera Company were in full swing. The committee had decided on 'My Fair Lady' as their late-Autumn show, but everything that could go wrong went wrong. There was always a certain tension and jealousy and a great deal of bitching but this production seemed to bring out the worst in everybody. The first problem was the director, a certain Jane Austin, but there, as Trevor stated, 'the talent stopped'. She was overweight and extremely bossy. She was a school teacher and made the error of assuming she could address adults as she did pupils. Needless to say open rebellion was on the cards and sarcasm was the order of the day. She had selected a fair soprano to play the part of Liza Doolittle over the top of their usual soprano. This did not help things as this virtually only left one other subsidiary role, that being Professor Higgins's housekeeper, Mrs Pearce, so neither of the singers spoke to one another at all. Trevor, never being short of sharp words, decided that the production should be renamed 'My Pear Lady' due to the fact that the lead soprano had an unfortunate figure of average height but with small shoulders, not a pronounced bust but very large hips and buttocks. Needless to say, when she heard of Trevor's bitchy comment, which had everyone in hysterics, the conversation between them ended abruptly and that was extraordinarily difficult, as Trevor had the lead tenor role.

The costumier stated outright that this musical was set in Edwardian London and the ballroom gown, which was the highlight of the show as far as the costumier was concerned said he would be the laughing stock of Walvern, that there wasn't any possible way of covering that backside, which could easily be mistaken for a rhinoceros from behind. The screaming and shouting was predictable.

'Come on, come on!' cried Jane. 'You are worse than students.' But to no avail and rehearsals had not even started. The auditions for the rest of the cast went on interminably with something wrong every time. After three weeks the cast was finally selected but no one, not even Jane, thought they could be ready for late autumn and so some smart lad in the chorus said, 'After twelve months of rehearsals we should be ready to go."

'Yes,' came Trevor's sharp reply, 'but where?' which had everyone laughing.

Carol Bing was the pianist as always, a gentle soul, until verbally insulted, then she turned into a tiger and the language was unbelievable. Occasionally she played well but for rehearsals she most certainly was not perfect. One smart member of the chorus suggested slamming the piano lid on her fingers. She slammed the lid down with a crash but her fingers were well clear of it. Then she snatched her handbag and stalked out, not before addressing the whole cast and telling them in no uncertain manner that they could all get fucked. Another rehearsal night ruined.

Trevor at this stage was sure that it would all have to be cancelled but on they went, with no fixed date for opening night.

'These costumes are shit,' said a girl in the chorus about the black and white Ascot outfits.

'If you think you can do better,' screamed the hysterical costumier, 'then do it yourself, you fat cow.'

'You bitch!' was the girl's riposte.

'And by the way, sweetie,' he said sarcastically, 'it takes an extra metre of fabric to stretch across your arse.'

'Please, please!' shouted Jane. 'This won't do at all. Now let's go through that scene again.' So Carol Bing pounded the keyboard and a wailing commenced that was supposed to be singing.

At the beginning of *My Fair Lady*, Eliza has to sit down on a sidewalk and sing while selling flowers. Sitting down was one thing but getting nimbly to her feet was another. As she rolled to one side and staggered upward, Trevor got the giggles every time. He looked at her and laughed. She stalked off the stage. Another night wasted. Jane was now beginning to feel that her talent as a director was wasted on this pack of fools but as she was paid she continued.

Every funny or bitter line that has to do with show business was heard in these rehearsals. 'Oh, you should be on the stage,' Trevor said to the leading lady. 'There's one leaving town in ten minutes.' This produced screeches of laughter, much to Jane's consternation. The stage was not enormous in the Walvern Memorial Hall and the flies were narrow so with the Ascot scene and the ballroom everyone jostled for the best positions. The result was chaos, in fact when one girl had her foot stepped on and assuming it was deliberate she launched a shove that sent another girl crashing to the floor. The expletives were sufficient for Jane to call a ten minute break and she was seen to take a handkerchief from her pocket and wipe her brow.

'Tonight was the pits,' said Trevor to Mary and Joseph at the Oriental, where he had joined them as usual for the Wednesday night dinner, but in his case a very late dinner. 'The Chorus is like a group of old tomcats on heat, the sound is appalling. This is the only production of *My Fair Lady* sung to the music of *Oklahoma*. You have no idea.'

Mary burst out laughing. 'It sounds fabulous.'

'Well, it's not. It's a fucking bore and the leading lady, well enough said. The costumier said this was the only production of My *Fair Lady* where he was forced to dress the star in a farthingale to hide the hips and arse.' Mary was hysterical.

Enid joined them, curious at the laughter and with Trevor recounting disaster after disaster the three of them had tears running down their cheeks. Trevor was a good story-teller but what he was recording was reality, not an elaborated tale. Between telling all about *My Pear Lady* and tasting a delicious meal prepared by Lenny Trevor he also noted that Joseph seemed different. He didn't know how or why, but he was. He seemed, according to Trevor, to have an inner confidence which shone out. Even Enid noticed it, and this radiance complimented his good looks. Joseph was patiently waiting for the weekend as Thomas had promised to join him but oddly he was not nervous. It was exactly as he thought it would be, a beautiful man that everyone liked, kind and considerate and to top it off sexy. Why should he worry? The same cannot be said for Thomas, who was agitated and as Friday night loomed up he became even more agitated.

'You must come, Rose,' he said in an urgent tone.

'Why?' she asked. 'You are an experienced young man. You don't need me.'

'Please, Rose. I will feel so much better if you come.'

'Don't you think your parents are going to wonder at the fact that we are house guests two weeks in a row? I'm sure they will, but it won't take them long to realise you have an ulterior motive.' He smiled and looked a little dejected. 'Very well,' she said, 'I'll play the cover for you but only this once. After that you are on your own – or with Joseph.'

'Rose, you are divine.' He stood up and kissed her. 'Thanks! I don't think I have ever been so nervous in my whole life.'

'Good,' she answered. 'You are maturing like good red wine.' He laughed and then in an instant was serious again.

'Rose, what if he isn't really interested in me?'

'That, Thomas, the two of you together will have to work out, but just remember he is a charming and seemingly innocent little brother of one of your closest friends. Tread lightly, Thomas.'

'I wouldn't hurt him for the world,'

'I certainly hope not,' came her reply.

* * * * *

'Come on, you lot. Let's have it again.' 'Oh!' was the response. It was the Ascot scene and some of the upper-class English accents were laughable. 'Everyone who's here is here', was translated especially by some of the chorus as 'everyone o's 'ere is 'ere' much to Jane's annoyance. A scream from her stopped them and they went through it again, exaggerating the accent so badly that she thought at the end of the rehearsal that 'from 'ere to 'ere' probably seemed better.

The tenor who had the role of Freddie, who sang 'On the street where you live', was particularly unpopular. He was the fully married man and had the most annoying habit of always prefacing every comment with 'my wife and I', which, as Trevor said, was a dead give-away, but he was so pretentious, every rehearsal with a different jacket with a neck scarf and matching handkerchief in his pocket, always so frightfully neat. During the song he was, according to Trevor's description, moving his arms like a windmill. A bright spark from the chorus yelled out, 'Does your mother know you're out?' which received howls of laughter and again rehearsals were brought to a halt. Jane now was becoming much more aggressive and, as Trevor said, she looked like a bull dike, in a loose man's shirt and trouser. 'Sensible shoes' was Trevor's comment, which again brought a giggle from a group on the side. Jane shot a look of death at them.

Because finance was very tight, the costumier, a certain Calvin Holmes, was forced to cut corners and what should have been miles and miles of ribbon, in black and white silk, turned out to be crepe paper attached to the frocks. From a distance it almost worked: up close it was very tatty and very easily dislodged. 'Just be careful', was the phrase that Calvin used continually but it didn't matter what he did with the two major costumes of the leading lady. They just looked awful. In desperation one evening he spun on her and spat out, 'Do you think we could beat the excess 20 kilos off?' The slap was well aimed and a scream and a return slap stopped the whole rehearsal again.

'Make your own costume, fatty. I only make costumes and good ones, not fucking circus tents.' This time he moved nimbly to the side as she took another swing at him.

'I'll flatten the pair of you,' yelled Jane, her patience almost at an end. And so this left Calvin working contentedly and refusing point blank to dress the dinosaur.

If there were problems with Calum, Ron the set designer, was in a world of his own. 'Ronny, dear,' said Trevor, sarcastically to this tall, thin man, 'I don't know if you have lost the plot but we are not doing *Annie Get Your Gun*, we are doing *My Fair Lady*.'

'Smart arse,' was the reply, but the stands for Ascot really did have a look of the OK Coral. 'He thinks it's a Western,' said a male friend to Trevor. 'You know, he might just be right.'

A part in the Ascot scene had every one moving about. One of the girls stepped on the back of another's long frock and there was a ghastly ripping sound. She swung around and supported herself on the racing stand so that the whole thing tilted for a moment and crashed down on top of the chorus. There were lots of expletives used to describe Ron's ability as a set designer but worse was to come. While the leading lady was singing 'I could have danced all night', Ron moved from in front of the stage with a large plank as he made his way up on to the stage. Suddenly Carol Bing's thunderous music stopped; everyone turned and looked. Ron was watching the front of the plank and not the back. It swung around and caught Carol Bing by surprise on the back of the head and almost rendered her senseless. Another rehearsal was brought to a sudden end.

'Imagine,' said Trevor, 'the fun. Searl is going to be reviewing this production.'

'Yes,' replied his companion. 'Why don't you tell him that we are doing *The Merry Widow*. We may as well confuse him.'

'If I tell him we are doing *My Fair Lady*, that's going to confuse him as well,' and they both laughed.

It didn't matter what Ron did, it didn't work. There was a scene where the leading lady had to ascend four stairs and exit through a doorway. This was done to a shrill scream as Ron could be heard yelling, 'Hold on a moment!' She had opened the door and instead of stepping onto a platform, fell, as Ron had not had time to put the platform in place, so down she went, as did the whole set as she had hold of the door knob. Jane was to be seen pushing both hands against both ears.

* * * * *

Friday evening saw Thomas, Rose, Mary and Joseph dining at the Oriental, with Enid moving in and out controlling everything. When she had a moment, she joined them to say that one of the guests had just received a telephone call from his sister to say someone had died as a result of a wrong mixture of something at the Stardust Hotel.

'He apparently bought something, mixed it with a strong drink and that was that,' Enid said.

Mary felt very uncomfortable. Although she knew Keven pushed drugs, she hoped desperately that he was not involved in such a terrible incident. But the evening moved gently along, with Thomas gaining the sure feeling that his attention and feelings were being reciprocated. This was enough. He knew that Joseph was going to be well worth waiting for.

Dining at the Oriental or the Travellers'Arms in Melbourne was now almost identical, except the Oriental was much larger and the food just a hint better, due to the free hand Lenny had in the kitchen. If there was something Enid was confused about or unsure, she drove to the Travellers' Arms for a lunch or dinner to see exactly how they resolved the problem. This was now become a thing of the past, as Enid had honed the running of this hotel down to a fine art. Nothing missed her eye and no detail, no matter how small, escaped her. The fresh flowers twice a week were a certain expenditure but these now turned out to be the trade mark of the hotel and everyone now expected them. The fact that Enid had driven a hard bargain with the local florist had nothing to do with the effect and it was Lenny, not Enid, who organised the floral display, much to her satisfaction and that of the guests.

Thomas drifted gently into Joseph's presence and the two of them spoke and laughed softly together, while Mary, Rose and Enid chatted on about Trevor and his part in *My Fair Lady*, which had them in hysterics yet again. Rose noted, as did the other two that Thomas and Joseph left the table and moved into the empty courtyard where the fountain was splashing. All the flowers in the courtyard were white, so in the evening their colour reflected the light - but neither Joseph nor Thomas noticed. In the soft shadows, Thomas held Joseph and kissed him. Strangely, for a very shy 23 year old, Joseph calmly accepted that this was the way things should be. His grasp of the harsher forms of reality seemed something that would never touch him, only this, this handsome, dark man with the electric blue eyes that could, with one look, make his whole world seem complete. For Thomas, it was much more complex. He was very experienced but not in this particular field, where he was not the aggressor. He found he had to wait for Joseph in an emotional sense and Joseph, though not by malice or in a calculating way, made Thomas as a result of his innocence 'tread' the line for him.

Thomas saw him alone on Saturday morning. He called early at Mary's knowing she was at the dentist's studio and Joseph had called Thomas earlier. So a morning of discovery took place, at times awkward for Thomas but not for Joseph. Thomas was infatuated with him; he was not pretentious, he was not interested in the same things as Thomas, except antiques but there was a bond and a very strong one and the more they were together the more confident this bond became. Just to be together alone was the tops for both of them; to hold and kiss was the subtle but sensitive beginning to something they both knew without a shadow of a doubt would mature into a real and concrete relationship.

'Can I come in,' Mary shouted, as she made her way down the corridor to find Thomas and Joseph having a glass of wine together. Thomas stood up and moved across and kissed her. 'A glass of wine?'

'Two, thanks. Hi, Joseph.' He smiled at her. 'The studio was so busy this morning. Thank goodness for Trevor. Oh, I hope you don't mind, I invited him for lunch.'

'Not at all,' Thomas answered. Joseph did not pass a comment.

Mary sat down heavily. 'Oh, I am dead!,' she moaned, only to hear the front door bell. 'Joseph, be a dear.' He stood up and disappeared.

'He is the most fabulous young man in the world,' insisted Thomas to Mary. She looked him straight in the eye.

'Be sure you do look after him, Thomas. He's very special to me.' Thomas kissed her on the forehead.

'I promise,' he said, very seriously and Mary smiled.

'I shall always remember that you promised,' she added. 'Well, here we are. Thomas, you look great. Sorry I couldn't join you last night, a private matter to sort out.'

'Well, Joseph,' he said, 'tell me you'll marry me and you can have one of the lobsters.'

Joseph just smiled. 'Thanks for offering, but I happen to be spoken for.'

'Really?' Trevor sounded surprised at Joseph's quick response.

'Yes,' and he walked slowly over to where Thomas sat, moved in behind the chair and put both arms around Thomas's neck.

'Well, well,' Trevor said, 'beaten again. The story of my life.' Everyone laughed, but inside Trevor was not so happy. He had courted Joseph for a long time and very carefully, due to Mary's threat and here was Joseph with his arms around his best friend. Trevor being Trevor kicked in with jokes and took over the kitchen. 'These are the last three lobsters of the week. Let's hope we can eat them.' Inside, a tiny empty space began to widen. The one young man he desperately wanted for his own had been snatched away by his best friend and all this was with, it appeared, Mary's blessing. It took the third glass of wine to settle him down. Thomas was oblivious to Trevor's problem, but Mary felt it terribly. She knew Trevor and Joseph would never have made it as a long-lasting relationship. Trevor was not the type and then she thought again nor was Thomas. The luncheon was hysterically funny, once Trevor had accepted the inevitable and as he also had more than just a feeling of friendship for Thomas he threw himself into preparing a splendid lunch and recounting the adventures of the Walvern Light Opera Company.

'Can you imagine! I have to dance with the bitch in the ballroom scene, darlings. You just can't get your arm around her - and two left feet! Her voice is OK but the dancing is atrocious. It's like dancing with a duck.' Everyone laughed. 'She has no idea and can you believe it, the other night when we were singing one of the girls in the chorus slapped another and then it was pandemonium. I don't know what happened but it was twenty minutes before we all got back to work. Oh, I knew I had to tell you something funny. The leading lady had her aunt make all her costumes due to Calvin refusing to make them and really I haven't seen them but one of the girls in the chorus has and said that they are ever so over-the-top that they seem ridiculous. As I said to her, 'Welcome to the show'.'

Saturday lunch was very pleasant. Trevor made an exit and Mary said if they were all going to meet at the Oriental at eight she would have to take to the her bed.

'Joseph,' said Thomas, 'would you like to see Killpara?' He said he would and so Thomas had Joseph yet again as his captive companion for the afternoon. Joseph had no idea of Killpara and was genuinely surprised at its modesty. He had thought it would have been a larger complex but with Thomas nothing mattered. The fact that he was with him was all that was important. After introducing him to all, they went for a walk in the late afternoon sun. It was hot but the sting had gone out of summer now and there was a slight hint of autumn on its way. The grass was still a yellow-brown as they walked down the hill from the house to the creek at the bottom, which had only a trickle of water flowing and lots of sticky mud. They walked on and up the other side to a large stand of eucalypts and sat down. Thomas was surprised that it was Joseph who instantly put his strong arm around his shoulders and drew him to him.

'I knew it would be like this,' he said in a genuine honesty that gave Thomas the odd feeling he was not totally in control of this relationship. As he kissed him, he knew he would not have had it any other way. They lay back in the warmth of the day and the cawing of crows and the agitated sounds of magpies. They both felt exactly the same sensation, a security that comes from trust and a chemical reaction that says 'I am yours'. Thomas realised that logistics were going to be a problem, but not insurmountable, with him working in Melbourne and Joseph here in Walvern. It was at this moment, when he looked at Joseph, that he realised he actually knew very little about him at all. He was Mary's brother and was a restorer of frames but that was it. And equally as suddenly he knew it was not important.

'Would you like to live in the country?' Thomas asked him. He smiled and looked at Thomas. 'With you, yes, but I will be happy wherever we are.' Thomas drew him into his arms. 'I may just have you living here.'

'Well, I'm sure we can make some arrangements,' Joseph replied and he talked on about what he wished to do in his life. Thomas realised he had no great single ambition but there were lots of minor adventures he wished to achieve. 'I like living in a big house,' he said suddenly. 'Before I lived with Mary it was terrible at home, Keven and Dad fighting all the time and the house was awful, always sad and cold. He wondered what Joseph thought of the interior of Killpara.

'Living with Rose is great,' replied Thomas, keeping the conversation flowing.

'Does she have a nice house?'

'Yes, a very nice house. She is very fond of antique furniture.'

'Oh, I like that too. I always go to Mr Ollies' Auction Rooms to have a look about. I bought a very damaged mirror a month ago.' He sat up and looked back toward Killpara. 'It's a fabulous shape but it's going to take some time to put it all back together. Jan is helping me.' He spoke with a sureness that surprised Thomas, this tall good-looking youth, with a mop of soft, light brown hair.

Thomas had assumed incorrectly that he was slow – not mentally, but someone who followed the rhythm of country life and as well was extremely shy, but he found that when he was in his company this description was inadequate. He was a much more complex person. It was as if he had just waited for Thomas, knowing that everything would work itself out. He had no friends as such, only Mary's friends, which she shared with him and although his social skills had improved enormously keeping up with Trevor was a test of anybody's skills. But keep up he now did, and occasionally he also threw a sharp line in. Joseph knew Trevor liked him but was not aware of Mary threatening Trevor if he ever made a move toward him.

They stood up and walked slowly back to the house, with each discovering a little more about one another and so a foundation was being laid for the future.

'What's that?' asked Joseph, pointing to a mass of cast iron.

'That just happens to be a birdcage in a thousand pieces.' He laughed and told Joseph the story. 'It's being restored bit by bit.'

'I dislike Barry Haughton,' Joseph said strongly. 'He's stupid. He thinks he is an important person and he isn't.'

Thomas looked at him. 'My father has the same opinion as you. I don't really know him. I don't think I have seen him in seventeen years or so.'

'You're not missing anything,' Joseph replied in an offhand way. 'But it's interesting,' he went on, pushing his hair back, 'that you five have remained friends for all your lives. I think it's great. I never had anyone a school I really liked and couldn't wait to leave. Mary always said I should have studied more and gone to university but that wasn't for me. I found I could only think after I left school, when I had time to. I don't feel a lesser person because I don't have a degree, in fact I feel quite happy, especially since I met you.' Thomas said thanks and held his arm.

'Hi, Thomas!' called James, as he began to herd the cattle toward the milking shed.

'Hi, James,' Thomas replied, as James came over. 'James, this is Joseph.'

'How do you do,' James smiled and put his large hand out to shake Joseph's. 'Are you a country boy or a city boy like this one, here?' he went on, grinning.

'I guess I fit somewhere in between.'

'Well, that's not a bad place to be, the best of both worlds. Oh, look, I have to leave you. Pleasure meeting you, Joseph.' He whistled and his dog ran around behind, bringing up two stray cows.

'He's nice. I like him,' commented Joseph, but declined to pursue the conversation on this level. In fact he changed it all together. 'Thomas, do you swim?'

'Yes, Rose has a pool, so in this weather every day.'

'Lucky you. I hate the local swimming pool and I don't think Mary will tear up her beautiful back garden to put in a pool for me so I guess I'll just have to wait.'

'Simon and Terry have a pool. I'm sure they wouldn't mind you using it every now and then,' Thomas suggested.

'No thanks. That is just too tricky.

'What do you mean?

'Well,' Joseph turned his head slightly, 'Terry makes me feel uncomfortable and Simon, well that's a very different story.'

'Oh, is it?' Thomas feigned jealousy and held him tightly.

'No competition, Thomas, you are a million times more me.'

Thomas looked at him and narrowed his big blue eyes. He realised that despite Joseph's comment about Simon he did feel a streak of jealousy sweep through him.

'Come on, we must get going or we shall be late to meet the others for drinks at Mary's and then on to the Oriental.'

They walked to the house, where Thomas went in to change. Joseph sat on the veranda and waited, until a voice said, 'Well, how do you do?' He stood up at once. 'How was the walk?'

'It was nice, thanks.' Rose sat down on the veranda with him. 'I'm afraid you must think me an awful woman.' When he looked surprised, she went on, 'Well every time we have met I haven't really spoken to you.'

He smiled at her and said, 'That's OK. When there is a lot of people I don't say much anyway. Thomas tells me you have a swimming pool.'

'Yes, and you are most welcome to come and stay and use it.'

'That's very kind of you,' he replied, and then, narrowing his eyes a little, said, 'You had better look out or I may just take you up on it.'

'I hope you will,' Rose replied with a smile. 'Thomas tells me you restore frames and furniture.'

'Well, I'm learning and I like it very much.'

'I saw the frames you did for Thomas. It's excellent work.'

'Jan helped me. The corners were a bit difficult for me, but I think they look quite good now.'

'They certainly do,' she said. 'You have a brother, don't you?'

'Yes, unfortunately. I hate him and everything he stands for. He is a real loser and he drags every one down to his level. 'He spoke easily about Keven as if he was explaining directions on a road map and Rose listened intently as he spoke on, about growing up in a house where everyone fought all the time. 'I am lucky now. I live with Mary and everything is looking much better,' he said, turning his head and running his fingers through his hair. 'I don't know why I was so reluctant to go and live with her. At the start I suppose I just wasn't sure about myself.'

'And are you sure about yourself now?' she asked with a wide smile.'

'Oh yes,' he replied, 'very sure. Thomas is great.'

'I heard voices so I knew you would be here,' and Joyce opened the screen door with one hand, swung around and joined them on the veranda with a tray with a bottle of wine and four glasses.

'Do open the bottle for us, Joseph,' she said, handing him the bottle and corkscrew. She had met Joseph only two hours before but she was speaking to him as if she had known him forever. She went on to pour them all a glass of wine, leaving one empty for Thomas.

'What do you think of Killpara?' she asked.

'It's a very peaceful place,' was his comment.

'Yes, it is. I'm afraid it's not very grand. That I will leave to Rose. I suppose I should have done more with the house but I just never got around to it. I shall leave that to the next person.' She smiled. You see, Killpara is important for Rose and me, as it was our grandparents who established this property and built this house, then they sold it. My husband Samuel's family bought it and then I married him, so the circle has now almost completed itself.'

'What do you mean, 'almost'?' Joseph queried.

'Well, I have this feeling that someone else is going to finish the circle, not me. Did you go to university, like Thomas?' When he said he didn't she replied that she was glad and reached over to hold his hand for a moment. Then she sighed. 'He's a nice boy, Rose. I am very pleased about that.' Then she spun off in another direction saying how hopeless she was as a gardener. 'I can't even grow weeds properly'. They all laughed.

'Do you like gardening, Joseph?' Rose asked.

'I don't know. I've never had the responsibility of a garden but I like them very much. Thomas says you have a beautiful garden.'

'Yes, but I didn't design it, though I like it very much. Now, remember the invitation is open to come and stay and enjoy it – and the pool – but you had better hurry up. Summer's coming to an end.'

'Thank goodness,' said Joyce. 'I am so tired of these hot nights. I don't sleep well at all.'

'Who doesn't sleep well?' asked Thomas, joining them having showered and changed.

'I don't,' said Joyce. 'Just help yourself, dear,' as Thomas poured himself a drink.

After another fifteen minutes of general chatter, in which Joseph held his own, the three of them bade goodbye to Joyce, who disappeared to feed her hens and they set off to Mary's for a drink before dinner at the Oriental with the others.

'I'll go with Mary,' said Rose. 'When you two are ready, join us,' and they left in Mary's car.

'Thomas!' came a call from the hallway and he put down his drink to go in the direction of the call, expecting Joseph to be ready but instead he stood there in only his underwear. He reached out and embraced Thomas, drew him into his bedroom and gently closed the door. He removed Thomas's shirt and laid it over the back of the chair and took him into his arms. Thomas felt a sure of adrenaline sweep through his body and an excitement that he had never felt before. He slowly undressed. 'Thomas,' Joseph whispered, 'I have never been to bed with anyone before.'

'Oh, Joseph, you are so beautiful.'

'So are you.' Joseph ran his hands over Thomas's body and the next moment they were in bed, kissing and caressing one another.

'Come on, said Thomas, twenty five minutes later. We shall be late.'

Joseph lay on his back, smiling at him. 'I feel fantastic,' he said, pulling Thomas back on top of him. 'You are fantastic. I didn't think it could be so wonderful.'

Thomas kissed him as he ran his hands over his chest and then to his lower abdomen.

'Thomas, will you sleep with me tonight. I want you to teach me everything.'

'That's quite an offer,' he laughed. 'Come one, up you get,' and he pulled him to his feet.

* * * * *

'We thought you'd got lost!' exclaimed Trevor, sitting closest to the fountain.

'No, we're here.' Thomas smiled but it was Joseph who gave the game away by simply saying nothing, while the generous smile betrayed him.

'We are late, I know, and it's not my fault,' insisted Simon, as he and Terry joined them.

'It's Pete's fault,' admitted Terry, 'and if he isn't careful, he may just find himself in Lenny's baking dish.' Everyone laughed.

'What happened?' Rose asked.

'Well, that beastly bird flew up onto the roof of the house so I had to get a ladder and Simon had to go up and chase him down and I had to catch him. He's getting so sneaky.'

'He sounds fun,' Rose suggested.

'Half an hour ago, fun was not an adjective I would have used.'

'Everyone has only just arrived so there is no need to worry,' said Rose and drew Terry into a conversation about porcelain birds, which he was genuinely interested in, allowing the others their general conversation that inevitably left him out. Enid joined them and sat beside Joseph for a moment before dashing back to see if everything was absolutely correct. 'Joseph, you look great,' she said, not aware yet of the connection between him and Thomas. 'Life must be agreeing with you.'

'Oh, it is,' he smiled and didn't continue the subject.

'Enid, you're wanted at the bar,' said a new attractive waiter and the two of them disappeared into the packed hotel from the courtyard. Joseph was just drifting in a sea of happiness and all he could think of was sleeping with Thomas that evening. There was absolutely nothing in the whole world he wanted more, and if he had known Thomas's thoughts, they were remarkably similar.

'Oh,' Terry interrupted, 'I forgot you are all invited to lunch at Rosebae tomorrow – very informal. If you want to swim, the pool's there and by the way you may just taste for the first time in your life roasted peacock,' which got them all laughing.

'How is the star of the stage?' Simon asked him.

'Don't start me. We are having two rehearsals a week and still there's no date for the production. I think they will put up the posters with a 'Coming soon' sign at the bottom. Last Friday, our Ron dropped a piece of timber and just missed someone below. The words uttered were not in the script. I have never known such chaos. Why Ron is working when we are rehearsing, who knows, and his cretinous offside plumed us into darkness for twenty minutes, having short-circuited the theatre. You have no idea! And the chandelier in the ballroom scene at a certain point is lowered. Why, no one knows. Jane, I think, thought it would be more dramatic and Ron got confused about the length of cord and so the lead soprano was waltzing away with moi when this damned light fixture plummeted down, missing us by inches. Jane has given up on the demure school teacher performance and in a rougher form of attire and the voice of a sharp fishmonger plus a range of expletives believes this is the only way to pull this unruly group together. 'Ron,' she screamed, 'put that bloody cigarette out. Can't you read?' as she pointed to numerous signs around the walls stating smoking was prohibited. Ron said something inaudible and stubbed the cigarette out. 'OK,' Jan yelled, 'Let's have "I could have danced all night".' 'I am right, thanks,' shouted a spirited lad from the chorus. 'Shut up,' she yelled. 'OK, Carol,' and off they went. Towards the end of this scene there is where the star has to exit the door at the top of the famous four stairs and return and then leave. The other girl, playing Professor Higgins's housekeeper, Mrs Pierce, loathed the lead soprano, as she's taken her role and instead of a gentle push to persuade her to go to bed, the thrust was so brutal that it sent her flat on her knees just in front of the door. 'You bitch,' screamed the soprano. 'Sorry, fatty,' was the reply. 'Cut the small talk!' screamed an irate Jane. The same evening the soprano was giving a very lack-lustre performance, much to Jane's annoyance, and she screamed, 'Suck in those buttocks and give me some sound.' The girl whose part had been lost to the soprano piped up, 'Oh, fuck, if she did that we would lose half the hall.' Ten minutes of hysterical laughter brought this part of the rehearsal to a halt. Carol Bing, who prided herself on being one of the more talented and well-dressed members of Walvern, always tottered about in the most extraordinary high-heeled shoes and 'tottered' is the right word. One evening she made a catty comment to one of the female members of the chorus about her haircut. It was later when someone spoke to Carol about how long she had been playing that the offended young girl loudly said, 'She is the only person alive who played the piano for silent movies.' It had an electric effect on Carol, who slammed the lid of the piano down and tottered off to the front door, clutching her handbag over her arm. At this point Jane seriously thought of bringing in a stock whip to get everything going the way she wanted it. Ron's sets were adequate and for one short scene he created a conservatory which was the best of the sets, with a little fountain, small window panes and palms, so that even Jane found it necessary to praise him. The ballroom props were another thing altogether. At best, it had an Edwardian waiting room in a railway station look about it and the very flimsy columns that surrounded the effect screamed disaster – and they weren't wrong. The yelling and screaming about standing on hems was due to Jane and Calvin deciding that as the girls needed to know how to walk in these garments the half-finished frocks were used right through rehearsals. It was meant to get them used to moving about and being careful about standing on one another's hems, but the boys inevitably did this, and ghastly ripping sounds were heard, followed by Calvin's shrill voice screaming 'Who was the fucking club-footed cretin' who had just ruined another of his creations. It just gets worse. I can't believe it.'

In between scenes, Trevor was not exactly knitting. He had in fact moved in on a not unwilling young man and was having a great time. The only problem was that this young man's wife was also in the chorus and not at all happy about the amount of time Trevor and he were spending together, laughing and joking, as well as making arrangements for appointments. So the tension for this production became more and more electric, less and less calm and verging on hysteria, especially when the first night date was determined, which gave them only five weeks more rehearsals. The orchestra was engaged and put in several rehearsals with the company, much to Carol Bing's annoyance. Instead of being the only provider of the music, she was now under the baton of a most peculiar conductor. Adam Adams was quaint, in that he never stopped smiling, almost as if he was embarrassed. He was short and over-weight, but attempted to dress at rehearsals like a teenager. The effect was laughable and this was the response he received. The orchestra was adequate but Carol Bing's thunderous production on the piano often had him stop the music and re-direct her, though smiling at the same time. 'He's like a fucking Cheshire cat,' she said in a bitchy tone one evening, as they left the rehearsals and she tottered to her car.

Rose thought it generous of Terry to invite Trevor to his and Simon's luncheon party and said so.

'Thanks,' said Terry with a weak smile, 'I guess we all have to move on.'

After dinner Thomas spoke quietly to Rose and said he would meet her the next day for lunch at Rosebae and he would come with Mary and Joseph. Rose smiled: 'I shall look forward to seeing you tomorrow.' Mary was not sure this was a good idea at all, but was trapped between her beloved brother and her beloved friend.

The night was everything Joseph had expected, for someone without any experience Thomas was surprised how adaptable he was sexually. The pair of them fell asleep in one another's arms, both independently secure that this was what they wanted for the rest of their lives. To wake in the morning and find Thomas beside him for Joseph was the closest thing to paradise he could think of and as it was such a natural feeling it never crossed his mind for a moment that Thomas was not thinking the same thing. He need have had no fear, as when Thomas opened his eyes and a beautiful young man with a mop of light brown hair and hazel eyes looked into his, he knew that it would not be long before Joseph himself and Rose would be having breakfast together.

Mary drove her car up the steep drive and onto the flat area at the back of the house which had been redesigned now as the front, to see Rose's and Patricia's cars parked side by side with a very plump peacock called Pete and a spotted hen called Tallula walking around these invasive machines just like parking officials.

'Come in,' cried Simon and gave everyone a hug. 'Come through.'

Thomas did not remember Rosebae very well : his memory was based on the past as a schoolboy when Simon's parents were resident there, but when he and Terry teamed up his visits stopped abruptly and the only place he saw him was at the Oriental with the others. He had a vague memory of Rosebae being gloomy, and that was it so he was surprised at the interior of the house, with a place for everything and everything in its place, as Rose described it later to him. The conversation was brisk, except between Rose and Patricia, neither fond of one another, but for the rest it was a very pleasant time. Trevor arrived late due to some predicament at home. Joseph and Thomas had changed into swim briefs as had Simon and they were swimming in the pool. Mary and Rose brought out a tray of drinks and joined them, while Patricia assisted Terry in his ever-so-organised kitchen. The boys were in and out of the pool, laughing and joking, but it was not only Simon who realised how beautiful Joseph was in a small swim brief and how well he filled it. It was also his school friend, Thomas, who looked every bit the ideal man. Mary and Rose were not oblivious to the scene of three very handsome men scantily clad, two being so dark and Joseph so light in contrast.

'They all seem so happy,' commented Rose.

'Yes,' replied Mary slowly. I just hope everything works out all right.'

'Oh, I wouldn't worry,' Rose smiled, as Trevor strode over to them, having changed in the house.

'Well, not bad at all,' he stated, looking at the three of them sitting on the edge of the pool. 'And look at us girls, all alone in the world,' and laughed. It was quite clear to everyone now that Joseph and Thomas were more than casual acquaintances and everyone, especially the men, had their regrets, but generously accepted the situation.

'Lunch is served,' came a shout from the house and everyone made a move, except Trevor, who dived into the pool and came up right beside Joseph. He put one hand on Joseph's knee. 'Well,' he smiled, wiping the water from his eyes, 'and don't little boys grow up!' Joseph laughed and pushed him back into the water.

The food wasn't good, it was fabulous :Terry had gone all out to impress. Rose enjoyed herself but of all the group it was Simon she liked very much, his soft manner and good, dark looks. 'Hm!' she thought, 'he would have been perfect for Thomas.' But she realised that Thomas's strong arm on Joseph's shoulder made it quite clear that we cannot select for others.

'I see Pete escaped the baking dish,' commented Trevor, making a conscious effort to be pleasant to Terry and draw him into the conversation.

'Only just,' came the reply.

'Listen, Terry, you could make some money. You could rent him to the production of *My Fair Lady*. He could fly across the stage. At least the patrons would see something smart.'

'I'll think about it,' laughed Terry, 'but I don't think he would be very co-operative.'

'Oh, he'd fit in perfectly with the cast then. Co-operation is one word that can't be used for this production.' And he went on to tell more funny episodes from the rehearsals. 'Three weeks to D-day. I can't believe it had taken us so long to achieve so little.'

Trevor was not the only member of the cast to think that. The back-biting was extreme and Jane really had had quite enough of it. Expletives flowed freely between all members of the cast. The regular members of the chorus for this production all turned into prima donnas, every one of them. The man who played Teddy Eynsford-Hill and sang *'On the street where you live'* now took to arriving with a huge scarf wrapped around his neck like a great opera star and behaved as such. Every attempt to send him up was followed by the cast and it was, as Trevor said, 'no holds barred'. Trevor was as bad as the rest. His vicious tongue got a lot of exercise at the rehearsals and not just in singing. One evening, very close to the opening night, he got into a verbal slinging match with the wife of the young man he was interested in. She was in the chorus. His bitchy remark that she really belonged at the back of the chorus did not go down well and was followed up with lines such as 'bitchy fag'. Jane once more had to intervene and once more restore the fragile calm.

After the splendid lunch and bright conversation it was time for all to depart. Thomas had only a moment to embrace and kiss Joseph before he and Rose headed off to Melbourne. Mary and Joseph went to Walvern with Trevor following and Patricia heading in the opposite direction to Killpara.

'Don't look so depressed, Thomas,' urged Rose. 'In another five days you can be in his arms.'

'I know.' Thomas smiled.

* * * *

Just up the road from Killpara, at Houghton Hall, Emily Houghton stood on a chair in the kitchen to retrieve a plate from an overhead cupboard and fell. Barry was not at home and his telephone was switched off, so she called Thelma to say she was on the sofa but in great pain. Thelma immediately hopped into her Range Rover and dashed to her sister's aid.

'Where's Barry?' was the first thing she demanded on entering. Emily said she didn't know. 'Well, we'll get you to the hospital at once,' and with a great deal of effort Thelma managed to half-carry Emily and put her into the Range Rover and off she sped in the direction of the hospital. Emily was diagnosed as having broken her leg and so left the hospital much later with one leg encased in plaster, hopping on crutches.

'You had better stay with me for a while,' suggested Thelma. 'Barry is obviously not going to be any use at all.' Emily said nothing, knowing that Thelma's prediction was very accurate. Now came one of the worse times in Barry's life : mother not at home at his beck and call and Aunt Thelma in charge. It was at this stage that Thelma, being Thelma, dictated to both Emily and Barry their futures. Emily's seemed feasible but Barry's was nothing short of a nightmare. Thelma in her own and not very discreet way demanded a good look at the finances of Houghton Hall, only to discover a less than miserable account and demanded to know why the property had been allowed to run down so badly and produce next to nothing. No answer was forthcoming. Thelma at this stage, with a now major logging company under her control decided that neither her sister nor her nephew was competent to run Houghton Hall, so single-handedly she took over. Barry's worst fears were realised. To his utter horror Thelma now controlled all the finance and that meant that unless he did exactly what she said it meant no money. So he was reduced to cleaning the drive, raking leaves. Every time she came to Houghton Hall she had yet another list of things for him to do. Being basically lazy, Barry saw her as the most pitiless monster in the world. 'You do this properly,' she shouted at him, 'or up you go to the sawmill and work as a labourer, and I am not kidding.' He knew only too well the threat was real. Emily's leg took longer to heal than expected and so Barry had to fend for himself and this made the reality of a gentrified life-style a farce. Even he knew it, but the biggest blow was when Thelma insisted that the old Mercedes that burned oil at the most alarming rate and drank huge quantities of petrol had to go. She organised a little modern car with two doors, in white, that did not send out clouds of black oil fumes from underneath. For Barry this was the end of the world and so when he went to Walvern now he parked the new car in a place where he hoped desperately no one would know it was his. Unbeknown to him, Thelma in her inimitable way, when Emily was her house guest and recovering, insisted that she re-write her will, pointing out that to leave everything to Barry was tantamount to throwing everything out of the window. Emily did as Thelma insisted and left everything under her control, including Barry.

* * * * *

A week before the opening night of the musical, tensions were high and tempers short. Any form of advice suggested was seen as personal criticism. Jane at this stage was using even sharper expletives to get the message across clearly. Full dress rehearsal night was, and could only be described as, unbelievable. 'Sharing a dressing room with ten Brad Pits, five Sean Penns and thirty Bette Davises meant trouble and not one Antonio Banderas,' said Trevor, but the drama went on. Calvin felt, as can be imagined, very nervous about the costumes and looked very nervous. The soprano's first scene called for a costume of a poor girl selling flowers but the costume was far too smart and so it looked ridiculous. Jane made suggestions, as did Calvin, but his were a trifle exaggerated. It was the ballroom scene that had Calvin in hysterical laughter. 'My dear,' he screamed out, 'you look like something out of Vogue. My God, are you out of vogue!!' As expected, there were screams of laughter. The frock, which was supposed to be an elegant Edwardian gown, was in fact the soprano's wedding dress but it just did not reach across the back, so she had had a panel that fell from the shoulders to cover up the gaps down the spine and at the waist. The problem was, it was a wedding dress and looked like it and it came with an extraordinarily long train. Jane knew this was going to cause problems before the Act even began and Trevor, when waltzing with the soprano, no matter how hard he tried, could not help standing on it. 'Get off it!' was the cry through the whole act. Jane wondered if training bears in Alaska would be as difficult as this.

The run through with the orchestra, sets, lighting and cast was a disaster. No-one it seemed really knew when to come on, or when to exit and Carol Bing interrupting the orchestra twice did not help the tension during the evening. Everyone left the final rehearsal complaining about something, but Trevor left with a smile on his face due to a rendezvous he had organised with the young man in the chorus. Needless to say, the wife was not aware of this arrangement.

Opening night was Saturday and nearly all the seats had been sold. Mary had bought seven tickets, one each for Joseph and Thomas, for Rose who said she just couldn't afford to miss it and also for Simon and Terry. Enid said she was working but planned a little after-show dinner at the Oriental and to her surprise from the morning when she had casually announced this after-show dinner by 2.30 in the afternoon every table was booked and Lenny began the planning for a light meal. Enid hired two extra young men, expecting a busy night and she was not wrong. Of the eight boys who applied for the jobs she chose the most handsome and then without pity took them through an immediate training course. To say they were surprised was an understatement.

But before this, a week after lunch with Simon and Terry, Joseph had caught the train and was collected from Flinders Street station on Tuesday morning by Rose, as Thomas had to finish off some work and from lunchtime on gave himself a break for the rest of the week, something he had never done before. He met Rose and Joseph at Albany Road for lunch and then took Joseph and Rose to several antique shops. They then went to look at the preview of the paintings to be sold the following evening at an International Hotel, organised by Betty Marshall.

Hi!' she shouted. 'How are you, Rose? Hi, Thomas – and who's this?'

'This is Joseph.' Thomas smiled happily at her.

'Well, you are a handsome lad,' she said. 'It's been frenetic here - so many people! I think the sale of paintings for the AIDS research is going to be fantastic, thanks to you, Thomas.' Joseph looked at him. 'This was Thomas's idea and has it borne fruit! I have your table organised for tomorrow night.'

Rose and Thomas quickly looked at one another. 'Oh, goodness,' exclaimed Rose. 'We need another ticket for Joseph.'

'Oh, don't worry about that. I'll work something out. You're on my table, so I'm sure I can sort it. Don't worry. Now have a look around, if you can push through the crowd.' She disappeared.

As they started to look about, Rose took Thomas's arm. 'We shall need a dinner suit for Joseph. You have two or three. When we get home, we'll try them on him and if there are any alterations needed I know someone who will do it for me at once. Or we can just buy him one, whatever you like.'

'Let's see what we have at home later,' Thomas replied. 'I just didn't think of it.'

The starting price on all the paintings was A$500 and under each one was a sheet as every table had a number and in turn every chair. You simply put your table and chair numbers side by side on the sheet and the amount that you wished to offer that was higher than the bid before. This had gone on all day and some of the sheets had had to be renewed due to important artists donating a canvas. The three of them looked around and Rose was very impressed by one particular canvas and as she knew the artist wrote her bid on the sheet. Joseph and Thomas wandered off, looking at the paintings. The one that caught Joseph's eye was a small one without a frame, as were many of the canvases. This one was of a lady in a fifteenth century turban playing cards, with an Italian landscape in the background, partly masked by a burgundy drape.

'Do you like this one?' he asked.

'Yes, I do. Shall we put in a bid on it?

Joseph smiled shyly. 'I can't. I don't have that amount of money.'

Thomas felt embarrassed that he had placed Joseph in this situation. 'Don't worry,' he said, trying to reclaim the situation. 'I'll put a bid in for both of us,' and he pulled his ticket from his coat pocket, copied down his numbers and wrote a bid considerably higher than the previous one. They then headed off home, with Rose very concerned that Joseph should not feel awkward the following evening.

He tried on Thomas's old dinner suit and where it was too tight across Thomas's chest it fitted Joseph perfectly. The trousers were fine, if a little loose on the waist, and Rose pinned them in. The shirts were a different matter. 'We'll get one tomorrow,' she said in a light-hearted way and moved to the telephone as the boys went up to change and then have a swim.

'It will be the last for the season,' she thought, for even though the sun was out one could feel a slight change in the temperature, which heralded autumn. She explained what she wanted, and then, 'Oh, that's so kind. I will send someone over with them now. Oh, really, that's so kind,' and she hung up. 'Anne!' she called out and the maid appeared. 'The seamstress will be calling by in about ten minutes. She was passing anyway. These are the trousers to be taken in. Tell her I must have them back at the latest by tomorrow lunchtime.' Anne disappeared with the trousers to pack them so they would be ready. Rose then rang her favourite restaurant and booked a table for three. After a swim and a drink in that order they all changed and set off. Rose was becoming more and more impressed with Joseph. He was completely honest. If he didn't know a particular thing he always asked, he never pretended that he knew. Both she and Thomas were very careful not to embarrass him with money matters and so every purchase was invisible.

Rose thought the next morning that this breakfast was historic as it was the first time in seventeen years Thomas had brought a man from upstairs down to breakfast.

'Good morning,' Joseph greeted Rose. 'Your house is just wonderful. There are so many, many things and they are all beautiful.'

Rose thanked him and said he was very kind, then he sat down in the breakfast room. Rose noticed that Thomas was the proudest man in the world.

'What shall we do today?' Thomas asked.

'You two will have to look after yourselves as I have a million things to do before this dinner at the hotel tonight, so what say we meet up here at no later than six o'clock for a drink and then we can go on from here. They agreed and just as they were leaving, Rose called Thomas back and whispered discreetly, 'Don't forget the shirt and whatever else you want to buy for him.'

Joseph couldn't believe it. He had been to Melbourne before but this was so different, to be taken to smart shops, and a wonderful lunch at the National Gallery Restaurant after being shown the Old Masters collection. While having lunch, Joseph looked across at Thomas. 'Thomas,' he said, 'you don't have to buy me, you know. I happen to love you and that should be enough, shouldn't it?'

Thomas smiled at him. 'I'm not trying to buy you. If I was, we wouldn't be together. For me to purchase a few things for you gives me the greatest of pleasures. I hope you understand this – and, Joseph,' he finished, 'I happen to love you very much.' Now it was Joseph's turn to feel a little embarrassed. 'Anyway, what about restoring some of those frames we saw this morning?' he asked, changing the subject, but wishing he could just reach over and kiss him.

'I should need Jan's help,' he laughed. He had a wonderful deep laugh and his whole face lit up. He was the most handsome 23 year-old in the world, thought Thomas.

They finished lunch and crossed the main road to the park where they walked slowly along the path, glancing at the gardens. It was then Joseph asked, 'Can we go back to Albany Road now?'

'I was just thinking the same thing.' Thomas squeezed Joseph's arm.

Rose was always buying Thomas elegant antique cufflinks, so Joseph had quite a box full to choose from. At 5.30 he tied Joseph's tie, kissed him and said he was just so beautiful. Joseph smiled and said quietly that Thomas was the same. They went down the staircase together and Rose joined them ten minutes later for the drink the boys had already started.

'Wow, you do make a striking pair! Just a moment,' and the elegantly dressed Rose, in a burgundy silk taffeta that was finished off with a splendid diamond necklace and earrings, returned with a camera, positioned the boys and took several photos. 'There,' she said. 'I need one for that silver frame over there. We shall see how they print up.'

The hotel foyer area was packed. Everyone was there and Rose, it seemed to Joseph, was known by all. He stayed very close to Thomas who just beamed with pride, as they all began to move into the banqueting area.

Betty Marshall, in a long emerald green gown stood up and took the microphone. 'Ladies and gentlemen,' and the din subsided to a mere buzz, 'before you sit down, you still have fifteen more minutes before the bell to check your bids on the paintings. Remember you ticket alone will allow you to pay for them and collect them.' The noise swelled up again. Rose moved over to check her bid in the room next to the banquet area. 'Shall we have a look at our bid?'

'Yes, let's,' Joseph smiled, feeling he was definitely part of the evening. As Rose returned from the exhibition space, to her surprise, she saw Rodney Marshall.

'Rodney,' she cried, 'how are you? I hope we are sitting together.'

'Don't worry, Rose, I insisted on it.'

'You are sweet,' she replied, kissing him on the cheek. 'Darling, I have the most amazing favour to ask of you.'

'Name it, Rose, and it's yours.'

'I knew I could depend on you. Thomas has a friend with him.'

'Yes,' came the terse reply. 'Mum told me. What's his name?'

'Joseph,' she told him. 'Darling, he's only a bit older than you and is not used to these affairs like us. A kind word might just make another person happy. What do you think?'

'Rose,' he began, but she interrupted him with, 'Thomas will always like you.'

'Great! But never love me.' He spoke in a rather superior manner.

Rose put her arm around his shoulders. 'Rodney, you can have Thomas as your fiend for life or you can make things difficult where he has to make a decision.' She turned and looked at him.

'You don't understand,' he began again.

'But I do. Don't ever make the mistake that friendship is a lesser state than love. That thought pattern is for very insecure people and the world is full of them.'

Rodney looked at her as if she had addressed him for doing something that was wrong and then he realised in a flash what she meant. 'Rose,' he said, but he didn't follow it up, as they walked arm in arm into the banqueting area.

As they approached the table where Thomas and Joseph were already seated, Rodney turned slightly, squeezed Rose's arm and gave her a wink. He marched around and put two arms around Thomas's neck from behind and kissed him on the cheek. Then he repeated the same spontaneous reaction with Joseph, except he said to him, 'Hi, I'm, Rodney.' Everyone took their positions. Rose sat between Thomas and Joseph while Rodney was diagonally across, but after a while he insisted that the person sitting across the table should change seats, so he ended up sitting beside Joseph.

Betty had thought she had organised the table well. The hotel management had objected that when all the tables were to be for ten this one had to be made for eleven. 'Bring out a larger top for this table, then.'

'But Madam,' he had begun, though to no avail.

'I,' exclaimed Betty in a determined voice, 'am organizing this event for the most important research necessary in this world, and you will reap a great deal of the benefits from this evening. My closest friend, Chris, who is the best fashion promoter in Melbourne may just be interested in returning here and making you money, if I have a word with him, especially after your shoddy performance last month. You have the most important Melbournians here this evening. Play it well and you may just win.'

'Certainly, Mrs. Marshall,' was the reply. Needless to say the larger table was ready for the evening.

Rodney chattered on to Joseph as if they had always been friends. It was a very anxious Betty, opposite, who thought things might have not worked out so well.

'I'm sorry,' said Joseph, 'I don't dance at all. It must be great. I have two left feet.'

'You don't. You just need someone to show you how.'

'It sounds easy but Rose tells me you are an expert.'

'She's exaggerating,' said Rodney, filling another glass. Rose looked across at Betty and Robert both on 'hot bricks' about Rodney's confessed love for Thomas.

Then the bell rang and all the bids were finished. Several young men that had been recruited from the public schools checked the results and found their way to table after table, handing a docket that stated that their bid had been successful. Betty and Robert's arrived first at the table, followed by Rose's and after some time Thomas and Joseph's. For Joseph it was like winning the lottery without having done anything. He felt for the first time in his whole life that he was genuinely part of a group, as well as the lover of the most beautiful man in the world.

The evening was a great success but before dessert was served Betty took the microphone and thanked everyone – she promised she would be brief! She thanked Thomas for his idea and everyone for their purchases and then just short of putting down the microphone she smiled and said, 'Everybody, thanks for being here and especially two people,' there was a pause, 'Joseph, who's with us for the first time but not the last, and Rodney whom I am so proud of this evening.' There was deafening applause. Thomas reached his hand around Rose from behind and squeezed Joseph's shoulder.

'Well,' said Rodney to Joseph, 'we love the same man but I don't think that should limit us being friends for life.' Unlike Rodney, Joseph instinctively knew what was being offered to him. He embraced him and kissed him on the cheek.

'You know, Joseph, if I can't have Thomas, I'm prepared to wait for you!' They both laughed. Rose gave an audible sigh and glanced at Thomas, who refilled all their glasses. The drinks waiter was then dispatched for yet another bottle.

The morning after was slow. Thomas and Joseph did not surface until ten: Rose had been a little more cautious in her consumption of alcohol but not so the boys. But it was another breakfast not far from Albany Road that was much more dramatic. When Rodney came down for breakfast, Betty and Robert were already there.

'Sit down,' said Robert stiffly.

'What's wrong, Dad?' Rodney asked.

Here, Betty took over. 'Darling we are so proud of you last night with your kindness to Joseph and especially as we know how you love Thomas.'

Robert interrupted. 'Your performance as a gentleman was nothing short of splendid and when - and it will happen, Rodney, you are young and good-looking - when the man arrives who deserves you and you love him I promise you the best reception Toorak has ever seen.'

Rodney threw his arms around his father's neck and held him tight. 'It's such a problem. I love Thomas,' he whispered. 'There are other Thomases in the world and it's up to you to discover them, and,' he said, raising his voice a little, 'and bring them home for us to meet.'

'I promise'. Rodney sat down beside Betty, who instantly put her arm around him. 'Darling, when this country finally gets itself in tune with the world, like Spain, the wedding reception we shall have for you will equal the very best. Darling, we love your desperately.

'And I love you both and you know it,' he replied.

The week swept by so quickly and soon they were packing up on Friday afternoon to return to Walvern. 'Thomas,' said Joseph,' give me the measurement of the picture you bought. I might just find a frame at Mr Ollie's. You never know.'

They had all been bidden to Mary's for dinner but there was no Trevor, due to the last rehearsal before the following night. Mary was now much more relaxed about Joseph and Thomas, as even she could see that they were totally engrossed in one another. Joseph was quite excited, telling Mary everything that he had done in Melbourne. She smiled. She had never known him so enthusiastic or so happy. She said to Rose that she had taken the liberty of having a very early, something before the show at her home with Simon and Terry and had invited Thomas's parents and Patricia.

'Well, that's very generous of you,' Thomas said.

'Oh, don't worry, it's just going to be a lot of finger food. Lenny has organised it for me, as we are eating dinner at the Oriental after the show.'

Rose left with Thomas for Killpara but not before Thomas made a promise to stay with Joseph on Saturday after the show. Joyce was very spritely when they arrived. After dinner and drinks were served she demanded to hear all the news about the art auction and who was there.

'If only we had more hectares,' Samuel said.

'What do we need them for?' Joyce asked, curiously.

'Well, Killpara can only make a certain return and no more due to the lack of land. We can't spell cattle and close off pastures for hay and still have enough over to make everything work, especially if we keep this number of stock. Perhaps this year we may have to purchase hay.'

'Goodness,' exclaimed a surprised Joyce, 'why didn't you tell me about this before?'

'I didn't want to worry you.'

'Well, you have now,' she said, speaking sharply. 'I have no idea why so much of the land was sold off. They probably got nothing for it.'

'Probably. But the land between Killpara and Houghton Hall – whose was that?' asked Thomas, surprised. He had never been interested before.

'It all belonged to Killpara, even part of Houghton Hall, plus the three farms that back on to this property,' Samuel told him.

'Are any of them for sale?' Rose asked.

'I'm not sure but there is a whisper that the land between us and Houghton Hall may come on the market if things don't pick up. You see, Rose.' continued Samuel, now addressing the conversation at her, 'when they cut up all these big properties into smaller holdings it was economically feasible, but today it's just not. We had a harsh summer last year and very little rain. This summer hasn't been much better, so these farms are not rendering as they would if there was more land.'

'What if we formed a company and began to re-purchase the land,' she asked. 'Thomas can look into the legal side of things. Our company can certainly purchase the land without any problems.' Thomas was not the only one who noticed the word 'our', in respect to Thomas and Rose.

'Well, that's certainly worth thinking about,' Samuel said. 'I'll bid you all a good night and we'll talk about it again in the morning.' At which he and Joyce left the living room. Rose began to collect the glasses.

'Well, said Thomas with a smile, 'thinking of becoming a country girl again, are we?' He laughed.

'You never know,' she smiled at him.

When in his bedroom, he thought of the great contrast between the house he was in now and the elegant mansion in Albany Road and wondered if Rose thought the same thing. As she undressed for bed, she also had many thoughts rushing through her head. It was hers and Joyce's grandparents' house and land. She had grown up close to it, in fact between Killpara and the village of Aspel, less than a mile away. Yes, she thought, we shall make this investment. As she turned over in bed, she was aware she was smiling.

But oddly enough Rose was not the only one with ideas about expansion. Thelma had sat down with Emily before she returned to Houghton Hall most nights, trying to work out a salvage plan for the place. Barry, she had given up on. He was a fat, lazy bastard. This had been Thelma's thought about him always but she was stuck with him : after Emily and herself there was only Barry. What a waste, she thought to herself. Thelma was now a very wealthy widow and a very hard worker. Every cent had to do a dollar's work.

'Emily,' she said one evening, 'what if we marry Barry off to a strong woman? This might solve our problem, because I am not going to invest in Houghton Hall unless I am sure that Barry is not going to fritter everything away, and he will. I know him. But with someone behind him the story might be different.'

'Who would marry him?' Emily asked.

'Him, I take your point.' Thelma sighed and poured them both another drink. 'How much actual land is left?

'Thirty six hectares.'

'Is that all?' Thelma exclaimed. 'Thirty six! What the hell happened to the rest?'

'It was sold.'

'I can't believe it! I always thought you were basically intelligent.' Thelma snapped at her. 'What! You have sold off most of the land and let what's left – oh, Emily, you must be on easy street.' This was said sarcastically and there was no reply. 'Listen, as your sister, you have got to start to look at what is happening. If you're not careful, you will end up in a housing commission flat with two bedrooms, Barry and you, and when you sit down in your tiny living room you will have both filled it.'

'Oh, it's fine for you to pass these comments,' Emily returned, angrily. 'Just because you have a beautiful house here on Aspel Drive you think you have made it.'

'But I have, dear Emily, but I didn't always live here. This is the result of getting up at 5.30 every morning and driving out to the sawmill where I oversaw everything from the cutting to the packaging – everything, for years. I have money now but I have worked bloody hard for it, as opposed to you, who have sat back as Mrs Eddie Houghton, who, by the way, drank and ate his way through his inheritance and has left you a copy of himself as Barry to carry on – and my, haven't you carried on, in exactly the same stupid pretentious way! The result being that you are now in dire straits economically and it's your own fault.'

There was a vicious silence. All the words Thelma had stored up for years were out but she still had some more.

'Listen, Emily, if your precious Barry isn't interested in women, and it appears at thirty six years of age he's never had any interest in them, it leaves only two alternatives.' Here Emily stiffened in her comfortable chair. 'There have never been any reports from the RSPCA, so that only leaves one alternative.'

The two sisters glared at one another, neither giving way. Thelma was in the winning situation but Emily refused to address this. 'Come on, Thelma said, in a much softer tone. 'What the problem? Look at the boys at Rosebae. Only a month or so ago they purchased that long run of two hundred hectares that joins their property at the corner and I am told they are going to run beef cattle. They will make a fortune. They are clever and just happen to be gay, so what's your problem?'

'I do not for a moment believe Barry is gay,' Emily stated very defensively.

'Oh, don't you? You wear your pearls with blinkers, do you?' Thelma was winding herself up again. 'Barry's friend happens to be that ghastly bitch Stewart Searl, who is the pitiful writer for the local rag. And don't try and tell me, dearest sister, he's not gay.'

There was dead silence. Thelma refilled the glasses without Emil refusing. 'Look,' she went on, 'you get good and bad with every group, that's a fact. It's just a pity that Barry seems to have attached himself to Searl.'

'He went to school with him,' Emily interrupted, defensively.

'So? Wake up, Australia. If we can't find him a woman, perhaps we should be looking for a man. I must say, Emily, that Simon Osler at Rosebae is very handsome indeed.'

'Really?' came the reply.

'Yes, really,' insisted Thelma, becoming tired of the cat and mouse routine. 'I'll tell you what. You think all of this through and we'll talk in the morning. But you have only two options. One, that you let me financially and legally take over Houghton Hall, or you make an application for a Housing Commission flat after you sell off the squalid remains of Houghton Hall. The choice is yours. Good night, Emily.' She stood up and left the room, with Emily looking into a half-empty glass of red wine with the developing feeling that Thelma was one hundred per cent correct. The thought of living in a public flat ran a shiver right up her spine.

The boys at Rosebae had indeed purchased a very neglected two hundred hectares that had been two farms, plus a house in Aspel that went with the deal, and set about putting things in order slowly. The price had been very good. The arrangement was the price stayed down if they purchased the two farms and the house as well. Originally they had no intention of buying two but as the price was so good they went ahead and did it. Thelma's informant was absolutely accurate. They did indeed intend to run beef cattle on one of the properties for now and then to see how things worked out. So for the boys at Rosebae it was all go. The bank had lent without any problem at all and the money paid for the properties and left a certain amount over to stock it, so it was all immediate. It was a very tired Terry and Simon who fell into their beds knowing that they had taken a big risk financially but also knowing it was the only way to survive in this day and age – to extend.

In the morning, Samuel and Joyce spoke to Rose and Thomas over breakfast and said they were in agreement with Rose and that Thomas should go ahead and draw up legal papers that would benefit them all and the moment that was done they would begin negotiations for the property adjoining them.

Rose finished her cup of tea and as she was about to stand up turned and look at Samuel. 'It's Saturday morning. Go and see the man next door and get first option on the purchase of the property. Get it written down and then we'll go from there.' Thomas was surprised that she was insisting that they strike so soon but he was to find out in the future the wisdom of it. 'Oh, by the way, Samuel, you're a surveyor. Get me a divisional plan of this whole zone, with Killpara in the centre.' Rose smiled at him.

CHAPTER 5

A Radical Change of Direction

CHAPTER 5

A Radical Change of Direction

Even before opening night there was more drama. The cast always had an after-performance party and assumed, because there was to be one at the Oriental, they were automatically invited. When they found out this was not the case, tempers ran high and to placate this situation Jane telephoned, at one day's notice, the local hotels for a late dinner. At such short notice this was impossible, as cast and friends and families ran to well over a hundred people, so the Stardust Hotel it was. They promised a flat rate and a space reserved exclusively for them. So the drama was reduced somewhat, but everyone knew Trevor was going to the Oriental and this bred contempt.

'It's not my fault my employer booked the table at the Oriental, not me,' he protested, very defensively.

Jane tried to sort out the mess but in the end just gave up. She came to the conclusion that they were all actually enjoying being unhappy.

The overture began to a giggle from the seats that could see directly behind the conductor. As he stepped in onto the podium, which was low, he pulled the little door closed behind him. A clever dick or 'smart arse' as they are generally known, had glued a horse's tail on the door facing the audience, so when he faced the orchestra it appeared that his tail had been threaded out through a hole in the door. This was just the beginning.

The conductor, smiling as always, was furious that Carol Bing took no notice of him at all. And what did our Carol look like? The hair was lacquered to a great height, the slinky costume was in pale blue jersey and lace and of course there were the extraordinary high heels and a make-up, as Trevor said later, that would have terrified horses.

It was the first act that changed the dynamics of the whole production. This was due to the soprano being over-dressed; a girl selling flowers in the late nineteenth century was most unlikely to have ever had the finances to purchase a garment with a train, especially in violet crushed velvet, but there she was. She began well, with Carol beating out her best on the piano, much to the orchestra's and conductor's annoyance. Half way through the opening song she moved closer and closer to the edge of the stage and then turned quickly before returning to the centre. 'Ham!' exclaimed Trevor loudly.

She did it yet again, but this time the train slid underneath her feet and being crushed velvet it was very slippery. It must have taken all of two seconds: she rocked for half that time and then both feet went from under her and she disappeared with a shrill scream into the orchestra pit.

'I said 'break a leg', 'smiled Trevor.

The audience was silent for a moment and then the laughter began. It was very infectious. Thomas gently held Joseph's arm as they laughed together. Obviously the orchestra stopped with a yell of 'Get off me, you big cow' which again had everyone in hysterics, including the critic of the night, Stewart Searl. An understudy was organised while Carol Bing played a piece of music by Rachmaninoff, which gave just the right level of insanity to the production. The soprano was carried out on a stretcher, having actually broken an ankle on the fall from the stage to the orchestra pit. There was no trained understudy, so it fell to the girl who thought it should have been her part anyway. The curtain dropped, Carol continued playing and the audience laughed. Then they started again : on with the show!

This time, in an extremely odd costume, but one denoting genuine poverty, it began with an hysterical Calvin being called on to produce the three major costumes for the star while the show was in progress. Lots of 'Oh, fuck!' and 'What the hell am I going to do?' were heard from a temporary workroom in the hallway. The production continued and as the first act finished, Calvin was seen as the hysterical costume designer attempting chic in crepe paper and pins. Carol helped out, playing assorted medleys to drag the interval out a little longer.

The next act was the Ascot scene, all in black and white costumes and Calvin was very pleased with the impromptu costume. Ron's scenery was a bit shaky, literally, as the stand of viewers at the races tended to move dangerously at times, causing Jane a certain amount of blood pressure. But, on with the show!

It then moved forward to the scene in the ballroom, which even from the first moment was doomed. Ron's flimsy Doric columns stood in a semi-circle at the back of the stage and the gracious chandelier dangled over the top. By this time, Ron was also feeling the stress and decided to have a cigarette, despite its being forbidden. As he held the rope that lowered the chandelier dramatically he lit a cigarette. 'Hm,' he said to himself and began on cue to lower it but at a certain point his left arm, being higher, caught the cigarette and it catapulted from his mouth onto the floor and rolled over in the direction of an enormous heap of tissue paper from Calvin. Fear instantly struck Ron's heart. He let go of the rope and raced for the cigarette which had ignited the first sheets of paper. He jumped up and down, extinguishing the fire. 'Oh God!' he shouted and glanced through the flies. The chandelier had crashed to the stage, missing the new soprano by centimetres.

'Keep dancing!' shouted Trevor, and they danced around the fallen chandelier to the applause of the audience. After the cigarette, the chandelier was seen to be hoisted up again very rapidly, giving more comedy to the production.

There was another disaster in the ballroom scene. Someone in the chorus moved in the wrong direction and bumped a column. Down it went - but not one, all, in a falling domino manner. They kept dancing! By this time, the audience was in hysterics. It was one thing after another and Jane was now ready to slaughter personally the whole company, including Carol Bing, who seemed to be playing something totally independent of the orchestra.

The other interesting disaster of the evening was in the gazebo act, when a clever spark set a large frog on a fake lily leaf. It had a long tube from its most personal part to a large plastic ball. When the ball was compressed, obviously the large green frog jumped. When it was activated the actress, not being aware of this addition to the show, in horror jumped backwards, upsetting everything including two false sets of windows which fell backwards with the scream of 'the fucking thing's alive!'

The audience by this time had not only got used to these disasters but loved them. Every time something went wrong they applauded all the more. Jane at this point was contemplating teaching Japanese in Somalia.

At the end, there was a standing ovation. Never had the locals had such a fun night and never had they seen a production of *My Fair Lady* like this, where the first one was carried out on a stretcher and the second was almost flattened by a chandelier. The applause never stopped and after such a disaster even Jane had to admit that comedy always wins over.

Thomas, as well as the others, was in a very elated mood. It had been a funny performance and genuinely entertaining but he, at this moment, was more elated, standing with the man he loved, waiting for the others to join them before they all headed off to the Oriental for a late dinner. As they walked out to their cars in the dark, Joseph slipped his hands into Thomas's. It was an instinctive gesture but for Thomas it was the most amazing sensation of acceptance. He turned and in front of everyone making for their cars embraced him spontaneously.

'Well,' thought Rose, 'this young man seems to have hit home base,' and smiled to herself.

The Oriental was fully booked and they entered into a very crowded space. Enid showed them to their table and a little later they were joined by Trevor. As he swept through the door, the tables gave him a round of applause.

'More, more!' he cried and laughed. He sat down with the others and went on, 'I must say,' as he glanced around, 'Noddy has a real eye for waiters.' He glanced at the two new staff.

'How would you describe the evening?' he asked Rose.

'Dearest Trevor,' was the reply, 'amateur theatre is well named.' This caused a burst of laughter all around, even from Joyce, who caught the nuance of the comment. Rose thought it interesting that Joyce did not seem concerned at all that for most of the evening Thomas had his arm resting either on Joseph's shoulders or on the back of his chair. Rose had never seen Thomas so totally devoted to a man in her whole life and though it was splendid, it seemed a natural, spontaneous response that was reciprocated.

Simon said to Trevor he was sure that he could have done a better job than the soprano. 'Of course,' was the response. They all chattered on, laughing, in fact the whole restaurant area was the same. It was a very pleasant evening and with Enid's sharp eye everything went like clockwork, with not a mistake from anyone, although if it be known the two new waiters were ever aware of Enid on the sidelines, watching like a hawk for the least error. Stewart Searl had a table with his friends, of whom Barry was present, and nodded graciously towards them, ever aware of Samuel's threat to strip and beat him in public if he ever did anything pretentious again.

While dinner at the Oriental proceeded smoothly under Enid's direction and Lenny's expertise in the kitchen, the same could not be said for the Stardust reception. There were two large groups booked in, it being Saturday night, plus all the locals from the district. The young and noisy were in a zone known as the 'Discotec' where lights and music blared continually. Although the reception area was on the other side of the hotel, the noise and the throbbing base sound penetrated there, much to Jane's annoyance. The food was self-service and although it was not expensive it was very second-rate : drinks had to be collected from the bar all the time. Still, the cast without Trevor prided themselves on having done a good job, despite circumstances. They were all very concerned about Stewart Searl's review, which would appear in the local paper on Thursday, as they still had three more performances to go.

'Anyone who misses the local production of My Fair Lady is missing a rare theatrical treat. Never have I seen a performance that equalled this in all my life. Every disaster was a winner. It is an evening's performance that can, if similar to opening night, have one in stitches of laughter. Well done, Walvern Light Opera Company.' This, needless to say, guaranteed a sell-out for the last three performances.

It was a most contented chorus 'girl' who spoke to Carol Bing, stating how pleasant it was that Trevor had not joined them but it was a discontented husband who sat at the end of a table, drinking heavily. It was this unhappy young man who, as the evening wore on, saw in front of him an idea to save his family's hotel. The Crown had been a favourite drinking place for a sizeable part of the population, not so smart or pretentious but as a family pub and now it was in economic hot water. Of all the people to save it, there she was, tottering about on extraordinary high heels, dressed in an outlandish costume for someone twenty or thirty years younger — our Carol Bing. Carol had seen herself as the star of the evening, the only one with enough common sense to keep the ball rolling. She became a little bored with both the food and the company, but obviously not the drink and moved to the black, lacquered grand piano in the corner of the reception area. She began to play. It had a magnetic effect of everybody singing along and the young gentleman called John suddenly realised that if he couldn't manage to have Trevor for the evening he still had in front of him about a hundred people singing and laughing together. This, in a quick calculation, equalled survival for the Crown and so it was that our Carol gave up her work as a receptionist for a local solicitor and took over as an entertainer at the Crown Hotel, and to everyone's surprise it worked. John called Trevor in to advise on decor and to his wife's extreme annoyance they spent many evenings together, and not necessarily at the Crown Hotel, working out details. Trevor was sure that as a type of Music Hall the Crown could survive and with Carol at the piano, why not? So it was that two of the five original hotels went ahead financially. The others closed, with the Stardust taking a great deal of all the young trade.

Trevor was a transitory lover. He never stayed long but with John, with an hysterical wife in the background, for some reason he began for the first time, a little like Thomas, to develop a stable relationship. Mary was the first to congratulate him but at the same time warn him of a possible future disaster with the wife, whom she knew slightly and as a very determined foe. Mary had now accepted Joseph's love for Thomas and the great fear, that Thomas would call and cancel the affair, began to dissipate. She saw Joseph as a new, confident young brother, who was now holding his own with everyone. She was amazingly proud of him and every second weekend, if Thomas was not at Killpara, Joseph was at Albany Road. She saw the relationship develop in a way she had never thought possible. Her best friend, Thomas, and her adored young brother, just folded into one another. There was no clash of cymbals — it was soft and serious and she knew that this was right for both of them.

Like Mary, Rose held the same sentiments. She adored Thomas and to see him completely happy with another person gave her a feeling of a confidence and security that she hoped Thomas felt as well, and this he most certainly did. To be with Joseph was his only desire. He thought of him so regularly as to be thinking of him always. But Joseph was different. He believed in love and it never entered his head that when he fell in love the other person was not as infatuated as he was. He accepted Thomas's love, both physical and emotional, as if it was expected and gave in return the same intensity of feeling. Unlike Mary and Rose, Joseph had no fears at all that he and Thomas would not be together always. He loved him absolutely and having waited until he was twenty three years old he knew in his heart that this was the man for him.

Joyce continued on her upward spiral, much to everyone's surprise and took to helping children read at St Mary's every Tuesday and Thursday morning, something that, in the past, would have been just unthinkable. She also took to filling the sitting room with fresh flowers in several bowls and could be seen quite often walking past them, stopping and arranging one tiny flower and continuing her daily tasks. It was as if she was a mouse, come out into the sunlight after a long, long time, and she developed rapidly. Her sense of humour, which could never have been said to be good or elevated now sparkled and at dinner parties with Patricia at home with Simon and Terry or at Rosebae with them, Joyce held her own, often to the surprise of Patricia, who wondered how on earth her mother found the smart repartee, let alone understood it. Joyce liked Joseph very much and Rose often wondered if she really grasped the relationship but as it was something that didn't distress or upset her everyone let sleeping dogs lie. In fact on two occasions Joseph remained a house guest at Killpara, with Thomas, in his room. Samuel said nothing. It was as if he wore blinkers. He saw straight ahead and in his mind this was all that was important. If his son and friend were happy then so was he : he and his philosophy were as simple as that. He was grateful to Joseph that he and Joyce now saw a great deal more of their son, as before, it was definitely a red letter day when Thomas made the trip to Killpara, so both he and Joyce now made a real effort to encourage the relationship as they in turn shared in it.

Patricia was totally indifferent to it, having no real feeling for either Thomas or Joseph, but a real friendship had developed in her with Terry and Simon. One evening, when Thomas was in Melbourne, a dinner party was organised at Rosebae and it was for five — Mary, Joseph, Patricia and the two hosts. Everyone was in fine spirits and great gales of laughter followed the nightly ritual of putting Peter the peacock to bed. But the strong hand on Joseph's shoulder made the ever-protective Mary slightly uncomfortable, and as much as she adored Simon she didn't want any interference in Joseph's relationship with Thomas. To her, it seemed Simon was more than just interested in her beautiful brother, who laughed and joked all night with everyone, seemingly unaware of this attention from Simon.

The next day at work Mary spoke in confidence to Trevor about the previous evening.

'Darling,' said Trevor, 'you can't control the world, you know.'

'I know, I know,' sighed Mary, 'but I am very worried. If Joseph becomes involved with Simon I know for sure Thomas will abandon him at once. I know Thomas only too well.'

'I don't think you have much to worry about,' Trevor replied. 'Joseph is 23 years old and totally in love with Thomas, and he with him. Joseph is floating on air. If he pays attention to Simon it's just that he's in love and everything is great.'

'Really?' Mary sounded most unconvinced.

'Believe me, darling, I have been there.'

'Yes,' came the sharp reply, 'with Simon, but not Joseph.'

'Point taken!'

'How can this relationship work out with one living in Melbourne and the other here in Walvern?'

'If you go on worrying like this, Mary, about Simon's hand on Joseph's shoulder, and construct all sorts of tragic scenarios, you are going to work yourself into an early grave.'

'I suppose you're right' she admitted, looking at Trevor in a lost way. 'And your set-up with John?'

'Oh, darling, that's another story. Our Marge is a real rattlesnake. She is a real bitch!'

'Well, in all honesty, I can't really blame her. Here you are, swanning in on her hubby.' She smiled, helping herself to another coffee.

'What do you mean?' Trevor cried, in a very dramatic tone. 'I happen to have been chosen by John as a lover companion and Mrs Dracula is swooping about like a vicious bat.'

'Trevor, you can hardly blame her. They are married.'

'Ah,' and he gestured with his finger,' but he doesn't love her and she isn't interested in him sexually. It's all a big front.'

'Well, I'll take your word for it.' She smiled. 'Come on, we have patients waiting, but in the name of mercy, be careful, please. I don't want to lose my closest friend to an irate wife who decides to cut your throat at midnight.'

'Don't you worry, Mary. She wouldn't dare.' She hugged him as they walked back into the reception area and then through to the surgery. But Mary was very worried about Joseph. He was, as she saw it, an introverted young man, but this wasn't quite the truth. Joseph belonged completely in his own world. He believed absolutely that when the right man arrived everything effortlessly would follow and in his case with Thomas it was so. But for Thomas, this was a revolutionary change in his life. For the first time ever he waited for Joseph to call him. At work, if he closed his eyes, all he saw was Joseph. He was for the first time in his life totally smitten with this young man and to his amazing satisfaction this love was reciprocated. Not to see him for a week was hell. He moped about, only to have Rose tell him that the weekend was only two or three days away. She had never seen Thomas so; he had always been Mister Independent, and the callers had come on their knees. For the first time, it was the reverse. Thomas lived only for one voice on the telephone or when the weekend arrived to collect Joseph from the town or if the other way around to meet him at Walvern and either stay the night with him at Mary's or now at Killpara. This was an interesting development. As Thomas's confidence grew with Joseph, he just assumed that his parents, as Rose would have, accepted it all. For Samuel it was awkward to begin with, but Joyce, the country mouse, now the lady about town, took it as accepted and as far as she was concerned Joseph was family. When he stayed at Killpara he shared Thomas's bed and Joyce thought nothing of it. She only once said to Patricia that she was so happy that Thomas had such a wonderful friend. Strangely Joseph and Patricia, with time, got on well and sometimes he would come and stay at Killpara without Thomas. Inevitably this meant a dinner at Rosebae with Simon always looking at an elated Joseph. Patricia found Joseph to be like a person from a fable, the gentle person who never does harm to anyone and strangely always need guarding, so she, when Rose or Thomas were not at Killpara, became, with Joyce, his minder.

Joseph lived in a country town, but not in the country as such. At Killpara he loved to wake to hear the magpies calling all to work first thing in the morning, and there was in a strange way no sound, or was it it that Joseph's predicted sounds of cars in the town just weren't here in the countryside? The throbbing of the milking machines, the barking of dogs, they were all so secure, these sounds, but to wake up with Thomas beside him and these sounds as well came as close to paradise as he could imagine. They had developed a sort of telepathy between them; one only had to think and the other automatically responded. Quite often when they went for a walk about Killpara they rarely spoke; because they were together often hand in hand, their feelings were transmitted completely, so words were unnecessary. Joseph accepted all this without worry or stress, but for Thomas this was new ground and it became Joseph that directed with very few words their pattern for the future. In Joseph's mind this pattern was like a gentle romance that one can buy at a newsagent's, filled with every possibility of happiness. Joseph only saw the rising sun and believed in it implicitly; after all, he reasoned, he had waited 23 years for it, so it must be right. It was Patricia who saw this more clearly than any of them. She dealt in books of this kind and in Joseph's uncomplicated concept of love, that once he had located the 'other half', everything would be happily ever after. So simple, she thought, but how wonderful, even if she thought her brother didn't deserve him.

Rose's thoughts of Joseph were remarkably similar but she saw him in a slightly more sophisticated way, like a piece of exquisite Meissen porcelain that complemented the thing she loved most in this world, Thomas, and she was now convinced that this partnership that she would never have chosen Joseph for Thomas but the combination was very, very successful.

* * * * *

Emily Houghton was grateful to be back a Houghton Hall, although she realised she missed her sister's company and began to see Barry as Thelma did. He ate voraciously, drank cheap red wine and slept, nothing else, hence his weight problem, which became ever more evident. Emily hadn't been quite the same since her fall. She seemed much more frail and had seemed to age somewhat. She was always exhausted and it was Thelma who came to the rescue in the form of a Mrs Talbot, who, at her own expense, she installed at Houghton Hall to look after the house and Emily. Mrs Talbot was fifty one years old, a stout figure and with a sharp tongue. She was divorced and this live-in situation suited her, as it allowed her to rent her own home, thus making much more money than just from the job. She was a whirlwind. She never did anything gently or slowly: it was always with great effort and enthusiasm and such was her way that in less than a fortnight she was running everything, much to Emily's relief and Barry's horror.

'Get on with it!' she scolded Barry, as he was forced to drag the hall runner outside onto the veranda and to make things worse was instructed to take a straw broom and clean it thoroughly.

'I'll be back to have a look in a minute,' she said, as she disappeared into the gloom of the house. With all the blinds now up, light streamed into the forgotten parts of a run-down, dust-filled house.

'No cats inside! Do you hear?' she cried as Barry made a sloppy job of cleaning and sweeping the very worn hall runner. Mrs Talbot now did all the shopping and with Thelma getting a weekly report, the two of them took over. A heavy downpour of rain showed water staining down the passage wall and in the big living room. Thelma was told immediately and the plumbers arrived a day later and began to replace the major part of the roof. Mrs Talbot had been horrified at the squalid little room off the kitchen that served as a minute living room with a television set and all the old newspapers rammed into the cracks around the windows. The TV set was removed to the larger living room and the little room completely stripped, and Thelma was notified.

Barry was now starting to become very worried. He was being ordered around from dawn to dusk and to his great annoyance Mrs Talbot had put him on a diet. 'It's for your own good,' she declared. 'At that weight, you will surely die of heart disease.'

Barry just shrugged his shoulders and glanced at his plate of vegetable soup with no bread allowed. 'I shall more likely die of starvation,' he began in his arrogant tone.

'Don't you speak to me like that,' Mrs Talbot shouted, 'or off you go to work at your aunt's sawmill.' A sharp sigh was the reply.

'The house is in an appalling condition,' she explained to Thelma when she met her in Walvern. 'There is six feet of dust everywhere and all the furniture is in a terrible condition, especially the upholstery in the sitting room. The cats have shredded everything. I have given them all short shrift but the damage remains. What shall we do?'

'Have them re-covered or pitch them out and buy a new divan and chairs.'

'I think the latter is the wiser,' Mrs Talbot replied, with an air of authority. The stench of cat spray permeates the whole house, especially all the upholstery and curtains. One set of curtains I took down and washed — or attempted to wash — and they just dissolved in a sea of brown water. I presume that the expense account you have given me covers this sort of disaster?'

'Of course,' Thelma sighed, with a weak smile, knowing full well that probably the whole house would have to be re-curtained, as her memory of them was of being in a very shabby state. 'And Barry?' she asked.

'Oh, such a lazy piece of work! If given a task, he takes all day and it's never done well at all. He is always moaning about the diet I have him on. He is so obese.'

'Yes, bone lazy,' Thelma agreed. 'Part of that is Emily's fault. She always gave in to him.'

'Well, I must say,' Mrs Talbot countered, 'that Mrs Houghton has been very supportive in helping me getting him to do some work.'

Thelma congratulated her and told her to keep up the good work.

Mrs Talbot swept into the curtain shop, selected what she thought suitable. The shop assistant took all the measurements and guaranteed that they would be ready in seven working days. Feeling pleased with her organisation and selection of the fabric, she then headed to the supermarket to do her weekly shopping.

Barry was really starting to resent Mrs Talbot and said so to his mother, but he knew no matter how much he protested he was unable to alter anything as behind every change was Aunt Thelma. Not even in a rare moment of courage would he ever have thought of challenging her. So little by little Houghton Hall began to lose its dilapidated look, though it still had a long way to go.

'She is just the most unbearable member of staff,' Barry said loudly to Stuart Searl. 'I can't really understand why Aunt Thelma has employed her.'

'Well, fire her,' was Stuart's reply. 'It's your house.'

'Yes, of course,' replied a very pretentious Barry. 'I must speak to Aunt Thelma. These goings on are just too much,' but he knew very well that words were cheap and he had no intention whatsoever of speaking to Thelma.

After her fall, Emily never recovered completely. She was always tired and looked very worn out. She began to lose weight, not that she had much to lose, and Mrs Talbot began to worry. Emily had forbidden her from worrying Thelma but a dizzy spell soon put a stop to that and Thelma's car was seen driving fast past Killpara to Houghton Hall.

'You look a wreck,' was Thelma's gentle greeting, not having seen her sister for several weeks. She moved Barry out of the way as she went to the telephone to call Dr James, saying the case was urgent. Half an hour later, the doctor arrived and was also shocked at Emily's condition, as he had seen her two months earlier when he had set her broken leg.

The next day, she was admitted to hospital and the tests began. Now Barry was really worried. If something happened to his mother, who was the buffer against Mrs Talbot and Thelma - his life would not be worth living, he thought. Emily was diagnosed as having stomach cancer and further tests showed that it had spread through her now very frail frame. The condition was so advanced that treatment, except to make her comfortable, was useless. Now Mrs Talbot took over completely. Emily returned home at her own insistence and Mrs

Talbot became housekeeper and private nurse all in one. Barry now saw the writing on the wall. His future life was to be managed by Thelma and Mrs Talbot, but he thought if his mother died he would inherit the lot, sell it and move into Walvern into a smart town house. Oh, what could be easier, free of Thelma for life? Good food and the Oriental, which had now become his favourite watering hole, due to Stewart! Oh, a future where for once he was free! His mind did handstands! No more privation called a diet! Oh, well, if the future called, he could only be the winner. This simple solution to his immediate problems was pathetic and his realisation of it when destiny took its path was to prove to Barry that a loser never wins.

The doses of morphine became high and higher as Emily fell slowly into a dream world where very little made sense. Everything with the doses became softer, like falling backward into a mattress of cotton wool and if she didn't recognise anyone it didn't matter. It was her world and her last moments and they passed with a softness supported by a decent dose of morphine very regularly. So, Emily, after only three short weeks, passed from this world to the next. One would have expected Barry to have been mortified that his woman who had supported him all his life had passed away, but in fact he was so off-hand about the death of his mother that Thelma thought seriously about giving him a good beating and Thelma, being Thelma, was quite capable of doing so. It was his arrogance that annoyed her more than anything, his lack of sentiment his 'faux grandure' about his mother having passed on. Thelma was furious at his total inability to grasp the fact that his mother had died. He was totally disengaged from the reality — he just wasn't interested. He was much more concerned about his own future and how he could live it to his own advantage.

He was now to receive the greatest shock of his life. After the funeral and still with Mrs Talbot in the house, he foolishly dismissed her, grandly saying her limited services were complete. A sharp telephone call to Thelma followed a very brittle reading of Emily's will, which left Barry with the feeling that going down with the Titanic was something he understood very well. Thelma had no pity at all. She inherited everything on the condition she made allowances for him. This was a grey area. She, Aunt Thelma, was perfectly ready to decide how these grey areas functioned and not one of them went in Barry's favour. She was set on sending Barry on unemployment relief and getting on with putting Houghton Hall in order and as she had no compassion or sympathy for him she simply offered him three possibilities, the first being work at the sawmill, which she controlled absolutely, or he was to take on one hundred per cent responsibility for Houghton Hall under Mrs Talbot's strong guidance or, as the last suggestion, go on to relief help and see what he could find. He was caught. He had nowhere to move at all. Thelma had won and he had lost and being a coward it hurt all the more, so his destiny became Mrs Talbot, as Thelma's henchwoman, dictating how and when. He was convinced to die would be an easy way out, but as he was a coward not even this was a real alternative.

Everyone locally had attended Emily's funeral and it had been a satisfactory but empty ceremony, as Emily, like Barry, had been — unlike her sister — very pretentious, so the local people felt the responsibility to attend the funeral as a formality but nothing else.

As Barry and Emily had sold off a good three quarters of the property sometime before, Thelma now made enquiries about how to re-purchase the land, and was surprised that the owners were co-operative, though the price they demanded was, according to her, 'daylight robbery' so she held off buying, but took a three month option on the purchase. She could only see Houghton Hall paying its own way if there was enough land to economically show a return. Mrs Talbot was now responsible for all the accounts and she and Thelma, every Thursday morning when Mrs Talbot was in Walvern, went over the expenditures. Thelma began to wonder about the sense of keeping this 'white elephant' going and sat down to see what she could gain if she sold what was left of it. She was dismayed to realise that the property was worth very little and the house itself practically nothing.

* * * * *

The weekend in Melbourne with Thomas was becoming a very regular event. Joseph would arrive on Friday morning and return on Monday, or, if Rose had some plans for him, much later. Having Thomas with her always as an independent nephew was one thing she enjoyed immensely, but she was now enjoying looking after Joseph, who was not so independent and taking him out and about to galleries or auctions or restaurants was also becoming part of her life.

After one of these pleasant stays at Albany Road, Joseph returned to Walvern to help Jan with some restoration work, much to Thomas's dismay, wanting him to stay the whole week. When he arrived at Mary's home, he unpacked and set about preparing to go to Jan's. When the front door bell rang, he opened the door and was shocked to see his brother, whom he had not encountered for some months, looking terrible. Keven's eyes were red, his skin blotchy and it looked to Joseph as if his hair had not been washed for months, as it hung in greasy twisted threads.

'I need a hand to collect something,' stated Keven, staring Joseph straight in the eyes.

'The answer is no,' Joseph replied, looking behind Keven to see one of his sidekicks sitting in a car waiting for him.

'All you have to do is pick up a parcel and bring it to me in the car tonight. Nothing else.'

'Why can't you do it yourself?' Joseph asked, defensively. There was a very good reason why Keven or his friend could not do it : they were both so well known that the minute they made an appearance the police would know automatically that they were collecting a dispatch of drugs. This particular situation was much more complicated, as Keven, over the phone, had agreed to take the 'stuff' and a price was struck, but somehow the police also had wind of the deal so the moment either Keven or his friend showed their faces the police would nab them at once and as this package had been organised at such a good price Keven could not afford to lose it, let alone let the police lay their hands on it. The dealers in Melbourne had already dispatched the stuff, so Keven was in a real bind if he didn't collect it as organised by the Melbourne dealers; they would not supply him again. So he needed a bunny, and an innocent bunny, hence he turned to Joseph. Keven was not an intellectual, but he was exceptionally streetwise and this deal was very important to him.

Joseph, for the second time, refused to have anything to do with it. Now Keven played his trump card. 'Oh you will,' he said, with a sly smile, showing his terrible marked teeth, 'or I'll go to Thomas O'Riely as well as Mary and tell them you have been dispatching stuff for me for ages and your trips to Melbourne are a cover for moving my merchandise.'

Joseph felt his blood run cold. What if, just what if Thomas believed the story? It would be the finish of their wonderful relationship. And Mary? What would she say? He just stared at Keven, not able to find words.

'Good,' Keven said with a smirk, 'I shall collect you at the corner of the street at ten o'clock tonight. Be there or I shall really do a job on you.' He turned and strutted down the path with his cowboy boots making a sharp sound on the brick path.

Joseph closed the door, went to the kitchen and sat down, staring at the garden through a wall of glass. What was he to do? Not turn up and risk losing Thomas if he told Mary? Would she really believe he wasn't helping Keven? He mulled these thoughts over again and again. Losing Thomas — this was his greatest fear, having waited so long and now being completely in love with him. And what if he didn't believe him? The more he thought of all this, the more confused and upset he became until he couldn't even reason.

At exactly ten o'clock, he climbed into the back seat of Keven's friends' borrowed car so no trace of recognition could be discerned. They drove with a white-faced Joseph, who never said one word through drizzling rain. Winter had really set in and the heating in the car was suffocating. He began to feel nauseous. The two front-seat passengers chattered on about clients and more so about the huge profit margin they were to share.

'They are fucking idiots in Melbourne. They didn't even realise the last time we shorted them $1500. They confused us with someone else. I told you they are real dickheads.' Keven continued in this vein.

This car of young men was not the only people who had braved this miserable wet Tuesday evening. Samuel, Joyce and Patricia were attending the opening of a local painter's work in the big room off the Library. It was an odd night for an opening but it had to do with the Mayor's availability, so Tuesday at eight it was. Samuel couldn't find a parking place close to the Library so with umbrellas unfurled they walked a block on a cold rainy winter's night to the building.

'How I hate winter; muttered Patricia. 'If I had the money I would spend winter on a tropical island.'

'Well, you are never going to have the money if you keep spending it on that enormous cast iron birdcage,' responded Samuel.

'Come on, you two, no arguing,' Joyce interrupted.

'Well,' Patricia went on, 'I may just go to the tropics next winter because I have made the final payment last Friday to the man who has restored all the pieces, so next week we can start assembling it.'

Samuel said nothing. He always associated the birdcage with Barry's arrogance, so he had no real love for it at all.

'By the way,' he said, 'I believe Barry is now toeing the line for his aunt and not before time.'

'Not only the aunt,' added Joyce, 'but Mrs Talbot as well. He won't be very happy about it at all.'

'Serves the pretentious fool right,' was Samuel's sharp reply.

The large room off the Library was packed, much to Patricia's surprise, having helped to hang the exhibition that afternoon and predicting two cats as company, she saw it was full. They moved about, having deposited their coats and umbrellas and Patricia dashed off to see if the cheese and wine were being distributed.

'Samuel, that's Barry's aunt over there, Mrs Thelma Smith.'

'Really?' Samuel looked surprised. 'She doesn't look anything like her late sister at all. She seems almost normal.'

'Sh! She may hear you!' Then Samuel noticed two men come through the door, Barry and Stewart Semi. He narrowed his eyes. Barry nodded formally and then quickly disappeared into the crowd, searching for the cheese plate and the carafes of red wine. He went over and said hello to Thelma, as he knew not to do so might mean bread and water for a month. She spoke to him and then made her way through the crowd to Samuel and Joyce.

'How do you do! I'm Thelma,' she stated in a direct way. 'I believe we are neighbours now.'

'Yes,' Joyce answered. 'I'm pleased to meet you. We didn't know your sister at all, I'm afraid.'

'Don't be,' she smiled.

'You will have your work cut out putting Houghton Hall back together. It's been allowed to run down.'

'It certainly has,' Thelma agreed. 'By the way, you have some unimproved land that touches Houghton Hall. Are you willing to sell it to me? You see, my stupid nephew, whom I believe you know —'

'Only too well,' came a quick response from Samuel. Thelma turned her head a little, detecting a no-love situation between Samuel and Barry.

'Barry sold off more than three quarters of the property some time ago and the people who have the land are willing to sell it back but at a prohibitive price.'

'I predicted that this would happen,' said Samuel. 'I'm sorry that you now have to pick up the responsibility of putting the property back together, but the land you have asked me about is not for sale, as later we plan to enlarge our herd and so we shall need all the land we can get, much the same as you, I'm afraid.'

Thelma smiled. 'Thanks, anyway. It's been nice meeting you both.' She moved back through the crowded room, wondering what Barry had done or said that must have angered Samuel.

'Well, you must be very proud of yourself,' said Joyce as the three of them, after the exhibition was over and they battled the rain as they hurried back to their car.

'Oh, it's coming down cats and dogs now,' Samuel complained, as they ran the last half block like everyone else. When in the car and shaking off the rain, 'I was so surprised there were so many people for a little show like this,' said Joyce. 'It was very pleasant. You are to be congratulated.'

'Thanks, Mum. I must say I was also surprised at the turn out, and, you know, I think they sold nearly all the paintings, so obviously we need to hold an evening like this more regularly.'

'I should say so. Oh, we met Barry's aunt, Thelma,' added Joyce. 'She seemed a down-to-earth person, not like Emily, who I don't think I said more than hello to in all my life — a very distant woman, but Thelma seems quite nice, I think.'

They chatted on about the paintings they liked and the others that they thought were not quite so good. Samuel had now left the town and was driving slowly in torrential driving rain, complaining that the visibility was terrible.

* * * *

'Now don't fuck this up,' threatened Keven, and handed Joseph a manila envelope. They had driven for some time to the rendezvous with a very nervous Joseph in the back seat, who now felt very frightened. The only thing that went back and forth in his mind was if Thomas might think he was an accomplice in drug dealing. The emptiness within him was complete. Why hadn't he had the courage to telephone Thomas and tell him about Keven's blackmail and why, oh why hadn't he told Mary?

The rain now was teaming down as they arrived at the appointed place and time. It was a service station in the middle of nowhere with one automatic pump and the torrential rain with the fluorescent lighting gave the whole place a theatrical appearance, completely unreal. Under the veranda section was another car. Keven's friend began to panic as he wasn't sure whether it wasn't a stake-out by the police. Keven plunged his hand into his coat pocket and withdrew a tiny plastic packet with two brown pills inside. He opened the packet and handed one to his friend. 'Take it!' was the command and his very nervous friend did as directed. Keven took the other.

Joseph moved across the back seat and got out on the side of the car closer to the other. He went across as directed, in the freezing wind and ran. He didn't see anything. He wasn't interested in anything. All he wanted was to be in bed with Thomas's strong arms around him. He handed the envelope over as the side window was wound down and in a moment a rectangular package was thrust into his hands and the other car drove off at high speed. Joseph returned to the car and Keven. By this stage the 'extra' he and his friend had taken was having an effect. Keven grabbed the package from Joseph and put it on the floor of the car between his feet. 'Go!' he screamed at his friend and the car swung about and headed back to Walvern at a dangerous speed, considering the weather. Joseph felt nothing. He was completely numb. The two in the front were now singing to loud disco music on a CD player but Joseph was only aware of the sound, nothing else. He had the distinct feeling he had done something very wrong and he would in one form or another pay for it. Keven's friend, who went by the name of Mark, was really 'away' with it, due to the special something Keven had given him and was driving on the wrong side of the road, giving an oncoming car so much of a fright that it ended up in a ditch beside the road, in this frightful weather, with Keven and Mark laughing hysterically. They now made the main road into Walvern, with Joseph, from this loud music and the oppressive heat in the car, feeling even more confused and nauseous than ever. The rain was heavy, the road slippery and Mark absolutely out of control. The car that was coming toward them slowly suddenly became a target for Mark and in this very limited visibility he planted his foot on the accelerator and drove like a maniac. Keven was not aware of the danger. He was feeling great, having ripped off these dealers before and with the quantity of what he had received this evening his profit margin was enormous. This was all he was interested in.

The impact was catastrophic. Mark's foot, as he came closer and closer to the lights ahead of him, pressed down harder as he became more and more excited.

It was eleven thirty when Mary's telephone rang. 'Oh, where is this wretched child?' she thought. She had been to dinner with Trevor and was surprised Joseph was not at home. She wondered why he had not called her to say he was working late with Jan. Then her telephone rang.

'Where are you,' she said, sharply. There was silence, then 'Mary,' came a voice she knew, 'it's Peter here.'

She knew him not only as the local constable but also as friend and client. 'Peter, what's wrong?'

'Your brothers have been in a fatal car accident. The three O'Rieleys are also dead. Mary, can you hear me?'

'Yes,' was the only reply. 'Yes.' She hung up. The whole room began to move and she was very aware she was breathing very heavily and not regularly. She punched Trevor's telephone number, or so she thought.

'Hello,' came Enid's voice.

'Enid,' said a bleak voice. 'They are all dead.'

'Where are you?' Enid asked. 'Are you at home?'

'Yes.' She hung up. She couldn't find tears : they just wouldn't come. It was the gasps of deep breathing that continued and she repeated aloud, 'They are all dead.'

Enid thrust a tray into a waiter's hands and made for the door, but not before explaining to Paul and Lenny what was wrong. 'One mistake this evening and you're fired,' she yelled to the staff as she raced past tables and out into the street and into Paul's car. She drove at breakneck speed through red lights — not that there were many in Walvern — directly to Aspel Drive, while telephoning Trevor and Simon to alert them of the disaster.

Trevor arrived first and the moment he held Mary in his arms the tears began, as Enid came in through an open front door and slammed it behind her. She witnessed the most tragic of scenes, with Mary having completely given way. Her gasps and tears were heart-rending. Enid helped Trevor support her to the settee, where they sat either side, holding her. All she could say was 'Joseph' and kept repeating it. Enid took over and asked her if she had Rose's telephone number. Even Enid knew this was going to be an impossible call. Mary pointed to her telephone directory and Enid moved into the kitchen to make the call. She could have called Thomas on his telephone, but something told her this was not the way to pass on the message. Meanwhile, Trevor had called his father, who came three doors down in the still pouring rain and administered a sedative which in a few minutes saw Mary in bed and sleeping.

Rose and Thomas had been out to dinner and had arrived back at Albany Road in high spirits, laughing about the events of the evening. Just as they entered the front door, the telephone rang. 'I told you,' laughed Rose. 'I'll bet it's that good-looking banker who was drooling over you all night.'

'Don't be silly,' he laughed. 'Do you want a night cap?'

She said yes as she moved to the demanding telephone. She removed an earring and listened. 'Yes, yes,' and she said no more. Thomas returned laughing. 'Who wins the bet?' and then he saw Rose's face. She sat down heavily on the chair beside the phone and just listened, becoming whiter and whiter. Thomas put the glasses down and moved quickly to her side. In slow motion she handed the phone to him.

'Hello, he said rapidly. 'Enid, what's wrong?' Unlike Rose his self-control was much less. 'Joseph,' he wept, 'Oh God, Joseph.' He felt an arm around his shoulder as Rose took the receiver from him.

'Enid, we shall leave now.'

'Come directly to the Oriental. I will have two rooms prepared. It's pointless going to Killpara and Mary has been sedated. She's not in a good state. I shall expect you both in less than two hours. I am so sorry.'

The two of them looked at one another and instinctively embraced. Thomas was, for the first time in his life, completely lost. He wept bitterly for his parents but as Rose knew it was for his beloved Joseph that the pain was the most tearing. She now took over. 'Get changed,' she said, 'and pack. You will need clothes for the funeral,' and left him and went upstairs as if she were on an escalator. It was as if her feet were moving automatically and the emptiness inside her was excruciatingly painful. Joyce had been her older sister who had always looked after her. They spoke every second day at least and just when Thomas and Joseph were fitting easily into this family scenario why, oh why, she thought, as she packed clothes into a bag. She walked as if in a dream. Nothing made sense. Why, oh why, she kept asking herself. She passed Thomas's room, only to hear the most heart rending sobs. She pushed open the door and he was lying on his bed, face down, holding in his hands the photo Rose had taken of the two of them in dinner suits. Her own pain and loss now took second place to his and she sat beside him with her hand on his shoulder, not saying a word. After several minutes of tears that Rose thought might never end, she stood up and packed his bag for him, his toiletries, everything. She stood beside the bed.

'It's time now, darling,' she said softly and he got up very slowly. 'Here, change into this.' She took his dinner suit from him as he changed into jeans, a blue shirt and a dark blue jumper. She handed him a jacket as she hung up his suit. He took his packed bag and like a child followed her down to the car parked outside the front door. It was a great contrast to less than thirty minutes before when they had returned from a dinner party, laughing and joking.

'No, Thomas, I'll drive.' They pulled out onto an empty, wet street and headed in the direction of the freeway that would take them to Walvern. There was no point in talking. Thomas couldn't; he was numb, his whole beautiful life with Joseph had vaporised in front of him. Everything he had planned to share with him was now finished. 'Nothing', that was the word he sought in his mind, 'nothing'. The rain had let up and the road reflected yellow shafts of light on the wet surface. The squelshing sound of the tyres did little to make either Thomas or Rose think of anything positive. She glanced sideways at him to note that tears were streaming down his face. She reached into her jacket pocket and handed him a man's handkerchief. He took it but not a word was passed between them; no word would have been appropriate to the situation.

At half past one Rose pulled her car up in front of a well-let Oriental Hotel. They got out only to find that the rain had begun yet again. They made for the front door to find it unlocked and walked into the most amazing scene either of them were to experience in their whole lives. As they crossed the hall, having rung the bell, it was a jubilant Enid who rushed at Thomas, kissing him and hugging him. Both Rose and Thomas were unable to grasp what was happening.

'He's alive,' cried Enid, with tears running down her cheeks. 'He's alive,' she repeated. Thomas stood like an alabaster statue, not moving a muscle. It was Rose who demanded an explanation. When the police had arrived on the scene of the accident, there had appeared to be three dead people in each car but by a miracle Joseph had been thrown forward with the impact into the cushioned back of the front seats and then catapulted back into the padded back seat and was unconscious. It was assumed that he too was part of the carnage of the evening. It was only later that it was discovered that he was alive. By that time Mary had been sedated and Enid thought it better to wait until they had arrived at Walvern. The others in the cars were not sci fortunate. The five of them had died on impact.

Thomas looked at Enid, then Rose, not sure if it was true or not and Enid repeated the story again as the realisation sank in. The two women witnessed a spectacle they both prayed they would never have to see again as Thomas slowly sank to his knees on the hall floor. His head touched the pavement and he began to sob but in a way that both women were particularly worried about. Enid went to help him up but Rose motioned her to leave him. The heart-rending sobs were for joy and relief; Rose and Enid watched the man they both loved cry for the man he in turned loved.

Enid had received this information about Joseph via Trevor, who had stayed at Mary's for the night. No sooner had Enid left and Mary slept sedated than the telephone had rung and Constable Peter had told Trevor that Joseph was alive and had been transferred to the local hospital where he would remain for the night and tests would take place the next day. After Trevor had spoken with Enid, she had already in her mind organised everything.

'Get yourself and Mary here for breakfast in my private dining room upstairs. We shall all feel better together, especially with this positive news.' She had then at this very late hour telephoned her head waiter. 'I want you here for breakfast.' When he exclaimed at the order, looking at his watch on the bedside table,' she repeated, 'for breakfast and double wages.' She hung up and telephoned Lenny, explaining all and asking rather than demanding (which was her usual way) if he would cook a breakfast for six or seven people. He agreed. So at eight o'clock Mary and Trevor walked upstairs, past the attractive young waiter, to Enid's dining room.

Neither of them had ever been there before. As they turned at the top of the stair, they saw Rose and Thomas coming toward them. Mary moved forward and held Thomas, with tears running down both their cheeks. The waiter behind them gently motioned them into the dining room. Trevor followed, with Rose. It was indeed a beautiful room, filled with antique furniture. The walls were the softest old rose colour, with billowing silk curtains that matched perfectly. The immaculately set table and the side tables held enormous bowls of white lilies. Everything had a cushioned effect, a delicate feeling, and Rose realised that it was a room that was obviously very rarely used. The tears gave way to question after question. Why was Joseph with Keven? Why had he not phoned Mary? And so the conversation continued.

A little later, Simon joined them and the old school group was together again, each person in their own way making tiny bridges to cross this abyss of unhappiness. It was Rose who felt a loss that was final. There could be no way Joyce could be brought back from the grave. Thomas, she thought to herself, definitely had his guardian angel in place. He had lost his family but he had at least Joseph. Rose had just lost. Of all the people at the breakfast, it was Enid who sensed this terrible emptiness in Rose and as she sat beside her she gently took her hand. No words were passed but just the physical contact of one person trying to support another was sufficient for Rose to hold Enid's hand firmly as the tears slowly streamed down her cheeks. Enid handed her a handkerchief which Rose took and with a weak smile thanked her. It had been the first time someone had thought of Rose's loss and not Thomas's. This Rose never forgot.

Both Thomas and Mary were desperate to see Joseph but, typically, Enid had phoned Constable Peter first thing in the morning to find out how the lie of the land was. She had received the hospital bulletin, as she knew one of the surgeons there who was a regular customer at the Oriental and always received special attention. Joseph, by way of a miracle, was physically in perfect condition, with not even a scratch, nothing, just bruised ribs. With the agreement of Constable Peter he was to be released from the hospital that morning but he was to be questioned in the afternoon, as Peter smelled a rat in this terrible accident, especially as he knew Keven only too well.

While breakfast was being served and a deluxe breakfast it was, Lenny going all out, the waiter, who was also being paid double, found the trek from the kitchen up the stairs to the private dining room a bit of a bore. It was Rose who noticed that this large dining table, groaning under the weight of crystal, fine crockery and silver, had two settings laid with two empty chairs tucked neatly under it. As breakfast began, the door opened and Paul entered, ahead of a white-faced Joseph. Thomas had his back to the door and suddenly realised everyone was silent. He looked across the table at Mary, who began to cry, then spun around like a spring let loose. His cutlery clattered onto his plate as he stood up, while Paul moved to the side and in three steps he had Joseph in his arms. He just stood there, unable to cry or laugh. When He felt Joseph's arms close around him he was immediately aware that had things been different he would never have held him again. Mary stood and moved around the table; Joseph moved from Thomas's arms to hers, then after a few moments she released him, and just before he went to sit down beside Thomas he moved over and embraced Rose.

'I am so sorry,' he whispered. 'It's all part of my fault.'

She hugged him. 'There's no fault, Joseph. What has happened has happened.'

He tightened his grasp on her and then sat down beside Thomas, who held his hand and then the questions start to come thick and fast.

'I was scared that you would both think that I was trafficking drugs with Keven,' he said. 'He threatened to prove to you that I was.' He looked down at his plate as the waiter offered him some of Lenny's delicious scrambled eggs, which he accepted. He didn't look any different after Paul had collected him from the hospital, with a clean bill of health. Paul had taken him to Mary's, where he had showered and changed and here he was.

'I hope the other car is all right,' he went on.

'What other car?' Mary asked, and he went on to explain that Mark had driven at a car and it had gone off the road, but he couldn't remember much about it.

'Were there drugs in the car?' asked Enid.

'Yes. Keven made me give the guys in another car an envelope and they gave me a packet.'

'Hm,' sighed Enid, 'this is not so good.'

'Excuse me,' interrupted the waiter to Enid. 'You are needed downstairs for a moment.' She stood up and disappeared as the waiter changed plates and yet another course was laid out for them.

They were all talking over one another when the door opened and Constable Peter Simons came in. 'Hello, Peter,' Mary greeted him, and the others exchanged greetings as well.

'I thought it might be a little less daunting if Peter spoke to Joseph now at breakfast as opposed to the Police Station,' said Enid boldly.

'You have tested clean,' Peter said, looking at Joseph and being offered a chair at the same time. The same cannot be said for your brother and his friend. What exactly were you doing with your brother last night?'

185

And before he could answer, Peter shot another question, 'and what was all the flour for?'

Joseph looked at Thomas, who was holding his hand in bewilderment. 'What flour?' he asked.

'There were no drugs in the car at all, just a large packet of flour, which had spread out over the front of the passenger side.'

'I honestly don't know what the flour was for.'

'It's very odd, 'Peter went on. 'Anyway, you seem to be the lucky one.'

'What happened to the other car that Mark drove at, that finished up on the other side of the road?' Joseph asked.

'Oh, so it was Mark, was it? Yes, it was reported last night, about two jerks having taken something special and ending up killing three innocent people and themselves. There will be an inquest but it appears it will be a formality.'

Thanks, Peter,' said Enid and Mary together. He stood up to leave. 'I am very sorry about your parents and sister,' he said to Thomas, and looked at Rose, 'and your sister.' He turned and left, with Enid escorting him downstairs.

Mary looked straight at Joseph. 'What exactly was in the packet you exchanged for the envelope?'

'I don't know. I was so frightened. I just handed it to Keven and got in the car.'

'Well, said Trevor, 'it appears our Keven was ripped off for once. Instead of cocaine he received flour. It's odd he didn't test it before he handed over the cash.'

'He was high with it by then. Mark was scared. He thought that the police were about. That's why they used me. They had taken something as I was getting the packet, because I remember when I got back in the car they were laughing and singing, so I guess Keven just thought everything was OK.'

'His mistake has saved you,' said Enid, coming into the room and overhearing the conversation. 'If that flour had been cocaine, Joseph, you would be charged with trafficking in drugs, which means a jail sentence. I've spoken to Peter, who is only too aware of what happened last night, so you can thank the saints that your brother was well ripped off.'

There was silence at the table, with Joseph feeling that he was being disciplined for his part in this terrible incident. It was Thomas's tight grip on his arm that made him feel not quite so alone.

The funeral was set for Thursday, the funeral, that is, of the O'Riely family. St Joseph's was packed and two very different events occurred on that day, the first being Stewart Searl's column *'In and Out of Society'*, which came out that day, where he viciously attacked everyone in the community who was a client of Keven's, stating without pity that they were directly responsible for the death of a complete family, as if they hadn't constantly demanded Keven's wares he would not have been on the road in that state on that night. As he was also very aware of the story behind the dreadful accident, 'Next time, 'he wrote, 'it may be your family who won't be spending Christmas with you'. It was a vitriolic attack on the young and not-so-young who took drugs and on the terrible accident. The police made a much more studied effort at the Stardust Hotel to catch whoever it was who would take over from Keven, distributing drugs.

The second odd occurrence was, as Rose dressed for the funeral, her telephone rang and she answered it. She didn't recognise the voice or the name when given and then the male voice introduced himself as the owner of the large property that was situated between Killpara and Houghton Hall. He offered his condolences but said he was in an awkward situation.

'What's the problem?' she asked, still dressing.

'I've decided to sell, as my kids are all married now and I have a copy of a first option that was made by your late brother-in-law and you.'

'Yes.'

'Well, I know it's not the time and I am sorry but I was contacted fifteen minutes ago by Thelma Smith from Houghton hall with a generous offer to buy. I just wondered whether, under the circumstances, you now might not wish to purchase the property. As I said, I am so sorry about the bad timing but Thelma wants an answer in half an hour and I am not sure what to do or even if you still want the property.'

'The option stands,' Rose countered sharply. The amount was agreed on legally and is what will be paid. Under the circumstances I know you will wait until Monday when we can organise this with our solicitors. Thank you so much for calling and thank you for your condolences.' She hung up and applied her make-up, wondering what sort of person this Thelma was, whether her offer was just coincidental or whether she was a vulture, waiting and preying on the dead.

The church was packed and a very sad sight of three coffins lying side by side made the feeling of loss even greater. Thomas and Rose stood side by side as the priest entered and the rite began. Joseph stood in the row behind, with Mary, Enid, Trevor, Terry and Simon, all feeling the sensation of morality.

The funeral that followed much later in the afternoon was a very forlorn event, with Keven's coffin standing alone in a nearly empty church. The same small group attended but apart from his parents most of the pews were vacant. It seemed to Enid a very sad and empty funeral Mass. At the cemetery Rose discovered that the term 'loss' or 'parting' were relative. Thomas's loss of his parents and sister was to a point nullified as a result of Joseph being saved. Mary suffered no loss as a result of Keven's departure and a great sense of happiness that Joseph was alive. It was when Rose, who felt an extraordinary emptiness at Joyce's departure, looked aimlessly about at the enormous numbers of flowers that had been laid around and on the freshly dug graves that her eyes rested on a bunch in colours of blue, with three peacock feathers in behind them. She lent down and read the card. 'We shall miss you very much'; it was signed by Terry and Pete. She stood up, looking down at the flowers and feeling very ashamed that she had never had a good relationship with Patricia, Simon's boyfriend and peacock who had sent their last regards to a new friend they had made, and were very, very sorry to have lost. It was then Rose realised that death is dependent on so many things in producing a response - a thought, a tear, who was it? were they close? - and here it was a little bunch of blue flowers from a friend and a peacock who were going to miss Patricia's call on her way home from work, for Terry the link between the group that seemed impossible and himself that had made fitting in with them so much easier.

Rose walked slowly back through the rows of gravestones toward the main gravelled space and the gates, feeling completely empty. She was surprised to find an arm sliding through hers and turned to find Simon smiling at her.

'Listen, Rose,' he said quietly, 'when you have to go and check up everything at Killpara and there's no-one to go with you, promise me you will give me a call and I'll join you for company. Going alone is not such a good idea.'

She turned and kissed him on the cheek. 'Thank you, Simon, I may just take you up on your kind offer, as Thomas is now totally pre-occupied with Joseph having been saved — as are we all.'

'Any time, Rose.' He kissed her and made for his car, where Terry was waiting.

She was not exaggerating. Thomas was now so intensively directed toward Joseph that he saw nothing else. He genuinely felt he had been given another chance at happiness and he now couldn't bear to be away from him. Just to hold him, in these early stages, to hold him seemed a gift from the saints. Had fate been different, he could have just as easily buried him with the others, so for both Joseph and Thomas this tragic situation had finished in a certain sense in their favour, but it pointed out to both of them very clearly that one's mortality might be closer than one thought. For that reason Thomas decided that everything in his life had to and would be sacrificed for Joseph, so they could be together for whatever time was allowed them, and to develop it to the maximum.

CHAPTER 6

Re-starting

Chapter 6

Re-starting

The solicitor was a very handsome man of about forty two, a charming man by the name of Brendan Crane.

'Please do sit down,' he said, as he fussed about with some papers, smiled, and then said, 'Well, the will is extremely clear and simple. It states that you, Thomas, and your sister, Patricia, are to take an equal share of the property. In the event of one of you pre-deceasing the other, the total goes to the survivor.' He went on and read the whole will, with Rose and Thomas wondering if he would ever finish.

'Thank you so much, Mr Crane,' said Rose. 'There is another matter I should like you to attend to,' and she explained about the property that would now be annexed to Killpara.

'Well, well, well,' he said, smiling, 'that is sure to put Thelma's nose out of joint.' He laughed and Rose stared at him, having no idea what the joke was.'

'I'm afraid I don't understand,' she said.

'You see, Thelma was here only three or four days ago. She was determined to purchase this property. You know how she is.'

'No, I don't,' replied Rose. 'I have never met her.'

'What did she come to see you about?' enquired Thomas, curious.

'She wanted to know if the first option that the late Mr O'Riely and you,' smiling at Rose, 'made was legal and if there was a legal way of purchasing this land without adhering to the first option.'

'Thelma sounds great,' said Thomas, in an off-hand way. Mr Crane laughed. 'Thelma is quite a character and not used to not getting her own way.'

Rose had an uneasy feeling that the now-enlarged Killpara was going to be sharing a boundary fence with someone she was absolutely sure was never going to be her best friend. She was absolutely correct.

'I shall begin the transfer of property tomorrow. I take it a thirty day settlement will be satisfactory?' he asked.

'Perfectly,' Rose agreed, smiling. 'Do let me know if you need any extra documents.'

She stood up and shook hands with him, as did Thomas, then they left his smart office and walked into drizzling rain. Pulling up an umbrella, Thomas said, 'Come on, let's go to lunch at Enid's. I think I could really do with a drink.' They walked the half block to the hotel, where Rose and Thomas were still staying. They had, in the last six days, been treated as super-special guests, with Enid taking great care that everything was perfect. She was much happier now, as Thomas was in residence, as the rest of the group ate there more regularly with him and Rose, and she was able to join them.

The following day at lunch, in a packed dining room, with Enid stalking about like a cat waiting for the first wrong move from someone, Rose excused herself and made a telephone call to Simon to ask if he would accompany her to Killpara that afternoon, as Thomas was seeing Joseph. Simon's response was in the affirmative and he said he would collect her from the hotel at two thirty. 'Simon, how kind, but as I have my car, why don't I stop and pick you up instead, on the way.'

'Rose, that's fine by me. Whenever you are ready.'

Rose was half an hour later than she expected due to Trevor joining them for lunch and then Joseph a little later still. Conversation-wise Trevor kept the ball rolling, telling funny stories and joking, which everyone loved: anything that short-circuited this terrible accident was truly welcome. Rose left them still laughing and went via a waiter to Enid where she asked for a bottle of whisky for James, the share-farmer, and if possible something she could take for afternoon tea with Simon and Terry. In an instant, in a delightful package, Lenny put together a feast in a box, and it was all done in ten minutes, so when Rose descended the stairs the good-looking young waiter had a basket with two boxes of goodies for afternoon tea, with a bottle of champagne tucked inside, and, wrapped separately, a bottle of whiskey. Rose thanked the young man who carried the basket to her car and wished her a pleasant afternoon, saying that he was looking forward to her company in the dining room in the evening.

Enid was clever. Now she was prepared to learn; put the equation together and you have success, especially on a financial level. The Oriental had never paid like this; the smart service, attention to manners, excellent dressing and an array of very beautiful – or should one say very handsome – waiters. Even now, when Enid had a night free, she would drive with a new waiter to the Traveller's Arms in Melbourne and watch every movement, which seemed so effortless, but the effect on the clients was a caring security that meant without any doubt a return to the restaurant. She was very slowly changing. She had been shown, via Trevor, a way to survive economically and the formula worked for her. She dedicated twenty four hours of every day, determined to make it work, and she did. Everything was perfect and just seemed naturally to glide, to make the clients feel that they were the luckiest people in the world. But all of this was the result of a relentless attention to detail on her part. Paul did exactly as she demanded. The mortgage to finance this change at the hotel had been almost paid back in record time, due to the fact that every evening there were disappointed patrons who sought tables that just were not available. It also had to do with Lenny, who, given a completely free hand in the kitchen, showed exactly what he was capable of. On occasions he and Enid locked horns, but although she had the personality to attack at once she always pulled back and gave in to him, knowing full well that without him the Oriental would be in real trouble. When they had very good months of work, she always gave him a percentage of the take. This not only made him feel that he was appreciated but he was also being handsomely rewarded as well, so his incentive to do better was always there.

'Simon. Do take the basket in to Terry and tell him we shall be back with all the news in less than an hour.'

They drove down the hill and back up the other side on a wet gravel road, with the rain having made tiny rivers in the surface. It was still drizzling and a cold wind swept across the hills, swaying the evergreen trees like kites in the sky. 'It's actually quite beautiful, isn't it?' she remarked to Simon.

'Well, it depends whether you have to work in these conditions or just admire them.'

She laughed. 'You are absolutely right,' she said, very aware that she was laughing. She drove into the drive and down to the side of the house. They got out of the car and went up the ramp at the side, then walked into the house. It had been less than a week since this house had been lived in, but in this short period something had been exhausted out of it. It was cold inside and there was the sensation of damp. And worse than that there was the eerie sensation of silence. Rose moved slowly from room to room, followed by Simon. Her eyes rested on nothing – it was almost like an eye-training exercise where one watches a pencil as it goes from left to right. Now, without Joyce bustling about, the house seemed to slump and its breathing was slow and irregular. Rose knew the house very well, but today it was more forlorn than ever.

'Do you believe that some people are given the opportunity to see the future?' she asked.

'Yes,' he replied immediately. 'I'm sure there are such people.'

'I think Joyce received this capacity to see her future. Don't you remember her birthday party? She changed from the full country mouse to someone determined to live every minute to the full. She bought younger-looking clothes, she tinted her hair, she wore make-up, she gave up two mornings a week to help children at St Mary's read. I am sure she knew her time was charted and she wisely made the most of every minute. I spoke to her about Thomas and Joseph: it was the first time in all our lives Thomas's sexuality was spoken of. In the past it was as if he were asexual, which was easier because one didn't have to think about any alternatives, but Joyce said to me that if Thomas was happy with Joseph then she was happy as well.' Rose spoke on about this subject and others as she and Simon walked about this empty house. He realised that Rose needed to talk about all these things to someone and he listened attentively, wondering what it must feel like to lose all one's family in one blow. He had lost his father and mother only one year apart and as a result had inherited Rosebae as the only son. For him it had been a loss in slow motion, as they had both been very senior citizens. He was considered very much an answer to a constant prayer. He was born when his mother was forty two years old, so he had been the child who was doted on, though he had never been arrogant or used this privileged role of being the only son. He had, like the others in their group, just fitted in and had fun.

They found themselves in the living room and Rose spun slowly around and looked at Simon. 'It may well be my grandparents' house and then Joyce and Samuel's, but it's really awful, isn't it?' She asked this in an odd way that left Simon in a dilemma as to how to answer.

'I'm sure,' he said, 'with good decoration you can do wonders.'

'I'm not so sure,' she said, slowly looking about.

A splendid afternoon tea was laid out by Terry and they all decided that champagne was better than tea, as they tucked into Lenny's delicious sweets.

'What do you and Thomas plan to do with Killpara?' asked Terry in a direct way, topping up the glasses.

'Strangely, we haven't spoken about it but as we have annexed the property at the side of Killpara it will allow for much greater development and on that subject I must sit down with you two and talk about it.

'Not with me,' laughed Terry. Simon is the expert.'

'I don't know about expert but if my development here at Rosebae works out, next year I want to employ a full-time share farmer to do the bulk of the work, which will leave me free to look at other ventures.'

Rose sighed. 'It's important to make these properties produce as much as possible. I shall have to study the books but I have this feeling Killpara is not producing as it should. Oh, by the way, 'she went on, 'do you by chance know Thelma Smith?'

Terry answered, 'She is Barry Houghton's aunt and a bit of a dragon. I have met her a few times, a very determined woman. You know when her husband died she bought overalls and a Jeep, drove out to the sawmill she had inherited and worked to develop Smith's Mills as the largest timber company in this zone. She built it up from virtually nothing. I don't believe she is known for pity.' He laughed. 'Barry is having a hell of a time as Thelma's henchwoman, a certain Mrs Talbot, controls him completely.'

'She sounds like a woman without many scruples,' Rose commented.

'The two sisters were like chalk and cheese,' Terry told her. 'Emily was like Barry, very pretentious and grand, whereas Thelma is a very, very rough diamond. She is very aggressive and competitive, so with you having snatched the big farm that she wanted, I would imagine she is not the happiest of women.'

Rose drove back to the hotel with many thoughts rushing around but she was unable to concentrate on any one, though Terry was correct. Thelma was black with rage when the farmer called and told her that the first option was legal and that he was selling the property on Monday morning to Thomas O'Riely. Thwarted in the purchase made the meeting she had with Barry in the afternoon extraordinarily uncomfortable for him. She demanded all the legal documents, a copy of the title to everything and to her annoyance Barry confessed he hadn't any idea where his mother had kept them. This only annoyed Thelma even more. Why the hell did the O'Rielys take out an option on the big farm? They have big holdings themselves, she mused, and why was the legal document signed and dated? Surely as next door neighbours and friends that shouldn't have been necessary. And then some tiny thought came into the back of her mind: Joyce's sister – that's who is in the middle of it all.

Rose was met at the door by the waiter and she handed him the basket that had held a very generous afternoon tea. Then she walked through to the second room with the glass wall looking out onto the fountain, which was refracting light from the splashes of water and rain over the pavement. The effect, with soft lighting, was very romantic, as it was now six o'clock and dark. She saw Joseph and Thomas sitting together and joined them with a large roll of paper under one arm. They stood up as she approached and came forward to kiss her.

'What have you got under your arm?' Thomas asked with a frown.

'All Samuel's survey maps of the area around Killpara. I took it from his office. We shall have to sit down and have a good look at them. I have been talking to Simon this afternoon and I think we need to overhaul Killpara completely.' It had been left to Thomas but he had shown no great interest in it and so Rose had taken it upon herself to take over. He had nothing against her taking control: for the last seventeen years she had organised his life and now his parents and sister were gone she became, for Thomas, an even more important part of his existence.

'Joseph,' she asked, as a waiter brought her a glass of champagne, 'what do you think of Killpara?'

Thomas took a deep breath. He was not sure exactly where this conversation was leading.

'I have only been there a few times but I like it.' He put his hand on Rose's and smiled. 'But I think the house in Albany Road is a million times better than the house at Killpara.'

'Rose smiled and Thomas knew instantly that Joseph had given Rose the response she wanted. 'Well,' she said, slowly turning her head toward Thomas, 'it appears that we must do something radical with the house. We have a town house and now I think the three of us need a comfortable country home. What do you think?' She smiled, anticipating the response.

'Rose, you can do whatever you like with Killpara and I really do agree – the house is small and not very outstanding, so anything you wish to do to make it better is fine with us.' Rose noted the 'us' and they all lifted their glasses and touched them together. 'To Killpara,' they chorused.

Both women would have been horrified if someone had suggested that Thelma and Rose were similar types and yet there were similarities. Both women never made a move financially unless they were absolutely sure of success. Rose never purchased a fine painting or a piece of furniture without doing her research first. She was never to be pushed into a purchase just because someone tried to insist. Thelma was the same. Their personal activities were totally different, but at this particular moment in time both women had an identical plan in their minds to enlarge and diversify their properties and neither was going to give an inch to anyone. Thelma had seen how swiftly the big farm between them had been annexed to Killpara and she was damned sure nothing like this was going to happen again. But the one great difference between them was the nephews: Rose had Thomas, a financier and investor, someone who supported her in everything she did, as well as being her greatest friend. Thelma on the other hand was thwarted at every turn by Barry, who undermined her if he could. He made no effort at all to help her and she, basically, aunt or no aunt, loathed him.

Over dinner, it was decided that they would all return to Melbourne the next day as it was now a week they had been there and business in town called. The following morning Thomas packed and then took Rose's car with Joseph to collect his things at Mary's. Rose took this opportunity to go to Enid to thank her for her support and kindness, as well as the excellent service for the week. She then asked for the account. Enid smiled.

'There isn't one. It's been great having you stay.'

Rose was quite taken aback and genuinely surprised. 'Enid, this is just far too generous. I must insist.'

'Insist all you like,' she replied. 'If I were in a situation like this, you mean you wouldn't show me support?'

'You know I would,' Rose said quietly.

"You see,' Enid went on, 'when I was at school, it wasn't easy for me but the group always came to my rescue socially and financially. At last I am able to pay back a little of what Thomas and the others gave me. So please don't take this away from me.'

Rose leaned forward and held her hand. 'I shall never forget your great kindness and thank you so very much, but I think in the future you will be seeing a great deal more of us as we develop Killpara. And you must promise, when we are in order, that you will leave the hotel for a lunch or dinner with us at Killpara.' Enid promised her.

Back in Melbourne, Rose found she had Joseph for a companion, as Thomas had returned to the office. They continued their same routine of auctions, galleries and restaurants, so time was not dull. One afternoon she spread out on the dining room table the large surveyor's charts she had brought back from Killpara and with Joseph she studied exactly what land they held and the possibility of gaining more. This was now a more urgent task as she was well aware that the woman she had never met, Thelma, was probably doing the same thing. They noticed that a parcel of unimproved land that touched the extreme corner of the property they had just bought, which could be used or developed as a passageway to several properties behind. Rose immediately phoned the real estate dealer she knew at Walvern and they waited for his reply.

'The house,' she lamented to Joseph, 'is so inadequate for us. I suppose we shall have to build something sympathetic on the side of it.' When he asked why, she went on, 'Well, for one thing, there is only one bathroom and the whole house is so disjointed.'

'The answer's easy,' he said, nonchalantly.

'Really?' She lifted her head and gazed directly at him.

'Of course. We simply buy a big house of the same style and join it on.'

Rose continued looking at him but not a word did she utter and Joseph began to feel awkward. Then, with slightly narrowed eyes, she said, 'Exactly, Joseph. That is exactly what we shall do, buy a big house and join it on. Of course. What a brilliant idea!'

When Thomas arrived home from work, he saw both Rose and Joseph scanning real estate on the internet to find just the right house 'for removal', but it appeared nothing was what they wanted. It was only after dinner and lots of discussion that Joseph returned to the computer.

'Would you like to live at Killpara?' Rose asked Thomas.

'I've never thought about it,' he replied, 'but why not share Albany Road with Killpara, half the week here and half the week at Aspel? What do you think?'

'It sounds find to me,' Rose said and began to speak about acquiring property. She was abruptly interrupted.

'I've found it, I've found it!' yelled Joseph from the other room. 'Come and have a look. It's just right. It's enormous.'

Rose and Thomas stood up and went to where he was searching on his computer.

'Look,' he cried, 'what do you think?'

Rose and Thomas stood either side of him and glanced at the screen. It was a structure similar but not exactly the same as Killpara but it wasn't a house, it was an old de-licensed hotel. It offered twelve bedrooms, five bathrooms, two dining rooms, a bar and various other spaces. 'In fair condition' read the bottom line.

'How much is it?' asked Rose, as Thomas asked, 'Where is it?'

'The price, 'replied Joseph, proudly, reading from the screen, 'is fifteen thousand dollars on removal.'

'But that's nothing,' said Thomas, running his hand around Joseph's neck. 'And where is it?'

Joseph mentioned the name of a sparsely populated area. 'Where's that?' asked Rose.

'Near Smith's Saw Mill,' came the reply.

'Oh!' and Rose once again saw that it appeared she and Thelma were crossing paths.

'Let's think about it and we shall decide over breakfast.' Thomas knew he did not have to work the next day; for that matter he did not have to work at all as the business worked perfectly if he was present or not, so there really was no problem.

It was a very excited Joseph, next morning, who waited for the judgement on his find. No one said anything for a few moments but it was obvious to Rose that he had probably not spoken of anything else since he went to bed with Thomas. 'Let's have a look at it today,' she suggested, casually, 'and then we can make the decision together.'

They left at a quarter to ten and by mid-day arrived, having first telephoned for an inspection. An indifferent woman of about thirty five showed them about without any enthusiasm at all. Rose thought perhaps she had shown hundreds of people through and was just bored with the routine, but on enquiry, Sandra, brushing back an amazing coloured mane of burgundy hair and with no make-up said, 'No one wants it. It's too big and in shit condition.'

Rose admired her truthfulness if not her use of expletives, but Sandra was right. It was in terrible condition. It would need a new roof to start with and heaven only knows, thought Rose, what the floor bearers are like, but she felt good in this large space and could mentally see it attached to the side of the old house at Killpara.

'All we need now,' said Thomas with a smile and a hand on Joseph's shoulder, 'is a tower.'

'Not so difficult,' said Rose, and walked back through the building. Many of the windows were broken and the smell of damp was pervasive. All that rain and a leaking roof, she thought. The lino covering the floors was torn and worn; the drab colours and the forlorn spaces without furniture left it just empty, but the building had the advantage of high ceilings right throughout. There was no skillion roofing at all.

'Are you interested or not?' asked a blunt Sandra, who was obviously feeling the cold. 'I can't stay here all day.'

'Who do we speak to about purchasing the building?' Thomas asked, as Rose and Joseph instantly turned their heads and look at him. 'We'll take it,' he said, in a determined and authoritative way. 'I don't suppose you know anyone who moves this type of residence?'

'Sure. My brother-in-law, stupid as a monkey, but he just happens to be an expert in this work. Just a tick. I'll rush next door and get his card.' She disappeared.

Joseph spontaneously seized Thomas and held him in his arms and began to dance with him, humming a jaunty tune. Rose laughed. Well, she thought, this, attached to Killpara with a tower, should give Thelma a run for her money, especially as Houghton Hall is not in such good condition.

When Thelma found out that Thomas had purchased the old hotel a quarter of a mile from her sawmill, she was irate. It was not that she wanted the old run-down hotel, but it was like the farm; it seemed that Thomas and Rose, as she had now found out her name, were making things very difficult for her and she was anything but pleased. She was not a snob, but it helped that Houghton Hall was the largest house in the district. She knew very well when she found out where the old hotel was destined for that Houghton Hall being the biggest in the district was going to be a thing of the past and she did not like it at all.

As they were only thirty five minutes from Walvern, Thomas telephoned Enid and said could they possibly have a table for three as they were celebrating purchasing a hotel. Enid was to say the least surprised that Thomas had thought to go into opposition against her and was rather brittle in giving the OK for the booking.

'You two go on,' suggested Rose. 'I want to see the real estate agent and will be back in fifteen minutes.' She disappeared.

'Good afternoon,' the receptionist said to her when she arrived.

'I'm here to see Jerry Taylor, but I'm afraid I don't have an appointment.'

'Not a problem,' the receptionist smiled and Rose was shown into his office.

'Hi!' he said, in a jaunty way, 'I haven't forgotten you, but I have been snowed under with work.'

'Do you have time to search the title and owner of the property I am interested in?'

'Yes, of course, and they are willing to sell it at this price.'

Rose took a deep breath. 'I'll take it. Do let me sign a sale note. I am in a bit of a hurry. You know my solicitor – he will handle everything and I think thirty days would be fine.' She signed the sale note, put a copy in her handbag and made for the Oriental, just down the street. As she hurried down, another woman, dressed in smart slacks and cashmere jumper with a heavy navy blue overcoat bumped into her.

'Sorry!' said the woman. 'It's been one of those days,' and disappeared in the direction of Jerry Taylor's Real Estate Agency.

And it had indeed been a day for Thelma. First she had found out Barry had used all the money in his credit account and had asked for more. He worked out that if he had to suffer Mrs Talbot and Aunt Thelma someone was going to pay, literally. Then when she had gone to the Council Offices for a copy of a surveyor's map of the district around Houghton Hall, she had been thwarted again. The plan she had ordered had turned out to be of another district, not what she had wanted at all. A sharp use of expletives persuaded the Council Surveyor that at the beginning of the following week they would have a copy ready for her. She had stormed out of the offices, slamming the glass door behind her and then a thought crossed her mind. Jerry Taylor must have a copy. She would borrow it or photocopy it in sections. Hm, the early bird gets the worm, thought Thelma, and made no real introduction but demanded a copy of the surveyor's plans for her district. The receptionist called Jerry.

'Hi, Thelma, how's it going?' he asked.

'It's not. Can you make me a photocopy of the land around Houghton Hall?'

'Sure, but it will be a bit small.'

'I'll see if I can enlarge it on the machine,' added the receptionist and took the sheet from the plan press. After some discussion they found the part Thelma was seeking. When it had been photocopied in four sections and taped together, she spread it out on the table.

'Listen, Jerry, what's this big section of land at the back of the Hall that seems to touch some undeveloped land? Just here – look!'

'That undeveloped land is part of Killpara.'

'Really?' She reacted sharply to the information.

'And the much larger piece of land you're looking at here – 'but she interrupted him with, 'Is it for sale?'

'Sorry, Thelma, I sold it this morning. There are one thousand and fifty two hectares. It's a big piece of land.'

'Who bought it?' she demanded and when told she snatched the photocopy and made for the door without any goodbye or thanks. The slamming of the door made it quite clear to Jerry and his receptionist that she was anything but pleased.

Enid had welcomed Thomas and Joseph rather formally, and Thomas was very aware of it. Joseph was so excited he didn't notice. 'We bought a hotel. Isn't that great?'

Enid's sharp face looked back at him. 'Wonderful,' she muttered, blankly.

'We are going to move it and join it on to Killpara to make a really large home.'

'What?' she cried. 'Run that past me again.'

Thomas interrupted a very joyful Joseph to explain what they had just done. Enid put her arms around each of them and gave them a kiss. 'I thought for a moment that you were going into opposition against me.'

'Enid,' said Thomas, firmly, 'to go into opposition against you would mean instant death!'

'You'd better believe it!' She smiled as she showed them to their table where a complementary bottle of champagne was sent in by a most relieved Enid.

Rose joined them and was shown to the table by the same young man that had looked after her for a week there. She thanked him and he smiled back. It hadn't been possible to pay for the week's accommodation but the waiter was most grateful for the generous tip Rose had given him.

'Well,' she began, smiling as the waiter brought her a glass and filled it. 'Let's drink to a new house and an extra one thousand and fifty two hectares.'

Thomas and Joseph just looked at one another. 'What! One thousand and fifty two hectares?'

'Oh, didn't I tell you? I bought it this morning. I must get on to Simon for some good advice about making it work.'

'Well, it has been a busy day,' said Thomas.

'Joseph,' Rose interjected, 'I hope you realise that you will have to take over a great deal of the administration of Killpara now, and obviously a wage will be paid into your account. It's going to mean commuting between Walvern and Melbourne, though it's only an hour and a half away, so I don't see any problems, do you?'

He glanced at her and a smile lit up his whole face. 'No,' he said, 'I don't see any problems.' Money had been a problem for Joseph. He worked with Jan restoring frames and furniture but it was Mary who paid into a credit card fund for him, so he had money to keep up with the others. This wasn't now necessary as Rose and Thomas paid for everything. It had been a problem neither Rose nor Thomas were able to resolve until now, as simply to hand Joseph money all the time was not very dignified and he always felt embarrassed, as he confessed to Thomas when alone: he didn't have money but didn't want hand-outs all the time. Now, with this new project about to begin, he was to be employed as an administrator for the work and the time he put into re-establishing Killpara. He would be paid like anybody else.

'I shall send a friend of mine, an architect, down next week to decide on the best way of joining the houses –'

'– and the tower!' teased Thomas.

'Oh, I'm sure Joseph will find one on the internet or we shall just have to have one copied. Thomas just laughed, saying, 'Of course.'

The next week in Melbourne was frenetic, with the architect, Rose and Joseph going over detail after detail until all the ground plans were thrashed out. Rose had also had some stocks cashed in to pay for the new properties and kept a certain amount back as she knew very well that this new Killpara was going to cost a great deal more than Thomas or Joseph realised. She also contacted Roaul to say that her garden in Albany Road, even thought it was winter, looked splendid and then introduced him to the idea of developing gardens at Killpara.

'Anything, Rose. Not a problem. We shall turn out a little Versailles!'

That's exactly what I want,' she laughed. 'Listen, could you and Andrew make it for dinner on Thursday evening? I need to talk to him about a great deal of furniture I'm going to be needing.'

'Rose,' he answered, 'we should love to join you. Andrew is dying with curiosity to meet Joseph. Men are all the same.' He laughed. 'We'll see you at 7.20 on Thursday.

It had been some time since Rose and Thomas had seen Roaul and Andrew and she was looking forward to it. But the thing that surprised her as she was dressing for the occasion was the fact that, with the purchasing of land and the hotel, all of this re-building or re-defining Killpara had to a certain extent deadened the effect of the terrible accident. It was as if the death of her sister, brother-in-law and niece was like a phoenix: it had to be destroyed in order to be re-born and in an odd way Killpara was determining her life as well as Thomas's and Joseph's for the future.

'Rose, you look divine – as usual!' cried Andrew as she swept down the staircase to meet the boys being shown in by the maid.

'Thank you, darling.' She kissed them both, accepting a large bunch of hothouse flowers which she handed to the maid and bade them take a drink in the drawing room.

'I'm so sorry I sold you that fabulous credenza, said Andrew with a smile. 'I could retire on it now.' They all laughed. It was to this laughter that Thomas entered with Joseph, who was a little nervous at meeting new people.

'Thomas, I hate you!' Andrew greeted him, giving him a kiss, then the same to Joseph, who was not sure what to do, so he wisely did nothing.

'I'm Roaul.' He shook hands with Joseph but did not miss the opportunity to kiss the man he adored. 'And how are you, Thomas?'

'I'm fine, thanks.'

They sat down, drinking and talking, with Joseph just listening. He didn't say a lot but just watched the dynamics of the conversation and it didn't take him long to work out that Roaul thought a great deal more of Thomas than just as a friend.

'How many rooms?' Andrew asked.

'With both houses together, twenty, I should think,' Rose replied.

'Well, you might just be in luck. The Ashfield House is going to be sold. I heard it on the grapevine the other day, so I phoned Anthea Ashfield to find out what was happening. She wouldn't tell me anything but I invited myself around for a drink.'

'As you do,' Roaul chipped in and received a sharp glance from Andrew.

'Well, it turns out that Anthea's husband, the ever attractive Timothy, has made some shocking investments plus a lot of fooling about on the horses and they are in hot water financially. They have a big apartment of her aunt's in Lansell Road but they are going to sell the house and contents. They don't want anything made public, so we just might be able to work something out. There are some beautiful pieces of furniture in the house – I should know since I sold Anthea's mother quite a deal of it, but I haven't any idea of what she's going to ask, price-wise. She's not a fool with money, it's just hubby.' They all laughed.

Rose had quite a bit of furniture in storage but it obviously wasn't sufficient to fill a twenty room house, so this idea of purchasing a large lot was more than interesting. Rose had known Anthea's mother but not well: she found Anthea insufferable, pretentious and extremely vain, so their paths rarely crossed and when they did the reaction was frosty.

'Well, what sort of garden is there at Killpara?' Roaul asked.

'None,' was Thomas's instant reply. 'To one side of the house is a drive, so called, which everyone uses and to the other side is a huge disused orchard where this old hotel will be situated, but not much else. There is a hedge on the far side of the orchard and a matching one down the side of the drive and a few random trees. That's it! I'm afraid my mother was not a gardener.'

'Aren't there any architectural features?'

'No, none at all.'

'We have a large Victorian cast-iron bird cage that just been restored but it's in pieces,' Joseph joined in quietly.' Roaul noticed, as did Andrew, the 'we'.

'Fantastic,' Roaul went on. 'At least we have a starting point and you obviously have space for a pool as well.'

Joseph's face lit up, a pool just for him and Thomas. Wow, he thought, and Rose immediately picked up his enthusiastic smile.

'Of course,' she said, 'we must have a pool. I am going to move the share-farmer and his family to the house on the property we have purchased between Houghton Hall and Killpara as all the sheds and equipment are much more up-to-date and if you,' she went on, looking at Roaul,' can use or re-develop any of the original buildings at Killpara, fine. If you can't, then we shall have them all demolished, except for the old stable block that I think we should keep.'

'I'll have a look at the place first and then we can all decide what we are doing and what we need.'

'Well, in less than thirty days we take possession of the property and then we can begin but the big hotel will be in position long before that, I hope. Now, come on, let's eat.' They all followed her into the dining room, chatting about the new house.

'Make sure you have a large entrance hall,' Andrew said. 'I know just where to find the most fabulous console and mirror. It's enormous. For that reason it's sure to be a good price. Are the ceilings high?' Joseph, joining the conversation, said that they were and that the rooms were quite large, and that there was a very generous hallway.

'Sounds fabulous,' Andrew commented, directing his attention onto Joseph. 'Do you know the people who own Houghton Hall?' Joseph said he didn't and Rose added that none of them did. 'In fact I have never been in the house, but I do remember Patricia told me that she once took some books to Emily Houghton when she was ill and she said it was extremely run down. But Emily's sister, Thelma, has apparently inherited it and I hear on the grapevine she is going to restore it.'

'Well in that case we shall really have to lay out a splendid garden,' laughed Raoul. 'Killpara must end up being the best on the block.' Rose agreed, still wondering who and what this Thelma was. Little did she know the woman who had humped into her after her purchase of the extra property in Walvern was in fact Thelma. They had been ships that had passed in the night.

'Where did the birdcage come from?' asked Raoul.

'Houghton Hall.' Thomas related the story which had everyone laughing at the prospect of Barry being whipped naked at the local cenotaph.

'So Houghton Hall must once have had a big Edwardian garden?' asked Raoul.

'I've no idea. We have the birdcage but if I remember correctly Patricia said it had to be hauled out of bushes and nettles, so I presume the garden is non-existent?'

'It's such a pity,' said Roaul, in a very serious way, running his hand through his bushy hair. 'Gardens are the most fragile form of architecture in the world. In only a short time they can disappear.'

'Well, that's not the case at Killpara, as there was and is nothing to disappear!' They all laughed.

'What sort of garden would you like?' he asked, directing the question to Joseph.

'Oh, that's easy. The same as the garden here at Albany Road. It's very beautiful.'

Roaul smiled and accepted the compliment from the very handsome twenty three year-old who just happened to be Thomas's lover.

Joseph did in fact take over the administration just as Rose intended he should. If he had a problem, he telephoned her at once, otherwise he made the decisions, gathered what documents were required from the Council for the old hotel, solicitors for transfer of properties and generally went as go-between for the share-farmer, whose wife, Paul, when told they would be moving to the other property was elated, leaving the dingy cottage behind her. It was, as she said to Joseph, 'fabulous – this place is no better than a small stable'. Joseph did make one telephone call to Thomas, which had him gritting his teeth, when he said he was more than happy to work with Rose's friend, the architect. Thomas felt it might be a good idea if he kept his hands on the plans and off Joseph's body. He repeated this to Rose the same evening and she made a telephone call. Whatever was said, Joseph had no more problems with a new, very formally behaved architect.

The hotel came in four sections over a three day period. The stumps were put in and a group of carpenters was ready to replace rotten beams, and so the building began to fit together little by little. After three days of yelling and shouting, the huge architectural mass fitted in neatly beside the old house, giving the effect of a giant derelict house, due to the different paint colours, although most of the bright blue had washed or worn off the hotel over a fifty year period.

The first task after setting the foundations in order was to tackle the roof and in this period this was not the easiest of work due to the rain and wind, but as so much rain had already poured in a bit more, Joseph reckoned, could not do any more harm. When they joined Joseph that weekned, they were very surprised at the size of the structure and its sad condition. Even Rose was starting to have second thoughts about the wisdom of installing it in what was once the orchard, but Joseph was elated. In his mind he saw it finished and every little thing the builders did was a step closer to making this image a reality. Thomas was not quite so enthusiastic, but with Joseph's arm around his shoulder in this ever drizzling rain he was prepared to secede everything to Joseph's dream.

Joseph had had a great deal of trouble finding a tower from a demolished house; in fact there was nothing available and so the architect drew up a small tower to be placed at the intersection of the old and newly arrived hotel. Joseph personally thought it a bit miserable but said nothing.

A few weeks later, one of the builders, a middle-aged man who constantly made jokes, was talking to Joseph, who confided that he didn't like the tower design.

'Oh, see if you can get Ted Wally to sell you his.'

'Who is Ted Wally?' Joseph asked.

'He lives about fifteen miles from here. He collects old and antique cars. He's got one.'

Joseph was surprised and asked whether it was attached to a building, but was told it was behind the huge tin shed where the man kept his cars. 'He's a bit cranky but go and see him. You'll find his address in the telephone book. Oh,' he went on, as Joseph started to hurry away and seek the address, 'don't tell him what you want. Just tell him you are interested in old cars. After half a dozen bottles of beer you should be able to begin negotiating. Joseph thanked him and rushed into the original part of the house in search of a telephone directory.

When he spoke on the phone, the first response was, 'Wadda you want?'

'Would it be possible to see your collection of cars?' asked Joseph.

'Anything's possible. When?'

'Why not this afternoon?'

'Why not?' and the line went dead.

Joseph was very excited about the tower, but what sort of tower would it be and how did a man who collects old cars end up with it, he wondered. He telephoned Rose to say that he was going to see a tower or the top part of one and asked what the budget on this aspect was. Rose said she honestly had no idea.

'Get a price, Joseph, and we will go from there.'

The rain had finally stopped and the hammering of new corrugated iron onto the new section of the house could be heard echoing right across the valley. Thelma, on one of her regular visits to Houghton Hall, stopped her jeep and just stared at the vast mass that was to become the new Killpara when it was finished.

'God!' she exclaimed aloud. 'It's like a bloody health resort!' She couldn't believe that that rundown blue-coloured old hotel was now snuggly attached to Killpara. This Rose has got big ideas, she thought, planting her foot on the accelerator and speeding onward to her destination and a very worried Barry, due to his over-spending yet again and on what was likely to be Thelma's attack.

'Anyone here?' shouted Joseph, as he rounded the large corrugated iron shed to find that there was another even larger one behind. A dog came around the corner, barking, but instantly recognised that Joseph was no thief and was quite happy to have Joseph pat and scratch his head.

'You make friends easily,' came a voice from behind him. He spun around and said 'Hi!'

'Toddy usually bites. I guess that makes you OK.'

Joseph said thank you a little nervously. 'Here, this is for you.' He handed Ted Wally a box of a dozen bottles of beer, to the response of, 'Nice of you. I'll show you around.' He took Joseph into the first shed, with Toddy following close behind.

'Good heavens,' Joseph exclaimed, 'I have never seen so many old cars. That one is fabulous.' He was walking toward a 1924 Austin, a huge rectangular structure in faded burgundy, with room in the back seating area for a party. 'Hey, this is the original stretch limousine.

'Yeah, they had style then.' And so the tour continued, with Joseph genuinely forgetting why he had come. Ted explained simply what these cars were and how he had come to acquire them, generally for nothing, just the cost of transporting them but as he said they were now as rare as hen's teeth. The second shed was large, with even more of these cars jammed in side by side, but this shed held more recent giants of the road, a huge Ford Galaxy, Fairlanes, all looking as if a good re-decoration would be in order. Joseph marvelled at the length of these cars and wondered about the problems of parking them.

'There's a couple out the back here,' said Ted. 'I've gotta get a guy with a tow truck to drag 'em in here,' at which they went out to see Ted's latest acquisitions. And there it was, sitting in tall grass, with about twenty wooden planks leaning against it. Toddy leapt forward, barking at a cat that was taking advantage of the few rays of sunshine after days of drizzling rain. It fled, with Toddy in hot pursuit.

'Where did this come from?' asked Joseph in amazement.

'Well,' Ted rolled down the sleeves of a very grubby dark blue track suit top, 'the bastards were going to chop it up for scrap. You see, it's a metal sub-structure.'

Joseph turned and looked at Ted. 'Sub-structure' seemed a very big word for Ted's vocabulary. 'It's the top of the tower of the old Post office in Walvern. No one wanted it, so I took it for twenty dollars or so, years ago. You can see the big circle under the top part that once held a giant clock but the rat bags dropped the mechanism form where it was attached and it smashed to pieces, not to mention the mayor's new car as well.' He roared, laughing. 'The bastard had the flattest car in Walvern.' He continued laughing. 'Serves him right for having the old Post Office demolished. I can't stand people,' he went on in a determined way, 'who want to destroy the past. They are all fucking vandals and yet they think they are so bloody smart.' Toddy returned for Joseph to pat him as a reward for removing a startled cat.

'Mr Wally –'

'Ted's the name.'

'Ted, would you sell me this tower top? I'll tell you why,' and he went on to say how they had saved the old hotel and were going to restore it.

'Nice idea, Joe. I like it,' though he made no commitment. They both looked at this tower top.

It was indeed on a metal substructure. The top section was from a square base swept up to a smaller square at the top. The sides were in slates and were swollen out so it had a very rhythmic look to it. The small square where this terminated at the top had a decorative cast iron gallery around, about eighty centimetres high and in the centre were the remains of a flag pole. Under the roofing section was an empty metal structure which, as Ted had said, had held the Post Office clock but it was now open on all sides, just metal poles supporting the decorative tower top. Ted rubbed his hand across his mouth.

'You know, Joe, you're not like the other young arseholes around here. Toddy would have a piece of 'em in a flash'. He laughed. 'Yes, why not? I'll never use it and you're an OK guy. Since you've given me the beer, the price is twenty four big cans of the best dog food for Toddy. How does that sound?'

'Sounds great to me,' replied Joseph. 'Shall I go and get them now?' He wanted to conclude the deal at once.

'OK, and when you get back, Joe, I'll give you the name of a guy that will move it for you.'

Joseph shook hands as he thought that was the way to do business and there was most certainly not going to be a receipt given here.

When he returned to Toddy's barking and his enthusiastic jumping all over Joseph, Ted said,' Strange. Toddy usually hates other people, especially young people.'

The two large boxes of dog food were deposited on Ted's veranda, which was covered with every sort of engine part imaginable. Joseph also put down another box of beer and returned to the car with Toddy leaping and barking at him. He unwrapped a paper and a large steak was quickly snatched, Toddy rushing off to devour the most delicious meal he had ever eaten.

'He was abandoned, was Toddy,' Ted told him. 'Some arsehole pitched him out of a car and drove off. We found him. He was skin and bone. I took him to the vet and he's recovered, the poor bastard. But I tell you if I get hold of the person that abandoned him to starve, I'll wrap a fucking monkey wrench around his neck.'

'And I'm sure he'll deserve it,' Joseph said, aware of Ted becoming very angry. 'Thanks again.' He took the sheet of paper with the name on it.

'Listen, Joe, leave me your address and I'll phone the guy. I know him real good. He'll give me a much better price.'

Joseph thanked him and left Killpara's address and his cellular phone number. As he drove back, for the first time, he realised that he was in complete control of his life.

* * * *

As predicted, Trevor became tired of John, not to mention the hysterical wife who was originally part of the entertainment, so he drifted back to the group. He saw Mary every day and she could see the inevitable happening, not that she thought the termination of this relationship was a bad thing. When Joseph was at Walvern, Trevor was once more in his company. Joseph's self-confidence was now so secure, due to Thomas, that he just accepted compliments from Trevor and Simon, leaving it at that. Not that he minded the attention at all. He did not tell anyone about the tower, deciding that it would be better as a surprise. He was still a Killpara on Friday morning when a truck with an attached crane arrived and deposited the tower quite a way from its final destination, due to the fact that the ground around the house was now like a quagmire and coarse gravel would have to be brought in to stop the trucks bogging down. The effect was like a battlefield, mud and gravel everywhere. If there had in the past been a semblance of order and a little bit of a garden, it was a thing of the past. The share-farmer and his wife complained bitterly about the mud everywhere as did the driver of the milk tanker.

Thomas left Melbourne early as Rose had developed a cold and felt miserable, so he came alone. He drove to Mary's house, expecting Joseph, but a telephone call alerted him to the information that Joseph was waiting for him at Killpara. Thomas deposited his bag and a box of documents which Joseph needed to copy and drove out to Killpara. As he passed Rosebae he stopped as he saw Simon collecting a parcel from the letterbox.

'Hi, how's the building going?' he asked with a smile.

'I'm just off to check,' Simon laughed. 'I believe we are seeing you tomorrow night for dinner at Mary's?'

'Great! Trevor's back on the scene – it appears he's become bored with love yet again.'

'Poor love!' Thomas laughed. 'Call in for a drink on your way back, if it's not too late.'

'Thanks. I don't expect to be too long at all. Bye!' Thomas drove on. As he arrived at the crossroads and turned right onto the asphalted road, he saw to his surprise this vast but dilapidated structure and on one extreme side a proud tower top. He drove in and pulled up, well away from the mud. Joseph came over and gave him a hug.

'Joseph,' said a startled Thomas, 'where on earth did you find this tower? It's immense. Don't you think it's a bit big?'

'Not at all,' countered a confident Joseph, with a smile. 'Do you like it?'

'Well, yes, it's fantastic but where did it come from?' And he simultaneously wondered how much it had cost.

'Come and have a look at the progress and I will tell you the story.' As they walked through the building by themselves, the workers having finished early it being Friday night, Thomas put his arm around Joseph's shoulders. As they went from room to room, he saw the smaller ones were in the process of being knocked into larger ones and were in sections. The walls did not exist, just the studs where there had once been some covering. The re-organisation of the space, now as one big house, was excellent, Thomas thought, perhaps a bit formal for the country but he was sure that with Rose's hand and the advice of her many decorator friends it would all pull together.

'What?' he exclaimed. 'Two large cartons of dog food! I don't believe it!'

Joseph went on to explain his adventure with Ted the previous Monday, which had culminated in the tower's being delivered that morning.

'How much did you have to pay for delivery?' Thomas asked.

'Well, that I don't know.'

'What do you mean?' asked Thomas, curiously.

'Well, when I asked the delivery chap how much did I owe him, he said that Ted and Toddy had sorted it out so there was no charge.'

'You really are the smartest guy around,' Thomas said. 'You must have really impressed Ted.'

'Do you know him?'

'No, not at all. But come on. You follow me and we'll have a drink with Simon and Terry, then go on to Walvern.'

Joseph followed him to the car, then to Rosebae. They entered into a warm living room. Even though it was officially spring, it was still cold, especially in the late afternoon.

'Take your coats off and sit down,' ordered Terry and a late afternoon drink with wine and an assortment of delicious small goodies straight from the oven made the cold outside forgettable.

'Oh, but I do know Ted Wally,' cried Terry, after Joseph had related his story. 'I can't believe that either he or the dog didn't eat you alive. He's a monster.' He went on to describe several nasty incidents that had occurred to people who had strayed onto Ted's property.

'He was very nice to me. He gave me a tour of all his cars – some of the early ones are fantastic.'

Terry, who sat opposite him, had his mouth open. 'No one, and I mean no one, has ever seen the collection – ever. And you bowl up, see the collection and get a tower as well. I just can't believe it. And that crazy dog!'

'Toddy and I got along really well.'

'I have never heard anything like it,' said a flabbergasted Terry. 'Your charm has won his heart!'

'And Toddy's, it seems!' laughed Simon. Joseph just smiled. He was so proud of getting this tower. His sense of achievement was sky high.

The same overjoyed state Joseph was in was not shared by the architect, who was obliged to alter the plans he had designed for the tower extensively, in order to take this extravagant structure Joseph had acquired.

Back at Aspel Drive and safe in Mary's home, Thomas felt a warmth that did not come from the central heating (which was certainly needed). Joseph had fitted into his life and he just couldn't imagine him not being there. This was Thomas's first real love affair and he cherished it very carefully. He could find no fault with Joseph and the

BRIAN PENTLAND

fact that he got along splendidly with Rose cemented this relationship into a positive and loving bond. With the surety of Thomas's love, Joseph, now in charge of the administration of Killpara, changed. He became a much more assertive figure. Whereas in the past he sat back and watched, he now was not shy in putting his opinion forward and expecting it to be heard. With the team of builders working at Killpara and often asking for clarification of certain points, it was to Joseph they turned and he had the instinctive knowledge to respond factfully and so the work went ahead much more rapidly under his direction. The weekend passed very pleasantly, but quickly, and Thomas left Mary's early on Monday morning for Melbourne feeling a real loss that Joseph was not coming with him. Their roles were changing a little. Whereas originally it was Joseph completely dependent on Thomas, now it was Thomas who felt an emptiness when Joseph wasn't by his side.

After Thomas had left and returned to Melbourne, Joseph headed, not to Killpara, but to the scrap metal dealer at the bottom of Churchill Street, near the football ground. He was searching for some decorative finials in cast iron, as the one from the original house at Killpara had long been lost and there was a place for another. He thought that the scrap metal man might have something. He parked his car and walked up a gravel track that was filled with pot holes, hence the huge puddles of brown water and shouted out but no one replied. He began to look around; the confusion in this very large yard was complete. He just didn't know where to begin, besides everything looked like industrial waste, not a decorative thing to be seen. He bent down to look at a piece of metal that might have been of interest only to discover it was of no use to him at all. He heard a crunch on the wet gravel and spun around to see a pair of legs that just seemed to go on forever. He abruptly stood up. The man was indeed tall, two metres at least, thought Joseph and he hurriedly introduced himself.

'Hi!' was the slow response. Jeffrey Anderson was indeed tall. He was two metres and two centimetres in height and as thin as a rake. He had a long narrow face that was topped with a thick mat of greasy hair, dark eyes and a heavy beard-line. In his outfit all in jeans, including trousers, shirt and jacket he looked, Joseph thought, like a rocker from the Fifties who had got it all wrong. Joseph explained what he was searching for and Jeffery Anderson beckoned him to follow to a large corrugated iron shed. He said absolutely nothing, which gave Joseph the impression that he was trespassing. The door swung open and banged against the wall; the interior was gloomy and Jeffery switched on the lights which were old fluorescent tubes hung at different heights all around the interior. It was, Joseph noted, drawing his coat closer to him, freezing in there. Jeffery pointed to a conglomeration of cast iron pieces in a corner and Joseph said, 'Thank you', then he went to have a look, with Jeffery standing rigidly like a totem pole. There was a pair of them, but one was broken, though the piece was there.

'How much are those?' he asked.

'What do you want them for?' was the dull reply and Joseph explained how they were needed.

'Hm,' grunted Jeffery. 'Forty dollars each.'

Joseph drew them out and pointed out that one was broken.

'It's the same,' said an expressionless Jeffery.

'I'll take them,' Joseph replied, quietly and at this moment the telephone rang. Jeffery moved over and picked up the receiver. His entire conversation considered of 'Yes – no – yes – no – yes – no – yes'. Joseph looked about while waiting for the man to finish. It was a wooden crate with the contents in chrome that caught his eye and he began to look through the objects. There they were, several old car mascots underneath old bathroom accessories also in chrome. Joseph began to drag them out and place them on the floor. There were three of them. Jeffery finished his riveting conversation and returned to Joseph.

'How much are these three?' he asked.

'If you take the finials and these, $150 for the lot.'

Joseph stood up and reached into his pocket, handed Jeffery the money but no receipt was offered. Jeffery just stood rigid without any expression on his face as Joseph made two trips to his car with his purchases. It seemed useless to say goodbye as after he had taken the last pieces to the car the shed door slammed shut and Jeffery was seen stalking off to a smaller shed that Joseph thought might serve as an office.

His first stop was a welder, in fact the same welder that had bit by bit restored the aviary that lay in sections in the grass at Killpara, to leave the broken finial for repair. Then he went off to the supermarket and then to Ted Wally. He hadn't remembered the road into Ted's being quite so bad and with the recent rain it was more like large puddles, some of them quite deep, than a roadway. He pulled up near Ted's house with the veranda groaning under the weight of the engines and car parts to see Toddy rushing around the corner and with wet paws jumping and licking him all over, making strange whining sounds. Ted, having heard a car, came out of the house with the screen door banging behind him, and carrying a shot gun under one arm. When he saw who it was he smiled. 'Hey, what brings you here, Joe?'

'I've found something for you. I hope you can use them. Just a minute, Toddy,' as the dog obviously had a very good memory. As he reached into the car and brought out a packet, the dog became hysterical, barking and jumping all over him. He unwrapped a steak and Toddy leapt into the air seizing the piece of meat and then rushed off to a position under the cypresses to devour it. Joseph swung a box of a dozen bottles of beer into the tiny space available that was left on the veranda.

'Here,' he said. 'I'm afraid it's not much, but thanks for organising the delivery of the tower.'

'A pleasure, Joe.' Joseph handed him the car mascots in a plastic supermarket bag. 'Joe, ya didn't have to do this,' he said, opening the bag. 'Fuck, Joe, y're a genius. I've been missing this one for years. Come and have a look.' Joseph followed him into the first shed and a very excited Ted set the mascot onto an old Riley. 'Look, this is probably the original. Fantastic! You're all right, Joe, you really are.'

'So are you,' Joseph replied, quietly.

'Any time y're passing, drop in.'

'I promise,' said Joseph, 'but I must dash now as the welder has promised to have some work finished for me this afternoon.' He shook hands and started back to his car. Toddy, having finished his steak, thought he might just try for another but to no avail, but there were lots of pats and licks, making it quite clear he also would be happy to see Joseph in the future.

Having collected the repaired finial, Joseph headed out to Killpara with his find and with a certain modification the front gable was adorned with a large cast-iron finial at the top. He thought it was not bad at all. The base for the first tower had been demolished and another, much sturdier structure with very imposing foundations, was beginning to rise, but the mud was everywhere. The workmen announced to him that they would take the base of the tower to the point where the part he had acquired from Ted would join, but until there were better weather conditions it would be impossible to bring a crane in to lift it into position because of the wet and slippery ground around the house. So they would finish both sections separately and later join them together. Joseph was a little disappointed but saw their point of view. In this soft, wet soil if the crane slipped with this enormous weight the tower top would be extensively damaged. The part of the tower top that was just metal uprights that had supported the part where the old clock had been was fitted with an arched window. In fact each side had a matching one and the metal disappeared under a covering of weatherboards to match the house. As the month drew on the weather did in fact pick up and the chill winds that blew across the hilltops began to evaporate a great deal of the surface water.

The interior, under the architect's direction, was now organised and a team of plumbers, plasterers and electricians began their tasks. The painters began the business of burning off all the old paint from the old house and newly installed section so it looked from the road even more derelict than before, but the pink undercoat began to unify the two structures as one.

Every Friday evening, Joseph organised, depending on how many men were working, beer after work, which was happily accepted by all. He was extremely popular with the workmen. He never became angry with mistakes, he diplomatically pointed out that they must be corrected and no one took offence. So when Rose came with Thomas after a break of three weeks, she was very pleasantly surprised at the progress on the house but shocked at the surrounding being still rather muddy and covered in gravel.

Thomas was becoming possessive of Joseph. It was a sensation he had never experienced in his whole life and to be four days without him each week had him very edgy by the time Friday evening approached when he could leave and hold him in his arms, his very own Joseph. Rose had always assumed that one day this would happen but she had not thought it would be as intense as this, as she watched Thomas with his arm around Joseph as he gave them a tour of the house. 'In a month's time we should be at a good point,' Joseph said, very professionally, and showed Rose through the new entrance hall that one entered under the incomplete tower, and through a pair of antique sandblasted glass doors that led to one of the sitting rooms, this one being the larger by far. To say Rose was impressed was an understatement. The house was now very grand, with big rooms, long Victorian windows; some marble fireplaces that had been installed and a riot of high Victorian plaster-work was well under way. Rose left the two of them together and very slowly walked about the house. How different, she thought as she opened a door to see an almost completed bathroom, from the time when not so many months ago she walked with Simon through the original part, feeling an emptiness and a loss. Now she felt a positive sensation. This enormous country house was now rising up on its knees and in a few more months it would at last be standing vertical and the thought of happy voices ringing through it cheered her up at once. She moved to the newer part and stepping over builders' materials found her way to what would be her domain, a bedroom, small sitting room, a dressing room and a generous bathroom. She walked around it with the satisfaction that a child has when receiving the birthday present he or she has always wanted. She looked through the window of her eventual sitting room, to see a jumble of builders' equipment and supplies all stacked up on what she desperately hoped was going to be a very gracious lawn or garden, depending on how Roaul saw it. Except for the two gable sections, the verandas now almost completely encircled the house and the decorative cast iron trim was now in some sections in position. It was possible to see the end in sight and Rose dismissed immediately the thought that she had had any doubts about the house not being a great success.

Everything in the house, space-wise, was generous, this being easy as they had so much space to work with and Rose was very pleased and also curious to see the tower when it was to be swung up into position. The painters had finished the top section, as it saved them setting up scaffolding later. As for the whole structure, the roofing was painted grey and the house a pale faded cream with all crisp white trim. But it was to be another month and a half before the major work was to be completed.

This weekend saw a meeting with two strangers that was to have a far-reaching effect on their lives and life-styles. Saturday morning Raoul and Andrew were due at Killpara and would stay at the Oriental as Rose did, whereas Thomas always stayed at Mary's with Joseph. Friday evening was spent at Simon and Terry's for dinner with Rose listening intently to Simon's ideas of redeveloping land and seeing at once that Killpara had to be totally overhauled from top to bottom and that would probably call for an injection of cash, as well as Joseph being trained to handle the project. She had the secure feeling that he was indeed up to the task, in fact he listened very carefully to what Simon was saying and was confident enough not only to ask questions but offer ideas as well. They had begun development on one section of the unimproved land, having a great many of the trees and saplings removed but had left a great many of the old mature trees and long windbreaks of trees obviously to limit the effect of the wind as it swept mercilessly across the tops of the hills but also against soil erosion. The large pastures that were recovered were at present being ploughed and levelled and Joseph was with this experience behind him looking carefully at the division of future fields in the last lot Rose had purchased of one thousand and fifty two hectares. The share-farmer and family, namely Lynette, were delighted with the shift to the house between Killpara and Houghton hall and that now left the small cottage vacant. It was also to play a major role in the future.

Saturday morning saw everyone at Killpara. Even Mary had taken time off to dash out and meet Roaul and Andrew. She stood in awe at the size of this house. She remembered the birthday party of Joyce's and the Killpara as it was then – but now! Raoul was a little daunted by the surroundings and the condition of them, not to mention the topography, a property that sloped from the entrance and just continued to do so all the way past the sheds to the creek at the bottom. Terracing, he thought, there is no other way.

'What an excellent idea,' said Rose.

'I'm afraid it's going to be expensive.'

'Not too expensive, I hope.' She smiled at him.

'It's the hire of the equipment to move the soil to make the level terraces.'

'I think I can find someone who will give us a good price,' interrupted Joseph, confidently gazing at Raoul.

'Well, in that case perhaps we can keep the cost down.' He walked around with Joseph, discussing soil levels and taking photographs. Joseph had supplied him with a topographical surveyor's map that they had photocopied from one of Samuel's maps, and he began to draw pencil lines here and there.

'Where do you think the swimming pool should go?' asked Joseph, grinning.

'What sort of pool would you like?' Raoul asked, knowing full well that whatever he wanted Thomas would insist that he have it.

'I would like it in a private space and not with a bright blue liner, a pool very similar to the one at Albany Road.'

This time it was Raoul's turn to grin. 'I don't think it's possible to make the garden here look exactly like Albany Road but we shall see what we can do.' They walked back toward the house where the others were exploring the inside.

'Oh, Joseph exclaimed, 'I almost forgot the aviary.' He led Raoul to a heap of layered sheets of cast iron that was the aviary. Raoul took out a measuring tape, while Joseph held the other end. 'It's considerably larger than I thought,' Raoul said, running his fingers through his hair. 'It should make a good feature for this garden. Are you going to use it for birds?'

'I believe so. Parrots were what Patricia wanted to breed.'

As they walked back toward the house, Raoul was not unaware of Joseph's attraction, tall, well-built but not heavy and with dancing eyes and a very soft, gentle smile. Joseph had the feeling that Raoul would need no encouragement if he thought of doing something with him.

'Don't tell me!' exclaimed Andrew with a theatrical swish of his arm and looking at Joseph, as he and Roaul joined them. 'You want a large chandelier in the living room.'

'But of course.' Joseph smiled and moved over to Thomas. Andrew, Rose and Thomas had done a tour of the house and Andrew had noted down what spaces there were and what furniture was required. He had been an interior decorator for years but in the last four and a half had just sold antique furniture, claiming he was too old to keep lifting fabric swatch books about. But this big house really interested him and Rose, little by little, began to apply pressure on him to take this project on. 'After all, Andrew, the architect does most of the work.'

'Really?' Andrew feigned shock, which had everyone laughing but he did take the time to go and have a look once again at the major rooms.

'I think we need to use some strong colour here at Killpara and make it as different as possible from Albany Road. You don't want to be moving into identical cocoons.' Rose agreed.

They had now all moved to Mary's for lunch. The conversation was brisk, with Jseph playing the barman and Trevor, who had just arrived, helping Mary in the kitchen.

'Thank God you've arrived,' she said to him in a desperate tone. 'I wasn't sure what to do with the meat but I've followed your instructions. Do have a look, darling.'

Trevor opened the oven door and began basting the roll of pork. 'Perfect, sweetie, just perfect!' He looked at Mary. 'I say, that Roaul is cute!'

'Yes, and his boy friend's nice as well.' She grinned.

'Bitch!' was Trevor's only response, as he carried more crockery to the dining room table.

It was an hysterical lunch, with plenty of wine and good cheer. The meal that was Mary's great pre-occupation had turned out splendidly, thanks, as usual, to Trevor, who took over the conversation with everyone laughing. The topics moved on to Houghton Hall and there were gales of laughter about Barry being tied down and whipped by Mrs Talbot, but although the tied down bit was not true the verbal whipping was.

Barry's life, having lived a life of self-indulgence always, was now unbearable. Thelma held all the money in her hands but if the truth be known Houghton Hall had no cash flow and if Barry was allowed a small spending amount it had everything to do with Thelma's pity and nothing to do with his grandiose ideas of family riches, which simply did not exist. Thelma was finding that organising and making a farm pay was very different from running a large sawmill. At that she was an expert, but property management was another thing. She made the investment and purchased back the land that had originally belonged to the Hall, plus another small farm that adjoined it on the other side and sat down to try to work out how the hell to make this investment pay. Here, she was hindered by Barry's stupidity: instead of helping, he made loud noises about Mother's jewels and Father's estates, which Thelma saw as downright embarrassing and silly. He made no constructive effort at all to help put Houghton hall back together. Thelma was furious and was now genuinely considering giving him a tiny living allowance and pitching him out of the front door. She was just waiting for the moment. Even when she thought Barry had gone just as far with this ridiculous pretentiousness as he could he went one better – or one more stupid. Thelma despaired. 'I can't make money with this lead monkey around my neck,' she said to Mrs Talbot. 'I think I shall have to get rid of him anywhere and as soon as possible,' when she was looking around the house after Mrs Talbot has called her out because the floor boards in the sitting room were now functioning as a trampoline, which to both women suggested the foundations had gone.

'I don't believe it,' Thelma snapped. 'This bloody house is costing me a fortune and now the stumps have given in. It's a white elephant, this place. I don't know why I bother to keep it afloat.' She didn't really see it as an economic advantage, but somewhere in the background, in the hidden recesses of her mind, there was a combative spirit and the other woman, that's to say Rose, was not going to win. This competitive drive kept her ever determined to develop and make Houghton Hall an economic reality. But from the dust of the ploughs and the chain saw noise from the back part of Killpara she knew the other woman that she had never met was challenging her and at this moment winning.

After lunch at Mary's, everyone returned to Killpara for three hours of planning, with Roaul re-checking measurements with Thomas and Joseph, while Andrew and Rose were indoors, going over ideas for the interior.

'I'm sure,' he said to Rose, 'that a great deal of Anthea's furniture would suit this house. I shall get on to her when I get back to town.'

'It might just be an idea not to tell her who the client is,' Rose suggested.

'Mum's the word,' and he laughed. They walked back into the newly enlarged sitting room with the last of the afternoon sun streaming in through the uncurtained windows.

'It's a nice room, this,' Rose commented, 'and the new cornice makes such a difference. The old cornices were so miserable in this house, just as most of the fittings were.'

Andrew didn't reply, but walked around as if he was in his own little world, glancing here and there, asking direct questions about colour and fabrics. He left Rose and went yet again alone through the house. She peered through the window to see Joseph and Thomas holding a tape measure and Roaul jotting down the resulting measurements that were necessary for constructing the large country garden.

When all these tasks were completed and it was starting to get cold, they decided to call it a day and planned to return the next morning just to re-check all their ideas. Dinner that evening was at the Oriental and Simon and Terry were invited, so it was the large table in the dining room that found them all seated after taking drinks in the back room overlooking the courtyard.

It was there, in that room, that Joseph noticed it first : it was a glance and a change from the normal conversation that he picked up. They introduced themselves to everyone again but it was the handshake that lasted just a few second longer than normal that gave the game away. No-one but Joseph noticed and he decided that he would for the moment keep their secret. Roaul looked directly into Simon's eyes and in that split second contact was made. Both were being extremely careful not to draw attention to each other, as both realised the consequences. Simon could not believe how handsome Roaul was. He noticed his dress sense, so neat, everything just perfect. His classical dressing of the grey flannel trousers, blue striped shirt and the navy cashmere jacket. It all screamed smart and understated and this was in fact a very accurate reflection of Roaul's character in life. He was the same, a place for everything and everything in its place. He constantly had short, discreet affairs but it was always home to Andrew. They had been together now for so long and any thought of change was really just too difficult – or was it? He was an excellent garden designer and had a great deal of work. He had an attentive staff who adored him and nothing he asked was too much trouble, but this Simon, he thought, he looks so much like Thomas, only a bit bigger or more broad in the shoulders perhaps.

He found he was having a little bit of trouble concentrating on the general conversation and as he had designed the courtyard at the Oriental Enid asked him discretely whether he thought the pots of annuals should be repeated as they were the previous year. He looked at her. 'I'm so sorry. What did you say?' he asked and this was the pattern for the night. He realised that if he were not careful this magnetic attraction for Simon would become obvious. 'I have so many ideas for Killpara running through my head I seem to be losing my train of thought.' He smiled, not daring to glance yet again at Simon.

Joseph was fascinated watching this encounter that was reciprocated by Simon and wondered if anyone else had picked it up but hoped desperately Terry hadn't. Full-scale drama just was not required this evening, but Trevor's usual banter and finishing up as the centre of attention which he adored short-circuited what could have been an explosive situation. Andrew loved Roaul and was not blind. He knew of his dalliances with other men and tolerated them but he absolutely refused to put up with a situation face to face. If Raoul stayed out late, OK, but if he had to meet the person, then the drama began, so it was a case of 'what the eye doesn't see the heart doesn't grieve about'.

CHAPTER 7

Defining Friendships

CHAPTER 7

Defining Friendships

'Oh, that will be great,' Roaul replied to Andrew's comment that he was going to take on the decoration of Killpara, but at the same time he gritted his teeth, thinking that this would not leave him quite the opportunity to develop something with Simon if he was constantly in the company of Andrew at Killpara, but he put on a good face. He and Simon were in regular telephone contact but there is only so much one can do on the end of the telephone line.

'Joseph,' Thomas asked, 'you said to Roaul that you knew where you could get earth moving equipment at a good price.'

'Oh yes. I shall go and ask Ted.'

It had been a conversation between two men that Joseph overheard while waiting for Thomas at the Oriental that shocked him or rather surprised him. The two men were talking about stock prices and how at present the only pedigree stock around that was still getting the top prices at auction for the best breeding cattle was Ted Wally's, who, as one man said, 'had the best Hereford breeding stock in Victoria'.

Joseph was confused. Ted had antique and veteran cars, but stock – he hadn't ever thought of it. Ted was Ted, but pure-bred Hereford stock? When Thomas joined him, he noticed he was agitated. 'What's wrong?' he asked, in a concerned way.

Joseph turned his head to one side. 'Thomas,' he said in a determined way, 'do you trust me?' Thomas smiled, with an interior warmth which made the answer unnecessary. 'Of course – with my whole life.'

Joseph took a deep breath. 'Thomas, on the one and a half thousand hectares Rose bought we are going to put pedigree Hereford stock.'

Thomas looked straight at him and sighed. 'Are you sure?'

'Yes, Thomas, I am.'

'You know Simon thinks we should develop this land differently, don't you?'

'He's wrong and besides he has something else on his plate now. I need a free hand.' He reached across to hold Thomas's, who replied, 'If we have the free cash, do it.'

'Thomas, I know I can do this. I just know it.' And they settled back into their chairs with the waiter filling their glasses at once.

The next morning saw Joseph, after a stop at the supermarket, on his way to Ted's.

'Get down!' he laughed, as Toddy jumped all over him, waiting for a paper package to be opened and showing just what the dog had been waiting for. As he lifted the dozen bottles of beer out of the car and moved toward the veranda crowded with vehicles, Ted came across from behind one of the large sheds.

'Joe, hi!' he called. 'Hey, you don't always have to bring a man a drink!'

Joseph laughed. 'Well, once in a while it's OK.'

'Yeah, Joe, once in a while it's OK.' Ted smiled, showing a missing tooth on the left side of his mouth.

They sat on the veranda in the tiny space left from the automobile parts.

'Ted,' Joseph asked, 'will you teach me about raising a pedigree Hereford stock?'

'Whadya talking about, Joe?' Ted asked, with a frown, and Joseph went on to explain what he thought would work for Killpara. 'I didn't know you were the expert in this field.'

'No one's an expert, Joe, always remember that,' he said, crossing his legs. 'No one. I make some good moves and every now and again a bad one, but I know what breeding is about. I am an expert in two things, stock breeding and veteran cars.' He smiled as Toddy returned from a delicious steak and jumped all over Joseph, who, when he jumped, grabbed him and pulled him up onto his lap. Toddy adjusted himself, took a deep sigh and allowed himself to be petted and caressed.

'He's crazy for you,' said Ted. 'He's a good judge of character. I'll tell you what, Joe, if you are about to buy out pasture now I must say it's a bit late and you still have a thousand or more to go. Yu won't be ready for stock before the end of next spring.'

'Won't I?' asked Joseph. 'But that's a year away.' He looked at his shoes.

'Listen Joe, I'll organise the stock for you and the best, but you have to have feed for them, and new pasture isn't going to take a big herd. You know that, don't you?'

Joseph looked at Ted. 'I'm sorry, but you're going to have to teach me everything.'

'No problems, Joe. I'll give you a hand to build up a real good line of these Herefords, in fact if we split some of the herd we can transfer back and forth as we need to. How about that?'

'It sounds fine to me,' replied Joseph with a smile.

'Careful with the development of the paddocks,' Ted went on. 'Keep your windbreak, but don't exaggerate and not too many large trees. Remember, where there are trees the cattle turn the ground under them into dust bowls and that doesn't mean feed, and that's what it's all about. You can't have stock and nothing for them to eat.'

'I'll remember,' Joseph said, seriously.

'Come on, Joe, let's have a look at your new venture.' Toddy leapt forward as Ted stood up and raced for the old jeep. He hopped up and looked very much the racing driver on the seat beside Ted.

'You'll have to nurse him. He gets a bit angry if he can't see out of the window,' so with Joseph holding Toddy on his knee Ted started out into his fields behind the big sheds that held his precious collection of cars. Toddy obviously thought it great fun to sit on Joseph's knee and have an arm around him as they moved into Ted's lower fields to see a large herd of Hereford cattle grazing lazily in the late spring sunshine.

'You see, Joe, now there's plenty of feed but in late autumn and winter you have to be prepared, which means hay. You have to have a good reserve of it.' Ted chatted on as the three of them moved about the stock and this hands-on lesson was to be one of many where Joseph, as a result of his trust in Ted, began to grasp the concept of raising a pedigree Hereford herd. He knew this was what he wanted to do and with Ted behind him he was certain that it would succeed.

The following day he made for Melbourne. He took a taxi after he got off the train and joined Rose for lunch.

'Darling, you look fabulous,' she commented, noticing a country tan as spring was now well advanced. She noticed that he now walked with much more assertiveness, his early awkwardness gone. He would soon be twenty four years old, but in one year he had matured completely. He now did not have to be asked if he would like a pre-dinner drink : it was accepted.

'Rose,' he began, 'we are going to develop the large undeveloped area you purchased into beef cattle, with pedigree Herefords.'

Rose stared at him. It all made as much sense to her as raising dinosaurs. Then, sitting down, he began to explain what he believed was the best for the land they had and as he had access to breeding stock via Ted he did not see any problem. And if there was one, Ted, as usual, would solve it. Rose thought for a moment. This idea was exactly the opposite of what Simon had insisted on. He had suggested an extension of the dairy farming.

'That's expensive for the return,' said Joseph, professionally, 'you would have to build another farm completely and an up-to-date one and employ another full-time share-farmer who would require a house and everything that goes with it.'

Rose was very surprised that he was so well prepared with his arguments. 'To me,' she said, as the maid interrupted her to say lunch was served, and she walked arm in arm with him to the dining room, 'to me your planning seems very logical and when Thomas comes home this evening I am sure he will agree. If Ted thinks we should start small and build up I am all for it, especially if we can reduce our overheads. Do you think the initial outlay will be expensive?'

'I'm sure,' he said, 'that, with Ted, no matter what we pay to establish this herd – and it will be registered at Killpara - we shall pay half of anywhere else.'

'Well, Joseph,' she said, and lifted her glass to touch his, 'here's to a Hereford stud that revels under the name of 'Killpara' and to the hoisting of the tower on Friday.' They clinked their glasses together.

* * * * *

The three of them left Melbourne early on Friday morning for Killpara and arrived at eleven, just in time to see the moveable crane being put into position. It had first moved the tower close to its final resting place, then the wheels were hoisted up as a result of the pneumatic supports being lowered, slowly, onto thick pieces of wood.

'Hold it!' yelled a man in a blue boiler suit and he re-adjusted one of the four pieces under the supports. Then they continued, and after settling it firmly in position the crane section was swung out over the tower and firmly attached by metal ropes.

'Looks as if we are going to have to repaint some of the bloody thing again,' complained the painter.

'Get back, all of you,' cried the man in the blue boiler suit. He revved up the engine and the tower very slowly left the ground. It swung dangerously close to the new veranda but did not touch it. It rose higher and higher. The four builders were already up on the scaffolding and as it was swung over its future base they guided it into position. When it was settled correctly they immediately began the process of securing it with huge metal bolts. Then, and only then, was a ladder used from the top of the scaffolding; the metal ropes were released and the crane was swung out of the way. Rose just stared at this addition to Killpara. The effect was better than she had ever imagined. It was certainly a very grand architectural detail, that changed the house completely and as it was located between the old and new parts it had the effect of unifying the two optically together.

'Joseph, it looks fantastic,' said Thomas proudly, squeezing Joseph's arm. 'It's just fantastic!'

'Congratulations, Joseph,' smiled Rose. 'An excellent choice of tower.'

'Well, I didn't have a choice. There was only one.' And he laughed.

The large truck with the crane drew up the metal supports and the truck again sank onto its tyres. After a quick conversation with the head builder the man in the boiler suit said goodbye to all and very slowly backed out, turned with the most amazing noise and headed out of the drive and back in the direction of Walvern.

As silence returned, the three of them entered the house for an inspection of the week's work. It was now starting to get to a good stage. The plastering was completely finished, the marble fireplaces were in position and it appeared that there was just the plumber's work to finish before Andrew took over. But the big change, with the exception of the addition of the tower, was the external painting. This was changing the whole look of the place. It was beginning now to look like one house, a very large one, but a unified complex. The three of them were more than pleased with the progress and only too ready to call Andrew and Roaul in to finish it off.

While Joseph and Thomas were looking at their part of the house, Rose wandered out onto the veranda, where the painters were still preparing the weatherboards for the final coat. Perhaps it was the smell of fresh paint or the chatter of the painters as they worked, but Rose felt that after all these years somehow or other she belonged there. She knew she didn't want to live there all the year round but she knew it wouldn't matter what the season was, she was without a doubt going to enjoy it.

Joseph did not return to Melbourne with them, much to Thomas's dismay. He missed not being with Joseph. This new experience, he told Rose while travelling back, was one he didn't like, even though he realised it was sometimes necessary. Loving Joseph had been the most rewarding experience in his life and he took every advantage to be with him as often as possible.

* * * * *

'What do you think, Ted?'

'Well, you sure fixed it up,' Ted replied, referring to the tower, which he stood looking up at. 'You fixed it real good.'

Joseph felt a swell of pride at being complemented by Ted, even if all the work had been done by others. They then climbed into Ted's jeep with Toddy's leash firmly attached to the steering wheel. He was at the window baring his teeth to a group of house painters who were more than pleased that he was securely locked in the jeep. They set off for this large tract of land that in Joseph's mind promised success with Hereford stock. Ted drove a little like a maniac determined to get to his destination as quickly as possible. Joseph got out and opened the gate for Ted to drive through, then got back into the Jeep to a very excited Toddy, who took his position on Joseph's knee. Ted drove about where it was possible and then they stopped and walked around, inspecting the site.

'It's OK, Joe, if you keep the guys that are ploughing and cleaning up the other section and when they are finished send them over here and just get going. It should work out well,' he said, scratching his unruly mop of grey hair. They walked about for an hour, with Ted constantly instructing Joseph what he must do. 'Get rid of all that scrub and only keep the really big gum trees – have the rest felled. They're no good for anything.'

And that was exactly what Joseph organised in the following months, as the dust from the clearing of one section of Killpara settled, it began yet again on a much larger scale on the other side of the property and the one thousand and fifty hectares of unimproved land began to take shape. The constant buzzing of the chain saws, although the sound was aggressively annoying, sounded progress. Summer now was beginning and the hot mornings gave way to even hotter afternoons. The work of clearing the new fields and finishing off the house became slower as a result of this ongoing heat. Andrew and Roaul were constantly back and forth between Melbourne and Killpara, and each time they arrived they duly unloaded yet more things that were necessary to complete their set tasks. Andrew had a free hand in decorating and was more than pleased. He said to Rose, 'I have a lot of quality stock stored and you can have it all for cost as I doubt I will ever use it now.' And with the painters and floor-sanders Andrew moved deftly about, taking measurement after measurement. Roaul's team, with the aid of the earth moving equipment from Ted, began to show progress at once, but the times Roaul was there without Andrew a telephone call beforehand assured him that Simon would meet him at Killpara and the now-vacant share-farmer's cottage became their secret meeting place.

Both Roaul and Simon were surprised by the intensity of the relationship they were developing. It was much more than just a fling and they realised that even though they spent as much time as they possibly could together it just wasn't enough for either of them. Lying in bed in the shabby share-farmer's cottage, Roaul looked about him while still holding Simon. The paint was peeling off the ceiling where obviously water was leaking in, the pale green walls were marked and some ghastly printed green and orange curtains were drawn, giving a half light, but he knew in his heart that he would not have chosen to be anywhere in the world except here with Simon. It was probably the first time that either of them had slipped into a relationship without thinking of the consequences. Just to hold Simon was for Roaul the most exciting thing he could remember; those strong arms that at present embraced him gave him the most exhilarating sensation and one he hoped desperately would be with him for a long time to come. He never even thought of Andrew. All he knew and felt was a love for Simon that turned his well-organised world upside down. The same magnetic sensual feeling was totally mirrored by Simon. It had been a long time since he had felt this sexual drive and a passionate love; together with Roaul he felt complete, but at the back of his mind was always a certain feeling that if Terry were to find out about this then high drama was on the way. So the pair of them, for these stolen moments, kept everything as discreet as possible, careful not to cause a situation that meant that they could not continue to develop this relationship, which seemed stronger than both of them.

'You have no idea how I have waited for this moment,' said Simon quietly.

'Oh yes, I have. Don't forget I am the other half of this splendid relationship.'

Simon rolled over and held Roaul tightly. 'You're just splendid. You're wonderful,' he said and kissed him. 'I don't know how we are going to resolve all these problems but I know we shall,' and kissed him again.

They rose, dressed and Roaul went back to supervising his team of workers to lay out the terraces and plan the steps but as he walked back to the work site he walked with a heart that was so light his feet barely touched the ground. He turned as Simon's car sped toward the gate, turned and then headed back to Rosebae. He smiled. Well, he thought, gardening in the country is not so bad at all. But Simon did not stop at Rosebae. He continued to Walvern and pulled up opposite the Oriental Hotel and went in. A good-looking waiter offered him a table but he asked if he could speak to Enid. The waiter disappeared and in a moment Enid appeared, dressed in a corporate style that suited her position.

'Hello, darling,' she said and gave him a kiss, but noted he was particularly rigid. 'Looks like you need a drink. This way, sweetheart.' She led him to a quiet corner of the second room and the waiter was summoned to bring a bottle and glasses.

'Well,' she said, taking a mouthful, 'who is it?'

Simon jerked his head up. 'Is it that obvious?

'Almost, Simon. You do realise I have known you for twenty years. Now tell me the problem.'

'I don't have a problem,' he muttered, looking into his glass and then downing half of it.'

'Oh yes, you do,' she replied, looking straight at him. She reached over and held his hand. 'You're in love, aren't you?'

'Seems you have a crystal ball,' was his comment.

'Darling, you are so transparent. Who is it?'

'Roaul,' was the quiet reply. She withdrew her hand and settled back into her chair.

'Well, you haven't let the grass grow under your feet, have you?'

'I have never felt like this in my whole life. Never.'

'Well, not quite 'never', Simon. I happen to remember when you were desperately in love with Thomas some time ago, so everything is relative and the fact that we are having a drink together and I am not taking flowers to your bedside in the hospital I deduce that Terry has no idea about this 'situation'?'

'Got it in one,' he smiled.

'I thought so. Now where do you go?'

'I really don't know. 'He looked dejected. 'As you know, Roaul lives with Andrew –'

''And you live with Terry,' she interrupted. 'Sounds like two unhappy families.'

'It's not quite like that. It, well, it's just different. Sure, I was in love with Thomas and I suppose, well, if he had asked me to go to bed with him.'

'I know, darling,' she smiled, 'a rat up a drain pipe.'

'Not quite.' He narrowed his lips.

'Come on, Simon, the only real problem you have is Terry. Now listen. He is not someone I warm to but he is not a bad gay. He loves you and together you seem to have worked out an arrangement that works so be careful. Don't throw everything out just for this moment. Neither you nor Roaul have any idea of what the future holds for you both, as, as I said, be careful.'

Simon looked into his nearly empty glass, which Enid then re-filled. 'You don't know what it's like to be with someone you really love,' he said, looking into his re-filled glass and not at Enid. There was a silence, which made him swing his head up. He saw Enid as he had never seen her in his life. She took a deep breath.

'You're wrong, Simon,' and she drank deeply from her glass and then tightened her lips. 'If you need a place to be with Roaul, all you have to do is ask me. There are plenty of rooms here.' She smiled in a soft, loving way that was most unusual for her. 'Darling, I must get back to the grindstone,' and she stood as did Simon. She held him in her arms. 'I haven't any advice except that, if you believe in him, and he believes in you, you can't go wrong, but for goodness sake be careful. Terry is not going to be understanding at all.'

Driving back to Rosebae, having stopped to pick up some supplies, he kept hearing Enid's advice and then the warning, and he knew she was one hundred per cent correct, but he wondered exactly what she meant when she said to him that she understood exactly what it was to be in love with someone completely. But who? he mused.

It took Enid exactly two minutes after Simon left to call Mary and insist she call in and have a drink after work. 'Without Mr Broadcaster,' she said, referring to Trevor.

'Oh,' was Mary's response as she stared at Enid. 'And Terry?'

'Yes, Terry,' came the reply. 'I think it's going to get very rough if he catches on to this.'

'I'm sure you're right,' replied a very concerned Mary. 'And if I were in his position, I think I would be much the same.'

'I don't like him much,' said Enid, referring to Terry, 'but the two of them have something going. I am not sure that Simon isn't just living a fantasy with Roaul.'

'How can one tell? Mary asked. 'I thought for months that this situation with Thomas and Joseph was destined for disaster and so I had all the safety nets ready, but as you have seen this relationship seems to go from strength to strength.'

'That probably has a certain amount to do with Rose,' suggested Enid, not very charitably.

'Thomas has been the best thing that ever happened for Joseph,' Mary said, defensively.

Enid re-filled Mary's glass. 'I suppose you're right,' she offered, in an off-hand manner.

'Oh, Enid, he's gay. Thomas is always going to seek out a man for love, as he has Joseph, but he is always going to be your and my friend forever and in the long run,' she went on, with a knowing smile, 'that's really not too bad.'

'I suppose not,' came the sharp response from Enid, who, although she liked Joseph, saw him as the one who had won, not her, and that wasn't the usual lifestyle that she wanted. She worked and succeeded but with Thomas even she had to admit it was an unachievable goal. 'Terry is going to find out,' she said bluntly. 'If you have a relationship with someone it doesn't take too long to work out something else is happening.'

'Really?' asked Mary in a playful mood. 'What's your experience?'

'Oh, come on, Mary! I have been married to Paul since I left school. No complaints.' She swung her hand as she said this. 'He has been a great companion and in the last eighteen months of development here at the Oriental so supportive. You know, Mary,' she said, downing what was left in her glass, 'I don't know who it is but Paul is very content and so am I.'

'So where does that leave you?' Mary asked.

'Secure,' Enid retorted with a smile. 'We have never made so much money as in the last year. I can't believe we were so short-sighted and the fact that Trevor took us in hand, well, I guess it's all history in a certain sense. We have survived and the other hotels are in real trouble economically. You know, Mary, without our ever effervescent Trevor we could also be in the same boat financially.'

'Getting back to Simon,' Mary said, 'do you really think that he is going to do something serious with Roaul?'

'No idea, but when I spoke to him this afternoon he seemed very determined.'

'Why are relationships so difficult?' wondered Mary.

'They have to be, or everyone would die of boredom,' Enid quipped, cynically.

'I hope it doesn't happen with Joseph and Thomas,' Mary frowned.

'It probably won't with those two. They will probably develop into a positive relationship where neither requires anything or anyone else.'

'Really?' Mary was expecting that Enid would knife the relationship as she still loved Thomas, so she was quite surprised. Enid beckoned to a good-looking waiter who returned with another bottle and a plate of delicious nibbles from Lenny.

'I shouldn't. I'm supposed to be watching my waistline,' said Mary, 'but as I watch it or look at it in the mirror every morning I may as well just move in.' She laughed. It had been a long time since the two of them had been together like this, laughing, judging and just having fun, especially as the wine flowed freely. After so long they opened up to one another.

'And your love life?' asked Enid.

'Oh, don't!' she replied with a laugh. 'I can't even spell the word, let alone know the experience, but I'm not complaining. As you said earlier, for me the most marvellous thing is that Joseph and Thomas are having and building a real relationship and strangely that's enough for me. With Simon, you and, as you so aptly named him, 'Mr Broadcaster', Trevor himself, it's quite enough. I suppose you know he is finished with John?'

'Yes, Lenny told me. Why the hell does he always chase and score, which I always find even more remarkable – married men! Why doesn't he just settle down with a gay guy and get on with it?'

'Because, sweetie,' replied Mary, helping herself to yet another tasty nibble 'most young men who are gay are obliged, due to peer group or family pressure, to marry and our Trevor collects them like sea shells on the shore only to break their hearts, every one of them.'

Enid sighed. 'I thought at once stage that Trevor was interested in Joseph?'

'He was,' Mary admitted, tightening her lips. 'I had to lay the law down there and I must give him credit, he didn't overstep the mark for once.'

'Wise boy! Death is for such a long time!' They both burst into hysterical laughter, with Mary's hand on top of Enid's.

'Oh, but I am so worried about Simon's discretion,' Mary said. 'I just know when Terry finds out it's going to be peacock feathers for kilometres.'

Enid laughed. 'I shouldn't laugh but I can just see it.'

'It must be very difficult for someone in Terry's situation. I do so hope Simon sees this as a fling and settles down.' Mary said.

'I'm afraid that's impossible,' was Enid's response. 'Terry is not the forgiving type and Simon, I know, when the fire is out, it's out.'

'Don't you think it's odd that Terry formed this strong relationship with Patricia before she died?'

'Not really,' said Enid. 'He has always felt on the outside with the group, as did she, and I suppose they automatically supported one another, probably at our expense.'

Mary didn't reply but looked at her glass and then at Enid. 'So our Trevor's on the loose again,' and smiled.

'Such a worry,' said Enid, very patronizingly.

'Oh, come on, Enid, you know we would both be the happiest in the world if Trevor ever found Mr Right.'

'Darling, with Trevor's track record, he's never going to make it, believe me. For him, basically, one night is too long.' They both began laughing again.

The staff stood back, watching this odd scene. Never had they seen Enid so elated and relaxed. She was always known behind her back to the staff as Mrs Commandanti and to see her in this state made the entire waiter staff feel very uncomfortable.

'Do you think Thomas will come to live permanently at Killpara?' asked Mary, casually, smiling, as Enid re-topped her glass.

'It depends on Rose,' replied a matter-of-fact Enid. 'She inevitably controls everything. Thomas won't make a move without her and Joseph is caught happily in the middle, so it seems. All's well that ends well.' And Enid drained the half glass.

'I suppose you're right,' admitted Mary, slowly looking at Enid and turning her head to one side. 'Hmm,' she sighed, 'she has a forceful personality, Rose, but she is totally dedicated to Thomas.'

'And now Joseph,' Enid interjected.

'Yes, now Joseph,' Mary agreed. She had seen Joseph slowly move out of her orbit and control and for Thomas and Rose to take over. Thomas, she didn't mind: he loved Joseph and Joseph thought of no one else, but Rose was another matter. Where there was Thomas there also was Rose but Mary consoled herself that with both of them looking after Joseph's interests it wasn't too bad at all.

* * * * *

Andrew rang Rose one evening in a very excited manner and said he was on the way over. She assumed it had something to do with the decorating of Killpara and she was correct but not prepared at all for Andrew's news.

'Darling,' he began, 'I must have a drink first.' This being done, Rose insisted that he pass on his piece of so-called news. 'Well, I went to Anthea's late this afternoon. In fact, I have just come from there, and it appears that when she found out who was interested in the furniture and artefacts she said she would rather burn the lot than sell them to you.'

'Bitch!' said Rose sharply.

'But I managed to convince her that if she wanted discretion, especially about hubby losing cash on the horses and making rotten investments, she could sell it all to me and what I did with it was my business.'

'And did she agree?'

'After half an hour, yes, but on condition you don't give a squeak about where all this furniture came from.'

'But, Andrew, I don't want all of it.'

'Exactly and this is why it took Anthea and me so long to agree on the pieces that I wanted for Killpara. You're right, she is a bitch, playing the fine Toorak matron but when it comes to money she shrieks like a fishwife. Oh, just so exhausting!'

'Well, what have we purchased and how much is it going to cost?' Rose asked, narrowing her eyes. 'Oh, and by the way, you will dine with me, won't you? The boys are out.'

'Love to. Seems we are both alone.'

'What does that mean?' she asked.

'Roaul has decided to stay at the Oriental for two nights as he says it is just too exhausting going backward and forward to Melbourne.'

'I see his point,' she admitted and then brought the subject back to Anthea, though she spoke rather sarcastically. 'Well, at least she has co-operated.'

'She had to,' Andrew said with a smile. 'Yes, I will have another glass, thanks, Rose. Would you like a top-up?'

'Very well, Andrew. What do you mean she had to?'

Well,' he said, smiling like the cat that had just had a bowl of cream, 'I had lunch the day before yesterday with Tilly Willson.'

'Good heavens, I haven't seen her for years,' said Rose.

'No, nor has anyone. You see she is now living on her parents' property in New South Wales. She was down here and gave me a call. I must say that heat and dust on that property have done nothing for poor Tilly's complexion. Her face looks like old pleated brown paper.'

Rose laughed. 'Andrew, you're dreadful!'

He smiled and went on, 'Do you remember Tilly's ex-husband?'

'Vaguely. He was considerably younger than her.'

'Exactly. And now that they have been separated for some time who do you think he is having an affair with?'

'No!' Rose exclaimed with a look of total amazement. 'Anthea?'

'Got it in one, sweetie. Yes, our very pretentious, self-righteous Anthea has been having a wild affair with Tilly's ex-husband. They are still on good terms, he and Tilly and he related the news to her and it then passed on to little me. You see, when Anthea decided not to sell me anything, I just happened to mention I had had lunch with Tilly Willson yesterday.'

'What did she say?' Rose was enjoying this delicious bit of social scandal.

'I must say it's the first time I have seen Anthea speechless and despite the extraordinary layers of that hideous brown make-up she turned whitish – or should I say, more correctly, beige.'

Rose was in hysterics at his vivid description of Anthea.

'Then we began to talk business and I found a much altered Anthea and the prices suddenly dropped to half with no screaming. Can you believe it?'

'Andrew, you're brilliant! I don't suppose we got the red lacquered Chinese grandfather clock, did we?'

'We did,' he told her, smiling. 'Rose, I'm starving. That stingy bitch Anthea didn't even offer me a cracker.

Rose stood and walked to the door, where she pressed a bell, still laughing, and explained to the maid that they would start dinner now, as Andrew was hungry. Over the meal he just kept going.

'Rose, do you think we should leave Anthea just one mirror?' When she asked why, he said, 'Well, it may just help her to cut back on that shocking make-up she is wearing. It must be something again smeared all over the pillow cases. Tilly's ex must be quite surprised at the mess in the morning.'

Rose laughed: 'The last time I saw her was at the races, months ago, though I must say the husband is very pleasant, but Anthea is a nightmare. She is so over made-up and her clothes, if I remember, were more suited to an eighteen year old, and we both know she is considerably older than that.'

'Considerably,' he laughed.

'I wonder if her husband knows about the affair,' Rose pondered.

'I don't think so,' Andrew returned, 'otherwise our Anthea would not have turned beige with fright.'

Rose broke into laugher again and so the evening continued in much the same vein, with Andrew explaining all the pieces one by one he had extracted from her collection, leaving her with the 'unusable bits'. He smiled in a catty manner at the thought. In all, he had obtained twenty eight good pieces of antique furniture, plus a host of other decorative items and some sumptuous light fixtures. These, plus all the furniture Rose had in store and what Andrew held in his antique shop seemed to him to be much more than sufficient to start work at once, and at once meant next Wednesday.

And so a large, unmarked truck collected from Anthea's house in Toorak the agreed pieces plus the other extras and very early in the morning smoothly moved out and down Toorak Road with no one any the wiser. The truck then took a detour to a furniture storage warehouse and then to a large shed at the back of Andrew's shop and then fully laden, under Andrew's supervision, headed out toward the freeway and on toward Killpara. The unloading was as simple as the collection and Andrew, knowing what he wanted and where it was to be placed, instructed the two men who had organised the exercise to unload the truck and shift the furniture into the room where it would remain.

His vision had been relatively accurate. Two or three pieces, with the painters to assist him, were later re-organised and his old assistant from the past, Tony, was called in to assist him for the week, hanging curtains and paintings and generally moving bits and pieces around until he, being Andrew, was happy with the result. Obviously there was still a great deal of fine tuning to be done but the bones of the house were now laid down. The seamstress had made a mistake with the main sitting room curtains, which caused even the hardest painters to lift their heads as a string of very sharp expletives was heard screaming from within the house.

* * * * *

'Well, how are you?' came a voice behind Joseph. Friday evening at the Oriental, where everyone had gathered, laughing and joking about things that were of no importance. Trevor as usual was on form and as Joseph spun around he saw a rigid face behind him that belonged to Terry.

'I'm fine. How are you?'

'Well, funny you should ask that,' was the acid reply. Joseph instantly felt that with this response there was trouble ahead.

'Well, it seems we have both been short sheeted.'

'Have we?'

'Well, I hope you are not the last to know.' This sharp reply came as they accepted hors d'oevres from a tray offered by a very attractive waiter.

'I'm not sure what you are getting at,' said Joseph.

'Oh come on, sweetie, you may be cute and twenty two years old –'

'Twenty three,' Joseph corrected him.

'Don't you think that both our companions (for want of a better word) are having it off together and after all this time isn't it just lovely?' Terry spat out in a sarcastic manner.

Joseph took a deep breath and weighed up the insinuation that Terry had thrown at him. Thomas and Simon: for a moment he held his breath and then all the pieces fell together. Terry knew Simon was having an affair with someone else but had made the error of assuming that the other person was Thomas, not Roaul. Joseph smiled and replied quite slowly, 'Wrong man, wrong love. Oh, I must see if Mary needs another drink,' at which he left Terry in an odd sate of not being sure of whether one went forward or backward. What the hell was Joseph implying – wrong man, wrong love? Why on earth wasn't he upset in the least by the revelation that Terry thought would turn him upside down. Now it was Terry who couldn't put the equation together and if he looked lost and confused this evening it was because that was exactly how he felt.

The days preceding this evening had been frosty to say the least at Rosebae, with both Terry and Simon being falsely polite to one another, each waiting for the other to make the first move. But it wasn't made. Simon's absences from Rosebae made it clear to Terry that there was someone else and he made the error of assuming that these absences corresponded with Thomas's arrival from Melbourne, and that the rendezvous was Killpara. On that point he was correct but it was the person he had wrong. After his encounter with Joseph, Terry began to wonder if Simon was really having an affair at all and perhaps he had over-reacted. This mental dilemma caused him in the following week to draw in his horns and step very lightly with Simon, who continued at every opportunity to enjoy Roaul's company.

The term 'enjoyment' could not be used to describe Barry's dilemma at Houghton hall. He had been virtually relegated to servant status by Aunt Thelma's henchwoman, Mrs Talbot, which he found degrading and most annoying. He knew very well that if he ruffled the feathers of Mrs Talbot it would have the immediate effect of Thelma reducing or totally eliminating his fortnightly income and for a pretentious man of no means at all this came very close to social death. He now used the Oriental Hotel as if it was his private club, as did Stuart Searl, but not as obviously as Barry. Enid tolerated them both: Searl was good for business, the chit chat in his social column in the Walvern Gazette virtually guaranteed the restaurant section would be filled for this or that evening, depending on which smart charity affair he was writing about, but Barry's conceit was such that just because he was present he assumed that Enid needed him or was overwhelmed that he deigned to attend her hotel and that she was completely captivated by his presence. Nothing could have been further from the truth. Enid had known Barry before, when he only ate at the Commercial Hotel and spoke badly of the Oriental. She knew him for what he was, a pretentious, overweight prig and if it had not been for Stewart Searl, whom she also disliked but was good for business and public relations, she would have joyfully pitched the pair of them out onto the street without any pity at all. Barry's pretentious fantasies knew no limits and there were times when even Stewart Searl found him just too much of an effort. Barry was oblivious to it all. He constantly spoke of his family having titles, of the family wealth, his mother's jewellery collection and the more he rattled on the more transparent his stories became.

Two separate incidents caused even Thelma to wonder about just simply poisoning him and digging a hole at Houghton Hall and just dropping him in, even if she did realise it would have to be an exceptionally large hole. She had employed a middle-aged man to clean up all around the big house, finally coming to the realisation that Barry was never going to do, or be organised to do, anything to help. When one afternoon Thelma had paid a visit to Houghton Hall, the said man cleaning up the debris of twenty or so years asked Thelma what had stood in a particular spot once, Thelma went over for an inspection and noticed a cracked cement base that was now clearly visible as the whipper snipper had levelled all the nettles. Thelma just looked at the old foundations. She turned her head to one side and frowned. 'I just can't remember,' she replied, as she glanced yet again at the large foundations as the front door shut it came to her.

'Of course!' she exclaimed aloud, and moved down to the sitting room to be greeted by Mrs Talbot.

'A cup of tea?'

'Why not?' Thelma looked about and noticed the living room looking both cleaner and neater. The new curtains were a neutral colour and hung well, as opposed to the old ones that literally hung in shreds due to the cats exercising their claws.

'Was the aviary here when you came here?' she asked.

'What aviary? a surprised Mrs Talbot answered.

'That large construction in rusted cast iron.'

'No. The place was just as I see it now, though it's now in much better condition.' Mrs Talbot smiled, feeling very secure.

'Where is Barry?' Thelma asked.

'No idea,' came the simple reply, 'but he might be back soon, demanding lunch.'

'Good heavens, is it that late?' said Thelma. 'I had so many things I was intending to do this morning.'

Mrs Talbot gave her a tour of the repaired house and received the comment 'not bad at all. As they headed for the front door it was opened for them by Barry entering in the reverse.

'Oh, Aunt Thelma, how are you?' he asked, grandly, having seen her Range Rover in front of the house.

'Fine, Barry. Just come this way.'

He knew this was not going to be good, but dutifully followed her to a now-cleared spot with old broken foundations.

'Well,' she demanded, 'what happened to the old aviary?'

'Oh! Oh!! Well, you know, Aunty, someone stole it.'

'Stole it? Stole it!! The bloody thing, if I remember, was enormous. How could someone steal it?'

'Well, that's what mother and I pondered for days,' he answered grandly.

'Did you report it to the police? And how the hell could you move this thing without you or Emily not hearing a thing?'

'Thieves are a very treacherous lot and so cunning,' he told her. 'We didn't hear a thing.'

Thelma was anything but convinced so she left it at that, hopped into her Range Rover and departed but as she passed Killpara she slowed down and to her surprise saw a small crane deposit on a complex base of cast iron a dome in rusted cast iron. She recognised at once the aviary, so she thought with a smile the Killpara group think they have got away with it, do they, and accelerated to Walvern and straight to her solicitor, Brendan Crane.

The dome had finally been fitted onto the base of the wall structure of this aviary and Roaul was very happy with the effect. It was a very large architectural feature of what was to become a very sophisticated garden. Yes, he thought, it's just right for the end of this terrace. One passes by, through the hedge, to the swimming pool. Perfect. Just as I planned - and he congratulated himself on yet another job well done.

'Thelma, are you sure?' asked Brendan. 'I can't believe it. Why would the O'Riely family steal a rusted aviary and then erect it for all to see? It just doesn't seem logical to me.'

'Well, we sue all the same,' stated a determined Thelma. 'Theft of an antique aviary.'

'Thelma,' the confused solicitor went on, 'what is it, a birdcage or an aviary?'

'Same thing,' she insisted bluntly. 'Now, where do I sign?'

'You don't, Thelma. I think there is something wrong. Why didn't your sister or indeed your nephew call and report this to the police? Don't you think it is a bit odd?'

Thelma looked at him dubiously. 'Thelma, if we go ahead with this charge for theft and it seems to me it's very shaky as Barry is the only person who knows anything about it as Emily is dead. I have this odd feeling the police are going to have a hard time prosecuting the O'Rielys, especially as Barry never reported a theft to them.

'Just begin the process,' Thelma said grandly and left the office. Brendan said,' Oh dear,' to himself and rubbed his left ear. Well, thought Thelma, as she slammed her car door, let's see how this Rose woman copes now, and she pulled out and drove off in the direction of her home.

Barry had not grasped the ramifications of what he had said to her. It was the same as everything he said: no-one bothered to follow it up. It was just Barry sounding off and who cared? But this was different, very different. Now the police were to be called in and his cover-up about the sale of the aviary was going to be discovered but in his mind it was just another comment, nothing to worry about, a similar comment as about his mother's jewellery collection, which was non-existent. But this aviary, now well re-constructed at Killpara, most certainly was a very tangible object and in someone else's now well-developed side garden.

When the letter arrived from the solicitor addressed to Thomas O'Riely, threatening legal action if the stolen aviary was not returned to the hands of the owners, Thomas was dumbfounded. He showed the letter to Rose as it had been sent to Albany Road.

'What on earth is this?' he asked in disbelief. 'I know Patricia paid for this thing, four hundred dollars. Terry helped her to obtain it after the run-in with dad, so what is this all about?'

'I smell a rat,' said Rose, slowly. 'Let me call Terry,' which she duly did.

'What!' was the cry of disbelief. 'I don't believe it! I have a copy of the sale note signed by Barry. Give me the solicitor's name and tomorrow I will sort it out for you.'

'Terry, you are so kind,' said Rose. 'However can I thank you?'

'It's a pleasure,' he replied. 'It's just a little thing I can do for Patricia.' He hung up, having got the solicitor's name and address.

'Well, said Rose, 'that seems to have sorted things out. By the way, Roaul seems to be spending a lot of time on the project at Killpara. I am more than happy. He must have so much other work and we seem to have received preferential treatment. Let's have dinner.' They moved to the dining room, still talking about the solicitor's letter about the aviary. But it was not so much preferential treatment that kept Roaul always at Killpara, it was a good-looking Simon that drew him like a magnet. Every time he thought of him he felt a genuine loss if he was not there, and when he managed this dangerous game and was in Simon's arms everything was worth the difficulties and danger.

The following day Terry, in his most haughty and grand manner, that only he could concoct, swept into the solicitor's office and demanded to see him immediately or he would call the police. 'Misrepresentation,' he said loudly and was shown into a smart office where Brendan Crane looked at the document, or sale note, and shook his head.

'I told Thelma that something was not right but she insisted. I am so sorry.'

'So am I,' retorted Terry. 'Photocopy the original and send it to your client and tell her she is damned lucky we are not thinking for the moment of prosecuting for deformation of character.'

The solicitor rubbed his eyes. 'Thank you,' he said in a dejected tone. 'I will call Thelma at once. I am so sorry,' he repeated.

Terry swept out of the office and into a bright morning's sunshine, strangely feeling very good indeed.

'What!!' came a sharp scream from the end of the phone. 'Are you sure?'

'Of course I'm sure, Thelma. I have a copy of the sale note in front of me. What on earth is Barry up to?'

'That I shall find out in exactly half an hour.' Thelma slammed the phone down. 'I'll kill him,' she said aloud as she grabbed her car keys and headed for the door. In less than the half hour she pulled up in front of Houghton Hall with the gravel being spat up in all directions. She stalked into the house to witness Barry with a glass of red wine in his hand watching television.

'Put the glass down,' she demanded, white with rage. Barry did as he was told. The slap was immediate and Barry recoiled in his chair, feeling the pain and shock.

'You idiot!' she screamed, bring Mrs Talbot in from the kitchen. 'Do you know what you have done?' Her voice grew louder and louder. 'Stolen? Stolen?! You sold the bloody thing. You liar! That's it! That's it! You can get to the workhouse. I don't care what promises I made your mother I am going to ship you to the South Pole, anywhere as long as it's away from here. You idiot! You fool! You have made me look totally incompetent in front of the Killpara lot and if there is any legal suit for deformation of character here you - 'and she waved her open hand at him, which had him reeling back in his chair, ' - will take the rap. Barry, do you understand me?'

By this time even Mrs Talbot had moved back toward the kitchen. She had never seen Thelma so angry before. With that, Thelma stalked out, slamming the front door and her car was heard to spit stones everywhere as she set off back to Walvern. To her annoyance, when passing Killpara, she noticed a man on a ladder adjusting a metal flag on the top of the aviary.

'It appears Aunt Thelma's a little stressed,' said Barry grandly to Mrs Talbot, who said nothing, but returned to the kitchen.

Thelma was a very good business woman and the saw mill was run very well. The drain on her resources was at present Houghton Hall, and the taxation department put a check on her movement of finances, assuming that her large claims on the Hall were a tax dodge. If there was one thing in the world that gave her blood presume it was the taxation department and after a week of intense investigation by them they accepted that she was not attempting to make fraudulent claims, and she was ever so happy to see the two tax investigators get into their car and return to Melbourne.

It was after this episode that she went to a gallery opening of a local woman's paintings in a part of the local library. As she entered she noted the same crowd, not that she expected otherwise. She looked at the paintings and was very interested in purchasing one of them. The room was crowded and it was difficult to see through the crowd, but then she heard Barry speaking loudly, not this time about his mother's jewels, but of Thelma's. He was saying in a loud voice, 'They are always kept well tucked away.' She was irate. She had just had a run-in with the tax department and had to declare all her assets and here was this cretin broadcasting to the world that she had a large collection of jewellery 'tucked away'. She angrily pushed her way through the crowd and with an open hand yet again struck Barry across the face. This time, though, he had a glass of red wine in his hand, which went everywhere.

'You irresponsible fool,' she screamed in front of a now-silent crowd, which turned to watch the drama. 'You,' she stormed, now toning her voice down to an icy manner, 'will begin work at the sawmill Monday morning, as your allowance is now non-existent – or you'll starve.' She stalked out of the gallery, this time determined to break Barry's stupid and dangerous behaviour or to happily throw him to the wolves. Barry was now extremely worried to have Thelma make this dramatic statement in front of his acquaintances. It deflated his bravado like a pin stabbed into a balloon and the thought of having to do manual labour . . .

'Oh,' he thought, 'this really is just too much,' and to his abject horror Monday morning saw a small truck drive up to the front of Houghton Hall and one of Thelma's employees who lived not far from him collected him and deposited him in front of Thelma at the sawmill. She threw a khaki overall at him and pointed to a pair of rubber boots.

When dressed in this outfit, she gave him specific instructions and thrust a large yard broom at him. So Barry's first ever day at work was hard and humiliating following Thelma's taking a sharp stand against him and his now five day work schedule, his mid-week lunch date with Stuart Searl just did not happen any more. But he did not change much. He began to lose a little weight, always complaining that Mrs Talbot's lunch that he carried in a plastic bag to work was always insufficient and if not too exhausted to go out on Saturday evening with Stewart, whom he told quite boldly that he was now helping Aunt Thelma in administering the saw mill complex.

Summer was now coming to a close and the evenings were becoming quite fresh. Killpara was virtually finished, at least the house was, and Andrew now had to just fine tune a few minor things. The new fields were all ready for sowing as were the lawns and the planting around the house, everything waiting for the last of the summer heat to finish. The swimming pool was not quite completed; Joseph and Thomas consoled themselves that it would be ready for use next summer.

Rose, Joseph and Thomas drove up on Thursday evening to Killpara, as this weekend was Mary's birthday and a scamper around the shops had been necessary to locate just the right gifts for her. Now, being residential in Killpara, the three of them enjoyed coming to the country ever so much more, although Joseph was at Killpara much more often than the others, due to the administrative work he had undertaken but there was a problem and that was staff. Thomas and Joseph made do in the kitchen but it was basically eating at the Oriental that was the order of the day. Saturday evening they arrived at Aspel Drive to find parking a bit of a problem and so walked half a block back to Mary's house with the three of them pulling on their jumpers as the evening had become a little cold.

'Happy Birthday!' they cried, as Mary opened the door. They handed her their gifts, as she thanked them and told them to come in. They went into her living room, which for once was being used.

'Trevor's playing barman,' she laughed, 'as well as the fool!'

'I heard that, you rattlesnake,' shouted Trevor as he made his way into the room with a large tray holding the drinks. 'Help yourselves,' he went on as he handed one to Rose. 'Your handiwork looks great,' he said, looking at the mirror frame that Joseph had helped restore, and which was looking suitably grand resting on the marble fireplace.

'Oh, you should see the entrance hall at Killpara,' said Rose, taking over the conversation. 'Joseph's restoration of the two very badly damaged frames that now hold the cleaned pair of family portraits look marvellous.'

'I am sure they do,' said Trevor with a wink in Joseph's direction. 'Oh, can you believe it? Noddy has finally deigned to take the night off, well not all of it, but she will join us later. But as we have a home-help this evening I shall not have to rush backward and forwards to the kitchen.'

'Really?' enquired Joseph. 'Who is it?'

'Mary organised her. I don't know her,' and the conversation drifted on about Killpara and Rosebae, when all of a sudden the doorbell rang and Mary was heard exclaiming, 'All together! Oh, what all for me? Thank you,' and she ushered into the living room Simon and Terry and Enid, who had arrived at the same time.

Conversation now picked up, with Trevor, as usual, giving his rendition of the story and the slap at the art gallery opening, which had seen Barry covered in red wine.

'Serves the cretin right,' said Terry, taking a stand and then giving his version of the aviary story.

'Well, all's well that ends well,' said Trevor, flippantly. 'He is now, according to a very reliable gossip, sweeping the floors in dearest Aunt Thelma's sawmill.' He waved his hand in a very dramatic way which had everyone, even Terry, laughing. It was after another round of drinks that Mary disappeared and then returned to announce that dinner was served.

The meal was delicious but the noise and laughter made it at a certain point difficult to hear everyone, but if sound was a problem, sight was not, and everyone at some stage of the evening glanced sideways at the person organising this birthday festivity. Beverly Evans was twenty nine years old but it wasn't that she looked older, just incredibly dowdy. She was tall, thin to the waist with no bustline at all and endowed with broad hips, but it was her face that was odd, straight black-brown hair, sad brown eyes and a most pronounced jaw with a cleft just like a man's and strangely a small button-like nose, no make-up at all, so what one saw was the real Beverly Evans.

The meal was pronounced a great success and they moved back to the living room laughing and joking. Even Terry was joining in the fun, despite there being no conversation between him and Simon, something everyone noticed. At a certain point Beverly, having put the kitchen to rights, poked her head into the sitting room and said good night to Marry and the others and then disappeared. The front door was heard to close behind her.

'Darling, where did you find her?' asked Trevor, looking at Mary, as did the others, who were also curious,

'Don't start, Trevor,' said Mary briskly. 'If you had had a miserable life like her you wouldn't be laughing.'

This comment brought the whole conversation to a halt. 'Well, what is the story?' asked Thomas, with one arm on Joseph's shoulder.

'That jawline . . .' started Trevor.

'Don't!' was Mary's defensive reaction. Beverly Evans was one of a family of five,' and she went on to give the background to the Evans family, but was interrupted by Terry. 'I know this family. One of the Evans boys was in my form at school, a nice guy, but absolutely not academic. I don't really know what happened to him or where he works.'

'You see,' Mary continued, 'I don't know anything about the rest of the family, just Beverly, as she has been a client of mine for years. She never says much but someone I know told me the whole sad tale only a week ago and as she is very short of cash I offered her the work of catering here this evening.

'Well, I for one,' commented Rose, 'think she has done a remarkable job,' and everyone concurred.

'Well, what's the story?' asked Enid.

'Well,' Mary started again, 'she was the bright one of the family, apparently she was top of her class always, but school girls and boys being as they are she, because of her appearance, suffered taunts all her school life. Her father refused to allow her to go to university and as she was not considered a great beauty she found employment impossible until two years ago she was employed on the checkout desk at the supermarket.'

'I knew I had seen her before,' said Simon.

'It appears that at seventeen, two local lads, and supposedly from good homes, raped her one night as she was coming home from the movies alone.'

Enid's face visibly tightened. 'I would shoot the bastards,' she spat out.

'So would I,' exclaimed Rose sharply. The whole group now was totally engrossed in this tragic story.

'What happened?' asked Thomas, taking another drink.

'Well, apparently the father, not wanting any trouble, did not report this to the police as he knew the families of the boys but when she became pregnant he went to the families and they decided to pay for an illegal abortion.'

'Good God!' said Enid. 'I don't believe it!'

'Well, it gets worse, unfortunately,' Mary told her. 'Beverly was well aware that she would, as a result of her appearance, probably never get a man, so she said she wished to keep the child. She was over-ruled and the backyard abortion went through without her approval. Apparently the job was botched and she later had to be taken to the local hospital where the doctor's report was that it was highly unlikely she would ever have a child, due to the shocking damage done by the abortionist, who, being warned, disappeared as the hospital reported this to the police at once.'

'How ghastly,' said Rose, slowly.

'She got part-time jobs cleaning houses but she wasn't popular and the jobs didn't last long, until the supermarket check-out position, but she has been fired and a brassy little piece of work with an enormous bust line that the manager of the supermarket is keen on has taken her place and so for Beverly it's back to square one.'

Everyone just looked at one another. It was Joseph who broke the silence. He looked at Mary. 'Do you know her well?' he asked.

'No, not really. She is a client, that's all, but the story is just so sad.'

'So sad!' cried Enid. 'It's damn well unbelievable that these two bastards have got away scott free and Beverly in a certain sense is still paying.'

'Just a minute,' said Joseph. 'Mary, is she an honest person?'

'As the day is long. Why?

'What do you think,' he answered, looking at Rose and moving his hand to Thomas's knee. Everyone glanced backward and forward between Rose, Joseph and Thomas. 'I think we should give Beverly a try at Killpara. We need a housekeeper. If I have to keep eating Thomas's meals I shall probably die of starvation!'

'Oh, thanks!' laughed Thomas. 'Very kind of you, Joseph!' Joseph put his arm around his neck and kissed him, a most unusual thing for him to do in public.

'I think it's an excellent idea,' agreed Rose. 'Joseph, you organise it and let's have a three month trial. She may not like working for us, you know, so let's just see what happens.'

Mary put her glad down, crossed the room and gave Joseph a hug. 'You're wonderful,' she said, quietly.

To say Beverly was surprised was an understatement. She most readily accepted the offer and the share-farmer's cottage was re-located. Andrew was called on to do an emergency decorating job inside it, the exterior had a new veranda attached and neatly trimmed with decorative cast iron, and so in less than two months the travelling back and forth from Walvern to Killpara was over.

For the first time in her life, Beverly Evans was independent; no parents demanding meals, no more unpaid washing and cleaning, it was all in the past. Joseph's spontaneous act of charity paid dividends in a million and one ways. There was nothing Beverly would not do to make the three of them feel comfortable. Her cooking was good, she was totally organised and now shopping for supplies in Walvern for Killpara gave her for the first time a sense of self-esteem. Rose decided that stretch jeans were not very flattering, so Beverly was given a make-over which included not only a smart uniform but also came with, as a bonus, a hairdresser's appointment once a week, so the dead straight hair now took, due to the hairdresser, a much softer, curlier look, which softened her face. A make-up lesson followed, but the jaw remained ever-prominent, but to all who saw her now everyone commended her on a great change for the better.

It was strange that although Joseph loved Thomas and adored Rose and Mary, from the time he had left home to live with Mary and now Thomas and Rose he had never returned to see his parents. He was capable of showing great kindness and charity, such as he had for Beverly, but as for his own parents, they just did not exist. Mary never spoke to him of them, as when she had originally he had said quite firmly he never wanted to hear of them again. Perhaps it had been a whole childhood of fighting with his father and Keven, the yelling, the bitter comments that never stopped, and when there was peace it was that icy silence that would, without a doubt, herald another shouting match. His docile mother just accepted it all without ever taking a stance or defending one or the other. She was a beaten woman, who just drifted in and out of this terrible household, who neither helped any of them or perhaps it was just that it was all too difficult for her. Joseph knew something very clearly, though, that that part of his life was finished, closed, and he was very determined that the only thing he would ever have to do with his parents was, with Mary, attend their funerals.

Beverly's experience with gay men was zero or as she worked out much later she simply had not thought of it, so after a few well-chosen words from Rose she found the position at Killpara not only offered her independence but also a security both workwise and sexually. The situation produced for the first time in Beverly's life an opportunity to go ahead without any impediments. She enjoyed, for the first time in her life, as Joseph had, responsibility; the running of this big home - because they were not often there together, perhaps just for the weekends - gave her the opportunity to do just as she wished and to indulge herself in the luxury of reading, without an aged parent demanding this or that.

CHAPTER 8

Finally a Meeting

CHAPTER 8

Finally a Meeting

With Andrew now well finished at Killpara and autumn beginning to set in, it left Roaul the perfect opportunity to stay for longer periods at Killpara. The sowing of the lawns, the planting of trees and shrubs, every excuse possible was brought to bear so he had an escape route to Walvern and Simon. Terry wondered if it was not Thomas then who the hell was it connected with the Killpara group that Simon was spending time with and as he thrashed it through his mind again and again came up with only one answer: if it wasn't Thomas, then it left only a very secure young man called Joseph. But occasionally he had doubts about that. With the improvements at Rosebae Simon was rarely at home in the daytime but he always dutifully returned in the evening, which confused Terry all the more, as a call to Killpara had Beverly responding to say the three of them were in Melbourne but would be expected back on Thursday evening for a week. Could she take a message? The answer was always in the negative. Terry was in the situation where although he was not having sex with Simon after all these years the emotional bond was stronger than ever and it was on this level that he was genuinely suffering. Who? Who, he wondered? And the most obvious person he missed completely.

The sowing of the new fields was complete as was the fencing. Now, all they had to do was to wait for a good rain fall and then spring. But as to be expected, the garden at Killpara took much longer to finish. Whilst the house was being finished and as they were only there at weekends, Joseph had asked Enid if Lenny would mind if Beverly assisted him in the kitchen of the Oriental during the week.

Enid agreed, Rose and Thomas paid Beverly's wages and Lenny had no opposition; as a top chef even Lenny was surprised at how quickly she caught on to timing, which he saw as everything. She never forgot a thing and even after a busy and tiring night when she arrived back at Killpara she took out a large exercise book and copied into it yet another recipe with all the bits and pieces that made it a masterpiece. This continued for two months and then Lenny was genuinely sorry to see her go, saying to Enid that Beverly had been the most intelligent assistant he had ever had. Enid sighed. 'Pity I didn't realise the potential before Joseph,' she said as she left the kitchen.

But strangely Beverly had left an imprint on everyone at Mary's birthday party, especially on Enid. She also came from a large family without finance as had Beverly, the difference being Enid was determined never to find herself again in this state, whereas Beverly had not managed until now to find a way out of her limited situation. Enid had never wanted children and this had had Paul at odds with her on the subject but Enid being Enid as usual had the last word. But the scenario of two well-to-do local lads raping Beverly and getting away with it angered her to the point of screaming. Why should they, she thought, the bastards, who the hell were they? And the more she thought of it the more determined she was to find out who they were. In a small country town, she thought, it's not going to be too difficult.

The Oriental at this stage was now in great demand for weddings and so it was not unusual to have a booking refused due to 'small and smart', as Enid always stipulated. No more than sixty or go to the Stardust, so big weddings in this area now if they wanted to do it well had several evenings before at the Oriental before the important date and it all equalled money. Enid's food was the top, the venue unequalled, the staff super-attentive, business was very good, the prices high but everything one could wish for.

Yet Enid dwelt on the problem or the past problem of Beverly. Perhaps it manifested itself as the result of her background, being the same as Beverly's - one never knows. But it began to become a fixation with her and she saw that these two boys, obviously men now, should not be able to get away with this ghastly crime 'just because they are men'. She did not have a Saviour complex; it was not that. She believed that it was more that someone had been taken advantage of and the result of it had been a hideous realisation that pregnancy in the future was out of the question. Inside, Enid boiled. Beverly left the Oriental, and it was not that Enid and she had any form of relationship other than as employer and employee; Rose and Thomas paid Beverly's wages. Enid began to hatch a plan. She organised Lenny to invite Beverly to dinner one evening at the Oriental when she knew the rest were in Melbourne and Beverly stepped into Enid's trap. It was a quiet night, with only eight tables, and Enid sat down with the very awkward Beverly for a meal. The conversation was, to say the least, slow but it began to pick up as both of them, due to Enid's honesty, admitted to a similar background and the same financial limitations – in fact there were moments of genuine laughter. Beverly was seven years Enid's junior but their extreme differences had the odd effect of linking them together in the strangest way. It was as if they were talking to themselves when they spoke together and if this was particularly strange for Beverly it was unheard of for Enid. Perhaps because they were such extreme opposites this odd bond was being forged, but if it was beginning to be formed into something concrete. Beverly was well aware that Enid wanted something out of it and so she did. She waited, like a cat that has caught the mouse, but for which the kill is not necessary, and then she sprang the trap. 'Who were they?' she said in a voice that transcended a demand or a plea and sat back in her chair waiting for the names. Beverly looked into her glass, not daring to glance in Enid's direction. She liked Enid, but at the same time was frightened of her. Enid was, for the whole of Walvern, a symbol of success, a fighter, someone without pity, a woman who would always win despite the odds and the Oriental was the living proof of this.

'What does it matter now?' said Beverly in a defeated way. 'Look, for the first time I feel I am going somewhere. I have been given charge of the running of Killpara. I have been given my own house. I am not complaining and it's all due to your friends. So thank you very much.'

'If I had been brighter you would have been working for me. Lenny tells me you're great in the kitchen.'

'He is a nice guy and good to work for. I really enjoyed the experience but I must confess I love working at Killpara. Everything is, well, how can you say it, smooth. Yes, that's it, smooth. No one yells, no one is inconsiderate, everything is wonderful.'

'I'm glad,' replied Enid with a sigh, 'but if ever you need a job, the Oriental is waiting for you.'

'Thank you, Mrs Wrighton,' she said, as Enid freshly filled her glass.

The conversation continued with a nervous staff watching this game. It was most unusual for Enid to sit and eat with anyone, so the staff, knowing Enid, realised she was after something. It took some time and every tiny bit of Enid's patience to finally draw out of Beverly who the two rapists were and to say she was surprised was the understatement of the year, but she under-played it and they continued and completed the meal with Lenny joining them for a drink later.

It should have stopped there. Enid had the information she wanted but it didn't. For some reason or another Enid saw this as a personal vendetta and she was out for blood. It had been many years since this heinous crime had been hushed up and our Enid was about to open up an old wound. It happened much more quickly than she expected. Paul took the call and made the bookings for the wedding and the florist. It was the usual gushing conversation that generally goes with these occasions and it was only when, two days later, Enid checked the weekly bookings and future bookings that she recognised a name, a name that Beverly had mentioned a few evenings before. So she thought this bastard is now into a society wedding. He was now well entrenched into his father's stock and station agency and ran the business. He was a physically a heavy man in his late thirties, ordinary to look at, drank heavily but not at the Oriental and very full of himself. The bride to be, as far as Enid was concerned, deserved him. She had known and disliked her for years. Now, Enid moved into top gear. She telephoned the prospective groom to call in and speak to her about the forthcoming event. He should have been more careful, but Daniel in the lion's den had nothing on the drink this man had with Enid. He had the odd feeling that he felt cold, but by the end of the five minute conversation he was sure it was warmer at the South Pole.

'Do sit down,' Enid said, as she ushered him to a chair near the large glass doors that overlooked the courtyard end. In this early autumn it was well past its best but the fountain splashed on just the same. 'I think we have something to speak about, don't you?' she teased him with the eyes of a hawk.

'Sure,' began the ever-assured groom-to-be. 'Everything's more or less organised. What do you want to check on? Listen, I have a lot to do so keep it short.'

It was very unwise to tell Enid to do anything, let alone keep her conversation short. 'Oh, I will,' she said, as she narrowed her eyes. 'I see there is a mistake on the seating list.'

'Really?'

'Yes,' she replied like the cobra now rising out of the basket and with no flute to keep it company. 'You seem to have left Beverly Evans off the guest list.'

He glanced at her in surprise but arrogantly. 'Never heard of her. Is that all you telephoned me to say?'

'Not quite,' came her icy reply. 'Rape is a serious legal charge, wouldn't you say?'

'What the hell are you talking about?' he said, now very disturbed. 'What do you want?'

'I haven't decided,' said Enid, enjoying the power game, 'but you are going to make some form of restitution in cash into Beverly's bank account.'

'And if I don't?' he asked, with an arrogant glance.

'Oh, but you will,' she smiled, 'or I shall cancel your reception here and make it very, very public about your brave sexual attack on a seventeen year-old girl. In fact, I may just use Stewart Searl to help me - a little article in his column a week before the wedding. What do you think, sweetie?' There was an acid touch to the voice.

'How much do you want?' he asked, looking behind him in case there was someone in hearing distance.

'Anything less than fifty thousand dollars would not be acceptable.' She smiled at him again.

He gritted his teeth. 'I should have to sell a property to realise that amount.'

'Do so, then,' was her sharp reply, 'and before the wedding, or else.' He was just about to use a string of expletives to explain what he thought of Enid personally but for once his sixth sense told him that would be particularly unwise. 'I will give you a copy of the bank account number and branch. I'm sure I can rely on your honesty,' she added insincerely. He stood up and stalked out of the hotel, with a dreadful feeling that when he returned the next time for his wedding he was not going to be feeling as relaxed as he had expected.

Round one, thought Enid. Now for number two. Number two was in fact a well-respected accountant at Walvern, married with two small children. Alan Simms had done very well. He had married the owner's daughter of this now growing firm and had a very good lifestyle. He often ate at the Oriental and considered himself a well-prized client, never refused a table, and so socially in this small country town he had a certain amount of social clout, as had the bride groom-to-be. It took Enid a week before she contacted him, as she had assumed that the bridegroom-to-be would have passed the message on but this was not what had occurred. Each, it seemed, had dismissed the past with a flick of the wrist and that was that. The subject was obviously never spoken of between them. So Enid, aiming her strike at Alan, took him completely off-guard. He never said a word. His mouth opened and shut like a goldfish. She, with her innate sense of survival, suddenly realised that he had not had any conversation with the other man at all and so she went for the kill. No picador could have thrust the swords so well or so deep.

'Match the fifty thousand or I shall expose you.' It was all she said. He stood up to leave. 'Oh,' she went on, and handed him a bank account number and branch office and smiled. A very nervous Alan Simms left the Oriental absolutely sure that when judgement arrived Enid would be sitting there with sword in hand.

In less than a month, twice Beverly had been to the bank as she believed there had been a mistake with amounts paid into her account. Each time it had been pointed out to her that there was no error, everything was completely correct. It did not take her long to check who had paid into the account and then put the story together. She had only told Enid two names and these corresponded with a certain amount that was sitting happily in her account. After visiting the bank, she went to the Oriental to speak to Enid, not that she really knew what she was going to say, but she felt she should do something. As she entered the hotel on a busy Thursday afternoon, having completed all the shopping for Killpara, and expecting a four-day stay with three dinner parties, she entered and saw Mary and Enid together at a small table near the glass wall of the courtyard. She crossed the floor and suddenly her courage fled. She wasn't even sure where she was going but these two women in front were well out of her league.

'Beverly!' cried Enid. 'Do join us.'

She couldn't leave, so to go ahead was the only way. She felt embarrassed but took the seat offered her and said nothing. It was unlike Enid but she leaned over and put her hand on Beverly's shoulder.

'It's not much, but we shall see if you need more in the future.'

Beverly went scarlet with embarrassment; to continue to blackmail these men in the future for more money had never crossed her mind, and for that matter it had not crossed Enid's but the glib statement gave Enid the most enormous amount of satisfaction, which Mary and Beverly noticed. Mary had been genuinely shocked when Enid had told her about the two rapists now paying into Beverly's bank account and said so. 'Enid, it's blackmail!'

'Yes, isn't it?' she smiled.

'But what if the police were drawn in to this?'

'Impossible, Mary. Both these bastards wouldn't dare. Their careers, not to mention their marriages would be finished in a flash. Would you like another drink?' she finished, flippantly.

* * * * * *

Rose was more than pleased with Beverly. Her manners were discreet; she showed utmost respect for them all, the house was spotless and the cooking wonderful. She now bought in the wines, after a few lessons she had had at the Oriental, but it had taken her a little time to get used to Thomas and Joseph being lovers. She had never in her life come into contact with homosexuality and if she had, she thought later, she probably would not have recognised it. But as Joseph and Thomas were so natural and Rose obviously so accepting of their love, she silently followed suit. By this stage Rose and Thomas knew all about Simon's affair with Roaul and were very careful not to make things awkward for Terry, so while the garden was still progressing, if Simon and Terry joined them for dinner and Roaul was present Rose studied the seating arrangements very carefully.

* * * * * *

It was nothing, in fact it was useless. It was an eight hectare site that flooded in winter and was as dry as a bone in summer. Its market value was very little and it remained wedged at the back of Houghton Hall and Killpara. Joseph, Rose nor Thelma had noticed it on the surveyor's maps, each assuming it was the property of the others and it remained like this until the owner died and left it to his daughter. She revelled under the name of Gwendoline. She was well into her fifties and dressed in a most obvious way, with clashing colours, clothes that might have suited an eighteen year-old, everything skin-tight and with stretch fabrics covering a very ample frame, platinum-dyed hair, heavy make-up and always in high-heeled shoes. She had married a certain Peter Sheffield and they had a small farm near Aspel. If Gwendoline Sheffield looked like a gaudy parrot, the husband was exactly the reverse, never or rarely speaking, and if you had to pick a colour to describe him it would be without a doubt a washed-out brown. He had extremely sad eyes and had a defeated look about him, whereas Gwendoline was definitely a go-getter, always out and about, showing all and telling everyone what they should be doing, not the sort of person one would choose to sit next to at a dinner party. But her social trade mark, apart from her exaggerated appearance, was her perfume. Gwendoline had a passion for perfume and usually used five or six different types together. The overall smell was asphyxiating in close proximity to her.

She was well aware of the competition between Killpara and Houghton Hall and foolishly thought that she would use the piece of land as a wedge to force her way into what she thought must be the two grandest homes in the district. She first contacted Thelma, who was, to say the least, very surprised about the tract of land, assuming it was Killpara's property, and Gwendoline then insisted she should speak to Thelma and took the liberty of inviting herself for a drink at Houghton Hall. Gwendoline was very pleased with herself, moving up the social ladder, she thought, as she wrapped the large cast-iron knocker on the front door, only to have Mrs Talbot open it. She glanced at Gwendoline's amazing costume – a red mini-skirt in some stretch fabric, a bright red jumper showing her ample breasts and very high heels, all this topped off with a battle jacket in fur of uncertain parentage - as the evenings had now turned very nippy.

'Do come in,' said Mrs Talbot, formally. 'Mrs Smith is expecting you,' and she was led down the long corridor to the sitting room, where Thelma was seated on one side with Barry opposite her. Gwendoline lost no time saying she would love a glass of wine and Thelma wondered exactly what on earth Gwendoline was using for perfume. It was extremely heady!

'What about this piece of land?' asked Thelma, coming straight to the point. Gwendoline was a triffle miffed at virtually being treated as a servant in Thelma's home. She had expected being asked to stay for dinner and exchanging all sorts of interesting gossip but she realised that this was not to be.

'Well,' said a sharper Gwendoline,' are you interested in purchasing it?'

'It depends on the price,' Thelma stated bluntly.

'I shall have to have it valued,' Gwendoline said, grandly.

'When you have done that, call me,' and Thelma stood up, this being the signal for her visitor to leave. Mrs Talbot showed a most dejected Gwendoline out. Thelma walked over to a table and spread out the surveyor's map. She looked at it carefully.

'Do you think we should purchase the land?' asked Barry pretentiously.

'You couldn't afford a packet of grass seed, let alone a piece of property!' she snapped and Barry turned his head in the direction of the television and watched his favourite quiz programme. Thelma looked at the map carefully. The piece of land is useless to me, she thought, it's in a difficult position, and she knew well that in winter a part of it was flooded so she just left it and went to see Mrs Talbot in the kitchen before returning to Walvern and home.

Gwendoline was furious that Thelma had treated her in such an offhand manner and told her husband time and time again. The following evening she tried the same approach at Killpara but was told by Beverly that Joseph would not be back until the following day and the rest were joining him the day after. Now Gwendoline was in a quandary. She knew Joseph did all the administration at Killpara and as it was a much larger and much more prestigious property than Thelma's she thought she had it, and would wait to see the whole group in a couple of days' time. Yes, much better, she thought, as she was more than curious to see inside Killpara and fascinated to meet Rose. She left her telephone number and hung up.

The next day, when Joseph arrived, he called Gwendoline to find out what piece of land she was talking about and she explained exactly what and where it was. He thanked her for the information and said he would call back when he had seen the tract of land. Gwendoline was anything but pleased with this quick dismissal: she had the sinking feeling that she might not even get a foot in the front door of Killpara. He looked at the map and located the piece of property for sale and then immediately drove next door to the share-farmer's house and they went to have a look at it.

'Oh God! I know the piece of land,' exclaimed James. 'It's useless but I thought it belonged to Thelma.'

'So did I,' agreed Joseph.

'It's in a terrible condition. It floods in winter if there is heavy rain'

'But can it be drained?'

'I suppose so,' James replied, 'but it's just over-capitalising. It's not worth it when you consider how much land we have added to Killpara. This is major work for no return. Let it go, Joseph. Let Thelma have it if she wants it, we don't need it.'

Joseph returned to Killpara and went over the map again: at Walvern Thelma was doing exactly the same thing.

The next day Joseph was expecting Rose and Thomas at about 6.30, so he offered to collect some things from the supermarket that Beverly needed as he had to go to Walvern. He went from the hardware shop to the supermarket and on leaving bumped literally into Ted.

'Hi, Joe!'

'Ted! How are you? Can I buy you a drink?'

'Sure.' So Joseph deposited his sacks in the car and they headed off to the Oriental for a drink. Joseph spoke to Ted about the small piece of useless land Gwendoline wanted to sell them.

'Why is it useless?' asked Ted and Joseph explained what James had told him. Ted ran his hand through his unruly mop of grey hair and asked what sort of trees were growing on it. Joseph frowned before explaining, 'Well, there are at the lowest point five or six weeping willows, some poplars and the rest are gum trees with a mass of blackberries.

'You know, Joe, weeping willows and poplars will only grow where there is plenty of water.'

'But in summer,' Joseph argued, 'James says it's as dry as a bone.'

'On the surface, yes, but obviously all this winter and spring rain filters into a large underground system that's full of water and what does stock want in summer?

'Water!' replied Joseph.

'I'll bet you could sink a bore and have unlimited water. Not bad, eh?'

'No, not at all,' agreed Joseph.

'But be careful, Joe. I know this Gwendoline. She's stupid but pretty cunning and I'll lay a bet the first person to invite her to dinner will no doubt get the piece of land. She's a terrible snob, though I don't know why. She hasn't got a thing going for her.'

'But, Ted, I don't think anyone else wants to buy the property. It's virtually landlocked.'

'You never know, Joe. Just be careful. Remember, Gwendoline is a real tough person. I have to rush. Toddy will be frightening everyone on the street. I've left him in the jeep. Thanks for the drink.' And with that he disappeared through the noisy bar crowd, leaving Joseph staring at a neatly arranged line of bottles behind the bar.

'Well, what do you think?' Joseph asked, as Rose and Thomas sat down for a drink.

'How much does it cost?' asked Thomas

'I don't know what she will ask, but when I was in Walvern yesterday, after Ted left me I went to the real estate office and asked what they thought the price should be estimated at and he said as it was virtually land-locked and was flooded in winter and spring he thought anything over five thousand dollars was robbery and thought a proper price was three and a half thousand, as it was useless to either Killpara or Houghton Hall.'

But twenty minutes after Joseph had left the real estate office Thelma also called in for some information only to be told Joseph was also interested. She left the office but couldn't work out why on earth Killpara, now with such large landholdings, would want a miserable eight hectares at the lowest part of their properties.

Joseph explained Gwendoline, via Ted's description, and with that Rose went to the telephone and called her. With a soft, charming voice, Rose began to search out what price she was asking and as Gwendoline was not coming forth on this and said quite bluntly that Thelma Smith was also interested in it, Rose remembered Ted's advice through Joseph.

'I think business deals over the telephone are so unsmart,' she said.

I couldn't agree more,' said a slightly more relaxed Gwendoline.

'I don't suppose I could possibly tempt you to join me for lunch tomorrow, could I?' teased Rose.

'Oh, well, I'm fearfully busy, but yes, I could make it.'

'Twelve thirty?'

'Yes, that will be fine,' and with that Rose said goodnight and hung up. 'It appears Thelma's interested in the piece of land. Do you think she has a notion about the subterranean water?'

'No idea,' answered Joseph.

Thomas, with an arm around Joseph's shoulder, wanted to know what time they were having dinner. Rose stood up to check with Beverly and returned to say, 'I was wondering, what is happening with Simon and Roaul and Terry?'

'No idea. I haven't seen Simon or Roaul for that matter,' came Joseph's reply. 'When I got here yesterday there were just the two girls working here.

287

'Oh, by the way,' Rose interrupted, 'dinner's in half an hour.'

Gwendoline was feeling very pleased with herself; a luncheon engagement at Killpara – oh, what a treat, she thought. No one in this area has had an invitation. Well, well, lucky me. I am sure I shall like them. It was then that her phone rang. When she said, 'Yes?' grandly into the receiver a voice said, 'It's Thelma Smith here. I am interested in buying that small piece of land. How much do you want for it?'

Gwendoline remembered getting short shrift from Thelma only a couple of days before and so now, in the power seat, she fired back, 'I haven't decided on a price, but after lunch at Killpara tomorrow I will let you know.' It gave her a great deal of satisfaction to hang up on Thelma.

Thelma was rather angry about Killpara, seemingly to have won again, but was also very curious to know why they wanted it and she didn't. She telephoned a surveyor she knew and asked him to come to Houghton Hall first thing next morning, which he duly did. They walked over the land and he said he didn't see a great value in it at all and then he noticed the large weeping willows and two well-established poplar trees in amongst the blackberries. 'Perhaps they want it for the water.'

'What water? There isn't any.'

'Thelma, these trees will only grow where there is water and a great deal of it. Obviously, it's just below the surface and a lot of it I would think.'

'Water – water!' she repeated. 'So that's what they want this for, water.' She went back to the house with the surveyor. 'But how did they know there was water?'

'I don't know,' he said. 'I am the only surveyor in this district and they didn't call me.' She invited him to have a drink but he said it was too early for him, though a cup of coffee would be treat. As it was Saturday, Barry was at home. He had refused to make the walk to the piece of land, considering the exercise a waste of time but he listened intently as he knew Thelma was not happy about the situation.

At precisely 12.30, a little red car beetled up to the front door of Killpara and out hopped Gwendoline. If Thelma had been surprised at her appearance two days before, the group at Killpara were overwhelmed by the platinum hair, lacquered into a sculptural shape, gold mini-skirt, a very tight apple-green fuzzy jumper with the usual low neckline, black stockings, and gold high-heeled shoes, all topped off with a gold silk-type scarf and a glomesh handbag on a long gold chain that hung from her shoulder.

'How are we?' she asked brightly.

'No, my name is Beverly. They are waiting for you in the sitting room.' With that Gwendoline tottered across the large entrance hall and into the sitting room. The boys immediately stood up and Rose slowly followed suit.

'How are we?' Gwendoline repeated and introductions were made all round. Rose instantly knew who and what she was dealing with and switched into full gear.

'What marvellously fresh colours you are wearing,' she said, wondering, what on earth was the perfume? 'I feel positively dowdy.'

'Oh, not at all. Some women can wear colour and others can't.' It wasn't quite a smile on Rose's face but she bore it well. Drinks were offered and Gwendoline was more than happy with champagne. 'It's the only thing I ever drink,' she lied and prattled on about the most foolish things. It was now taking Rose some effort to keep up and propel the conversation forward, never once mentioning the piece of land, for she knew tactically that it would be most unwise.

'It's such a nice house you have, Rose.' Gwendoline had immediately moved to first names without a blink of an eye and went on to praise the interior and also give a few hints about freshening it up. Thomas was having a great deal of trouble keeping a straight face. He thought the whole idea of Gwendoline giving Andrew hints on decorating very funny. Joseph eyed her curiously, remembering that his brother had once had a girlfriend just like Gwendoline and wondered if she was the same person. Gwendoline could not be stopped. At the dining room table no one got a word in edgeways; all the local gossip, beauty tips, you name it and Gwendoline rattled on about it, quite unaware she was making a fool of herself.

'She must be a lesbian,' she remarked.

'Really? Who?' Rose asked out of curiosity.

'Why, Thelma. Always in trousers, short hair, drives a jeep, though I don't suppose you know, but she runs a sawmill. Oh yes, obviously gay. I haven't a thing against it, but that dyke look I just can't stand.'

At this point Thomas thought he was not going to be able to control his laughter but he managed with a smile from ear to ear.

The meal finished and everyone passed their praise on to Beverly.

'I haven't eaten so well since my cousin's wedding,' Gwendoline smiled. 'Oh, I almost forgot,' she continued as she took her coffee in the sitting room. 'That piece of land. Are you still interested?' She addressed this question to Rose as she had with most of her chit-chat at lunch.

'Well,' smiled Rose, 'if you have someone else you would rather sell it to . . .'

'Oh no, Rose. I want you to have first offer.'

'Gwendoline, how very kind you are.' Gwendoline thanked her and belched loudly. 'Oops! Must be the bubbly.' She giggled.

'What sort of a price are you looking for?' Rose asked.

'Well, I'm not going to be ripped off, but I'll tell you the truth, Rose, seeing as we are such good friends – 'Thomas saw Rose gulp – 'you know,' and she dropped her voice, which was the first time in the afternoon, 'it floods. Dad could never use it. He used to have an old horse on it. I wonder what happened to it?' she said, turning and looking at Joseph who just shook his head. 'Well, I want four thousand dollars for it but I'll sell it to you, Rose for three thousand. How does that seem?'

'It seems a reasonable price, I think. Shall we use the real estate office or do you prefer to deal directly with my solicitor?'

'Direct, Rose. I don't see why we should pay the Real Estate lot anything. No, your solicitor.'

'Monday at 10.00,' and Rose gave her the address. Gwendoline staggered out at five minutes to three, leaving three exhausted hosts - and then the laughter began.

Gwendoline arrived home only to have her lacklustre husband inform her that she was to telephone Houghton Hall. 'Really? Who does she think she is?' she asked sarcastically.

'Oh no, it was Barry.' She stalked off to the telephone.

'Houghton Hall,' was Barry's introduction.

'Oh yes. Gwendoline. I do remember you'

'Aunt and I have been talking and I believe you are going to return our land to us.'

'What land?' cried Gwendoline in an excited manner, the result of a great deal of alcohol consumed at lunch.

'Your land? You can drop dead, Barry!'

'Really, Gwendoline, you have obviously been drinking.'

'You pretentious pig|! I wouldn't sell you the land if you were the last person in the world.'

'Sell? You should give the land back. It's part of Houghton Hall's heritage.

'Go fuck yourself, Barry!' and she slammed the phone down. 'Fat Bastard!' She swayed past her husband to have a lie down as she suddenly felt extremely tired.

But this was not the end of it. Sunday morning, very early, the telephone rang on Gwendoline's bedside table. 'Yes?' was the groggy response. 'Who?' and she sat upright in bed. 'I've had your stupid nephew on the phone and I'll tell you as well that the land is not yours and this rubbish you two are going on about returning Houghton Hall's heritage is just all bullshit. And Thelma,' she said in a loud, sarcastic manner, 'you will be pleased to know the land is now not on the market as a result of a sale. And anymore of this rubbish about heritage you can just forget it!' She slammed the phone down, pulled up the cover around her neck and wondered if that arctic rabbit fur jacket at Nelson's in Walvern was her fitting or not.

Thelma was furious, partly that she had lost the eight hectares to Rose, as it annoyed her that she always seemed to win, but also because of Barry. What an idiot! He had been the cause of the deal not going her way. She thought of tying him to a large tree trunk and having the sawmill blades cut the two of them in half. It wasn't completely true that it was Barry's fault. If Thelma had not been quite so offhand with Gwendoline initially, she might well have pulled off the purchase, but to have Barry add insult to injury was just too much for her.

Monday morning saw them all in Brendan Crane's office and in fifteen minutes all the papers were signed and a thirty day settlement was decided on as Gwendoline was desperate for the cash. She had been to Nelson's first thing that morning and put some money down on the white arctic rabbit jacket. The saleswoman was quite surprised that a woman of Gwendoline's age would be interested in such a jacket.

The four days passed pleasantly, with a dinner party every evening, Mary being present at all, as was Trevor, who kept everyone laughing. The second evening, Simon and Terry joined them but the tension between them was very evident and both Rose and Mary sought to soothe matters though it wasn't easy. Terry was brittle and if comments were passed in his direction his replies were very curt. Rose was ever so grateful to Trevor, who kept the ball rolling with one funny story after another. Even Terry had to admit they were entertaining.

When they returned to Rosebae, Terry had had just enough alcohol to have it out with Simon, and as they entered the house he started and expected that as usual Simon would play second fiddle. But this evening Simon had had enough, and to Terry's utter surprise he attacked him verbally.

'What is the point of you coming to Killpara? What do you want – a round of applause just for attending?' He caught Terry by surprise, as it was he who had intended to begin the evening's battle. Before he could even reply, Simon attacked again. 'I am sick and tired of your limited attitude. I have cared for you and always will but just lay off the martyred routine.'

Terry stalked through to the kitchen and returned with a can of beer, a bottle of red wine and two glasses. He poured and sarcastically said, 'Well, where do we go from here?'

'You tell me!' responded Simon, crossly seizing his glass but without waiting for a reply shot an arrow in Terry's direction. 'If you stopped being so defensive with all my friends, life would be easier for us all.'

'For you, you mean.'

'No, Terry, for you. I can go out and enjoy myself with or without you, but I am happy if you come. Do you understand me?'

'Perfectly.' The reply sounded icy. 'And now that we have got to this stage,' he went on, gathering momentum, 'what, or should I say who, are you having an affair with?'

'That is entirely my business,' smiled Simon.

'I'm afraid not. That is a child's way of resolving a problem and as neither of us can claim to be children you will have to do better than that.' Terry smiled falsely at Simon. There was a deathly silence that seemed to last hours. It was finally Terry who again took over. 'If I am supposed to support you emotionally then the least you can do is to be honest.'

Simon knew Terry was within his rights. He should be honest with him but something held him back. He knew if he told him about

Roaul there was going to be a screaming match, so he hedged the question.

'Oh, what does it matter?' He spoke wearily.

'It matters quite a deal,' Terry replied slowly. 'You see, I find myself in a situation like this evening where everyone I am sure knows of your affair – if I may be so bold as to describe it as such – and the most affected member of this group being me knows very little at all except that everyone is offering me small talk and pity. Charming, just charming wouldn't you say?'

Simon refilled his glass and the thought that went through his head was why the hell wasn't he in bed with Roaul and not having this electric altercation with Terry? He suddenly, as a result of this thought, decided to fight fire with fire.

'What do you want to do?' he demanded of Terry.

'And what is that exactly supposed to mean?'

'Well,' Simon began, summoning up his last remaining courage of the evening, 'I happen to be in love with someone.'

'Obviously not me,' came the razor-sharp reply.

'Our relationship is different.'

'Different or indifferent?' asked Terry, emptying the last drop of beer into his glass.

'I'm afraid I'm just too tired to keep this argument going,' Simon said wearily.

'But not too tired to have sex with this person,' spat Terry. Simon stood up. 'You make the decisions, you always do. Please yourself. Good night,' and he left the room and slammed his bedroom door.

Terry sat looking at the room around him. An emptiness crept into him and the ability to get rid of it just wasn't there. What was he to do? It wasn't that he couldn't find other accommodation easily, but Rosebae he had put his whole life into. He had shared the ups and downs with Simon and all of a sudden this safe little world was like a box of chattels turned upside down and scattered carelessly everywhere. He went to stand up but his legs felt like jelly. He knew all the smart descriptive words for the situation but it was rejection that sounded like a trumpet in his ears.

* * * * *

The return trip to Melbourne was just Thomas and Rose : Joseph, because of a legal problem and wages to pay, would follow the next day.

'Who is this Ted?' asked Thomas.

'Well,' Rose told him, 'he seems to be someone after our better interests, wouldn't you think?'

'I suppose so,' was the reply.

'Thomas,' Rose looked toward him as he drove through the autumn drizzle. 'What's the problem?'

'Nothing,' was the blunt reply.

'Thomas, what's wrong?' she asked again. There was a silence as Thomas pulled out and overtook a large semi-trailer that was well-laden.

'Well,' he said, looking ahead into the light-splashed road, 'we don't even know who he is or what he is.'

'Thomas, Joseph loves you. Haven't you worked that out?'

'Of course,' he replied rather defensively.

'Darling, why don't we have Ted to lunch. It can't be any more difficult than Gwendoline,' she said, laughing.

'The perfume – where on earth do you think she bought it from?'

'Probably the hardware shop, I should think,' and they both laughed.

'Well, that's settled. We shall invite Ted to lunch or dinner and thank him for his help and not only that, his kindness in assisting Joseph to work out the management of Killpara. What do you think?'

'Yes. Of course'.

But it didn't work out quite like that. When Thomas told Joseph of this arrangement, Joseph telephoned Ted. 'It's nice of you, Joe, but, well, it's not me to go into these big homes, you know. Why don't you come and have dinner with Toddy and me?'

'Love to,' was Joseph's reply. 'What shall I bring?'

'Nothing. I'll have it all done. What about next Saturday night. Six thirty to seven, as it's getting dark now.' Joseph told him that would be great and they'd be there. Then he hung up.

The following day, when Joseph arrived in Melbourne, he took a taxi direct to Albany Road to find Rose waiting for him. 'Really, Joseph, I thought that as a matter of respect for Ted he should dine with us, or we should be more than happy to host him at the Oriental.'

'He wants to do it his way.'

Rose sighed. 'Yes, and we must respect that, as he has been so good to you and directly to Killpara.'

The rest of the week in Melbourne was frenetic, with so many things to complete but one occasion it was not possible to dismiss. Betty Marshall had organised a dinner party for Wednesday evening and said if the three of them were not present she would never speak to them again as it was very special. And so they duly arrived on a cold, blustery evening but for once there was no rain, and entered Betty's warm home in every sense of the word. But as they went forward it was Rodney who swept forward and kissed them. 'Come and meet him,' he chanted, 'he's just the tops. If I can't have you, Thomas, or should I say a better man has you, well this isn't too bad.'

Rose laughed. 'Do tell, Rodney. He must be gorgeous.'

'He is, Rose, he is.'

Betty moved forward and said, 'Oh, let me save you from our love-stricken son. Come and have a drink.' They moved into the sitting room, where Robert stood up and welcomed them. 'I am so glad you could come,' he said. 'A dinner party for seven is such a magic number.' He smiled. Rose had known Robert and Betty for well over thirty years but she detected in Robert this evening a pride that was just about to burst out of his heart.

'Well,' said Betty, taking over, 'Rodney, make the introductions.'

'This is my lover,' Rodney smiled.

'Hello,' Thomas greeted him, extending his hand to an unusual-looking young man. He was tall, very thin, with black eyes and a mane of black hair and very olive skin.

'Hi,' he said softly, obviously feeling a little overwhelmed at Rodney's parents' acceptance of his love for Rodney, who was floating on air and in the highest of spirits. As they moved into the dining room, Rodney held Joseph from behind. 'I thought I would die when you and Thomas got together but now everything with Angelo seems just perfect.'

Joseph spun around and embraced Rodney. 'You see, sometimes you just have to wait.' And he hugged him.

'I'm still green with envy, but I love you both.' He laughed. 'Mum's put out the full spread tonight, so don't worry. I think she is expects us to marry at St. Patrick's.' He burst into hysterical laughter.

Betty had indeed pulled out all the stops. The meal was excellent, as were the wines. It was a very public statement that Betty and Robert had made together and they were so proud to introduce Angelo as their new and permanent member of the family. Rodney didn't stop. It was his night and he had a great time. It was Angelo who was more than just interested in the couple Rose escorted, Joseph and Thomas, and he instantly knew exactly what Rodney had confided to him about Thomas.

'You must come and stay with us at Killpara,' said Rose. 'In fact, I insist. The house is finally finished and the garden has a bit to do still, and it does look a bit sad, but come spring it should take off – or so Roaul says.'

'How is Raoul?' asked Betty. 'He hasn't been here for ages.'

'He has his hands full at Killpara at present,' answered Thomas and smiled. 'The pool is finished and so there will be time to swim, eat and drink.'

'Oh, Rose,' Robert exclaimed, 'I'm so envious of you.'

'Good heavens, Robert, why?

'Well, the three of you have worked as a team and you now have a house in the country to escape to.'

'We've been dreaming about it for years,' Betty interrupted, 'and now we have an extra member of the family,' she smiled at Angelo. 'A house in the country near you all would be just perfect. Is there anything for sale, do you know.'

'I'm afraid you will have to ask Joseph, as he is the man on the spot,' Rose replied and all eyes turned to Joseph.

'I can check, but just near Killpara I don't think there is a large house on the market at present. But you never know.'

'Promise me you will call me if anything comes up,' added Robert.

'Oh, it must have a tower like Killpara,' Rodney cried laughing, having heard the story.

'Why don't you come and stay at the end of the month for a few days and see how you feel about the district? Perhaps you mightn't like it,' said Thomas.

'If Rose likes it, as you do, Thomas, then we shall love it,' insisted Rodney, with a wicked look in his eye and one arm around Angelo's shoulder.

'And we shall all look forward to the end of the month,' added Betty. 'What a great idea.'

Robert agreed absolutely and Rodney just winked at Rose, who smiled back at him. 'Just think, Angelo, swimming from one end to the other of that pool naked. How fabulous!' and he laughed, though the rest of the company didn't. Betty turned her head in Rodney's direction to notice Angelo had gone red with embarrassment and stared at Rodney as did the rest of them. He immediately put his arms around Angelo and said very determinedly, 'I'm sorry, Angelo, if I have embarrassed you. It wasn't my intention at all.' There was a silence and then he said in a much quieter voice, 'I am sorry – I love you.'

'Me too,' was the reply.

'Joseph!' He turned toward Robert. 'I need to ask you a favour. I wish to leave in your hands a power of attorney, so if we are not here and a big home comes up you can sign for us, because, as you said, these properties don't come on the market every day.

When Joseph looked surprised, 'Don't worry,' said Betty. 'If you have done everything for Killpara I am sure you can do this little favour for us.' Joseph was not so sure that he wanted this responsibility but accepted the trust they obviously had in him.

Rose went on to say how exceptionally pleased she was with Beverly now running Killpara like clockwork and Joseph interrupted to inform everyone that she was a great cook, then changed the subject to describe luncheon with Gwendoline, which had everyone laughing.

They all left Melbourne on Thursday in the late afternoon and expected Mary and Trevor for dinner. All three were quite curious about the dinner party at Ted's on Saturday evening. Not even Joseph had got beyond the veranda covered with engine parts and so he had said to Rose and Thomas they had better be prepared for anything.

'Oh, that's all right. When I was young and living in the house near Aspel, there was a strange lady who lived alone, a Mrs Tackaberry. If I remember, it was a wooden cottage with lots of chimneys and it was completely overgrown. There was just a green tunnel from the front gate to the veranda. In those days Mrs Tackaberry administered hyperdermic needles for things like tetanus, I think. I fell on a rusty sheet of tin once and I was bustled off immediately for the shot. It was amazing inside, so dark if I remember, but she had four large angora rabbits in there. They were white or cream, I don't remember, and were not afraid of anybody. They made us children forget the pain of those old fashioned needles. I wonder if the house is still there?'

'There is a cottage with lots of chimneys but it's not overgrown. Just near Aspel. It's been done up and looks quite smart,' explained Joseph. 'I passed it last week when I went to Ted's.'

'Well, at least they haven't pulled it down,' Rose said.

'With four rabbits dashing about in the house it can't have been too hygienic,' said Thomas.

'I just don't remember,' said Rose, 'but they were quite a sight for us youngsters.'

They arrived as bidden at seven with the autumn weather well set in. The trees were beginning to change their colour quite rapidly, yellows and russets a great contrast to the olive-green eucalypts. The road into Ted's had been difficult for Joseph to manage as the potholes had become mini-lakes. As the jeep came to a halt Toddy leapt forward barking and jumping on to the door of the jeep as he knew this jeep well and it equalled Joseph and food.

'Get down, Toddy!' cried Joseph, but to no avail. Then he unwrapped a piece of meat. The dog seized it and raced off to devour it, totally unaware of Rose or Thomas.

'Come in,' called Ted. 'This way.'

They climbed the three steps onto the ever-crowded veranda. Joseph was surprised to see that Ted had on a white shirt and black trousers with an ample dark blue woollen jumper. They all filed in.

To say they were overwhelmed was an understatement and the looks on their faces was such that Ted laughed. 'It's home! A drink!' They all chorused their thanks and he showed them to seats in the sitting room. The three of them just looked about in amazement, saying nothing at all. Ted returned with a bottle of champagne and placed it in a silver wine cooler. Yes, the interior they found themselves in was as if they had been thrown back in time to about 1850. It was in spotless condition and if someone had entered the room in period costume it would only have made the three of them feel even more out of place.

'Ted, it's fantastic!' exclaimed a surprised Joseph and the fire crackled in the big cast-iron grate.

'Thanks. Things haven't changed here at all since my great-great grandfather.'

'I think it's just beautiful,' Rose said and then realised that she had forgotten to hand Ted a box of chocolates she had purchased. She apologised, and Ted's easy manner won the day. He gave them a tour of the house and each room was exactly as it had been furnished in the 1850s. The only addition since that time was the telephone and electricity. The curtains and upholstery were in immaculate condition.

'I've had the curtains re-made,' he explained. 'A lady in Walvern copied them identically, so we have the complete look.'

They returned to the living room, glancing in all directions at this step back in time. Ted poured himself a glass of beer but kept the champagne glasses well topped up.

'I must thank you very much,' said Thomas, 'for helping us as well as helping Joseph with all your knowledge. I'm no use at all on that front.'

'It's a pleasure, Thomas. Joe's a great guy. Toddy gives him full marks.' He laughed and then they moved into the dining room, lit only by candles and kerosene lamps. The soft glow was very romantic. Again, everything was in perfect condition, the silver gleaming, not a dusty item to be seen. The only modern thing was a large cane basket with low sides and lined with a tartan cushion which was obviously for Toddy, who at a certain point arrived and headed obediently to the basket and sat with his head on his paws, watching and listening to the conversation.

The meal was excellent.

'Ted, you're a wonderful cook,' Rose congratulated him.

'Thanks. I rarely get the opportunity to throw a proper meal together so for me it's a nice change.'

They discussed all manner of subjects from farming to Gwendoline with great gales of laughter and then in a more relaxed mood went on to talk about stock breeding and the subject arose about Houghton Hall.'

'It was once a fine property,' said Ted, 'one of the largest, and it produced very well. I remember my mother telling me, even in her time, the house had an indoor staff of four, which no one else had around here. And then Emily married this pretentious twit and they sold it all off bit by bit. And that fool Barry is no help to Thelma, so I don't know what she's going to do in the future. What do you think?' he asked, looking at Rose.

'I've no idea. I've never met her.'

'Oh, really?' Ted laughed. 'I would love to be there when you finally do,' and laughed again.

The evening passed very smoothly but Thomas had the odd feeling Ted was sizing him up, as he occasionally noticed him staring at him. Everyone congratulated Ted on his fine hospitality and his wonderful home. As they all stood up this was obviously the signal for Toddy to leap forward and accept pats from Joseph. Both Rose and Thomas held back. 'It's OK,' said Ted, seeing their nervous faces. 'If Toddy is with Joe, there's no problem.'

Driving back to Killpara the autumn drizzle began again. The conversation was electric and did not stop even when they entered Killpara.

'It's just fabulous,' Rose insisted. 'I can't remember an experience like this I my whole life.'

'Not even Mrs Tackaberry's rabbits!' laughed Thomas. 'But it is in immaculate condition. From the look of Ted you would never dream he lived in this wonderful cocoon of the past.'

'Well, if you see Ted in the dirty track suit and his hair everywhere, the contrast is even greater. Tonight he had really scrubbed up and even shaved,' laughed Joseph.

Thomas was so much more content now that he had met Ted. It wasn't that he was jealous, but then perhaps he was. These new experiences for him were quite worrying but having Joseph beside him this evening reassured him of Joseph's love, which was most assuredly reciprocated.

Sunday morning Beverly took a call and said, when everyone was up they would reply at once. Rose being first up returned Mary's call and Mary said that she had taken the liberty of inviting them to a showing of a local painter's work at three o'clock in the library at Walvern, and they just must, after Mass, have lunch with her and then go on to the exhibition. No was not acceptable. When the boys finally made an appearance at 9.30, Rose gave them the programme for the day. Joseph and Thomas had planned on this cold autumn day to spend it in front of the fire, drinking and relaxing, but it was not to be.

After the eleven o'clock Mass in Walvern, the black Jaguar eased its way back to Aspel Drive to a lunch that Mary and Trevor had organised. Much laughter and joking was the order of the day but not one word about Ted's dinner party. Joseph had said that if he had kept his house a secret for all these years and decided to share its secret with them, then a secret it should remain. Thomas and Rose concurred and so every subject was attacked but not Ted. Gwendoline did not get off so lightly, with Trevor doing imitations of her with a white tea-towel over his head to take the place of her platinum hair.

'Do we really have to go to this opening?' asked Joseph.

'Come on, sweetie. A little bit of local culture won't kill you,' said Trevor.

'I hate these turns.'

'We won't stay long,' said Mary.

'When we are finished, why don't you both come back to Killpara for dinner? I'll just call Simon and Terry.' Rose took the liberty of using Mary's phone. 'Oh,' she said, when she returned, 'I don't think all is well at Rosebae, but the invitation has been given.'

It was difficult to get a parking space near the library so they had to walk a block back in cold, blustery wind with the plane trees hurling their yellow leaves at the passing pedestrians.

'Quite a crowd,' remarked Mary, and they eased their way inside.

'Rose! It's nice to see you again,' and Gwendoline forced herself between two people, speaking with a glass of red wine in her hand and the identical outfit she had been attired in for lunch at Killpara but with the addition of an odd fur battle jacket on top of it all.

'Hello,' was Rose's reply, dreading the fact that Gwendoline was going to remain stuck to them for the afternoon. Fortunately this was not to be as she flitted from group to group, passing her knowledgeable opinion about art and generally having most people gasping for air as a result of the extremely heady perfume she was drenched in. When she returned at one point, with the group laughing about Trevor's description of a woman at the exhibition, she descended yet again.

'Dear Rose,' she said loudly, 'that's the dyke over there,' and pointed in Thelma's direction. Rose and Thomas spun around together to see a very countrified woman with masculine dress sense but Rose noted at once that it was an expensive dress sense. Rose looked again and turned back to the conversation: so that was Thelma - she was much different from what Rose had imagined.

Thelma was extremely well tailored, neat, nothing out of place, hardly a look that could be called lesbian at all. Rose had no idea why Gwendoline had labelled her as such but then thought again that every woman in this room was probably a dyke in Gwendoline's eyes, as a result of her own bizarre dress sense.

'So you see,' Gwendoline went on to Thelma, now more than under the weather as a result of many glasses of red wine - to keep the cold out, she said – 'that's the smart group I sold the land to,' and suddenly realised she had missed someone and sped off, lurching through the crowd with the ever half-filled glass of wine in one hand. Thelma turned very slowly to see this Killpara group. None of them did she know. 'Hm,' she thought, 'the young one is Mary O'Farrell's brother and the other one must be Thomas O'Riely and that must be her.'

Rose turned back to the painting she was considering purchasing. Well, she is a very elegant city woman, she thought, swinging around and having a second look. Odd she should be an expert in acquiring property.

'Let's go,' urged Joseph. 'This is terrible.'

'Just a minute, junior,' said Trevor, and introduced Rose to the artist. They spoke for a while and Rose was taken by Trevor to see what he thought was the best piece in the exhibition. Rose glanced at it. It was indeed a fine still life of fruit in an almost photo-realist style.

She looked at it again and had to admit it was the best in the show, although she said to Trevor, 'the frame is hideous.'

'True, true,' and they walked back to the others. She looked at the catalogue and the prices. They were probably high for the local market, but Rose thought she just might have it as there were still a few blank spaces on the walls at Killpara. As she was about to leave, she said to Trevor, 'Just a minute,' and she drew out her cheque book, wrote a cheque and said to him, 'Can you organise this for me?' Then she followed the others out into the drizzle that was falling yet again. 'Wait on the veranda for me. I'll get the car,' and Thomas, with the keys in his hand, rushed off to do so.

Thelma had had the same idea to leave and get home out of the terrible weather. She returned her glass and spun around, deciding she would take the painting after all, only to see it being taken down and Trevor doing all the organising. 'Well,' she said to him, moving across,' you were quicker than me.' She smiled.

'Hi, Thelma, no, I didn't buy it – Rose did.'

Thelma said not a word but made for the door, only to see Rose and Joseph arm in arm talking to Mary. She had to pass close by to go down the steps to the pavement. It was then both women glanced at once another, neither giving anything away.

Back at Killpara, in the large living room, conversation moved to light-hearted subjects, with Trevor as usual taking over. The door knocker was heard and Beverly opened it to Simon. 'Do come in,' she smiled, 'you look cold.'

'I am a bit,' he said and joined the noisy group seated near the fire.

'Where's Terry?' asked Rose.

'Long story. But he says thanks for the invitation.' There was a silence, which meant that everyone understood that the situation between Simon and Terry was anything but fine. As the evening moved on and just as the others rose to go to the dining room, Thomas took Simon's arm and they remained behind alone for a moment.

'What's happening with Terry?' he asked quietly. 'There doesn't seem to be a solution to this one.'

'I just don't know what he wants to do, but he most certainly isn't going to tolerate Roaul.'

'Are you sure you can't come to some arrangement?'

'Certain. I would be terrified he would put rat poison in the first meal for Roaul.'

'That bad, is it?'

'Worse,' came the reply, as they moved into the dining room,.

Simon was not exaggerating at all. Rosebae was a house that, when one opened the door, electric tensions were shot out in all directions like a neutron explosion. Terry specialised in drama and he was in his element now, but not enjoying it at all, although his comments, if he deigned to speak to Simon, were acid. The silence was to Simon's ears much, much worse. The evening meals were as if someone had pumped frost into the room and it hung on everything and there was little or no conversation to thaw it. The evenings became more and more unbearable for both of them, each hoping the other would offer a solution that was acceptable to both, but both of them knew that this was now impossible.

Roaul came up to Killpara and had organised a meeting with Simon. When alone he noted Simon's handsome face looking very tired and stressed and after an afternoon of love-making Simon held him in his arms as he looked vacantly across the room.

'What do you want to do?' asked Roaul, as he snuggled back under the covers and held Simon.

'I want to be with you,' he replied softly, 'but how the hell are we going to manage it?'

'Well, what are our choices?'

'I don't think we have many, do we?'

'One or two.' Roaul pulled himself up on top of Simon's body. 'You've just acquired another farm, haven't you?' Simon kissed him and said yes he had.

'Well, there's your answer. All the land you administer, but some distance from Rosebae is the other house at Aspel that came with the property. Offer Terry the house to live in, rent free. You needn't have anything to do with him at all then.'

'And where do you fit into the scenario?' Simon tightened his grip on Roaul.

'Well, I have to work but I now have a good business and a reliable team of workers who are great, so apart from the initial organisation and planning of the gardens my time is my own – and yours.' He said this with a wicked grin. Simon rolled over on top of him. 'I wonder if it's so simple,' he said, and was then lost in the splendid sensual exercise of love-making. For the first night ever, he did not return to Rosebae but shared it with Roaul at the Oriental.

If this act of determination on his part was to unnerve Terry, it worked one hundred per cent. Terry sat staring at the place setting opposite him. The emptiness of it was final. He knew, with this move, he had lost everything. There was now no possible way he could continue, as the last emotional blackmail card had been played and lost. Terry had few friends. He had acquaintances but no real friends, hence his insecurity. He had put everything he had into this relationship, admittedly on his terms, but a genuine commitment it had been. As he poured another glass of beer and played with the evening meal, he gave a deep sigh as he ran his hands through his blonde hair. He had never imagined that the relationship would ever finish. Sex, yes, but the bond they had built up was now in small pieces, scattered everywhere and he ran this through his mind until he was totally exhausted. He cleared all the dishes away and went to bed, where, for the first time since he could remember, he cried himself to sleep in a state of complete hopelessness.

The following late morning saw Simon's car pull up in front of Rosebae and he entered to see Terry aimlessly watching television. He closed the living room door was a slam which startled Terry. He swung around expecting trouble and he wasn't wrong.

'Would you like a drink?' asked a calm Simon. The answer was not in the affirmative. Simon poured himself a glass of red wine and moved to the television set and turned it off. Terry settled back in his chair like a coiled spring, ready to attack.

'We are going to resolve this situation now,' Simon began, steadily, and had a mouthful of wine. 'I am going to give you two options and two only.'

'And if they don't suit me?' asked Terry, arrogantly.

'Then you can pack and leave by tomorrow afternoon.'

The air was electric sharp and clever repartee had no part in the discussion. Now it was survival and Terry well knew it might not all be in his favour.

'The first option is this, but it won't work, I think. It is that you continue to live here and accept the situation.'

'You are correct,' snapped Terry. 'What's the second?'

'The second is this. I purchased, eighteen months ago, that large piece of land that adjoins Rosebae. There is a house and all new farm buildings that go with it, but,' he paused, taking a deep breath, 'that house will be for the share-farmer who begins Thursday week, so all the old farm buildings here, that are really out-dated I will have demolished. But with the purchase I also acquired a house in Aspel, a Victorian weatherboard house, similar to Rosebae and it is now untenanted. I am offering it to you rent-free for whatever length of time you wish to use it. With your private finance it should mean no hardship for you at all.'

There was silence.

'Well, who's idea has this been?' asked Terry.

'Do you want the house or not?' Simon replied, side-stepping the query.

Now that Terry realised that all was not lost, he swept back to his old self and defiantly began to spit venom.

'Don't!' Simon interrupted. 'I give you, or should I say I offer you, this house and that's it.'

'And everything at Rosebae?'

'Take what you want. I don't care. But when I return tomorrow you either accept this or make your own way. I shall always be your friend, no matter what, but your negative attitude makes continuing to live with you impossible.' He took his glass to the kitchen, washed it and then collected a few clothes. Without another word he left and drove to Killpara for lunch with Joseph and Roaul.

Terry sat as if in a trance. 'Dismissed, that's what this is', he thought angrily, dismissed to make way for someone else. He stood up and walked through the house, mentally calculating what he would take, this and this, and in a moment the thought of dismissal or loss had passed. He put on his coat and went to the door, climbed into his car and went to have a look at the house in Aspel. He pulled up in front of a double-fronted Victorian house in apparently good condition. He went for an inspection tour of it. To his surprise, the back door was not locked, so he entered and walked through the empty house, but the sensation of emptiness was different from Rosebae. Rosebae had been built up by two people. It took only the loss of one to make it empty, whereas this house only needed the addition of one to fill it up.

It had been a little easier than Simon had expected, but as he knew Terry he knew the drama was not finished yet. It was Roaul in the following week, when he spoke to Andrew about Simon, who received a very big surprise. 'So,' said Andrew,' where does this leave us? Do we sell the house?'

'Not at all,' Roaul replied. 'I would like to spend half my time with you and half with Simon.'

'Oh, would you? I presume that leaves me with the same option.'

'But of course.'

'Well, I must say your choice of man is good, and I am not sure why I am being so co-operative and understanding, but there it is. I suppose after so many years relationships have to be fine-tuned and the fact that I have you for half the time is not much different to now, is it?' Andrew narrowed his eyes a little. 'Don't tell me you want me to decorate the new country house.'

'But of course. There is no one else I would ever consider using.' Roaul laughed and left the room, only to return with a bottle of champagne and two glasses. 'Let's drink to –'he stopped a moment '– what shall we drink to?'

'How about real friendship.' They clinked glasses together. 'What's the house like,' Andrew then asked.

'Well, I think the expression 'the pits' is applicable.' Andrew laughed. 'Oh, I forgot to tell you, there is a small cottage, all to be re-arranged, but it's yours, of course.

'Of course,' came the reply.

'Now, do I tell Rose or do we?'

'I think 'we' would be a more civilised way of doing things, don't you?'

'Absolutely,' and Roaul stood up, crossed the elegant living room to kiss Andrew on the forehead. 'My shout! What about that divine restaurant in Richmond? Shall I give Rose a call and see if she can make it?'

It was fine by Andrew, so Roaul went out, while Andrew looked about the gracious room and took a deep breath. Their relationship had always been open-ended and he knew that one day the one night stands were going to eventually turn into something more concrete but they had always been honest with one another. The drama was there, but underneath it all was a stable relationship, one for the other, and even if Roaul were in love with Simon this didn't break their original bond : it strangely cemented it. This relationship could only be said to be in marked difference to Simon and Terry's. Rose was exceptionally careful at dinner not to make any mistake about times and places as she had known about Roaul and Simon for some time, so she directed most of the conversation at Andrew, which made a much-relieved Roaul smile.

When Simon had returned to Rosebae after giving Terry his ultimatum, some time had passed, mainly at Killpara as Rose and Thomas had arrived and joined Roaul at the Oriental so it was thirty six hours later when he pulled his car up and went inside. He was shocked at the interior. There was nothing, absolutely nothing remained in the living room. It was empty. Terry had taken him at his word and the moment Simon had left he called a removal firm and literally emptied the house. The only room not touched was his own bedroom. He looked about in sheer disbelief. There wasn't even a chair to sit on, not a dish, a glass, not even the refrigerator; no curtains, or carpets. It was as if a giant vacuum cleaner had totally denuded the interior. Not a picture. Nothing. No note – all gone, just as he had wanted but what was he to do now? He instantly called Roaul, who claimed it was a blessing, having only seen the interior of the house once and he explained that Andrew would have everything organised very shortly. And he did like the interior of Killpara, didn't he? Simon felt very weak and walked about the empty house and found that there wasn't any point bring a chair from his bedroom to the living room as that was even more depressing, so he shut himself up in the bedroom, glad to be without Terry's drama, but a house he had grown up in, all the bits and pieces that make up a nostalgic past were gone; his parents' furniture, everything. 'The prints on the walls, even the food from the cupboards,' he said forlornly to Rose. 'It's all gone, everything.'

'Let it go,' Rose advised him. 'You now have something much more important with Roaul's love. You can totally start again and until you do you absolutely must stay at Killpara. I insist.'

And that was what happened, though it was a very lost Simon who, for some weeks, returned to a cold and empty house that had been his childhood home. He thought of prosecuting Terry for theft but Joseph assured him that it was not worth it, and when Roaul arrived he concurred with Joseph. But Simon was not feeling at all secure. Rosebae denuded of everything was as if a part of his life had been stolen or even worse just cast away. Each time he returned to the house it was even sadder and more forlorn. The cracks in the walls seemed vast. The little marks here and there seemed great smears on the plaster, but it was the cold that he noticed more than anything and that manifested itself into abandonment. Nothing, just cold, empty spaces, and as the house was very large, one room after another in this condition made it even more sad; his bedroom still being furnished tended to make the whole scene even more ridiculous.

CHAPTER 9

The Beginning of Two New Lives

CHAPTER 9

The Beginning of Two New Lives

Thomas sensed that Simon was very unsure about everything and spoke to him. 'Look, when we began work here at Killpara I had no idea what would eventuate. You remember Killpara before and look at it now.'

'I see your point,' Simon said, with downcast eyes, 'but I have a feeling Roaul is going to want to overhaul Rosebae from top to bottom.'

'What a good idea! Look, I could never have done this transformation without Joseph's enthusiasm and anyway the past is the past. You need to start again with Roaul.'

'But how much is this all going to cost?'

'Talk to Roaul. Be honest with him about finances. He will organise it all. Don't worry.' Thomas put an arm around Simon's shoulder. 'Everything will work out. Don't worry about Terry stripping the house. You realise that apart from the two portraits that Joseph repaired the frames of, there is not one piece of the original furniture or fixtures from the original Killpara. It has all been recreated and I have to say I think it's great.'

'Do you think Joseph could find me a tower?' Simon joked.

'If that's what you want I am sure he could. Come on, let's have a drink. By the way, did Pete go as well?'

'Yes – and Touolula.'

'Well, that will please the neighbours,' and they both laughed.

The following weekend saw Rose well and truly in command. She had invited Andrew and Roaul to stay and she knew well having spoken to Andrew privately that a mature if not totally stable solution had been arrived at. The weekend was oddly relaxed, with Simon feeling the most awkward about the situation. It was after lunch on Saturday that Andrew asked Simon would he take him and show him Rosebae.

'Certainly,' was the reply.

'Alone,' was Andrew's second request.

When the two of them arrived, in wintery conditions, it looked sadder than ever. The house seemed to have just given up as if it were too exhausted to keep going. Andrew was shocked at the emptiness of it. He knew the story via Rose but the cold, desolate rooms, stripped of everything, completely naked, with nothing at all to recommend them, presented, especially to him, an overwhelming sadness. He said nothing as they walked from room to empty room in the large house and Andrew sensed Simon's anguish. He laid a hand on his shoulder. 'It's a disaster now but by the summer we shall have it all in order. Don't worry.'

Simon offered a forlorn thanks.

'And do I have *'carte blanche'* with the house?' Andrew asked.

'Sure. There's nothing left.'

'Perhaps that's for the best. Sometimes you need to get rid of everything and begin again. You see somehow your environment stops you from going ahead. You now have a clean slate, so there are no dilemmas of should I get rid of it or not? Terry has probably done you a great favour.'

As they walked into yet another denuded room, with not even a carpet, 'I see,' Andrew smiled.

'You're telling me exactly what Thomas said yesterday,' as he stared at the square space of unpolished boards in the centre of the room.

'Well, we can't both be wrong, can we?'

'But the expense of all this . . .' Simon sighed, glancing at the curtainless window.

'Listen, Roaul and I have spoken about your relationship and the situation that goes with it.' Here, Simon held his breath. He knew that the following conversation was exactly why Andrew had insisted that they speak alone at the now empty house.' Roaul and I have been together for years and we always will be in one form or another and it's the other that I think you and I have to talk about.'

Simon felt a swell of nausea. 'I would offer you a chair but as you can see, Terry took me at my word.' He smiled weakly.

'It's not a problem. I was impressed that you had offered me the cottage here so in a way I still share my life with Roaul and now with you. I shall confess I am completely envious of Roaul's having chosen such a handsome companion but I am conceited enough to think that perhaps that is a reflection on me.' He smiled as he said this. 'It's all right, Simon. I think, in one way or another, we can solve all the problems, even an empty house. Did Terry take all the contents of the kitchen cupboards?' He glanced around the old-fashioned kitchen.

'Yes, everything. The only room he didn't strip was my bedroom.

'He sounds a fair bitch,' Andrew laughed. 'Look, I still have furniture over from Killpara, so don't worry. There must be a chair or two.' After Simon had quietly thanked him, he went on, 'May I have a look about by myself?' He pulled from his coat pocket a biro and notepad and wandered through the large empty house making notes. 'Simon, why is the front door at the back of the house?' So Simon explained the story of the new road in front being cut two metres deeper down and thus leaving the front of the house trapped on an upper level with a hedge protecting it from the cold winds which swept up from the valley. 'So Terry changed it back to front so to speak,' said Andrew.

'Well, thank goodness the house is weatherboard. We can move it about.'

'Can we?' asked a very surprised Andrew.

'Of course! Look at Killpara.'

Andrew saw the point but felt that all of his control of the property not to mention his energy was slowly but very surely slipping away.

When they returned to Killpara, Simon felt marginally better. There had been no drama with Andrew and it crossed his mind that he really didn't think he had offered the cottage to Andrew at all. Obviously this had been Roaul's doing. Oh well, he thought, looking across at Roaul, who cares? He asked for a received a large sheet of white paper from Beverly and laid it on the table. From his tiny notepad he sketched up a floor plan of Rosebae. Simon was to say the least surprised that from less than half an hour in the house Andrew had remembered so much. Rose moved closer and looked at the layout.

'We shall move the house much further back on the property and swing the front to the side road and plant an avenue. What do you think, Roaul?'

'Yes, but it will have to go back quite a way and remember there is a swimming pool somewhere there,' as he looked at the design on the paper.

Rose instinctively slipped her arm through Simon's, as she could tell he was feeling left out of all of this.

'That shed has to go and the cottage can be moved here,' said Roaul. 'That gives us a much larger garden space near the pool.'

'I think the veranda should be extended on all sides and the living room changed to here, with French windows. Oh yes, a much better idea. Knock these two rooms into one. There is plenty of space in the house so we don't have a problem. A few more bathrooms, one here, what do you think?' Andrew looked at a very lost Simon and it was

Roaul who suddenly realised Simon's predicament. He swept up and held his other arm. 'We want a large bathroom with a double shower, don't we?' he asked, looking at Simon and squeezing his arm. Simon just nodded.

'Good,' said Andrew. 'All decided. I know exactly what I am doing now,' and turned to look at Simon. 'You know, Terry will be furious, but he has done you a great favour emptying out Rosebae. It saves you a great deal of work and expense.'

'I suppose so,' he replied, and realised he was holding Roaul's hand quite firmly.

They moved back to the fire when Simon's phone rang. He moved into the entrance hall and replied, then slowly walked back into the living room with all eyes upon him. 'She's died,' he said softly and Roaul was instantly on his feet with his arms around him, holding him tightly.

'Who has died?' asked Thomas.

'Auntie Elizabeth. She died in her sleep a few moments ago. The nursing home director said she died very peacefully.'

Simon's Aunt Elizabeth was ninety two years old. His father's sister, she was the last of that generation to survive and Simon had dutifully seen her every Thursday for years when he went to do the shopping at Walvern. She was his only relative and the small bunch of flowers every week was for her a living symbol that she wasn't alone. That evening in bed, Simon was aware he was holding Roaul quite tightly and the strength in his strong arms around Roaul seemed to dissipate the passing of his aunt, Terry leaving Rosebae stripped and the plans to completely overhaul it – all these things slowly evaporated and he felt Roaul's lips on his and snuggled close beside him, not saying a word, but exceptionally grateful he was there.

The funeral was the following week and the church was packed for the funeral Mass. Aunt Elizabeth had been an exemplary woman and one who had managed to move across three generations with ease. The packed church of mourners was proof of this. Simon had always taken care of her legal matters and as he knew her will nothing was a surprise to him. Being her only relative and a much-loved nephew, he inherited everything. The house on Aspel Drive had been tenanted for years and time after time the tenants had pressed Simon to sell it to them, so it wasn't a problem to sell the house at all. And for all these years he had, every six months, written a cheque to Anderson's Warehouse & Storage Company as, when his aunt had moved to the nursing home she placed all her furniture and belongings in storage. This was now another problem he would have to resolve. He did not remember much about the contents of Aspel Drive, as it was now a long time since it had gone into storage. He had never told Terry about it and never knew why in all these years he had kept it a secret. It was not logical, but a secret it had remained.

A week after the funeral and as he was still staying at Killpara, he and Joseph in torrential rain went to see the furniture at Andersons'. A dash from the car with their coats tightly held as a protection from the rain and wind convinced them winter had really set in.

'Good morning. I called about Miss Elizabeth Osler's furniture. May I see it?'

'Well, some of it,' said a hefty young lad. 'I have moved some of the stuff but not all. It's just too difficult. Are you going to take it?'

'No, not for the moment. We just want to have a look at it.'

'Well, over here.' And they walked down a passageway that was created by furniture and boxes with huge tags on them and numbers. They rounded a corner and went up to another landing. 'Here's some of it,' said the lad and left them to themselves.

'Wow!' exclaimed Joseph. 'It looks really great. Look at that cabinet. It's all inlayed like the one at Killpara.'

'Gosh,' said Simon in amazement. 'I don't remember any of this. Look at the big gilt mirror.'

'Hey, look, there are two more here.' They spent an exciting half hour searching and climbing over boxes and furniture.

'How many dining room chairs are there?' Joseph asked.

'I haven't a clue. Why?'

'Well, there seems to be lots of them over here, with the same lot number as the rest of the stuff. How big was the house your Aunt lived in?'

'I haven't been in it for fifteen years. I haven't any idea, but you're right. It seems a vast amount of furniture for one house, doesn't it?'

'It sure does. I think you're going to have to call Andrew in to sort it all out. He's the expert in this field.'

'I suppose so,' Simon agreed, looking across at Joseph.

'You know, Simon, I think Rosebae, sitting up on all those huge drums, looks great.'

Simon laughed. 'I'll tell you I got quite a surprise seeing how easy it was to move it once they had demolished the chimneys and cut off the water and electricity. But you must admit it looks a bit sad, doesn't it?'

'A bit. But come on, I'll shout you lunch at the Oriental. I phoned Enid this morning.' They made their way to the hotel, after explaining to the lad at Andersons' Storage that a certain Andrew would be in very soon to check out all the contents of Miss Elizabeth Osler.

If Terry thought he had won the day, he was very wrong. He had made one alarming error and that was size. Rosebae was a very large house and what he had been given rent-free was much, much smaller, so he had in his greed or revenge in taking everything filled virtually to the ceilings the house with furniture. To return some of it was out of the question, but what to do with it was the most pressing problem as he wove a path from an over-crowded kitchen through to the sitting room or what had been a sitting room. There was space on one side for an arm chair and in front on a piece of furniture was perched the television set and a small electric radiator separated them. Terry was in a real mental dilemma as returning the excess furniture to Simon was out of the question, but to sell what was in excess seemed like defeat. He had even had the removal firm take Pete's large cage and to say that Pete was happy about the move was evident in that he refused to come out of it and sulked in the corner, with Touloula scratching about in what was a very overgrown back garden. It was a very hollow victory for Terry but if he was in a dilemma with the furniture that was nothing to his utter surprise when he passed Rosebae to go to Walvern to shop only to see the house on huge drums up in the air and now on a different site altogether. He stopped the car and just stared. Sure enough, there it was, at least twenty metres or more back from the road and the front of the house was now facing the road, but with a window in place of the front door. 'What the hell is Simon doing?' he said aloud as he placed his foot on the accelerator and turned the corner onto the bitumen road and headed into Walvern.

Simon had discovered, when the house was moved, that great sections of the bearers on which it was constructed were in very bad repair. Several were so rotted that they just fell apart when the house was jacked up. Andrew had insisted that when Rosebae was in position it was to be placed a good sixty centimetres above the ground to let the air move through and to avoid rotting in the future, as the main part of the house had been constructed more or less on ground level. As the work progressed Simon was genuinely surprised at the cost. Both Roaul and Andrew had called in old friends and they had worked for 'mates rates'. Even so the bills were mounting and Simon decided to sell Aunt Elizabeth's house to cover costs.

The speed with which Rosebae was restored surprised another person who in her jeep often passed on her way to Houghton Hall. Thelma was surprised at how large the house was. Before, only a part of it could be seen from the road as it was hidden behind the hedge system, but now, relocated and clearly visible, it was, she thought, almost the size of Houghton Hall, but she couldn't work out why there was a window in place of the front door. There now was not much difference in size between the two houses, due to the fact that Thelma had demolished the entire old servants' wing, due to its dangerous condition and dry rot through most of it, so Houghton Hall now looked smaller and Rosebae larger. But as Thelma turned and headed to Houghton Hall, she passed what was now the largest and most gracious of the three houses, Killpara, with the large tower standing majestically and determinedly signalling that fortunes had changed.

Andrew was elated with the furniture of Simon's aunt and was telling Rose all about it while having lunch with her at Albany Road. 'It's actually good quality stuff, mostly Victorian but there is also some nice Georgian pieces – a lovely bed.'

'I'm so glad you are going to be so close to Killpara,' said Rose.

'Yes, so am I. When Roaul told me about Simon I really thought things were just going to be difficult but with my own cottage everything is working out well. You know the plasterers are in next week and then off we go. Roaul is going crazy about the garden. He has his team in, planting trees everywhere. I must say it's going to look very smart. Simon won't know it when it's all finished.'

'I'm sure he won't,' Rose smiled.

If Simon's aunt's death had brought him a certain gain, another death a month later brought only tragedy and pain. Simon and Joseph kept one another company when Thomas was not at Killpara and before Rosebae was completed, although throughout the day time Simon had his work cut out organising the new share-farmer and changing gateways and water troughs to link the old property with the new as well as demolishing all the old sheds that Andrew deemed unsmart. This Simon took in good spirit.

'Joseph, may I have a word with you?' Beverly asked one morning. 'I should like the day off as I have a real family problem. I have left lunch for you and Simon and all you have to do. Come and have a look.' She led him to the kitchen, a realm Joseph rarely entered. 'Look, you just take this out of the fridge and put it in the oven. I have written down the temperature and time. I hope you don't mind. I will be back this evening.'

He said it was not a problem and asked if he could help her but she said not and soon her black Volkswagon was to be seen going up the drive and heading off to Walvern. Beverly had been contact by her mother, whom she saw very little of, to say that her elder sister had died. If Beverly had little contact with her, her parents had none at all with her sister. She knew that she had a real problem with drugs and was completely dependent on them. Her husband, less so, but the combination did not make for a happy home. They had a daughter, Anne, who was now eighteen, but there was a little boy of six years old. He had been the tragedy in this sad story. Beverly's sister's habit was expensive and so she had taken up with a wealthier solicitor and thought to divorce her husband and marry him, but as the solicitor was already married he had no intention of doing what Beverly's sister wanted, so her sister did the obvious. She became pregnant by him and attempted to blackmail him. If worked for a while but the husband, who knew full well the little boy who went by the name of Michael was not his son, made life difficult for both of them, though he accepted any of the extra money that was floating about as a result of the child. But with a mixture of drugs and alcohol, Beverly's sister's husband became violent and often took it out on Michael, who was a very frightened introverted child.

It was into this sad scenario that Beverly entered. It had literally been years since she had seen her sister's husband and time had not been kind. He was just as aggressive and arrogant and now very worried. His finances, as a result of the blackmail, had dried up. He had contemplated continuing it and had approached the solicitor, who in no uncertain manner threatened to hand him over to the police, so he decided not to risk that, as he had three police convictions before him, and knew another would almost certainly mean a jail sentence. So he was anything but co-operative this late morning.

After the funeral, the family returned to Beverly's parents' home, where a very scrappy lunch was served. 'He's going to a foster home,' was the reply to Beverly's question about Michael. She looked across to the forlorn little boy, lost yet again, and then it came to her. She had a house, a permanent job, no prospect whatever of a child, and it all flooded back of what it was like to be really all alone. She remembered the lonely days she had spent with no one to talk to, just listening to orders being shouted at her. She knew she couldn't negotiate this: her sister's husband was antagonistic and if she made an offer to take Michael, he would refuse out of spite, especially as he was not the father. It was a very heavily weighed down Beverly who left the house as the yelling began between one of her brothers and her sister's husband. She sat alone in her car, staring out of the windscreen but not seeing anything. Her preoccupation was for Michael and then she thought he was so much better off in a foster home, away from this dangerous world in which he survived, and for a reason she never knew, but, having parked her car, she walked across the road in teeming rain to the Oriental Hotel. She went through to the room overlooking the now rain-splashed fountain and just sat there with an empty feeling and without any energy to do anything or go forward.

'Well, what a surprise!' came Enid's voice, which saw Beverly sit upright as if she had received an electric shock.

'Oh, hello, Mrs Wrighton, how are you?'

'I'm fine, but I can see you're not,' replied Enid, signalling a waiter and sitting down. 'I'm sorry your sister has died.'

'I'm not.'

'You'd better tell me what's wrong.' Beverly knew from the previous interview that there was no point not telling Enid what she wanted to know. 'I see. How old is he? Listen, don't move. Have a drink. I'll be back in a moment.' She disappeared, only to return with what might have been described as a smile, a rare occurrence in her case. 'I have just hurdled the first problem. Rose does not see a problem at all, providing the child does not interfere with your work schedule and she says they are all happy to work around any problem that occurs.'

'Oh, Mrs Wrighton –'

'Just a minute! We now have the second hurdle, the boy's father, or supposed father. I think a certain payment should get him off our hands. Are you prepared to lay out, say, five thousand dollars for Michael?'

'Oh, much more!'

'Oh no, that won't be necessary. Just leave it to me,' she said, continuing to smile.

'I don't know how to thank you,' Beverly said, and began to cry.

'Hey, none of that,' Enid said. 'You'd better go and do some shopping for Michael. Come back here in a couple of hours.'

Enid knew who the sister's husband was; in the hotel trade, word passes around very quickly. She went to her computer and put together a letter. She made up the legal heading and having experience with such documents drew up a letter where the sister's husband would, for the offer of not five thousand dollars but one thousand, hand the boy over legally into Beverly's care until he was eighteen years old. 'Not bad,' she muttered to herself. She flicked through the telephone book and dialled a number.

'Yeah, he's here,' was the reply from Beverly's brother.

'Put him on,' was the sharp command.

'Yeah.'

'Get yourself to the Oriental Hotel now if you are interested in one thousand cash and bring Michael – and I mean now!' She hung up and went downstairs to wait. As she passed Lenny she asked, 'Could you put together a little something for a little boy?' and walked on. In less than twenty minutes a wreck of a man, hardly in his forties, appeared at the door of the dining room, having been shown in. He shakily sat down. Enid directed one of the waiters to take a very bedraggled but beautiful child to Lenny for something to eat.

'You will sign here in a moment when I call for a witness.'

'What's this all about?' he demanded arrogantly, slightly slurring his words.

'I will tell you what it is all about,' she snapped. 'For this small, how shall we say, 'offer' of goodwill you will sign Michael's future over to someone who will care for him until he is eighteen years old.'

'What sort of a father do you think I am?' he retorted.

'I would say, without any doubt, hopeless,' she smiled sweetly at him, 'especially as you are not the boy's father and a DNA test will prove that easily. I believe a certain solicitor in Walvern might be closer to the DNA, wouldn't you say?'

'How much?'

'Just a minute. These are the terms. A small sum, and you will have nothing at all to do with Michael, and don't think you can come back here and demand more, because I have heard on the grapevine of a robbery and bashing at the service station at the corner of Elm Street. Now if I just have a little chat with a good friend of mine, Constable –'

'OK, I get the point.' He spat out the words. She stood up and called in a waiter. 'Sign here and here,' she said, and the husband did as demanded. She signed, as did the waiter. She then dated the letter and handed him an envelope after the waiter had left. 'There is a thousand dollars in one hundred dollar notes. Don't spend it all at once and if anyone says I have given you this I shall call the police about the job at the service station. Three, isn't it? Previous convictions? This time they will throw the key away.'

He went to stand up. 'I haven't finished yet,' she went on in an icy tone. 'Remember and remember well, the child is not yours and a DNA test will prove it. You will never see him again, as he isn't yours anyway. Do you understand me?' He stood up and started to leave.

'Perfectly,' he spat back at her and left, with the envelope clutched in his hand.

Beverly went back into the Oriental well before the two hours was up, only to find a very contented Enid sitting gazing out of the window of the room overlooking the fountain with Lenny, and a small boy seated between them, hungrily eating Lenny's offerings.

'Well, it's all solved,' said Enid in a rather superior way. 'He is now legally your responsibility and I think you will find that everyone at Killpara will pitch in to help.'

'Mrs Wrighton -' Beverly spoke as she put down her handbag and withdrew her cheque book.

'Put that away,' Enid commanded, smiling. 'You are going to need every cent for the future, especially for this good-looking young man.'

* * * * *

You did what?' exclaimed Mary. 'I don't believe it. Enid, you are turning into a criminal, blackmailing these men. It's against the law. Don't you realise that?'

'Keep your voice down. We now have a happy home. Not bad, eh?'

'Enid, really this must stop. Eventually someone is going to lay charges against you and you could go to prison,' Mary cried, gulping down a glass of wine.

'Don't worry. I don't think I will have to do it again.' She laughed. 'Remember, I am the saviour of the down-trodden women of Walvern.

'Be that as it may, and I think what you have done is splendid, but Enid, it's all against the law.'

'Don't worry, Mary. I am dealing with men. If it were with women I would obviously have to be much more careful. By the way, I believe Rosebae is up in the air – literally.'

'Well, it was,' Mary replied, feeling very nervous about Enid's latest escapades, 'but the house is now on new foundations and when I went to see Joseph the other day the veranda had grown and wrapped itself all around the house, complete with cast-iron trim. It looks great.'

'And Terry?' asked a curious Enid.

'I don't know anything at all, except a friend of Trevor says that he is living in a furniture storage depot.'

'What!' Enid exclaimed in amazement. Mary, with a few giggles, explained that he could hardly move from the front to the back of the house due to all the furniture he had taken from Rosebae.

'Serves him right,' said an uncharitable Enid. But she had not quite finished her little intrigue, and as she knew, as a friend, the solicitor that had fathered Michael, and was the legal hand that did all the work for the Oriental, she invited him to dinner one evening, on a slow night, so she could have him all to herself.

Brendan Dane was a good man, hard-working and, as Enid said, basically honest. He had formed a disastrous relationship with Beverly's sister and things had gone from bad to worse.

'Do sit down, Brendan,' Emily smiled and the waiters sprang to attention. It was unusual on an evening for Enid to sit and eat with anyone. She actually disliked doing it, as she felt she was not completely in control. She need not have feared, as the well-trained and well-paid staff were ever attentive.

'Do you need me to sort out a problem for you?' Brendan asked as they moved onto the main course. Enid had kept up a smooth banter about Walvern and especially about the Stardust Hotel that was now in financial hot water due to poor management and the constant problems with violence and drug pushing.

'No, Brendan, everything is fine here. We have been very lucky and thanks to your guaranteeing the loan a few years ago for the renovations we are now doing quite well.'

'Quite well indeed!' he replied. 'You have to be someone very important now to even get a table here.'

She laughed and then began her game. She reached out and put a hand on his arm. 'You will always be welcome here, Brendan, no matter what.' She withdrew her hand and Brendan felt a shiver run right up his spine. He knew Enid only too well and he knew what she was capable of. He lowered his eyes and looked directly at her.

'Why did you invite me here for dinner?' he asked, slowly. She picked up her glass and held it in both hands, looked at the contents and drank from it and in slow motion returned it to the immaculately white, laundered tablecloth. Whether it was his sixth sense or Enid's supercilious smile, he knew he was in for trouble.

'No doubt you have heard about the funeral,' she said in a casual way that had him reaching for his glass. 'I have taken it upon myself to move the boy to a safe home, as I am sure you would wish.' He said nothing, but found swallowing the red wine difficult. 'Don't worry, darling,' she added with a smile, 'the secret is safe with me.'

He was absolutely sure that this was not the end of the subject and he was right. 'Have you seen Michael?' she asked, raising her eyebrows. He knew he could not get out of this trap. It had been laid too well and the bait he had taken without even thinking.

'Yes, once or twice. Where is he now?'

'He is now officially in residence at Killpara.'

'What!' he exclaimed loudly and then looked around to make sure he had not attracted any attention. 'Enid! Killpara! They are clients of mine!'

'Yes. I thought you would like that. Everything in good hands. He is living now with his aunt, Beverly, but as I know Rose it won't be long before he is taking advantage of her generous hospitality.' He gulped. 'Don't worry. There won't be any more blackmail.'

At this point he blanched. 'How the hell do you know about all this?' he demanded.

'A little bird told me, darling. Now to get down to tin tacks. I think the least you can do is pay for his education, don't you think? God knows, you have wasted a fortune on his stupid drug-addicted mother. I hope your investment with her, how should we say, has been worthwhile?' She smiled again, not altogether sincerely.

'This is blackmail,' he muttered.

'No, darling, this is called, in this day and age, responsibility and you will pick it up.' She spoke in a very determined manner that made him feel very uncomfortable. 'You can either pay the fees at St. Mary's through me, or pay them directly, whichever you think is the most discreet. I am only too willing to help you in this delicate matter.' Not only had the mouse been caught but the cat was slowly strangling it.

'I don't know how I got caught up in all this mess,' he said, looking at his unfinished meal. 'I started out so well, no problems, a bit of fun on the side and then everything went wrong.'

'Darling, you were not born yesterday. You should have known. Anyone who is drug dependent is completely without scruples when there is no money for a fix.'

'Yes, I suppose so. What does he look like?'

'He's very beautiful. He is six years old and has a mop of thick, black, bushy hair and electric blue eyes. Just like you.'

At this point he leaned forward and buried his head in his hands. 'I have really fucked it up, haven't I?'

'Well, darling, you can't be accused of being careful sexually, if that's what you mean.'

There was silence. Enid strangely felt sorry for Brendan. She had always liked him and Michael was the son his wife and he were unable to have, so the blow was double for him.

'Of course I'll pay his school fees. I might send the money through you so as not to cause any ripples at home, if you don't mind. It's good of you to have offered, and thanks for taking the initiative and saving the boy from that hell hole. I always felt helpless. I guess I knew the money went direct to drug dealers but I tried to justify it, thinking at least some would go to Michael. I guess I was stupid.'

'On that point, yes,' she said, baldly. 'Come on, Brendan, all is not lost. Your son is now not only in good hands but the best. He will now have the opportunity to develop to the full and I am sure as time goes on you will be able to have a certain access to him, but not just for now. Let's get him settled first. Remember, he is a very frightened little boy who has had a very rough time.'

'It's all my fault,' he said in a remorseful tone.

'Yes,' Enid spoke sharply. 'It is. If you men took a look before you went into situations like this, sad stories like Michael might not happen.'

Beverly had no religious convictions but accepted what Enid had virtually dictated. He was instantly transferred from the government school to St. Mary's, and as the bus passed the front gate each morning he was seen hopping on board in an immaculately pressed uniform and as time slowly moved on his oppressive past became dimmer and dimmer in his memory. Michael, little by little, became the fulcrum at Killpara and everyone made a fuss of him. He was particularly attached to Thomas for some reason and was always ecstatic when he was present at Killpara but he was also very fond of Joseph, especially when he took him to see Ted and Toddy, who adored him, taking him by the sleeve to show him about.

It had now been a year since Terry had left Rosebae and it was now unrecognisable. When Andrew said it would be smart, he wasn't playing with words. This large house was painted the palest of pinks, almost a cream pink, with all crisp white trim. The garden, after a year of careful curating by Roaul, was looking splendid. There were no real problems between the three of them and Simon had never been happier or more content. The cottage had had two extension added in the year and was quite a sizeable house on its own: 'totally co-ordinated' was Rose's comment. Aunt Elizabeth's furniture fitted in perfectly, and with new upholstery here and there, and a few new paintings, Rosebae became the fine house it had never been, especially when viewed through an enormous set of antique wrought-iron gates, supported by two large brick pillars topped with urns. When everyone was at either Killpara or Rosebae their evenings were always filled with laughter and fun.

But 'fun' could not be used as a word to describe Houghton Hall. Thelma had great problems turning the economic table around and although it was not paying for itself it was on the way to doing so. Barry was as obnoxious as ever, according to Thelma; his outright stupidity never ceased to annoy her. He was doing manual work at the sawmill: this, she hoped, would break down his ridiculous, pretentious manner. Alas no! Barry, when in company, was exactly the same. 'Of course,' he was heard to say at the Oriental with Stewart Searl one Saturday lunchtime, grandly, 'there are only three major houses in the district, Houghton Hall, as well as Killpara and Rosebae, which I am constantly invited to.' Never was a lie said so loudly and not one of the group he was with believed him, knowing full well the inhabitants of Killpara and Rosebae. But as he entered the hotel, he, being as pretentious as ever, arrived at Stewart Searl's table and as he sat down the waiter asked a breathless Barry, who had had to run down the street in order not to keep Stewart waiting, 'What would Sir like to drink?'

'The usual,' Barry declared, somewhat rudely.

'Really, sir,' replied the sharp waiter,' and what is the usual?'

Barry, flustered as usual, answered, 'Dry vermin and dry.'

As quick as a flash, the waiter retorted, 'Would Sir like the tail in or out of the glass?'

Stewart was unable to contain his laughter, but Barry was most confused at the joke, not having realised he had confused the words 'vermin' and 'vermouth'. This became a standing joke at the Oriental for some time to come.

One Friday evening, whilst having her evening meal alone, Thelma came to the conclusion that she had made a great mistake with Houghton Hall. It had only caused her worry and great financial expense and she still, after almost two years, was not showing a profit. She lifted her glass of red wine and rested an elbow on the table, only half-watching the television news. She slowly came to the realisation that Houghton Hall was never going to show a great profit. It was in fact a lousy investment and she wondered what its worth was on the real estate market.

Michael had indeed taken over Killpara. When they were all in Melbourne he slept in the cottage with Beverly, who was an exemplary, caring guardian, as well as an aunt, but the minute he knew the group were returning from Melbourne this tiny youngster took it upon himself to take up residence in the main house, much to Beverly's embarrassment, but as Rose explained to her the small blue bedroom next to Thomas and Joseph's was just perfect for him. He loved nothing better than to jump into bed with the boys first thing in the morning, laughing and making a lot of noise, sometimes to Joseph's annoyance though he tolerated it.

The old stable block had been totally restored at Killpara and now housed two horses and a pony. Rose had insisted on the purchase of the pony for Michael, so in good weather the three of them would go riding, Joseph being the most unsure of the three. James, the share-farmer, whenever he had a spare half an hour and when the boys were not in residence, came down and took Michael riding, which he adored. He fitted in perfectly at Killpara, with day to day duties being sorted out by Beverly, but it was the Thursday nights he waited for, when he was in Thomas's arms. Rose never arrived without just another little something for him, and, as Beverly said to James's wife, Paula, whom she had now developed a firm friendship with, Michael was the best dressed youngster in Australia.

Betty and Robert Marshal, Rodney and Angelo, arrived again for a long weekend. They adored Killpara and Thomas insisted that Rodney and Angelo, who was anything but certain about it, take the horses for a ride with Michael giving orders to everyone and laughing as Thomas lifted him into the saddle. They all watched the group slowly move out of the stable yard and into the field, with James watching to make sure all went well.

'Rose, the house is so divine! It's just so right and the tower, Joseph! Rose told me all about your adventure obtaining it. It's marvellous! 'and she went on to say how they just must have a house like this somewhere nearby.

Saturday lunchtime and they were invited to Rosebae and needless to say Michael would not be left out of the festivities. Again, Betty and Robert were overwhelmed with Rosebae as well. 'Chic, darling,' she said, as she linked arms with Roaul. He gave them a tour of the new garden, with Angelo wondering if all their friends had such splendid country mansions. It was Simon, after lunch, who noticed something he thought was extremely strange. He had never thought of Thomas as having any parental feelings at all; hedonistic, yes, but parental, no. But here he was with a young boy who had become sleepy as a result of racing about all morning with the guests and settled into Thomas's arms, resting his head on his shoulder. The other thing that struck him, as it did the others, was how similar Michael and Thomas were physically: black bushy hair, electric blue eyes.

'Well, well,' thought Betty, 'it seems Killpara is quite the happy family.'

Saturday evening they all made it to the Oriental and Betty, Robert, Rodney and Angelo were again surprised to sit and eat in a very sophisticated atmosphere in the country and they were loud in their praise to a glowing Enid.

She had, also, for what reason she did not or could not work out, become attached to Michael when he was brought in for a lunch or dinner with the others. She was aware she was making more effort for him than she would ever do for another child who had accompanied his or her parents. But even Enid had to admit, as she did to Mary one evening, 'It's uncanny. You would swear Thomas was the father. They are absolutely identical, and Michael is picking up some of Thomas's mannerisms.'

The evening meal with the Marshalls went very well, with Rose and Betty catching up on all the Melbourne gossip, when at a certain point Michael became tired and as usual ended up in Thomas's arms. It was Rodney who lent over to Joseph and whispered, 'I would have killed to be in Michael's position,' and they both laughed. 'Aren't you a bit jealous?' Rodney asked.

'No,' Joseph laughed. 'You see we share him when Thomas is here. Michael is always in his arms and when he's not, I get to look after him. He's a great kid and he has had a really rough life, but he's now putting all that behind him. If we love him, Rose is crazy for him. She adores him, so I guess his future is pretty well looked after.'

'He's a lucky guy,' agreed Rodney, as he squeezed Angelo's hand.

Michael, as a result of a good home, a pony and lots of love began to blossom from the timid, frightened little boy. He began to open up. His schooling was proving to be challenging but he rose to the occasion. He was a good student and, like Thomas before him, fitted in very well and was liked by all. Beverly was extremely proud of him and after the initial adjustments didn't mind sharing him with the others at all.

One evening, a month or so later, Enid had to deal with a very emotional situation. Rose, Joseph, Thomas and Mary, with the ever-present Michael, were having dinner at the Oriental. Another table across the room held a husband and wife team. As usual, as the night wore on, Michael was to be found in Thomas's broad arms. The wife at the other table left it to cross the room and speak to a friend of hers, so Enid took the opportunity to stand beside Brendan Dane.

'How are we?' she asked.

'Fine! Thanks for everything.'

'It's a pleasure, and if you look at the table with the group from Killpara, you will see how well Michael is being looked after.'

Brendan spun around like a released spring and there he was in Thomas's arms, with his head turned in Brendan's direction. Michael's arms were well-locked around Thomas's neck. All of a sudden, Brendan realised he couldn't see properly and turned and attempted to dry his eyes. 'He's beautiful,' was all he could say and the tears ran freely down his cheeks, which he quickly attempted to wipe away. 'Would you like to meet him?' Enid asked quietly.

'I don't think I have the courage.'

'It's up to you,' she said, kindly. But he stood up and Enid took him over to the table to introduce him to everyone. He knew them from legal work he had done for them but this was the first time he had met them socially. Enid produced a chair and he sat down, but he couldn't keep his eyes off Michael. Then he noticed how similar Michael and Thomas were and it gave him quite a start. Michael turned his head and looked at Brendan and then returned it to Thomas's shoulder.

'I had better go. I see my wife has returned. It's been very pleasant seeing you. Goodnight.' He left, and when Mary swung round to see the wife, she was very surprised to see Brendan holding a handkerchief to his eyes. Mary had known the story from Enid but the others did not know of Michael's father and they, that is to say Enid, Mary and Beverly, had decided to leave it like that. Brendan suffered a great deal as a result of this introduction to his son. He couldn't believe he was so beautiful and so wonderful. He searched his brain for more adjectives and found them easily. He now found himself trapped in a situation that he couldn't escape from; the thing he wanted more than anything else in this world was his son and the doors to this avenue were closed tightly. To confess all to his wife meant, as he knew only too well, divorce or a very restricted living situation, but, oh, he was beautiful! His eyes! He ran every scenario through his mind and always ended up with the same answer, that Michael was with them, not him. Paying his school fees via Enid was the only thing he could do, absolutely nothing else. As he sat at his desk in his office he realised once again he was having trouble seeing and this emotional situation would continue for him all his life. The child he had always wanted, this beautiful boy, as a result of his stupidity and dishonesty had been taken away from him and it was all his own fault.

If Brendan was suffering, Michael was not. A day or two with Mary and Trevor, this group tightened up to support him. Financially there were no problems and now he had so many supportive bastions that kept him well clear of trouble he was having the time of his life. He and Trevor joked and played for hours.

'You are a bad man!' he exclaimed to Trevor.

'Darling, marry me!' at which he swept up a surprised Michael into his arms and kissed him. 'Ok, beautiful, let's see if we can find Mary. I just happen to know she has some ice-cream hidden in the fridge.' Michael yelled, 'Oh yes!' and off they went to find the hidden treasure.

He worked as a catalyst for this group. They could all contribute easily but the return he gave was unconditional love, and every one of them saw this as the most expensive currency that existed.

Beverly boldly walked into the Oriental and asked to speak to Mrs Wrighton. When a voice from the side door said hello, she began, 'I won't take up your time but I thought perhaps you might like a copy of this as you have been so supportive.'

'What are you talking about?' Enid asked.

'It's the school photo and each student has his photo taken professionally. I have received a letter to say I can order copies. Would you like one of Michael?'

'May I have two large ones? I am sure that when you ask the rest of the tribe they will also want some.'

'I'm sure, but I have asked you first,' Beverly replied nervously.

Enid breathed deeply. 'Thank you, Beverly, thank you very much.'

Beverly hastily made her exit and phoned the so-called 'tribe', as Enid had put it, to order the portrait photographs that are done each year. Enid kept hers in a silver frame on her dressing table and was never sure why she did so. The other copy she had framed and when passing Brendan's office stopped and gave it to him. She was surprised. Brendan was tough, he was a go-getter, but with this photo of Michael once again the tears flowed freely for the son he wanted so desperately and couldn't have.

Rose, needless to say, went one better, and had a great friend of hers up to stay, who was surprised to see her painting hanging in the living room, the painting Thomas and Joseph had purchased at Betty Marshall's art auction. 'This is only a photo, but do you think you could manage a portrait of Michael?' she asked.

'Well, let's see,' and a weekend with lots of photos and with the artist's keen eye, the portrait eight weeks later was hung in the large sitting room at Killpara. When Michael saw it for the first time, he turned and looked at Rose.

'Rose,' he asked, 'will I always look like this?'

'No, darling, you will a little later I think look like Thomas.'

He was excited by this and hugged Thomas, almost upsetting his glass. 'I think that will be nice, don't you?' he directed his question to Thomas, who kissed him and said that he thought it would be very nice. Michael than dashed out to feed his pony, leaving the three of them digesting Michael's enthusiasm.

Thomas then stood up and moved to the settee where Joseph was sitting and put an arm around his shoulder. There was no conversation, just the absolute sureness that these two men loved one another completely and this gave Rose the greatest satisfaction she could have imagined. It didn't peter out; it just matured, this relationship with Joseph. This was the only thing Thomas lived for and it was totally reciprocated.

Thomas now spent a great deal more time at Killpara than he did in Melbourne and obviously Joseph was the reason. Rose moved between the two places and fitted in without a problem but as Joseph now organised and took complete control over the administration of Killpara he was obliged to be in the country more than the others, and missed Thomas desperately. To have to share him in bed with an excited Michael was one thing but no Thomas was a very empty alternative. Mary never really believed Enid's view that the relationship between Thomas and Joseph depended on Rose. She was Rose, the dynamic centre of this group but Mary always thought that if the magic or love, call it what you will, wasn't there between Thomas and Joseph, nothing would have happened and there they were, more in love now than ever, and supported by Rose and a noisy Michael.

Killpara now was a well-developed and supervised property. The dairy part was well organised by James and the Hereford stud section was beginning to show fruit. Joseph had had the eight hectare part fitted with a pumping station and as a result Killpara now did not lack water. This pumping station supplied water to the cisterns that eventually filled all the water troughs for the cattle but also the water supported the now large garden that surrounded the house, as well as topping up the pool.

Beverly was always chatting to Paula, James's wife and often they went to Walvern together, shopping. One Saturday morning, early, Beverly realised that she had not dropped off some letters to Paula that had been delivered by mistake to Killpara. She collected them and dashed out to her car as she knew no-one would be up before nine and hurried down to the share-farmer's house but just before the gate she saw a Range Rover at a very strange angle as if it had just slowly run off the road and gently run into the shallow ditch. She drove past to speak to and deliver the letters to Paula. 'Has the jeep near your front gate broken down?' she asked.

'What jeep?' was the reply and they both walked out on to her front veranda to see the stationary jeep.

'Oh, I hope everything is all right. Let's go and have a look. It's very strange to leave a jeep in the middle of the country. No-one came asking for help her.' Paula sounded worried and the women hopped into Beverly's car and drove the short distance to the vehicle.

'That's Mrs Smith's jeep,' cried Paula. 'Oh, I hope there's not a problem!' and with that the two women jumped out of the car and went to have a look.

'Oh God!' cried Paula. 'She's in there. Look!'

Beverley opened the passenger door to see Thelma slumped half on the seat and half on the floor. She leant over and felt her pulse. Beverly jerked her hand back at once. 'I think she's dead. She is as cold as ice. Quick! I'll stay here, you go back home and call the Ambulance and the Police at once.'

Twenty minutes later both were heard tearing up the road past Killpara.

'Is she – alive?' asked Beverly, as a white-faced Paula held her arm.

'No. It appears she has been dead for some time.'

'Oh, I don't believe it. What happened to her?'

'We won't know until we have an autopsy, but my guess is she has had a massive heart attack.'

Beverly left Paula after the ambulance had removed Thelma's body and hurried back to Killpara to pass on the sad tidings. The police continued to Houghton Hall to inform Barry.

'What!' exclaimed Rose. 'Dead?'

'Yes, and they think she had been dead for some time. Perhaps this happened some time last night.'

'Oh how awful!,' said Rose, during breakfast, as the two boys joined her.

'Dead!' Joseph was surprised. 'How?'

Rose repeated what Beverly had told her. 'I don't believe it. That now leaves Houghton Hall in a real mess with that idiot to run it.'

Meanwhile Barry walked back to the living room after hearing the report from the two policemen at the front door. He thanked them, grandly, and closed the door. 'Well, well,' he thought aloud, 'now it's all mine, and probably the sawmill as well. Free of them at last.'

But not quite. As Mrs Talbot came in, not having been told of Thelma's death, Barry swung around and fired her. 'Get out, now!' Mrs Talbot thought perhaps he had been drinking but at this hour of the morning!

'Watch yourself, or I shall have a word to your aunt,' and started to leave.

'She's dead,' he said in an offhand manner, 'and you are now officially discharged.'

'What!' she shouted. 'Dead? How? Do you know?'

'The police were here only ten minutes ago.'

'Oh, poor Mrs Smith.' She spoke with genuine sentiment and started back to the kitchen in a daze. She sat down at the central table and looked about her, completely lost.

Barry was now gearing up for what he honestly believed was his due. He had suffered Mrs Talbot for more than long enough. Now not only was she to go but Aunt Thelma was gone as well. No more manual work at the mill, money at last, money and no Aunt Thelma.

The coroner's report read as the ambulance driver had suggested: Thelma had suffered a massive heart attack and been dead for fifteen hours, so it was assumed that she had died the previous evening whilst going to Houghton Hall. Barry had never known such relief and unfortunately did not contain his enthusiasm for a happier, lazier life to come, and most people who knew him considered his behaviour callous and vulgar. The funeral was for Wednesday and when it was over it was an excited and anxious Barry who swept into Brendan Dane's offices to hear the reading of the will, expecting great things. But he was to be exceptionally surprised when Brendan explained to him what Thelma had done with her money. She had left Barry not a cent. All her assets went into a co-operative fund to keep the sawmill working, thus keeping her large staff fully employed, with the exception of Barry, whom the will stated was not to have any access at all to the fund. All the land Thelma had purchased and annexed to Houghton Hall, which was legally all hers, was to be sold and the profits were to be put into this co-operative fund.

'And what about me?' Barry protested.

'You have nothing at all from your aunt's estate, nothing at all. You have just the 36 hectares and the house that sits on it, called Houghton Hall, and, Barry, I'm afraid that's it.'

'I'll sue,' he said, rising from his chair.

'You can't,' was the reply. 'This will was written only seven weeks ago and your aunt made very sure that you cannot legally touch a cent of her money. That's the way she wanted it.'

Without another word Barry left the office and slammed the door, leading Brendan to detect that Barry was anything but pleased! Barry was now in a very difficult situation financially. He literally had virtually no cash. He knew that the credit card that occasionally Thelma paid into was empty. He was discharged from the mill ('Thank God' he thought) and the thing that ran through his mind was a form of extreme fear. What was he to do? If he floated a mortgage from the bank on Houghton Hall, they wouldn't give it to him, simply because he had no job or the prospect of one to pay the mortgage back. It left him only one possibility and one only, to sell Houghton Hall and the 36 hectares as quickly as possible, but even so, if, just if he was lucky enough to find an immediate client, thirty days was the contract. What was he going to do with not a cent for a month. He pulled a twenty and a ten dollar note out of his pocket and some loose change. He drove back to Houghton Hall, a very dejected and unhappy person. He knew that even in death Thelma had won:

everything she had threatened she had gone through with. Oh, how he hated her! She was more trouble to him dead than alive, he thought, and then, turning off the sand road, having passed Rosebae and onto the bitumen road, he passed Killpara with its huge tower reflecting the late morning sun. 'Killpara' he thought, that's my way out,' and on his return to Houghton Hall with Thelma's Range Rover parked out in front, he boldly swept up to the telephone.

'Good morning,' came Beverly's voice.

'It's Houghton Hall here. I wish to speak to the controller of Killpara.'

'One moment' and then Joseph answered.

'Oh,' was the reply. Barry had assumed he would be doing business with Thomas or Rose. 'Oh well,' he continued, 'I suppose I can deal with you. Do you think you could come to Houghton Hall now?'

'Give me fifteen minutes.' Joseph hung up and turned to the others. 'This is going to be good.' He collected his car keys and made for the door.

'Be careful,' warned Rose, with a knowing sound to her voice. Joseph smiled and said he would be, and in less than the fifteen minutes he had pulled up behind Thelma's jeep.

Barry let him in and led him down to the sitting room. Joseph looked around, at a very ordinary interior, he thought, as he had never been to the house before.

'It appears that Aunt Thelma was not in her right mind when she wrote her last will, so I will get straight to the point,' Barry began, as he lowered himself into a comfortable chair. Joseph had never seen Barry up close before, only a table or two away at the Oriental, but nothing closer. He was much more overweight than he had realised and his blotchy skin and thinning red blond greasy hair did nothing to recommend him.

'I have decided to sell. The sad memories of my late mother and aunt are just too much for me. Are you interested in purchasing it?'

'How many hectares are there?' Joseph asked, knowing full well the number.

'There are 36.'

Joseph exclaimed in surprise, knowing that there was considerably more than that in the estate. 'Why only 36 hectares?'

'That doesn't concern you,' Barry retorted, grandly. 'Are you interested or not?'

'We may be. It obviously depends on the price,' at which Barry mentioned an incredibly inflated sum.

'You're wasting your time and mine,' said Joseph, standing up. 'These 35 hectares are the ones closest to the house, I take it, and they include the house. Don't be stupid. No-one is going to pay that for 35 hectares. That will never give anyone a living.' Barry said nothing, but moved uneasily in his chair. It annoyed him to have, as he saw it, a junior dictating to him what he could or could not do, but he knew very well Joseph was probably correct.

'I'll tell you what, Barry. When you get a real estate valuation on the property and give me a copy I will tell you if we are interest, but not before.' With that Joseph swung about and left. Barry sighed as he heard Joseph's car move down the drive.

When Joseph returned to Killpara, the three of them discussed Barry's ludicrous offer and then Joseph excused himself, and with the aid of the telephone directory, telephoned Brendan Day, whom he knew was Thelma's solicitor. He informed the secretary who he was and was connected to Brendan, who instantly thought something had happened to Michael. He was genuinely pleased when Joseph asked him what was going on with the property of Houghton Hall. Brendan explain it all to him very carefully, that all the land Thelma had annexed to Houghton Hall was to be auctioned as soon as possible and that it had nothing to do with the 36 hectares that was Barry's from his mother's estate. He thanked Brendan and walked back to the living room, sat on the arm of Thomas's chair and explained the situation. 'I can't see this land going for a high price at all,' he said. 'I think I shall just give the Marshalls a call and see if they are ready to buy. Houghton Hall seems fine for them and then we had better see how they are going to auction off Thelma's land.'

'What do you mean?' asked Rose, curious.

'Well, the land was not all purchased in one lot, so I suppose they will sell it off as various lots.'

'I think you're right,' Thomas agreed. 'Are we interested in any of it?'

'Oh yes, the lot that Thelma brought back originally, when she took over, that joins on to the side of where James and Paula live. I think, if I remember, it is three hundred hectares, but Thelma paid quite a bit for it. I'll have to check.'

The rest of the evening was spent discussing land acquisition and the excited and positive comments from the Marshalls, who just happened to be in America for a three-week holiday, about Houghton Hall, and would Joseph kindly begin negotiations.

A week later, Barry telephoned Joseph to say he had had a valuation of the property and if he was interested could come and discuss it with him. Joseph lost no time in arriving at Houghton Hall but this time, before he used the front door knocker, he glanced about him. The grounds around the house were just rough grass, cut back with a 'whipper-snipper', unevenly. The hedges were just rows of trees and everything was shabby and in Joseph's opinion not worth much at all as it would all have to be totally redone and he knew from the accounts at Killpara that it was not going to be a cheap venture but the thing he hated the most was the colour of the house, a brassy blue. He genuinely wondered about the taste of Emily Houghton.

'Come in, 'said Barry grandly. 'The staff are not here today. Everything is chaotic with poor Aunt Thelma's parting. I don't know what I am doing.'

'Where is the valuation?' demanded Joseph, finding that being in Barry's company was not a pleasant experience.

'Here,' and he thrust a Real Estate valuation into Joseph's hand. Joseph looked at the price, less than half Barry's original quote. Joseph thought it a reasonable price and said that his clients would accept the offer and he would sign the papers on Tuesday morning and it would be a thirty day sale. Barry agreed, so Joseph left and returning to Killpara passed a removal van heading for Houghton Hall. Barry had put the whole of the furniture, artifacts, everything inside the house, to Mr Ollie's Auction Rooms for the following week's sale. Through Stuart Searl Barry managed to locate a small house for rent in Walvern at a very low rent. The condition was that he would upgrade it; the future showed that Barry did not adhere to his end of the bargain.

Tuesday morning, Joseph signed the papers for Houghton Hall, a purchase made without Betty or Robert seeing the property. Obviously Joseph was a little nervous, a 25 year old deciding on a country residence for the Marshalls unseen was quite a responsibility and he confided this to Simon.

'Don't worry, Joseph. When the Marshalls take possession, I will make sure Andrew and Roaul are there with you, and you know how enthusiastic Andrew is. Anyway Betty Marshall, Rose tells me, has known both Andrew and Roaul for 20 years or so, so don't worry.'

But it was a worry for Joseph and as he said to Thomas, 'What if they hate it?'

'Joseph,' he said, with his arm around him, 'they will love it. Remember what Killpara and Rosebae for that matter looked like less than two years ago.'

'I suppose so, 'smiled Joseph weakly.

The thirty days passed for everyone quite quickly except Joseph, and Rose noticed this and called Betty. 'Rose, I am not worried in the slightest. Tell Joseph that as long as it is a large house, Andrew and Roaul can just take over. Rodney is ecstatic about it and is demanding all sorts of things that I will leave totally up to Roaul and Andrew. And you must be our house-guests whenever you want as you obviously can't live in it for a while.'

So the following month marked officially the beginning of summer and the possession for the Marshalls of Houghton Hall. Betty was prepared for the worst but was more than happy with the empty spaces inside and over lunch at Killpara with Robert she withdrew from a handbag a long rectangular box and handed it to Joseph. 'Darling, this is just a little something to say thank you so much for everything you have done for us.'

Joseph was genuinely surprised and open the wrapping paper to find a long burgundy box with 'Cartier' neatly printed in gold on the lid. On opening it he saw most beautiful watch, a very elegant evening watch. To say he was delighted was an understatement.

'How much of the other land did you buy?" asked Robert.

'We purchased the 300 hectares that butt onto Killpara, behind your thirty six hectares, and good for us, but you know we paid at least a third less than Thelma had paid two years ago.'

'Listen, Joseph,' said Robert, now addressing all business in Joseph's direction. 'These thirty six hectares of ours - I want you to use them, as they will never serve for us, so you will be doing as a favour if you graze them down for us.'

'Thanks, Robert,' he smiled. 'I'm sure we can do that for you.'

A great part of the following summer was spent between the swimming pools at Rosebae and Killpara, with an excited Michael learning to swim. He was forbidden to go near the pools without someone to supervise him so whenever anyone was at Killpara there were yells and screams to go swimming. The pastures that had been sewn onto the cleared land at the back of Killpara were now starting to show promise. The small Hereford stock was growing and the land supported them well. Joseph hoped that with Ted's help the following year should see an enlarged herd. The dairy section with the addition of the 300 hectares of good pasture and the extension of the milking shed and a local boy to help James was showing a great financial growth, much to everybody's contentment.

The Oriental continued its growth pattern as well. The Stardust had ended up in the most terrible financial mess and had been sold to new owners, but they also found that it was not a good investment and although the young still attended at weekends in droves, for the rest of the week it was virtually empty. One of the closed hotels re-opened and to a meagre cut of the market. Those that didn't want to go to the Oriental, or the Crown, could now attend the Star; the old bloodhouse was now under new management and they did reasonably well, but it was the Oriental that was the top hotel in Walvern and that, due to Enid, was as it stayed

Trevor was, as Enid called him, Mr. Broadcaster, but he witnessed something and kept it a secret all his life and never told a soul. He was at the Oriental one evening and looking for Enid, who was not there due to collecting a friend from the railway station.

'Oh bugger!' exclaimed Trevor and he telephoned Enid. 'Where are you?' he demanded.

'At the railway station, and the train is fifteen minutes late. What a bore! Listen just go upstairs to my private dining room and in the drawer of the sideboard are the documents Mary wanted. Just go and get them. I'll see you later,' and closed her telephone.

So Trevor went upstairs and as he walked down the well-carpeted hallway in the direction of the dining room, he saw the door slightly ajar and heard voices speaking softly. Trevor, being Trevor, moved stealthily forward like a cat and peered in through the opening to see Lenny and Paul talking in hushed voices. He was about to knock to announce himself when he saw Lenny reach forward and kissed Paul and then they held one another in their arms. Trevor slunk back downstairs as quietly as he could and ordered from his favourite waiter a glass of champagne and just waited until he saw both Lenny and Paul come down the stairs separately. This being done he went back upstairs, retrieved the documents for Mary and returned to his drink, and with a smile he thought to himself, 'Well, well, if only Noddy knew!'